COYOTE WIND

❖ AND ❖

SPECIMEN SONG

COYOTE WIND

AND

SPECIMEN SONG

THE FIRST TWO MONTANA MYSTERIES
FEATURING GABRIEL DU PRÉ

Peter Bowen

St. Martin's Minotaur ★ New York

ISBN: 0-312-26514-X

D10 9 8 7 6 5 4

Coyote Wind

❖

For Nancy Stringfellow

✤ CHAPTER 1 ✤

Du Pré stirred in his sleep. His eyes fluttered, opened, he looked up at the ceiling. He squinted, raised his head, glanced toward the rising light in the east, out the window of Madelaine's bedroom. Little spikes of frost reached out from the corners of the wavy old glass.

A pebble rattled against the window.

Du Pré decided it was not a dream. He slipped from the bed, a warm breath of air thick with the scent of their bodies rose from the bed. Madelaine's lips bubbled softly, it was as close as she came to snoring.

Du Pré looked out toward the street, saw a crooked shadow on the short white picket fence. White hair askelter as a forkful of hay. Old Benetsee, the fool, the drunken old breed, a singer, once a dancer, old enough to have been most anything outside of town.

"Shit," Du Pré whispered, annoyed at coming out of warm sleep for this. It passed. The old man always had a reason for bothering Du Pré, even if it sometimes took Du Pré years to see it. Benetsee. Du Pré could see him long, long ago, dancing in the deserts, his head one day smiling from a platter at while the king's wife swirled in silks and scents. God damn. Loony prophets anyway.

"Du Pré!" Madelaine, now up on an elbow, rubbing her eyes.

"Benetsee," whispered Du Pré. "I must go out, see what he wants."

"Take him a glass of wine," said Madelaine. "Don't tease him."

Du Pré shrugged into his clothes, pulled on his boots, one leather mule-ear pull came off with a final chuckling rip. His heel slid down. He walked to the stairs and placed his feet carefully going down, the resinous yellow pine steps creaked five times before his boot touched the worn woolen carpet at the bottom. He went to the kitchen, took a jug of cheap white wine from the icebox, poured a big glassful, lit a cigarette, went outside.

The old man was shivering, leaned up against the Russian olive tree, his bright old eyes brilliant black in his brown creased face.

Benetsee nodded, took the wine and gulped it down.

Du Pré waited, respecting the old man. He had been a good friend of Du Pré's grandparents, long dead now. Plastic flowers on their graves, dust ricking in the petals. Du Pré washed them with holy water on saints' days that had been dear to them.

"I dreamed of a coyote last night," said Benetsee, "he went up a draw, sat and howled by some people's bones."

Du Pré nodded. Benetsee's damn riddles. He wished the old fart would come to the point, which was probably five dollars. So I just give him the five dollars and go back to bed? No, the old man was not just a pest.

"Then you come and sat down on your heels and looked and looked," the old man went on, in his slurred Coyote French, "but you never saw till the coyote come back and scratch the earth."

Now my days got skeletons in them, thought Du Pré, but if the old man go to the police they throw him in jail for drunk. Me, I look at burn marks on cow asses for part of my living. It's cold out here.

2

Benetsee cleared his throat, waved the empty glass, looked at Du Pré hopefully.

"You have another drink you go to sleep," said Du Pré.

"Madelaine don't mind," said Benetsee. "She's a saint, you could learn from her."

Du Pré snorted, shook his head, went back in the house and got the old man another belt. Someday I find him dead in the frozen mud where he pissed his pants and passed out and stuck there, but for now, he's happy. He heard Madelaine on the stairs, she came into the kitchen, her wool robe clutched tight around her against the cold.

"He can sleep in the shed," Madelaine said. "You take him the old sleeping bag in the hall there. Also tell him good morning and when he wakes up I will make him eat something."

Du Pré smiled. Madelaine, she would feed all the earth, soothe its pains and hungers. She was as simple and straightforward and generous as the sunlight.

And she knows what's bothering me before I do, Du Pré thought. He smiled at his luck.

Du Pré opened the door and pushed the storm door away with his foot, scooped up the sleeping bag. A slop of wine drooled down his hand, he smelled the alcohol.

The old man sniffed the wine happily, drank it in a single long draught.

"Madelaine says you got to eat, you wake up," said Du Pré.

"I do what Madelaine say," said Benetsee, taking the sleeping bag and walking off toward the shed. There was an old army cot in it, on the duckboards. Flowerpots and bags of fertilizer, garden tools on nails, sanctuary.

Du Pré watched him go, smiled, went back in the house.

✦ CHAPTER 2 ✦

Du Pré signed off on the two truckloads of steers. The brands were good and the destinations usual. Feedlots in Nebraska, then to pot roasts in Chicago or St. Louis. The drivers pulled away, the long double-deck trailers stinking, green shit running down here and there from airholes, ammonia and bawling. The buyer's check had been handed over to the Oleson brothers, Ike and Earl, in their sixties now and bent as any other old cowboys, a life of fractures and strange strains of work which bowed the bones and made the hands grow huge. They knew horses, wore farmer shoes and tractor-driver hats, claimed it was so that folks wouldn't think they were just truck drivers.

"Some fine day," said Ike, wiping sweat from his forehead with a hand gnarled as old roots. "Earl busted his ankle again chowsing them cows outa the brush. I was too old for this forty years ago, thought I'd maybe do something else, but here I gone and done it anyway."

Du Pré chuckled. What was this place, Montana? Breeds, and squareheads from Scandahoovia, other families from the common American ruck. The land was tough and poor and so were the people. Old cars and old shacks fell into the earth, people starved out in the twenties, left the dried-out dust-eaten little ranches with their homes in their hands. Too poor then to buy grease for the axles of their

4

wagons. The wooden wagon beds could be found beside hundreds of the little trails, gone silver from the sun, parts of them charred from the wheels catching fire where they rubbed the axles to flame.

"When you going to fiddle again?" Du Pré said, looking at Ike Oleson. The old cowboy, never married, a Hardänger fiddler, two extra drone strings on his sawbox. Du Pré fiddled, too, but just the old four-string kind, like his ancestors, the voyageurs, with their red sashes and little tobacco pipes, tasseled caps and the beaded moccasins.

"Sunday afternoon," said Oleson, "at the bar in Toussaint. Good Swede music, then we let you play to clear the hall."

Du Pré heard the squak squak squak of his two-way radio, the dispatcher's stripped voice. What's this? Well, sometimes I get to play lawman, when the Sheriff's deputies are all tangled up. I even have a gun somewhere in that car, I think the trunk. Maybe under the front seat.

Du Pré walked to his old Plymouth, actually bought from the cops, shorn of lights and siren, but still with clips on the door for a rifle and one small bullet hole in the rear window.

"Du Pré," he said, pressing down the red button on the mike.

"Gabe!" boomed the Sheriff's voice, big loud man, everyone liked him even though he sometimes hurt their ears.

"Yes."

"We got a bad wreck on the highway near the Res—and Toomey is off with that busted arm. Them rich drunks own that big house in the foothills of the Wolf Mountains, you know the place?"

"Yah," said Du Pré. Everyone knew the place, ten thousand square feet of house, bigger than the high school in Pomeroy, for Chrissakes, looked like it dropped from space. The people in it came from East Coast money, lots of it, enough to hire help for everything.

"One of their hands claims he found a plane wreck and some skeletons or something up in a dry draw, up high, he was looking around, he said. Probably chasing a deer he shouldn't have shot. Wonder if you'd go look?"

"Don't the FAA handle that?"

"I called them," said the Sheriff. "They got no record of any missing plane could be where the cowboy says it is, so they want proof it is one 'fore they get off their asses."

"Can I get a horse there?" said Du Pré.

"Talk to this guy found it, name's Bodie, I'd think so."

"Am I gettin' paid for this," Du Pré wondered loudly, knowing the answer.

"You know we ain't got that kind of money," said the Sheriff.

"For my gas, at least?"

"Yeah, yeah." Bullshit bullshit.

Du Pré wondered if the cowboy had got kicked in the head or something, was seeing things, like Benetsee.

"OK, I'll do it," said Du Pré. "You call Madelaine, tell her I be late, hear?"

"SURE!" boomed the Sheriff. Du Pré winced.

"What's that all about?" said Ike Oleson.

"I dunno," said Du Pré, "some shit about a plane crash in the mountains. I got to go look at it."

"Up past them rich shits, in the Wolfs?"

Du Pré nodded.

"Hell," Ike said, "I bet them people see things like that all the time. I saw Mrs. Fascelli out there once, she sashayed buck naked across the lawn wavin' an umbrella, singin' she was Mary Poppins or some damn thing."

"No shit," said Du Pré. "Well, they drink a lot, I guess."

"Glad I don't have money," said Oleson.

Du Pré nodded, and got into his car.

✦ CHAPTER 3 ✦

Y ou don't look like no cop," said the young cowboy,
Bodie. He looked very stupid. Ragged dirty shirt,
stained old wool vest, brand-new jeans with the price tags
still on them.

"Auxiliary," said Du Pré.

"What's that?" said Bodie, his little eyes narrowing. Too
many syllables, Du Pré was making fun of him.

"Part-time," said Du Pré.

Bodie considered the hyphenate, spat in the dust.

"I need a horse," said Du Pré, "and you guide me up
where you found this wreck." You stupid son of a bitch.

"You think I'm lyin'?" hissed Bodie. "It's a plane, pro-
peller and everything, lotta bones, couple skulls."

"No, I don't think you lyin'," said Du Pré. I think you're
so fucking dumb you probably found an old campfire and
two white rocks or something. And I pick out the horse I
want, they must all hate you a lot.

"Hey!" A shout from the huge stone and glass and
redwood house, a fat red face hanging out a window.

"Who the fuck are you?" said the face. Someone inside
pulled, the face disappeared.

"Don't mind him," said Bodie. "He's about ready to go
off to the dry-out place again."

7

Bodie walked away, Du Pré followed. He had stopped at a little grocery and beer place on the way, bought jerky and candy bars and a couple butane lighters, case he had to stay out overnight. Late as it was, he would.

Bodie threw Du Pré a catch-rope, pointed to a small cavvy of horses, began hauling saddles, blankets, and tack out of the shed. Clouds were stacking up over the wolf country, high, stuck on the peaks. Du Pré saw an eagle floating motionless. Good. Never mind he had to hold the road map out as far as his arms could stretch to make out the names of the larger towns. Glasses had a way of getting lost and broken.

The trail went straight up through a big fenced pasture, overgrazed, though the fences were so new and well done they could only belong to an owner who needed more to lose money than to make money in the cow business. Bodie rode ahead, fighting a little with the movements of his horse. One of those lousy riders who will never get any better. The horse kept swinging his head side to side, obviously pissed off.

Du Pré looked up at the island mountain range, the nine peaks, robed round with bluffs and foothills. They rose up strangely from the high dry plains, catching enough water from the eastering clouds to make them green with trees and shrubs. The sight of them against the northern sky was as familiar to Du Pré as the house he was raised in and lived in still. Strangers to the country remarked on their beauty. Du Pré was uncomfortable in lands that didn't look like this. It simply was meant to look like this. Home.

Bodie's horse shied, a rattlesnake had sunned upon a flat warm spot on the trail. The bad young cowboy flew hot in rage, beat on the horse until the animal reared and fell over on its side. Du Pré thought he heard Bodie's leg snap. He hoped he had.

"Goddamn it to fucking hell," the boy screamed, hands clasped to thigh.

Du Pré swung down, dropped the reins. His horse stood there, knew Du Pré's hand, knew him. Bodie's horse trotted away, once stepping on a rein and jerking his head. Du Pré knelt by the cowboy, felt the leg. Not broken, but the muscles torn and swelling.

"I'll shoot that fucking horse!" Bodie snarled through his pain.

"No you won't," said Du Pré. "You're not bad hurt. Now, I go catch him for you and you ride on back and you be good to that damn horse. I get back and see his mouth's torn or you hurt him, then I kick your stupid teeth down your throat."

The cowboy gaped at Du Pré.

"It ain't broken?" he said.

Du Pré spat, walked back to his horse. He swung up, went off after Bodie's rangy gelding. Idiot. Shoveling life's shit with a broken handle.

The pony stood waiting, looking back at Du Pré. He grabbed the reins and led him back.

"He'll take you," said Du Pré. "Now where you find this wreck?"

"Little dry draw third shoulder over," said Bodie.

"You just let that horse carry you back," said Du Pré. "I hope he dumps you and kicks you to death. He does, I buy him, feed him oats and carrots every day, molasses. You're too stupid to live."

"My leg . . ." Bodie whimpered.

"Fuck your leg," said Du Pré. He rode on. Before the trail turned he looked back. The cowboy was struggling to mount, the horse's ears were back.

More in the world like him than not, Du Pré thought. God damn it, be like that. Shit.

♣ CHAPTER 4 ♣

He found it right where Bodie had said it was. A mess, yes, but a very old one. A juniper had grown up through the metal frame of a seat. Rusted engine half-buried in the yellow earth of the draw. Bones were scattered around, the coyotes and skunks and badgers would have come along and supped. When this had happened the draw had burned, maybe it had been a rainy night, but it had been a long time ago. The plane had been a light, flimsy one, the marks it would have made when it hit so long ago had been erased.

Du Pré stamped his feet. It was cold, maybe ten above. He had spent the night crouched over a little fire, a saddle blanket on his shoulders.

Candy bars and stale water for breakfast. Madelaine was in bed. Missing him. He hoped.

The light rose. Du Pré cast around, quartered back and forth. He looked down at the place where the sagebrush trunk went into the ground. A jawbone, human. The skull then rolls downhill. So he walked straight down, like water would run. The draw was pretty steep, not much water had moved through it.

The skull was nestled under a flat rock which crossed the little streambed. The spring melts were running through the gravels underneath the slab. Lucky the skull was still whole.

Du Pré knelt, looked, crossed himself. Some days he

10

didn't believe in God, but he did believe in crossing himself.

"Maybe this let you sleep now," said Du Pré. He picked
up the white skull, the color of the giant puffball mushrooms that came up in pastures in the wet years. The
mushrooms were bigger, and startling in the green.

"Now I got someone's head in my hands, I thinking on
frying mushrooms," Du Pré said aloud. "Dumb bastard."

Du Pré turned the skull in his hands. A neat hole in the
forehead of it. Something rattled inside. A thin bone at the
back, near where the spine joined, had been chewed
through by a coyote, so the brains could be licked out. A
slug fell out of the hole, landed on a bed of broken lime
between stones. Dull gray, dull green. Copper jacket then.
Du Pré stared at it.

He looked again at the hole in the skull, punched when
the bone was living, dished, like an awl hole through tin.

Du Pré put the slug in his pocket, snapped the flap shut.
He looked up toward the place where the rusting engine
stained the earth. The sun was up enough now to begin
making clouds, little misty wisps, from the flanks of the
mountains where the frost had bloomed the night before.
They would gather above the peaks, be thick by afternoon.

He put the skull and jawbone in a saddlebag, picked
again over the ground, found another jawbone. Older,
drier, the teeth had slipped from the sockets. If there had
been teeth in them. Well.

Du Pré stood up, arched his back, still cramped from the
night's cold.

"Enough," he said. More than. Now the FAA cops
would come and sift carefully for all the remnants. Haul
the engine down the mountains. Ask tough questions of
the hawks and coyotes? A lot of years ago.

The case would get filed and jawed over in the saloons,

but nothing more, no plane supposed to be here at all. File and forget. A bullet hole in the skull.

Du Pré picked his way back down the draw, leading the horse. The pony was gentle as a puppy, unwilling to give trouble where none was offered, like most creatures. Damn that fool Bodie anyway, he give a bad name to men.

I just don't think they ever find out on this one, not ever. Du Pré whispered a novena, looked back at the place of death. Well, every place was that for something. Du Pré stepped on a spider.

The horse knew the way home, snuffled a little. The sounds of his hooves picked up tempo as the grade flattened. Maybe he thought Bodie had been replaced by Du Pré, now the opportunities for goldbricking would be greater and the new rider wouldn't rip his mouth up with a bad hand on the reins.

Du Pré stopped for water at a little spring purling out of a red band of stone, wreathed in watercress shiny with little black beetles. He plucked a few leaves, shook off most of the bugs. Chewed. The bitter crispness freshened his mouth, the sour taste of old candy bars left.

By sunset he was at the Sheriff's office, the Sheriff chewing mints to mask the Saturday whiskey he allowed himself in adult portions. Let others arrest the amateur drunks, I run this outfit. Nobody should be Sheriff who wants the job.

"Fuck," said the Sheriff, looking at the skull, the hole in it, the jawbones, the slug Du Pré dropped on the counter for punctuation. "Now them FAA's got to come." He turned the slug around in his fingers. "How come you didn't put this in an evidence bag?"

"Didn't have any," said Du Pré. "Remember, I inspect brands. They don't make evidence bags big enough put a cow in."

The Sheriff looked at him hard, fuzzed up, trying to come back but too much Canadian hooch on his tongue, just sitting there.

"What about that cowboy found this?"

"Oh, no," said Du Pré. "That dummy, he wasn't even born this happened. No. Anyway, he's too stupid to do any killing, 'cept maybe his mother or girl when he's drunk. He'll end up in Deer Lodge, he's dumber than a box of rocks."

"What do you think of this?" said the Sheriff. He was staring up at the ceiling, trying to get sober.

"I don't," said Du Pré. "I don't understand it. I'm glad I don't have to."

Du Pré dusted his hands, picked up his hat.

"Where you goin'?"

"Confession," said Du Pré. "I go to Mass in the morning."

"Well, good luck."

Du Pré's eyes crinkled. He laughed.

✤ CHAPTER 5 ✤

I'm still living in sin with Madelaine Placquemines," said Du Pré, to the dim shadow behind the confessional screen.

"Good," said Father Van Den Heuvel.

"Also I wanted to kill somebody." Du Pré thought of shooting Bodie. It made him happy. Bodie bled in the dust and the horses smiled at Du Pré.

"Did you?"

"No," said Du Pré. Good idea, though.

"Two sins. Good week. Got any more, I'm running a special."

"Don't think so."

"Couple Hail Marys. The words are pretty, you'll like them."

The priest absolved him.

Du Pré struggled out of the booth, looked at the few others who were waiting. His daughter Jacqueline, pregnant again, flowing.

Du Pré the grandfather, at forty. Five times over. She started young with her man. Fifteen, him seventeen. She wanted twelve. Du Pré didn't want to remember that many names, but he supposed he could.

He stopped and bent over to kiss her. She smelled beautiful, no perfume, just her.

"You come by, eat?" Jacqueline murmured.

"Sure," said Du Pré, "what we bring?"

"Wine and your fiddle."

Du Pré walked out of the church, smiling. His wife died so suddenly, cancer of the blood, seemed like a bad cold till she died just like that, less than two weeks. The two girls, four and nine then, very bad time. Jacqueline got very mad personally with Death, take one of hers she send back twelve till Death give up. Just you wait and see, for sure.

And my other daughter, child of the times, Du Pré thought, grimacing. Horrible, loud, mean music, forty lipsticks all at once, the only roached hair in the town.

Poor Du Pré, the mothers of the families said, while their children got drunk and knocked each other up or finally got through school and went off to the service or college

14

or, often enough, to Deer Lodge Prison when the judge's patience ran clean out.

He wondered for a moment if Maria was still a virgin. Probably not. All things taken into account, probably none of Du Pré's business. She was a young woman of fourteen, going on twenty-five. When she got to twenty-five, she'd look back and wince. Like everybody.

I don't know the proper noises to make, Du Pré thought. I could threaten her with convent boarding school. She'd laugh. She keeps trying to piss me off. I think. If I get mad, she cries. I do not understand any of my women.

He drove out of the town toward his house. Maria's boyfriend's old pickup truck was in the driveway and loud horrible noises came from the house. Some people might think it was music, but Du Pré knew better.

Du Pré parked his car, went on in. The two had been necking on the couch or whatever, Du Pré had enough sense to flick his headlights coming up the drive and smoke a cigarette before coming in. When you just walk on in like a dumbass you deserve what you get, anyway.

The living room smelled of beer. Lust. People.

Maria and her boyfriend—what was his name, Raymond? Dark and surly kid with high-top running shoes, embarrassed at not knowing what the fuck was going on anywhere, like any other boy his age.

"TURN THAT SHIT OFF!" Du Pré roared. His head hurt. Maria, pouting a bit for appearance's sake, punched the button on the record player, and it died.

For this, no resurrection, Du Pré thought. Hah.

"Good evening, Raymond," said Du Pré to the boy.

"He's Billy," said Maria, eyes narrowing, "and he's been Billy for some time."

Du Pré nodded.

"Sorry," he said. I'm not, either.

Billy looked at the floor and his untied shoelaces.

"You got a report card?" said Du Pré. I play father, maybe she be nice and not laugh at me in front of Billy, here.

Maria brought it. She got very good grades, though Du Pré had never seen a textbook in the house. Just magazines.

"Very good, daughter," said Du Pré. "All A's, one B, who was this prick anyway? She didn't get this from me.

Maria smiled, they would hug later.

If she needs me to take care of her some way I'll do it, thought Du Pré, but I am afraid to try it on my own. He looked at Billy. Was I as dumb, clumsy, and loutish as this boy? Undoubtedly. It's a wonder there are any people at all, something didn't eat us all a million years ago. I see Billy, I cannot believe in evolution. It is not a religious matter.

Don't make fun of the boy, it hurts forever.

"We go to dinner at your sister's tomorrow?" said Du Pré.

"No, I got something else," said Maria. She didn't like her sister these days, having beautiful babies, being a real woman, damn age anyway.

Du Pré thought Maria would shoot out of this place like a missile, get an education, and what Du Pré thought of that no matter. He thought it was wonderful, but didn't want to screw anything up by approving at the wrong time.

I don't know how to do this, Du Pré thought, Jackie and Maria do. I think. I hope.

"I'll be at Madelaine's," said Du Pré.

Like I always am, and all the kids will be drinking beer here and maybe smoking a little grass, but I have never come back at a reasonable hour of the morning to find the place not cleaned up, so I suppose she is not trying to tell me anything.

I don't understand any of my women and I am not going to, it is beyond me and that's that.

He walked down the gravel walk, looked out at the horse pasture and his six head, standing there in a circle, plotting something.

"Just keep quiet, Daddy Du Pré," he said to himself, "An' let your daughters take care of you, or if you don't, make noises, they will *really* take care of you."

Know that for sure, yes I do.

✤ CHAPTER 6 ✤

Du Pré was prepared for complete assholes, these FAA's. But they turned out to be pleasant weary professionals who sorted out death and destruction, maybe save someone's life down the road. Unlike the FBI and BATF agents, who were jerks to begin with and then exiled to Montana to boot. Made them vicious. Take Leonard Peltier, for instance, take Wounded Knee. The second one.

Their work made the FAA inspectors direct.

"You Indian?" one said. Not "Native American."

"Some," said Du Pré. "A lot, really. But Frenchy enough so the anthropologists don't bother us."

"A blessing," said the FAA man. "My sister was married to an anthropologist for a while."

The FAA men had come in by plane and a helicopter had been chartered from a local cropduster. Du Pré hated helicopters. The fucking things could not possibly fly, or anyway not long enough. *Whack whack whack. I ask you.*

Du Pré sat by the pilot to point out the way.

The flight was short, a few minutes. A horse gives you time to get there, Du Pré thought. The noisy shaking machine touched down on a barren flat spot less than half a mile from the crash. The FAA agents, just two of the four, the others would come the next trip, got out with their cases of cameras and metal detectors.

Du Pré had helped sort through one other crash, but it was fresh and stinking. This was very old, here. The only smell was pine and sage.

Du Pré helped carry the equipment, his load a tripod and a heavy backpack full of something or other.

He led them up, the older agent wheezed a little.

Du Pré stopped by the rusting half-buried engine. The two FAA men looked around, whistling.

"Long time ago," said the older man. He'd got his breath back.

"Beats intestines hanging from the trees," said the other one. With such a job black humor let you sleep at night, among other things.

"I suppose I stay out of the way?" said Du Pré.

"Oh, no," said the older one. "Mr. Du Pré, we're city folks. If you could look around, maybe spot something. You'd be better than us at seeing things that were out of place."

Du Pré nodded, rolled a cigarette and smoked, watching them set up their cameras and take out tape measures and a box of plastic bags. For parts of planes. Parts of people. Long time ago.

Du Pré looked up the draw, up at a weathered cliff, the common gray stone of these mountains. There was a yellow scar of fresh rock thirty feet from the top. He won-

18

dered if the plane had hit there. Bounced back. Wait, an old Ponderosa pine rotting into the ground, laid out like a pointer from the scar on the rock to the engine buried in the yellow earth. A spray of rotted branches clustered round the little block of steel. The trunk of the tree was slumping into dust, spilling red sawdust from the jaws of the big black carpenter ants.

"Hey," said Du Pré, "I think maybe it hit up there, then land in the crown of the tree. Maybe the tree was already dead, they get hit by lightning. Then it went over, roots rotted out."

". . . And then the engine and such landed here when the tree come down. Maybe. Maybe I'm full of shit, too."

"I like this guy," said the younger FAA man. "Sounds good, even the full of shit part."

"Can we get up there?" said the older man, pointing at the scar on the cliff wall.

Du Pré looked. "Need a rope, you can't climb this rock, it's too rotten. But anything hit there, it should fall to that ledge below, should still be there. I can get to that, easy enough."

"If you find Judge Crater or Nixon's integrity or anything, you call down, we'll bag it up."

Du Pré climbed up slowly through the rubbled rock the ledge had shed to frost. When he finally rolled up on to the flat he sat up and saw an easier way, good game path on it, fifty feet away. Always worked out like that, life.

The grass and shrubs were sparse, spalled scree littered the ledge. Good place for rattlesnakes. He quartered back and forth, saw a square black corner, tugged a radio from the duff, beneath it was a gauge of some kind with the glass broken out.

"I found a radio and a gauge," Du Pré called down. "You want to come up or I just bring it to you?"

19

"God damn it, look again, and don't see anything," the younger man laughed. He picked up some plastic bags, slung his camera and bag on his shoulder. He started up the way Du Pré had gone.

"It's easier over there," Du Pré called down, pointing to his right.

Du Pré looked down at his boot. There was a coyote turd there, a rope of deer hair from a scavenged kill, and the gleaming tiny skull of a shrew.

Du Pré put the scat in his pocket, snapped the flap.

✦ CHAPTER 7 ✦

How nice you come see me now and again," said Madelaine. "I already have one husband run off, now my boyfriend is practicing, yes? Hunh?"

Du Pré grinned at her. His wife dead, her husband gone crazy, maybe even dead, gone three years, not a peep. She wanted to divorce him for desertion but the Church says wait. I want to marry this woman but God won't let me. Bullshit.

Father Van Den Heuvel says about the same thing. No wonder he's here, ass end of nowhere, him a very educated man. Among the heathen I should wear my red sash more.

"I marry you today, Madelaine," said Du Pré. "Go and roust the Judge."

"I don't care what the Judge think," said Madelaine. "I care what God may think."

A good girl, four children, not wanting to blow Paradise.

God, He ought to get to work on time, stay later, tend to business.

All four of her kids were doing good in the schools, happy kids, poor, lots of love here and Madelaine firm on doing one's best. And working in the huge garden out back, where the stuffs they canned for the winter grew. When you sweat to grow what you eat it fills you up better.

"So what's this airplane's name? Uh. Debbie?"

"Bonnie," said Du Pré. An old and loving game they played.

"Well," said Madelaine, letting her robe fall open, "I 'spose I love that you still have some time for me, you bastard."

They went to bed, hot flesh, need, lay spent.

"I got to go out northwest for a while," said Du Pré. "I got a feeling someone is maybe selling beef too quick."

"Who?" said Madelaine.

"Oh," said Du Pré, "I don't know, be a brand inspector, you just got to show up a lot of places where you not supposed to be at all. You know, kill a beef and sell it out of your car to people. Or back up a small truck with a portable chute, load it quick and take the cattle to a small slaughterhouse, the owner pays in cash, good deal for everyone but the poor rancher."

"Now I got to worry, a cow," said Madelaine. "What's her name?"

"Josephine."

"I got a daughter named Josephine . . ."

"She's six, too old for me," said Du Pré.

"Beast."

Du Pré got up, dressed.

"Du Pré," said Madelaine, "that daughter you got, she

21

could come live here, you know. I make her put her hair back nice."

"Oh," said Du Pré.

"Oh. What. Oh? She shames you running around like that with that worthless stupid Billy."

"I'm not shamed by her," said Du Pré. "Thing about Maria is she's her own. They both are."

"That damn hair."

"Madelaine," said Du Pré, patiently, "I know that you want to help. Well, help me. You try to run Maria, she'll buck. She's a good girl, she just doen't want to be a breed girl in bunghole Montana. She'll go away, find that there are worse things to be, try some of them. My daughters take good care of me."

"How's that?"

"They don't tell me everything," said Du Pré.

"Women don't never tell everything," said Madelaine. She grinned.

"Josephine, I'm coming," Du Pré sang. He had a good tenor, good for the chansons, good for the reels. Sometimes when he sang he felt his people back there a couple centuries, little French-Cree-Chippewa voyageurs, singing while they hauled the heavy packs of furs to Sault Sainte Marie for the Company of Gentlemen Adventurers of Hudson Bay. The HBC. Here Before Christ, to some.

They sweated and starved and froze, those little voyageurs. The men who made the money off the furs died of gout and port.

"Say," said Madelaine, "I want to hear you fiddle some this time soon—I see there is a fiddler's jamboree on Saturday. Maybe I even let you drink too much wine."

"Sure," said Du Pré.

"If Josephine let you go," said Madelaine, pouting.

"I ask her," said Du Pré.

Madelaine threw a shoe at him.

✦ CHAPTER 8 ✦

The big old saloon was crowded, it had been built back in the days when ranchers had lots of hands instead of lots of machinery. A lot of fiddlers here, even some college boys from somewhere, all trying to make authentic music. They didn't seem to know what music was, but they were hell-bent on authentic.

Du Pré set his violin case down on a small table, helped Madelaine with her coat.

"Josephine says I can stay late, drink a lot, stop off and see her on the way home," said Du Pré.

"Moo," said Madelaine. "I want some wine."

Pink wine. Sweet. Kind she liked was made out of bubble gum, Du Pré thought.

Du Pré got her a big glass, himself some whiskey. The woman behind the bar had a lacquered beehive hairdo, blond and white, with dark roots. Her hands were red from washing everything.

The Oleson brothers came in, dressed alike, new denims and the railroad red cotton kerchief. Ike was carrying the mangy case his curly-maple Hardänger fiddle slept in.

Du Pré hated Hardänger music. He claimed it had been invented to scare herring into the nets. *Scree. Scraw.* But he liked Ike Oleson.

23

The college boys were murdering "The Red-Haired Boy," a tune Du Pré would like to have heard in other than a tortured state. While the boys screeked away, they stared at Du Pré and the Olesons. Jesus Christ, Justin, there's some real ones. Right, Nigel.

"You look good there," said Ike, coming by, taking his hat off to Madelaine. Elderly bachelor, always a gentleman to the ladies, who scared him witless.

"You lookin' good, Dupree," said Oleson. Du Pré wondered what chickenshit television program the old fart had been watching. Du Pré indeed. These English, even if they were Swede.

"You play that Injun fiddle, eh?" said a big half-drunk man, so drunk it seemed a reasonable question to him.

"Wahoo," said Du Pré, turning away. The man went off.

"Play 'The Steep Portage,' Du Pré," said Madelaine.

"I want to wait a minute," said Du Pré, "see them tune." There were a dozen fiddlers twisting keys, the college boys would be tuned by the century's end.

Du Pré looked down at his feet, beaded moccasins in red and turquoise and yellow and black. Old Nez Percé woman over in Idaho did them. Du Pré had asked her if they were old Nez Percé designs. She had said no, she got them out of a book in a language she could not read.

"What language?" Du Pré asked.

"Japanese!" said the old woman, laughing.

"Hey! Du Pré!" Buster Lacroix from fifty miles east, played the rib bones.

Du Pré fiddled, Buster thocked out the rhythm hard. He made the good ringing bones from the third rib of a fat steer, aged them in the shitpile, or so he said.

The college boys looked hungrily at the two of them. Go

24

be some professors, Du Pré thought, we got to work our lives.

Some of the Métis women began to dance, the old reels and Cree glories, leftovers from the days when the Red River carts with their huge cottonwood wheels skreeked and scrawked down from the north to hunt the buffalo. The Métis drove the buffalo into stout blind corrals or drove the herds from swift surefooted buffalo ponies. Make everybody meat for the winter. The carts sounded for many miles over the prairies. At night the men gambled. The leaders were all poor, like those of the Indians who were the lost generous and humble. Wealth was a sign of a bad heart. The more power you had, the less you owned. Nobody who ever wanted a chief's job got it.

Take that, you white fools who want to be president.

Madelaine got up, joined the ring of dancing women. Her heavy breasts swung while she danced. She threw back her head, laughed, her white even teeth startling in her brown face. Her black hair flashed crimson, sheen of fire.

Long ago the English hanged poor mad Louis Riel, him with his visions and little talks with God, Jesus, the Holy Ghost, the saints Louis had heard of. Many of the Métis came down to Montana. To the old buffalo grounds, just before the buffalo were all slaughtered, just before the great cattle drives began. North to fatten scrawny Texas steers on good Montana grass, Texans came with the cattle, and Montanans hated them then and hate them still.

Gabriel danced too much and fiddled too much and drank too much. Madelaine danced too much and drank too much sweet pink wine and she flirted with the men, who laughed and nudged each other.

When they left, the fiddles were wobbling in search of the right notes.

25

Gabriel was too drunk to go to confession, so was Madelaine.

In the night the telephone rang. It was the Sheriff's office. Maria and some other kids had been busted, beer, a little dope. The Sheriff would let her go if Du Pré came to get her.

"No," said Gabriel, "I leave her there till morning."

Madelaine was half-asleep, but she woke up for that.

"You won't go get your own daughter out of jail?" she said.

"It would just make her mad with me if I did," said Du Pré. "See, that girl likes taking her licks for her own doings, you know? They are both pretty tough, my girls."

"I don't know," said Madelaine.

"My girls, I do," said Du Pré.

He went and fetched Maria early in the morning. They said nothing to one another while he drove her home.

She kissed him on the cheek and said a soft "thank you."

That be that, thought Du Pré. Whew.

✤ CHAPTER 9 ✤

Du Pré came back from checking out a long stretch of fence that was seldom watched. Ranchers were so pressed for time that often they did not miss stolen stock until the fall roundup, if the thieves repaired the fence. Du Pré watched for tire tracks in the barrow pits, fences a little saggy, maybe new wire bright on a splice. You could get a couple thousand dollars in a truck in a hurry. Beat wages, yes it did.

But he hadn't seen anything. Times like this he had his gun on the seat, in its holster. He'd arrested two men a few years before, one of them actually reaching for a rifle when Du Pré had shot and winged the bastard, shattering the man's upper arm. Then the judge let the guy off easy, on account of the trouble of his arm.

"He reach that rifle, maybe I'd be dead," said Du Pré. "Damn his fuckin' arm anyway."

No one paid any attention to Du Pré. The man got a year. Suspended.

So much, thought Du Pré, for my fuckin' civil rights, like breathing.

When he had offered that opinion the judge threatened him with jail for contempt.

The world was in a sack, for sure, Du Pré thought.

Used to be, Montana, you just shot them, said to the judge that they needed killing, went to the saloon.

Du Pré looked down the road from the top of the Big Bench toward Toussaint. The yellow-gray packed dirt, ribboning down to the shabby little town. The Sheriff's big fat cruiser, more damn lights on it than a Vegas hotel, coming up toward Du Pré.

I don't like this, Du Pré thought. I am a cow-ass man. A specialist in burnt skin and hair. Pyrography, I think that they call it. Shit. He hoped the Sheriff's car would blow up or something.

Du Pré pulled over to a snowplow turnaround, big pile of sand to spread on the icy spots, little gravel in the sand so big trucks can blast holes in your windshield when they pass you. He got out, rolled a cigarette, smoked it, wished he would quit. Bad for you, but I like it.

The Sheriff's cruiser slowed, turned in, parked beside Du Pré.

"Du Pré," the big man boomed, "I got news. That plane

went down thirty-five years ago, rancher and his wife from the Dakotas, someplace, Pembina I think. Didn't file a flight plan or nothing. You know how the people are around here. Government *says* I *got* to do something, fuck them till they ask politely, then maybe I'll think about it."

Du Pré nodded. He knew what the people around here were like, sure enough. Hell, when Montana convened its first legislature the first elected governor refused to swear allegiance to the damn Yankees, claiming that Pemberton's Missouri army had just marched northwest and was still in the game. The legislature removed the offending language from the oath of office. Kill a Montanan, you got to cut off their head, bury it where they can't find it.

"There's parts of three people up there, though. They got most of two skeletons. And another skull and extra fingers and hand bones."

"Sonofabitch," said Du Pré. "The Headless Man."

The Sheriff nodded.

A generation ago, when Du Pré was still a boy, twelve, maybe, a rancher found a corpse without head or hands, pretty rotten, too, dumped in a culvert. Not a tooth or a fingerprint to go on. Guy had an appendix operation scar, couple other dings. No clothing. Du Pré remembered his father talking about it, the year before he died.

"Bloated up pretty good," said Du Pré's father, a brand inspector, too, quiet guy, called "Catfoot" because he never wore anything but moccasins and barely ruffled the dust when he walked.

"We haul him out, coroner let the gas out of him, man, what a stink. So we send the meat off to the state lab, they send back a paper says the guy is dead, sure enough, so we wouldn't worry, and without anything to identify him with. They ask around, see if anyone got a head and a pair of hands, want the rest of the act. But no. Guy was about thirty-five, white, and that's all anyone ever knows. Had his appendix out, but it didn't help him much, I guess."

"Long before my time," said the Sheriff, "I didn't move here from the Bighorn country till seventy-five."

"Well, maybe," said Du Pré. He wondered why the Sheriff always shouted. Maybe he was deaf, too vain to wear a hearing aid. Maybe he was just a loud bastard.

"Report's at the office," said the Sheriff. "Maybe you could look at it."

"I ain't a cop," said Du Pré.

"Yeah," shouted the Sheriff, "But your people go back more'n a century here, maybe you know somebody knows something."

Du Pré spat at a beetle struggling through the gravel under his boots.

"I mean," said the Sheriff, "you ought to be a little curious, at least."

"No more than to lean over, someone telling the whole story in a bar," said Du Pré.

Du Pré got in his car, drove off toward Toussaint, and the Sheriff's office in Cooper, few miles on.

"Why," he said to himself, "would somebody go to all that trouble, kill someone, cut off the head and hands, hump them up into the Wolf Mountains, stick them in an old plane wreck. Knew the country good, knew about the plane wreck. Knew it better than all these folks who spent their lives poking around in this country, find the Lost Bullfrog Mine or something."

Or was it something else?

Du Pré thought. He remembered spitting on a dirty rock once, and a head rose up out of the coils, and the rattle started.

But before he spat, it was just a rock, you hear?

✤ CHAPTER 10 ✤

Du Pré hadn't liked reporters since he met one. They had very bad manners and they always got everything wrong or if they got anything right they misspelled it. One had come a few years back to do a piece on the fiddlers and he spelled Métis "Metissé," like a goddamned movie writer or something.

The movie people were so much worse they were kind of fun. One bunch had hired Du Pré at two hundred a day as a "consultant" while they made some piece of crap about a Sioux kept a pet grizzly—they thought grizzlies ate soybeans or something—and every time this Sioux killed a buffalo he held a wake for it. All the Sioux's relatives keening over this fine buffalo, good fellow, strong, brave, great singer and dancer, forgive us for making stew out of you our brother. The Sioux was extreme badasses, and before the whites give them horses and guns they was eating each other and any Cree that they could catch. As in, "We feeling peckish, so it is you, Least Muskrat. Apologies to you for we are eating you our brother." But never mind.

The deputy got the report for Du Pré, passed it over the counter, right under the nose of some watery-eyed asshole from the *Great Falls Tribune*. The reporter very much wanted to talk to Du Pré, as Du Pré had found the wreck.

"No, I didn't," said Du Pré. "The wreck was found by a cowboy named Bodie, works for the Crossed Eyes Ranch.

Big house, looks like it belongs in a big city, up the road toward the Wolfs."

"The Crossed Eyes Ranch?" said the reporter.

Du Pré nodded.

"Oh, bullshit," said the deputy. "It's the old Higgins place, but he's right about the house. Bodie's gone, though."

"Gone?" said Du Pré.

"Yeah," said the deputy. "Seems he owed a bunch of child support and his name wasn't Bodie anyway. So he's in jail in Miles City."

"Ho," said the reporter. "So I could talk to Mr. Dew Preee?"

"He's dead," said Du Pré. The deputy pointed and rolled his eyes.

Du Pré grunted, reading the simple report. Remains of three people, two had died of impact and fire, most likely, and the one extra skull with a bullet hole in it, the slug was probably a .38, but so weathered all the striations had long since worn off.

The hole in the skull was the sort a .38 could make, or a pole barn spike, or a meteorite that size. The skull with the hole in it lasted longer because it was not all crunched up when the plane hit and probably had arrived there at a later date, maybe.

The examining pathologist signed off, probably laughing at the very thought of ever finding out any more about this particular homicide, maybe, by bullet or pole barn spike or meteorite, maybe.

"Could I see that?" said the reporter, looking at the paper in Du Pré's hand.

"Sorry," said the deputy, taking the paper. "It's a murder under investigation." (Fuck You.)

"Could I talk to you, Mr. Dew Preee?"

31

Du Pré looked at the asshole. "I'm a brand inspector," he said.

"But you found the plane."

"Yeah," said Du Pré, "but I got a bunch of cow asses I got to go kiss. I ain't a cop. I don't have anything to do with this."

Du Pré walked out, got into his car, decided to go on home, maybe see how Maria was and if she wanted to talk to him, which she probably didn't.

He hoped the reporter would go up, talk to the rich drunks, get his shoes puked on.

Du Pré turned down the side road to his house, saw a crabbed figure tacking and yawing on the right side, sometimes throwing up his arms and tossing his head back. Nearly falling over.

Benetsee. Three parts drunk out of a possible two. Headed for Du Pré's house. First time, since Benetsee used to come by, see the Catfoot, the two of them would go and pick arrowheads out of the plowed fields in the spring, pull mussel shells out of the creeks for their wives to make buttons from.

Benetsee, now, he tells me about the coyote howling by the bones up the in that draw, tells me I'll figure it out when I see Coyote scratch the earth. They scratch the damn earth all the time. The old fart knows something. Probably everything. I think I don't want to talk to him.

Someday I'll be senile, won't know anything at all, whew.

Just like God, maybe He's senile.

Du Pré pulled up beside the old man. The drunken old fart was singing, high thin voice, Coyote French, love song for a voyageur's girl. Pull on the rope, bring me home. Benetsee was carrying a little bundle of dried flowers.

32

Du Pré rolled down the far window. "Want a ride?" he yelled.

Benetsee glanced at him, went off singing again, made an obscene gesture. No, and go do things to a lame coyote.

Du Pré shrugged, drove on. Now I got to go look for him at sunset, or maybe he freeze to death tonight. Damn.

Maria had the stove in the kitchen stoked up so it was red hot. It was so warm she was washing the dishes and cleaning up in a bra and panties. When she heard him come in she grabbed a robe, wrapped it around herself.

My daughter's a woman, good-looking, too, thought Du Pré. Ass like her mother's. Figures.

"You want something to eat," said Maria. "Billy brought us some venison, I got some other stuff at the store."

"Sure," said Du Pré. "Old Benetsee may show up. He's drunk."

"He's always drunk," said Maria.

"He bother you?"

Maria shook her head. "He's just like that, but a good man," she said. "Lots worse things to be than drunk."

"You want to talk to me?" said Du Pré. Make a stab at being a father, I don't know *how*.

Maria shook her head.

♣ CHAPTER 11 ♣

"That girl ever talk to you about the other night?" said Madelaine. She poured them coffee. Her children were off at school, except for the littlest, Sebastian, who had a cold. The kid kept coming into the kitchen, snuffling and sniveling.

"She don't need to talk," said Du Pré. "Thing about Maria is she's a good girl wants us to think she's bad."

"She needs a mother."

"She had one," said Du Pré. "Now all she got is me. And, Madelaine, I don't want you trying to mother her, it just upset both of you, and then, of course, it upset me."

"I just want to help."

"Sometimes the best help is no help at all."

Sebastian wandered back to his lonely bed of pain, a cookie in each chubby fist.

"See," said Du Pré, "when my wife was dying and she knew it and she made her peace with God and sent her love to her people and told me what to feed the dog and the cats. Took care of everything. So I took the little girls, four and eleven, into the big hospital in their little white dresses. Their eyes were very big, Mama was dying, she was going up to heaven, and my wife told me to leave the little girls with her a minute and go out into the hall and wait, she had to talk to them some, women things . . ."

Madelaine was looking very hard at her coffee, more than it deserved.

"So I went out in the hall and the little girls were in there for maybe fifteen minutes, I don't know. And my wife, she went into a coma that night and she never woke up. When she die, I have a house full of relatives, of course, and the priest, and all that, and I go out—it's summer, when she had that bad cold killed her—just to get away from all the people . . ."

Madelaine coughed some, sipped some coffee.

"So I'm sitting out there by the little creek, on a log, glad I don't have to hear someone tell me how sorry they are—I loved her a lot, you know, tore my insides out to lose her—and I looked up and there are my two little girls, one has a sandwich for me, the other a half-bottle of whiskey . . .

Madelaine scratched her neck.

"So I say thank you, I eat the sandwich and have some of the whiskey, and Jacqueline says 'Mama told us to take care of you. So we do that. I'm older, so what I'm gonna do is get married soon as I can and have a lot of babies for all the babies that Mama couldn't have for you . . .' "

Du Pré choked up. He caught himself, went on. Madelaine took his hand.

"And then little Maria, who's four, says that while Jacqueline is busy having all those babies she'll take care of me just as good as Mama did, do a real good job for sure."

Madelaine squeezed Du Pré's hand.

"So they raised themselves always thinking got to take care of Papa, don't upset Papa. All I can do is not get upset with them. They have done very well, better than I could have done for them, if I knew what to do for them, which I don't, I think."

"They're jealous of me," murmured Madelaine.

"So you drop dead, Maria will fix her hair back and start

going to Mass and confession again," said Du Pré. "Not that I like the idea."

"I ain't going to drop dead," said Madelaine. "They don't need me mothering them, I guess."

"They might need it," said Du Pré, "but they won't have it."

"You've been a real good father to them."

"I keep my mouth shut, let them take care of me," said Du Pré. "Worst of it was to have a eleven-year-old and a four-year-old do all the cooking. Some of the things I ate, smiling, I still have bad dreams on. But they got better at it and I lived."

Madelaine laughed, a long deep throaty one.

"I'm jealous of them, too," said Madelaine.

"Why?" said Du Pré.

"They got some of you I can't have," said Madelaine, "and I got some of you they can't have."

"Sometimes I feel like a piece of salt-water taffy," said Du Pré.

"Poor Du Pré," said Madelaine dryly. "All these women fussing over him and he feels bad used."

Du Pré grinned. "Not a bad life," he said.

Madelaine yawned. She'd been up all night with Sebastian, in the rocking chair, holding him against the pain.

"I got to go," said Du Pré. "They're shipping some of those Crossed Eyes cattle, I got to sign off on them."

Madelaine nodded.

Du Pré leaned over and kissed her good-bye.

✦ CHAPTER 12 ✦

Du Pré watched the brands closely. Always. A steer was a wad of hundred-dollar bills on the hoof, and it always paid to run a few weren't yours on through. Anytime.

Bodie was out of jail and still limping. He took one look at Du Pré and went as far away as he could without quitting the ranch entire. He spat a lot.

Du Pré looked at the brand. Five fours any old line, couple slashes. Crossed Eyes would have been better. He wondered if the red face that had asked him who he was was strapped to a bed somewhere, screaming.

Shipping two hundred and thirteen head. The trucks backed up and loaded their forty or whatever, two tiers. B A A A A A A A W W W W L L L L L L L L L L L L L L L L L. S S S H H H H H I I I I I I I I I I I I I I I I I I I T T T T.

Cows don't got much of an act, Du Pré thought.

Loaded up, Du Pré signed off. The cattle went down to Wyoming, someone had come into a little money and hated having it, bought cattle. Well, it always was a funny business.

Du Pré saw an old, old cowboy across the way, carrying a plastic sack of garbage to the slit trench where the offal was dumped, then covered with earth dumped by a backhoe every evening, or they would have skunks in numbers, and one skunk was plenty.

Booger Tom. That was the man's moniker. As opposed

37

to a name. Du Pré remembered him from the rodeos of his childhood. Booger Tom had seemed old then, helped in the chutes, too old to ride pickup or play the clown.

"Booger Tom!" Du Pré shouted, the old man was likely deaf.

The old cowboy stopped, stared over at Du Pré. Gabriel walked over to him, hand out.

"Why, if it ain't Gabriel Du Pré," he said. "You're old Catfoot's boy. Yes, well, I ain't seen you in years."

They talked of nothing much, the water or lack of it, weather, dust, cattle, a few men now dead they both had known.

"You always work here?" said Du Pré.

"Forty year. Worked for the Higginses, then these people," Tom said, spitting in the dirt, these people. "Get to my age, it's hard to get work."

"When did Higgins sell this place," asked Du Pré. His mind was prickling.

"Sixty-eight," said Booger Tom.

Gabriel nodded. Maybe. Time was a little close, though.

"But these Fascellis, they leased the place starting in sixty-two . . . waited a while to drop the hammer."

Du Pré's mind prickled a lot.

"Well, who owns it now?" He looked up at the Wolfs.

"Them kids, old man Fascelli died. Them two in the house are his son and daughter. But they ain't around even if they are. They drink. Their mother's in a nursing home. Checks come out of Dee-troyt. Regular about that, anyway."

"Well," said Du Pré, "they seem to be having a lot of fun I guess you'd call it. Jesus."

Booger Tom looked up at the ridiculous house with an old and rarefied hatred.

"When they first come here there was four of them

38

kids," said Booger Tom, "all wild, now there's just the two."

The fat red face Du Pré recalled staggered out of the front door of the gross house, lurching like his feet had forgot where his body was. The man found a lawn chair and fell into it. He turned to the house and yelled something Du Pré couldn't make out. A maid hurried to him, bearing a tray with bottles and an ice bucket on it.

"I got to go," said Booger Tom, staring hard at the drunk.

Du Pré started walking to the man sprawled in the lawn chair. He was drinking something brown out of a tall glass, and spilling it on his shirt. Shaking his head as though confused.

But by the time that Du Pré got there he was cold sober.

"May I help you?" he said pleasantly.

"Gabriel Du Pré," said Du Pré. "I just inspected the brands on your cattle. All in order, too, I signed off on them."

"I should hope so," said the man. "Drink?" He waved a red hand at the tray, the bottles, his life.

Gabriel nodded. The man put a double slug into a glass, added ice and water, handed it up.

"I'm Bart Fascelli," said the man, offering his hand.

The change fascinated Du Pré.

Gabriel shook the hand.

"So," said Fascelli, "you inspect brands. Do you know horses?"

"A little."

"Come and look at my pasofinos."

He led Gabriel to the horse barn, a new one, white with blue trim. It would have looked good on some millionaire's racing farm, in Kentucky, here it looked like it dropped from the moon.

They talked about horses. Then Bart walked Gabriel to his car.

"Come anytime," said Fascelli, his big red hands on the window.

Du Pré nodded and drove away.

"Now what's this shit about?" he said aloud.

A woolly bear caterpillar crawled across the dashboard. The orange band was wide.

Sign of a hard winter, some said.

✤ CHAPTER 13 ✤

Du Pré stood up and cheered loudly. Maria had just sunk a long jump shot and put her team ahead. The girls raced downcourt, set themselves in their defense. The crowd was fiercely partisan. Three fights had already broken out.

Girls' basketball. They were fast and graceful. This was fairly new, Du Pré thought, all them years when no one taught girls to move their arms when they run or shoot a basketball. They were good, damn good, and much fun to watch.

"Look at them now," said Madelaine. "These girls, they are very good. Your daughter, she's the star, see her shoot!"

Madelaine's oldest, Suzanne, was the center. Tall, like her vanished father.

Toussaint had no high school, the kids went to Cooper, the other team was from Fort Benton. Better team, lots more kids to pick from.

The breeds yell for Toussaint, the whites yell for Cooper, same team, Du Pré thought. What a bunch of fools we all are.

Maria fouled out. Du Pré saw her roached hair in some sort of cartoon whirligig, he expected to see dust, fist here, head there. She always fouled out. The Crusher, her teammates called her.

"My daughter, she take life very seriously," Du Pré muttered.

"What?" said Madelaine.

I don't understand any of my women, even when I do.

"Nothing," said Du Pré. He muttered to himself, came of working alone, someone to talk to.

Madelaine huffled, mad he wouldn't tell her.

"Du Pré," said Madelaine, "you go talk to your daughter, there."

Maria was on the bench, slumped over with her head in her hands.

Du Pré picked his way down the creaky bleachers.

"Child," he said, behind her, his hand on her shoulder. Maria turned. She had been crying. Her eyes crinkled up.

"I wanna play football, sack quarterbacks," she said.

Du Pré touched a bruise on her forehead, right above the eyebrow.

"You go sit there," said Maria, "right there." She pointed to an empty spot on the bleachers behind her. Du Pré sat. She walked round the bench and came and sat next to him, leaned against him. She smelled fresh, young sweat without much sin in it.

They watched her team lose.

"We wait for you, buy you a pop or something," said Du Pré. "Now where is Billy?" He looked back for the boy.

Maria shrugged. Billy was not doing good with her, for sure.

41

"Well," said Du Pré, "you want the pop or you got more fun folks to be with?"

"I bother Madelaine," said Maria.

"She bother you."

"S'pose I ought to learn to put up with her," said Maria.

"Hey, make it easy on your papa. Damn women anyway."

Maria laughed and went off to the showers.

Du Pré and Madelaine stood waiting for their children. Other parents slapped backs, exchanged dinner invitations, replayed the game, the shots, the errors.

Two men began shouting and swinging at each other.

Maria came out first, scruffy clothes, torn jeans, cheap boots that crumpled around her ankles, one papier-mâché earring. All clean, mind you. Du Pré wondered if she broke her clothes in with a hatchet.

"I want to go dancing," said Maria, "but there's no place to go."

"Who you gonna dance with?" said Du Pré. "Since Billy's went missing?"

"Myself alone," said Maria. Whatever the trouble, she was really mad with him. Billy should switch on his old truck, suck the tailpipe good and hard.

"OK," said Du Pré. "You dance with your old fart father, bar in Toussaint's got a jukebox."

Suzanne's fella was waiting on her, glands visibly throbbing.

Du Pré, Madelaine, and Maria got into the old cruiser and he drove to the bar in Toussaint. They took a little table and Gabriel bought soda for Maria, pink wine for Madelaine, whiskey for himself.

Du Pré danced with his daughter, danced with Madelaine, and then Maria danced by herself. A young half-drunk cowboy asked to join her. She nodded. The two

42

slouched together on the slow songs, danced far apart on the fast ones.

Du Pré walked out to Maria, nodded to the cowboy. "I got to go and you got to come with me," he said. The bar rules were that children were OK, but with a parent and no booze for them.

After they had dropped Maria off, Madelaine asked to go back to the bar for one or two more. Du Pré nodded. He was tired but not sleepy.

I'm listening to a record, he thought, the needle is whispering over the blank grooves, the song hasn't started yet.

But could you dance to it? Have fun?

The Toussaint bar was empty, the woman behind the worn bartop was washing up. Madelaine sat down at a table, Du Pré went to the bar, got a couple for them.

"This all right?" said Madelaine. "You pretty tired. We don't got to stay long."

Du Pré shook his head. "Just a little tired but not sleepy," he said.

Benetsee shuffled out of the men's room. He came over and stood for a moment, swaying a little.

The old man reached in his coat pocket and pulled out a knife, one mostly gone to rust. The elkhorn handle had been gnawed by pack rats.

"This was up in the wall of your shed, there," said Benetsee.

Du Pré picked it up. Handmade. Catfoot used to make knives. Knives for everything. He had more than fifty, Du Pré remembered. Made them out of old sawmill band saw steel.

The knife blade had a skin hook on the tip, a thick curved blade. Half of the top was toothed. Catfoot could skin out a deer, use the saw blade to saw through the joints in minutes.

Benetsee shuffled out the door.

Du Pré slipped the knife into his pocket.

Good steel, he thought.

Benetsee, he is telling me something.

What?

❖ C H A P T E R 1 4 ❖

B art Fascelli sat well on his horse. He shrugged inside his long slicker, taking the binds out before riding. Du Pré looked away. Was this the man who had screamed at him from the window?

He was sober now. He had called, wanted to see the place where Bodie had found the wreck. In the rain. He offered to pay Du Pré but Gabriel had refused.

I just listen, that song, someday I know all the words, Du Pré thought.

A maid came out of the house, she had a pair of saddle-bags, one in each hand. She wore just a thin white uniform, hunched herself against the splacking drops.

Probably snowing up there, the Wolfs, but it was early, not like the last time, they'd have light to make camp in.

Du Pré tied the bags behind him, they were fairly heavy. Du Pré wondered if there was a portable sauna in one of them. But Fascelli was sober, no reek of alcohol. Even if he'd been drinking yesterday he'd still smell.

Du Pré couldn't figure him out. He had a twin brother, maybe?

No.

There were two Barts. Maybe more. Time to time he went off his head. Did he want to go up there, see if he remembered it? When he had a sack across his horse? A sack that dripped little streaks of watery red?

So we go to a place of death and puzzles. Du Pré remembered Catfoot taking him, a child, to an old battleground, the air was sad there, Du Pré had been frightened. A place of bad hearts.

He crossed himself, felt the lump in his shirt pocket.

The shrew skull in the coyote scat. Du Pré had put the hairy turd in a little black plastic box, one that once held a hundred rounds of .22 ammunition. Gopher loads.

I don't think I probably want to know the answer to all this but I'm going to out anyway, Du Pré thought. A small cascade of icy water sluiced off his hat, onto the narrow strip of skin between his sleeve and glove. He moved his hand out of the way. The horse chuffled, swung his head, Du Pré had bumped the bit a little.

Du Pré clucked to the horse, a fine-gaited pasofino. Little, but tough. He wondered how much the horse cost. Bart wouldn't care about that. Why did he care about this?

They got to the foothills, Bart pulled up, swung down, put his hands in the small of his back and stretched. Snow clouds were huddled against the peaks. It would be damn wet and cold up there, the kind of wet weather kills people. Hypothermia. Eats flatlander backpackers. Not often enough. All the streams were polluted with *Giardia* now, the ninnies always brought their dogs, the better to spread it further.

"Some country, isn't it?" said Bart, banging one gloved hand into the other.

"All I know," said Du Pré, "but I like it pretty good."

"That plane went down in . . . 1959?" Bart asked.

45

"Fifty-seven," said Du Pré. Bart was close. These Fascellis, they came in '62. Did he come up here in '62, young then, on fire for the mountains? Find the wreck, keep it close against his need?

Long damn time for all these questions to wait.

Du Pré wondered why something kept nibbling out on the edge of his mind, telling him he didn't really want to know about this one. But he had to know now, even if he didn't want to.

Bart swung back up, headed up the trail. At the gate in the high fence he got down, opened the lock, swung the green pipe gate back to let Du Pré through. Gabriel reached for the other horse's reins and tugged the horse along. Bart locked up, swung up, they went on.

He was in good shape, for sure. Bad drunks now, their muscles melt away and they shake, too weak to do anything close to this.

They rode up into timber. A grouse banged off beneath Bart's horse. The animal skittered a little, Bart calmed him, another grouse boomed away from a bush. But the horse was used to them now, didn't even snort.

"You lead," said Bart, moving off the trial. "Where is it anyway?"

"Three miles, maybe four," said Du Pré.

"You think Bodie is stupid?" said Bart.

"Very," said Du Pré. "He's a bad hand with stock. You should fire him. He hurts them."

"Consider it done," said Bart.

"Booger Tom work for you all these years, eh?"

Bart nodded. "He's a nice old man, allowing for cowboy quirks. I like him, he hates us, how could he not? Rich, drunken assholes is what we are."

Du Pré looked away. What about this?

"Runs in the family," said Bart. "We aren't smart

46

enough to be artists. We could get away with a lot more if we were."

Du Pré laughed. He was beginning to like this Bart. The other Bart was a bastard and he hadn't met the rest.

Du Pré flicked his eyes left, right, up, looking for sign, the leaf without the raindrops on it, the shadow in the grass where feet had pressed it down, the branch swaying wrong, where the eagle had lifted off, great wings beating.

They came to the little meadow at the foot of the draw. Du Pré saw a pile of duffel, a big tent all up and taut.

The place where the helicopter had landed.

"I'm staying up here a few days, maybe," said Bart. "Had this stuff flown on up. You do what you want, but I need to stay."

Du Pré looked at him.

"Why you need me to bring you up here for, you knew where it was already?" I got work to do, this ain't it, for sure.

"I didn't really," said Bart. "The flying service just landed these things for me where they came before. I need you to show me where the wreck was, of course."

"OK," said Du Pré. Must be nice, call a helicopter to do the heavy work, say send me the bill.

They grained the horses, hobbled them, turned them loose.

Du Pré led Bart up the draw.

The trail was slick and wet, their boots were not much good for hiking, high heels, slick soles.

They sweated inside their slickers. When they opened them to cool down, their shirts steamed.

✦ CHAPTER 15 ✦

Du Pré stood by the hole in the ground where the little engine had been. The earth had been turned and raked, looking for bits and pieces. They had waved metal detectors, sifted, a lot of hours.

"The plane hit up there," said Du Pré, pointing. The yellow scar on the gray rock was barely visible through the light rain.

"Quick, anyway," said Bart. He walked round, hands in his pockets. The little watercourse was chuckling with runoff. Stunted chokecherry bushes lined the sides of the stream. The place where Du Pré had found the skull was a foot under water.

"It'll snow tonight," said Du Pré. The air smelled of it, and snow was falling hard up higher.

"Tore it up, didn't they?" said Bart. The FAA people had been very thorough. Du Pré could see where someone had even rappelled down the rock face, to measure the scar on the rock. Thirty-odd years and it still showed yellow. These mountains, they rotted very slowly.

But rot they did.

"You going to stay tonight," said Bart, coughing.

"Yes," said Du Pré. Why not, I can't read this man, make anything of him. What do I know to be true about this all?

What in the hell happened here, exactly? And why?

Du Pré rolled a cigarette, flicked his lighter to flame. His mustache was wet. The cigarette turned brown. He cursed and threw the sodden butt away.

Bart pissed. The yellow stream steamed, white tendrils. "I'm just going to wander around," he said. He walked up the path, stooping from time to time.

Du Pré always thought he could think better if he was moving, it probably was just foolishness, like most of life. In a little patch of grass and brush near him he saw a smooth, rounded boulder, a kind of rock from someplace else to the north. The glaciers had covered this place long ago, and crept down from Canada carrying pieces of other mountains in their guts. A close-grained reddish stone, with black mica in it.

Du Pré wondered how far it had come.

The FAA people hadn't cast out this far, the grass hadn't seen a foot on it. Du Pré went to the rock, sat on it, felt the cold through his slicker and jeans. He tilted forward, unbuttoned his slicker, brought out his tobacco pouch, rolled a cigarette, wiped his mustache hard. He lit the smoke, hid under his hatbrim, back to the little wind.

The Olesons ship their stock the day after tomorrow. So I'll go back in the morning, see Madelaine, get a piece of her sweet ass.

He dropped the cigarette. The butt hissed in the wet sparse grass, brown stains shot through the paper, it went out. Du Pré stared at it idly.

A little fleck of white down there between his boots. He poked at it with a finger. A tooth. With a filling in it.

Another one, white with dried brown roots.

Du Pré slipped his pocketknife out of his pants, dug carefully Three more. One had a filling in it, too. Hoo boy.

Du Pré put the teeth in his shirt pocket, next to the little box with the coyote scat. He snapped the flap.

Now what about this?

Whoever hauled that head up here had used this stone for an anvil, knocked the teeth out of the head, probably pounded most of them to dust but these got lost.

Was it coming on dark?

Maybe the guy was working drunk.

Now I got to tell the Sheriff. Now we got a little more, maybe the Headless Man begins to speak.

Or maybe a drunk just fell on this rock, knocked out his teeth.

But these are molars.

The rain ran off Du Pré's hat, a filmy sheet.

Du Pré saw a flash of movement off at the edge of his vision. He turned his head, slowly. A coyote, yellow-gray. The animal's head snapped up. Du Pré had been sitting still thinking and the wet held his scent close.

The coyote was gone, like so much smoke.

God's dogs, the Cree called them. Smart sonsofbitches. Du Pré had seen one robbing a bees' nest once, big clumsy bumblebees. The coyote had waved his thick tail at the nest, the bees attacked it. Then the coyote had turned slowly, the bees kept after his tail, and the coyote gobbled down the honey and larva while the poor bees tried to sting through five inches of fur on the tail. Poor, dumb bees.

I feel like them bees with this murder, here. I'm probably after the wrong end.

Du Pré heard a small plane snarling overhead. In this muck? Better be above it.

Du Pré stood up. He looked again where the coyote had been. The animal was long gone, and surely looking back at Du Pré from some safe and hidden place.

When I die, Du Pré thought, I want to come back as a coyote. If they *are* God's dogs they must know about everything important. Me, I tell my dog everything.

I like it when they sing.

✤ CHAPTER 16 ✤

The snow rattled on the tent, the size of little hard kernels of corn.

First time that I have eaten caviar in the wilderness, Gabriel thought. First time. Catfoot used to make good caviar from them paddlefish eggs. This stuff comes from Russia. Probably even up trade, ounce of gold, ounce of caviar.

And I am liking Bart here. He needs a job. Maybe I tell him, Bart, just sneak off, ride the rods to Portland, get a job as a dishwasher, you'd be happier. Get killed by another hobo on the way, you'd be happier than you are now.

Du Pré was sipping whiskey. Bart was drinking pop. His face wasn't red, he didn't look like he had hanging out the window, cursing.

We all need something to do. Trouble was, Bart would think he had to be the best at whatever he did, make up for the rest of his life. Me, I'm glad I didn't have money waiting on me.

"You like that caviar, eh?" Bart said, grinning. In there, a generous man, really.

Du Pré nodded. "I make some a little different, out of the paddlefish eggs. Put just a touch of the hot pepper sauce in them. The eggs are a little bigger, not much."

"What in the hell is a paddlefish?"

Du Pré described the big fish, sometimes a hundred and fifty pounds, he'd heard it was a relative of the sturgeon.

51

Catch them in the Missouri, the Yellowstone. Bottom feeders, mussels, crawfish, what have you. Maybe stirred the bottom with the paddle on its nose.

"Makes his own caviar," Bart murmured. He stared off far away to someplace cold.

"I barely know how to do anything," he said finally. "My résumé would be short. Drink. Write checks."

Suddenly he grew agitated, scratched himself. Closed his eyes and shivered. When he opened his eyes they weren't the same eyes, they were darker and very desperate. He scrabbled in the box where he had the booze. Lifted out a fifth of vodka, chugged half of it down, choked and heaved, forcing himself not to throw up. Then he sat back, eyes closed again. His hands gripped folds of his trousers. The tendons stood out, practically twanging.

Du Pré watched, wondered. The poor son of a bitch.

Bart let his breath out slowly. His eyes opened.

"Happens when I go off it," he said, "about the third day. Docs tell me I'll die of it sometime. Heart attack or seizure or something. If I jerk and foam, just leave me alone. It would be better than this."

Du Pré nodded. Well, Bart had the comfort of knowing the manner of his death. You could get used to it some that way.

A sudden bash of wind slammed into the tent, lifted the uphill side, nearly blew the thing over. Cold air knifed through. Du Pré buttoned his down vest.

Du Pré rolled himself a cigarette, lit it, didn't look at Bart. Maybe I end up riding down the mountain tonight. He remembered where the ax was, outside, buried in a stump. What do I know about this?

Du Pré had seen a lot of crazy drunks but they always got nuts after they had been drinking for days. But no one he knew had enough money to do that very often. You got the

D.T.'s, dried out, went back on the job. But this poor guy was a real pro, some life.

Bart cooked steaks on a gas grill. Fresh asparagus.

Du Pré had spent a lot of time up in the mountains, but the menu had been jerky, sardines, fruit leather, tea. Maybe rabbit.

Bart opened a bottle of red wine from France. It was very good. Probably sold for the same price as Du Pré's house, a case of it.

"I'll be OK now," said Bart. "I didn't find anything much up there. Did you?"

Du Pré shook his head, scratched the teeth through the cloth of his shirt.

"Your family all gone?" said Du Pré. Probably better they were.

"Well, mostly," said Bart. "Father and mother dead. One sister lives down in that house with me. She's worse'n I am. Hires studs, flies them out. Other sister went straight, sober, she's in Seattle works as a counselor there, alcohol. My brother died a long time ago."

Du Pré's ears pricked, went up, like a coyote's. He thought he heard one howl. In the blowing snow? They howl when they hunt, try to scare up a rabbit. But not in blowing snow.

Blowing snow, they try to sneak up on grouse buried in the drifts. Get hungry, get bold, go down and cut a sheep out of the flocks. Though not so much now the ranchers using those dogs, Maremmas, those others look to be all covered in noodles.

"He just disappeared from Chicago," Bart went on. "Last seen at the airport, had a flight to Denver. We thought he might have come up here, but he didn't. Never a trace."

"He sick like you?" Du Pré wanted to bite his tongue.

"Gianni? I don't know. Maybe he hadn't been at it long enough. All I remember is he had his appendix out. Sixteen or so."

Du Pré thought on that one, gummed it round. Lots of people have their appendix out. The Headless Man did, for one.

They talked of nothing much, slept.

In the morning Du Pré had coffee, saddled up. The cold leather creaked, snow bowed the firs down.

"You want me to take your horse, send the helicopter for you?" Du Pré said.

Bart nodded. He was a little shaky, pulling on tomato juice with a lot of vodka in it.

"Please take the horse," he said, looking close to tears. "But don't have the helicopter come for a couple days. I don't want to go back down at all, truth to tell. Couple days, I'll be all right."

"You not going to be all right, do this," said Du Pré.

Bart nodded.

But he didn't want to talk any more.

✦ CHAPTER 17 ✦

Yeah," said Du Pré, "he about shit I told him all that."

Madelaine swirled her sweet pink wine in the glass. She smiled, looked up at Du Pré.

"What did he do with the teeth?"

"Last I saw, he was looking at the teeth, they was sitting

on his desk, he was dialing on the telephone. I am out of it. I don't want any more."

"And Foosli is still up there?"

"Fascelli? Yes. I don't know. I feel damn sorry for that poor son of a bitch. Here's Foosli one minute, next he's gone. Fascelli, I mean, damn you."

Maria brought her hamburger to the table. She sat, demurely spread her lap with paper napkins. Still the torn black jeans. Du Pré wondered maybe she wanted part of her bad ass hang out of it.

"What happened to this counselor you had to go see?" said Du Pré. Used to be, kid get caught with beer, they got yelled at by a cop, parents made them stay home for a while, dance with the chickens. Now they got lame social workers all over them. No wonder they're more homicidal.

Government peckerwood wants to help, that *never* add up.

Maria shrugged, wrinkled her face like she had a bad smell under her pretty nose.

"He wanted to know you molest me or something," said Maria, she looked down. She was laughing.

"WHAT!"

Du Pré stood up, white with rage. Who the hell are these people anyway?

"So I told him lie down on the floor, suck himself," said Maria, "and I walked out."

My child, my child, thought Du Pré, now she tell me who I got to kill.

"You really say that to the man?" said Madelaine. She was trying to look shocked.

"I really say that to the man."

"What he say?"

"Nothing. I holler back that I tell my papa he ask me

55

such a filthy question my papa probably blow his shit brains out."

"Where this guy come from, anyway?" said Du Pré, steaming good.

"It's Bucky Dassault."

"Bucky Dassault! Jesus, that drunk? He maybe get arrested, drunk driving a hundred times, rape his sister once."

"I know," said Maria. "He go off to Galen, get a certificate, now he wants to help. Everything he done the bad alcohol and drugs make him do. Now he's sober, he says, wants to help."

"Well, you tell him," said Madelaine. She drank her pink wine.

"I tell him. Damn, he's a piece of shit drunk or sober, now he got a counselor's job. He's a *professional* . . ."

Du Pré sat back down. He wanted to start strangling people right away, begin with Bucky Dassault, end with the governor, not miss anyone in between.

"Du Pré," said Madelaine, "calm down, she already tear his balls off."

"So what I do with that bullshit, heh?" said Maria.

"What bullshit?" said Du Pré.

"Judge say I got to go talk to Bucky Dassault, go to AA for a while. Otherwise he send me to some place the state run to help me."

"How come this is the first I hear of it?" said Du Pré.

"Because I tell these assholes they talk like that to me in front of my daddy he probably kill them, scalp them, piss on what's left."

"I take care of it," said Du Pré.

"I don't want you to take care of it, Du Pré," said Madelaine. "I don't want to have come see you in Deer Lodge."

"Well, I go see that damn judge for sure," said Du Pré. He knew the guy, used to be a lousy prosecutor, always getting things wrong. Now he's a JP, way things going he be moving up to the Supreme Court next week. The one in D.C.

My daughter's a fine young woman, kids with beer, like kids ever and for always, now it's a big fucking deal. These people can't lie on the ground without a law says they have to.

Guy tries to kill me, I shoot up his arm, he gets a suspended sentence on account of his shot-up arm. My daughter gets busted with some beer, she gets gang-banged by a bunch of assholes ought to be hung 'cause they dumb and ugly. Shit.

Du Pré drove Madelaine home, took Maria out to the house. He thought he'd sleep there tonight, take her with him in the morning, straighten this thing out.

"Du Pré," said Madelaine, "you watch your temper, hear? When Albert run off, I had to get food stamps for a while, you wouldn't believe the shit I had to go through to get them. Them social worker people are crazy and worthless and they know it, know you know it."

"What is all this?" said Du Pré, pounding his hands on the steering wheel.

"We women, we're used to eating shit," said Madelaine. "You go careful tomorrow, that dumb judge throw you in jail for thinking he's dumb."

At home, Du Pré sat out on the porch in the cold. He was very hot and when he was mad he burned.

"Papa," said Maria from the doorway, "I know you can't sleep. Here you drink this, please, for me."

She handed him a tall glass, hot water, whiskey, a little lemon.

57

"I'm going to bed now," said Maria. "I think I won't go with you tomorrow."

"Why the hell not?" said Du Pré.

"Well," said Maria, "if I am right there and they get snotty, you get really mad. You don't have me there to protect, maybe you don't get so mad."

Du Pré nodded.

My child, she take good care of me.

✦ CHAPTER 18 ✦

Bucky Dassault wore the smarmy look of the saved. Once he was blind, and now he had an office and a diploma and a steady supply of people to mess with and fuck up, and he was a very happy asshole with a lot of undeserved clout. A Pro-Fess-ional, like Maria said.

Why the fuck don't we take fucking Charley Manson, Du Pré seethed, make him director of social services. He had a lousy childhood, you see. This would make him extra helpful to troubled folks.

Du Pré was very calm. Bucky was not fooled.

"It's the law," said Bucky.

Du Pré looked at him, didn't say anything.

"Du Pré, the State of Montana takes alcohol and drug abuse very seriously."

"Then why they hire you," said Du Pré, "they take it seriously?"

"Du Pré . . ."

"You were a piece of shit born and I don't think much

changed," said Du Pré. "Leave my daughter alone. I don't tell you that again."

Du Pré left. He thought about getting drunk before going to see this jerk judge, judge throw him in jail for contempt, sentence him to go talk to Bucky . . . Deer Lodge Prison, sure.

The food there was very lousy, no pussy, Du Pré would hate it.

Government, they can't do anything right.

Any self-respecting kid sneaks off, do some beer, smoke some dope. Now it's a big damn deal, got professionals for it. Like goddamned Bucky Dassault. I kick his ass I get thrown in jail, which make me so mad I *will* kill him.

My daughter's raising herself just fine, spite of my best effort and that is all a kid ought to have to put up with.

Du Pré ran into the Sheriff at the courthouse in Cooper. The big loud cop was there to testify in a drunk driving case.

"Guy hit a car," said the Sheriff. "Bounced up on my sidewalk, through my hedge, stopped with the hood all folded around a tree in my yard, fer Chrissakes. Three o'clock in the morning."

The Sheriff had made his own arrest. Call "60 Minutes."

"What are you here for?" he said, looking at Du Pré.

"My daughter was partying with some kids, had some beer, got caught, now they want to make her go listen to Bucky Dassault. Attend AA. She already goes to Mass. I am damn mad."

"The Judge is a pussy," said the Sheriff. "Don't scare him."

So Du Pré kept his mouth shut. Good thing, too. The Pussy Judge did all his talking for him anyway.

"Sssince you are in . . . Lawn Forcement . . . waive . . .

to your custody . . . don't want to see her here again . . . serious matter," said the Pussy Judge.

This so fucking serious, why that damn Bucky Dassault, thought Du Pré, while he looked respectful.

Du Pré said he took the whole matter very seriously.

The Pussy Judge went on to other matters, just before Du Pré would have lost his temper he had to stand and listen to any more of this bullshit. Which would have been tragic for everybody.

Du Pré asked God Who the Fuck was Minding the Store outside on the sidewalk. What the hell ever happened to kids will be kids, and kids do this sort of thing, practicing to be screwed-up adults like everybody else? Huh?

Du Pré drove back to Toussaint, sat in the bar which was empty except for the lady with the beehive hairdo who was washing everything. Du Pré drank whiskey, wished someone would come in he could kill—a Texan would be nice, can't get convicted of killing a Texan in Montana. Maybe I go find a dog with a calloused butt and kick him.

The telephone rang, the lady at the bar looked at Du Pré. She pointed at the pay phone on the wall by the front door. Du Pré walked over to it, picked it up.

"Papa," said Maria, "are you all right?"

"I just pissed off," said Du Pré. "All these people butting in business isn't any of theirs. Anyway, you don't have to go and talk to that damn Bucky Dassault or any of the rest of that crap. But you not to get caught again, you hear? I don't think it a bad thing that kids drink beer, long as they don't drive around. But now you got a bunch of bad people paid by the government to mess with you, call it help, and that is a lot of trouble."

"I know," said Maria. "I get caught with beer again my papa gets sent to prison." She laughed. So did Du Pré.

"I love you, Papa," she said.

"Love you too," said Du Pré. "Hey, I come and get you, we get Madelaine, we eat dinner here maybe."

"I pick up Madelaine," said Maria. Du Pré considered the fact that his daughter now had a car and a driver's license, or anyway a car. Du Pré, shut up, he told himself.

"OK," said Du Pré.

I know I don't do this father job so good, so I wish you luck, Maria.

"When you get this car?" said Du Pré.

"I love you, Papa," said Maria, hanging up.

Maria came to the bar alone. Madelaine was feeding her kids, she would come when they were cared for.

"Where'd you get the car?" said Du Pré, trying.

"Let's dance," said Maria. She put money in the juke-box.

♣ CHAPTER 19 ♣

It has to be the Headless Man," said the Sheriff, "the report says the teeth have fillings in them and appear weathered."

"Very interesting," said Du Pré. "I got back to inspecting cattle right now. I got five shipments here, four there, I am a very busy brand inspector." All yours, Jack.

"Where'd they bury the Headless Man, anyway?" asked the Sheriff.

"I don't know," said Du Pré. "Potter's field, maybe."

"Never heard of it," said the Sheriff.

"It's back of the old Mission church in Toussaint," said

61

Du Pré. "Where all the drunks freeze to death their families too poor to bury buried."

"Why there?"

"What?"

"Why behind the Catholic church?"

"The poor people around here are mostly Catholic," said Du Pré.

"Are you Met-isse?"

Du Pré nodded.

"Well, what are they? Indians?"

This son of a bitch here since '75 and he don't know what Métis are, Du Pré thought. "Red River breeds. they come down here after the Rebellion in 1886, some come before, this was the old buffalo hunting grounds. Come down in their Red River carts, get winter meat. The Métis were Cree and French, little English maybe. You know all them stories about the *voyageurs?* Métis."

"What rebellion?" said the Sheriff. "I thought the Red River was in Texas or something. John Wayne did a movie, yeah."

Du Pré had seen it, pretty good movie.

"Red River of the North," said Du Pré, "flows to Hudson Bay. See, I think the Missouri only flow like it does now since the last glaciers, ten thousand years or so. It used to flow into the Red River of the North."

"Red River Rebellion?"

So Du Pré told him about poor crazy Louis Riel, the saint, who led the rebellion and the English hung him. About little Gabriel Dumont, Riel's general, who would have destroyed the British troops but Jesus told Riel not to let Gabriel do it. The priests betrayed Riel to the English, Dumont tried to rescue Riel, bring him down to Montana. So for all his days thereafter Gabriel Dumont never once again spoke to priests.

62

So the Métis come here. Big families, couple horses, little blankets, a kettle, a wooden plow, a hoe, an ax.

"We still here," said Du Pré. "Still poor, still Catholic."

He left the Sheriff, drove off to his first inspection, small one, but he wanted to take his time. He didn't exactly think that the rancher was a thief, but he didn't exactly think that he wasn't, either.

He found them ready, a couple of stock haulers waiting. They ran the cattle by him, the brands looked OK, except for two might have been worked over a little.

"My youngest sort of screwed them up," said the rancher. "Had to touch up these two later . . ."

The story sounded OK, didn't sound OK, maybe, maybe not, was it worth skinning the steers, seeing what the original brand was. Du Pré subtracted the added scars, couldn't come up with a brand he knew.

Du Pré nodded. Not enough right now, but if someone came up missing a few head he'd be on this guy. He was half on him now. But you can't say "Judge, I have this feeling . . ."

"OK," said Du Pré, "everything's in order."

Or maybe the kid did screw them up, I'm just out of order.

The rancher tucked a chew in his lip.

"Du Pré," said the rancher, "seen in the *Tribune* about you finding that plane wreck and the rest of the Headless Man. Said you thought that the killer would be found pretty soon."

Du Pré nodded. That asshole reporter, don't get the quotes right that he likes, he makes them up.

"How's the investigation going? Any suspects?"

Television. What did those new shows call bad guys? Perps?

Jesus.

"I didn't say that," said Du Pré. "I don't know what the Sheriff is doing." Neither does the Sheriff.

"Oh."

"I look at cow asses," said Du Pré. "They just didn't have anybody to send so I went. I don't know much."

"Oh."

"Well," said Du Pré, "I got to go."

"Want some coffee?"

"No, I got another shipment, I got to run."

Du Pré drove away.

Perps.

Shit.

The next three shipments were all out of the same corrals, small lots of fifty or a hundred head. And a banker waiting to take the checks from the cattle buyer. Guy in lizardskin boots. Some banker.

The ranchers were going under, for sure, all working as long-haul truckers, just raising a few cows because that's what they'd always done. The brands were all good, Du Pré had known these people all his life.

He drove off to the last loading, some ten miles away. One of the bigger outfits, out-of-state money, probably a tax dodge.

Du Pré nodded at the foreman. He'd busted the man once. Before the man lost the ranch he tried one year to slip forty head of someone else's cattle past Du Pré. Well, it is pretty easy to spot bright new scar tissue, hardly had the scabs off, hard to sketch in a forged brand with a running iron and get the size right.

The man did a little time without complaint, and was always courteous to Du Pré.

Du Pré hadn't liked busting the guy. Now some assholes the government paid to lose money on cattle had the man's place. Including the little graveyard where his folks were buried.

The foreman lost the place, lost his money, worked for someone else on his family's land. Made that one try, he'd have done better to rob a bank, maybe.

The cattle marched past. Du Pré had to look hard at only one brand, had a bad tear across it, probably the animal fell onto a sharp rock or something. Just a rip across the brand, I know that's OK.

"Thanks, Du Pré," said the foreman, when Du Pré signed off.

"You bet, Jim," said Du Pré.

I still feel bad about busting him, thought Du Pré as he drove off. I always will.

✦ CHAPTER 20 ✦

Du Pré pulled his car over to a turnout on the dirt road, high up on the Bench, to look down the high plains toward Toussaint and Cooper and the blue haze beyond. He could see fifty miles south and east from the shoulders of the Wolf Mountains.

He rolled a cigarette, lit it, walked to the edge of the scraped dirt where the fireweed rattled. Late fall, soon on winter. Hadn't had a winter in a long time, but the summer had been cool and wet.

The winter right after the poor Métis fled south to escape the wrath of the English was the worst anyone remembered, 1886–87. That year there was no summer, two springs, the lilacs bloomed twice, some said because of the eruption of the volcano Krakatoa in the East Indies.

In December the winds howled high overhead, the air unstirred on the ground. The sky was pale gray and glittered. Snow began to fall, snow so fine that the cattle and horses inhaled it and froze their lungs and died of pneumonia. The temperature dropped to forty, fifty, sixty degrees below zero.

Then the Blizzard came.

The winds came.

Coulees a hundred feet deep filled with snow. Cattle wandered out into the flat white, sank into fluff. In the spring, the tops of the cottonwood trees had dead cattle in the forks of the branches.

Ninety percent of the range cattle in Montana died. The Texas herds had overgrazed the plains, too, so the cattle went into the winter lean and weak.

The Métis huddled in their tiny cabins, boiled moccasins for thin, stinking soup.

Corpses were stacked in the woodsheds, the ground was frozen many feet down.

Hard winter. There would be another someday.

Du Pré spat. He pissed, looking down at a couple of pickups racketing along the low road, one had a horse in back. Drivers were going too fast but everybody did here, you'd never get anywhere if you didn't.

I drive too fast. Now where the hell is Benetsee? The old man came and went, dropped his riddles. The old fart knows something. If the Headless Man is Gianni Fascelli, is who killed him down there right now? Could I see him if I had my binoculars?

Play my fiddle at midnight in the graveyard, summon up the Headless Man, have him tell me who? And this Headless Man, what would he speak with?

A rifle sounded, far away. Up in the mountains. All the hunters from the Flat States come here, think the game feeds on the snow up top of the peaks or something. Very little game up there in the deep green trees. Nothing for them to eat. Down here, there is a lot for them to eat. The haystacks of ranchers, for one.

I ought to go hunt this weekend, make winter meat.

When Gabriel Dumont led the buffalo hunt, he wore his red sash. I'll wear my red sash.

Benetsee. The prophets must have been a lot like him. No damn wonder folks killed them. Irritating sonsofbitches.

Where had Benetsee gone? Some city, sleeping in doorways in his old clothes, begging quarters?

I could find the old bastard, lock him in a room or something. Say, Benetsee, I got this wine out here, you tell me stories that I like, you get some. But not till I really like them damn stories.

I got no talent for being a bastard, torture a harmless old man. Leave that to Bucky Dassault, other helpful bastards. The Sheriff's such a fool, he think Benetsee's one too.

I got to find that old man, ask him, please, here, take this wine but tell me what you know. I won't tell anyone else, I tell you before God (who is deaf, or was when my wife died) but I need to know.

Coyotes sing now, they make the hairs on the back of my neck stand up, there. Real straight.

Du Pré looked down on some fine big country. He thought about the skreeking Red River carts, the people, the buffalo driven into stout log pens to be killed at leisure, the meat sliced off their bones in sheets a quarter-inch thick, hung on willow racks over fires, baled up and tied with sinew, bundles stacked in the carts and then everybody turned around and went back north.

At night the fiddles came out, the people danced, the men smoked and played cards on a blanket.

They smoked that meat right down there, went round the mountains to the east, played the fiddle right down there, made babies, longed for home, the priest.

The Black Robes, they come, have incense, golden kingdoms up above. But what good are priests, anyway, won't make medicine help you to steal more horses? Send smallpox to them damn Blackfeet and Sioux. Protestants even sorrier, not even incense, they get called Short Robes.

So I find that old man, see if maybe he tell me something.

'Sides I miss him, he comes from another time, like them buffalo hunters, like my grandfathers.

Red River.

✦ CHAPTER 21 ✦

Old Benetsee was at his shack, carving pipes from the red, close-grained stone quarried for five thousand years over near Pipestone Pass. He would fit them with a willow stem, hang a few chicken feathers on them, spread them on a blanket and wait for shoals of tourists.

Benetsee's hands shook quite a bit, but when he bent to dig another bit of red stone out of the deepening bowl they didn't.

"Ho Benetsee," said Du Pré. He had a jug of cheap white wine in a paper sack. He felt like a turd.

The old man looked up and nodded.

"I been expecting you," he said. "How are all your beautiful women; Jacqueline, Maria, that nice Madelaine?"

"Fine," said Gabriel. "They ask about you some. Wonder if you all right, hope things go well for you."

"I got no pretty women," said Benetsee. He seemed relieved about it. "If I had one now I'd be doing too well. Better this way, I don't have to wash so much."

Scritch scritch on the pipe.

Fifty centuries of that sound. Make that a couple million years. Some old fart going *scritch scritch* on the whatever, punctuate his teasings of a younger fool. Lot of men, stand where I am now. This dust is full of them.

"You hear about I find these three skulls where there should be only two?"

Scritch scritch nod.

"Well," said Du Pré, "what about that, you know?"

Benetsee looked up, head cocked, eye bright as a bird's.

"Coyote tell me much," said Benetsee, "but it very hard pick out just what he is saying, how much he is playing with me."

Tell me about it, thought Du Pré.

Benetsee dug at the pipe bowl. He seemed to have forgotten that Du Pré was standing there.

"You want some wine?" said Du Pré. Now maybe you remember me.

"Good morning to drink wine," said Benetsee, putting down his pipe, the little black awl with the deerskin wrapping the end held in the palm.

Du Pré handed Benetsee the jug.

The old man took a long pull of the gassy cheap wine. He belched and handed the jug back to Du Pré. A whiff of the wine hit Du Pré's nose, his mouth ran water, he felt like throwing up.

I am drinking too much whiskey these days, Du Pré

69

thought, I know better but when I drink a lot of it I don't grind my teeth in my sleep so much.

"Have some wine, good morning for it," said Benetsee. He looked far away, up to the Wolf Mountains. Little sharp face, Du Pré thought of the shrew's skull in the coyote scat. In his pocket.

Du Pré choked down some. Jesus, like drinking bubble gum.

"Whew," said Du Pré, "you much man, drink that."

"Poor man drink that," said Benetsee. He looked at his fingernails, rimmed in black, clawed old hands, the veins and tendons seen easily through the transparent skin.

"So what you want to know?" said Benetsee. "I don't know too much. Coyote knows a lot, but me, not too much."

Du Pré felt the warm bloom of the wine in his stomach. A nice warm peaceful feeling, he sat down next to the old man, put his elbows on his knees, rolled a cigarette. Gave it to him, rolled another for himself, lit both.

"Brings me wine, brings me tobacco," said Benetsee. "Hard to find a respectful young man these days."

"The Headless Man," said Du Pré, "how did his head get up in the mountains, in a place a goat wouldn't have, next to a wrecked plane fell down so long ago they think maybe it just flew to heaven."

Benetsee reached for the jug. *Glug glug glug.*

"Well," said Benetsee, "somebody very angry, of course. So you kill someone, you put the head and hands with some other bones, let the magpies and coyotes and skunks stir them. So maybe no one will know, what happened."

"I got that," said Du Pré.

"How long your parents been dead now, Gabriel," said Benetsee. "A bad day, that one."

Very bad day. Papa drunk and Mama deaf, car stall on a railroad crossing, didn't find a piece of either of them big enough to call Mama, Papa. Closed coffins at the funeral, coffins very light to carry, too.

Good people. Du Pré had loved them both. Killed while Du Pré was in basic training, Fort Ord. Du Pré, eighteen, only child. His mother always shamed she couldn't have more babies, like a good Métis woman.

"You know," said Benetsee, "most times there is a killing, there is a pretty woman in it somewhere, you know?"

Du Pré thought. His mama? Jesus, no, the two of them loved each other, make a pass at either, whoever, they wouldn't even notice.

"What the hell you mean?" said Du Pré.

But the old man had picked up the pipestone again.

Scritch scritch.

✦ CHAPTER 22 ✦

I tell you, Madelaine, I like to strangle that old bastard," said Du Pré. Diddle me out of that wine, leave me more confused than a newspaper.

"Well," said Madelaine, "you men get crazy, kill each other over us, you know. But you right, I don't see where he's pointing."

Early morning, her kids were stirring, time to get ready for school.

Du Pré rolled on his side, held her sweet warmth close.

71

"Got to cook them breakfast, see about their clothes," said Madelaine. "Old Benetsee, he talk to me, maybe?"

"Don't know."

Madelaine nuzzled his neck.

"Long time ago," said Madelaine. "Who around then? That old priest, Father Leblanc?"

Du Pré remembered. Father Leblanc had retired long ago, moved back up north to Canada, the fathers had a rest home there.

Red River.

Madelaine got up, Du Pré slept till the door banged to for the last time. He heard the grind of the school bus going off. Madelaine had four kids, they left Du Pré alone, he left them alone. But the oldest boy was needing a man to learn from.

I don't know what to do for my daughters, thought I at least would not have to not understand a son, too. Jesus, she got three more of them. Life, it get you every time.

Du Pré dressed, walked to the kitchen, carrying his boots. Madelaine dished him up some scrambled eggs, salsa, a couple slices of her good bread with chokecherry jam.

Du Pré ate.

"I got some fence to fix," he said, "check my place out." My few cows, horses, brushed-up little creek. I fix it up, work hard, lose more money.

He drove home. Maria was gone, off to school, bad-ass girl on the Honor Roll. People she hung around with probably couldn't read well enough to see her name, she's safe.

What about all this.

Du Pré filled a pocket of his down vest with fencing staples, took a fencing tool, a shovel, a topper's ax.

When he heaved against the rusty barbwire gate the top

72

strand broke, so he had to go back and pull a coil of wire off the spool. He fixed the gate, shut it, began to slowly walk the fence. Do a mile or so today, then more some-time. If his cattle got out they would be hazed back by the neighbors. No bitching, no cattleman needs the brand inspector pissed off at him.

Du Pré topped a little rise, looked down, saw four of his neighbor's steers at rest in his pasture. They got up when they saw him, trotted back home. Du Pré followed them to the downed fence. A post had rotted off, a cow had leaned against it until it snapped and the fence went down. Lots of tracks both ways.

I'd better fix this fence, here. Not too good a neighbor, me.

Du Pré cut a new post from a dead juniper, dug out a shallow hole, set and tamped the post. He stapled the wires back on.

The four steers looked glumly at him from the neighbor's pasture.

Spoilsport.

Du Pré saw his horses, one was limping. He hadn't worked his stock, they looked at him and trotted off, all but the one who was hurt in the foot.

"Tch tch," Du Pré clucked, coming up to the gelding. The oldest one, twenty years, gentle old fellow.

Du Pré patted the horse's neck. He lifted the left front hoof, saw the bad split.

Du Pré slipped his belt off, put it round the horse's neck, led him back to the little tumbledown barn. Got to fix these hinges, too, whole place is slumped and tired.

Us Du Pré, we been here a while.

Du Pré found the old inner tube, the rope, the Epsom salts. He went to the house, made up a batch of warm water, poured in the salts. He carried the kettle back out to the barn and slipped the inner tube over the horse's leg, tied it up, rope over the horse's withers. Poured in the warm drawing water, the horse danced a little at the strange feeling.

"Hohoho," said Du Pré. The horse stood, liking the warmth on his sore hoof and leg.

Du Pré left him there, went to the house for lunch.

He found a can of sardines, can of tomatoes. What the West was built on, cowboys ate and drank these. Piles of rusty cans at every good place to stop and have lunch. Ghost meals.

Du Pré went to the living room, cluttered with the magazines Maria brought home, but clean. He looked at the pictures on the mantel. Catfoot and Maman. Maria. Jacqueline, big smile, first baby, boy of course, Gabriel, of course.

Du Pré at a fiddlers' contest, first place, Du Pré half-drunk in the picture, little cheap trophy in his hand.

Picture of his father's sister, Aunt Pauline, with one of her husbands.

Aunty Pauline, blond, brown-eyed, good-looking woman. Trouble woman, she'd had three husbands.

Aunty Pauline, used to ride trick horses in the rodeo.

She'd be maybe sixty now? Du Pré hadn't seen her in more than twenty years.

Aunty Pauline.

Who Mama wouldn't speak of after that one time.

Du Pré didn't know what had happened. Long time ago.

Where was Aunty Pauline now?

Red River.

❖ CHAPTER 23 ❖

Du Pré was flicking his eyes over the brands, the cattle bawled in the chute. Funny job he had, no one needed him, then they opened the newspaper, saw prices up, or the banker didn't want to extend the note and they all wanted him right now. He'd be working till midnight tonight, for sure.

Pretty dull, too. While I'm here, somebody within twenty miles is losing cattle. The thieves pay attention to the market price, too.

"Du Pré! DU PRÉ!" the rancher yelling, right in Du Pré's ear.

Du Pré didn't take his eyes off the stock.

"All hell broke loose up to that rich folks' place," said the rancher, "the Sheriff's been shot dead."

"What?" Du Pré took his eyes off the stock.

"I got a scanner," said the rancher. "Deputies screaming, say the Sheriff's dead on the lawn and people are shooting from the house."

Du Pré looked back at the stock, found his place. Brands all OK. So what's this? Shit.

"Don't you need to get over there?"

"No," said Du Pré. "I need to see this stock loaded, then I got to go over to Koch's to see about theirs. There's nothing I can do about . . . all that crap at Fascellis'." Dumb bastard, that Sheriff.

So they loaded the cattle, Du Pré signed off, got in his car, cursed a while, turned on the radio.

"DUPREE DUPREE DUPREE GOD DAMN IT COME IN DUPREE DUPREE!" said the dispatcher, sounding hoarse.

"Yes," said Du Pré, very quietly.

"DUPREE!"

"Yes," said Du Pré, "it's me. And the answer is no."

"Get over to the Fascellis right away, the guy shooting says he will come out but he wants you there, wants to walk out with you. Won't have anybody else. MOVE IT."

Shit. SHIT.

"No," said Du Pré. "I don't do that, no."

The dispatcher started screaming, so Du Pré switched off his radio. Rolled a cigarette. Smoked it. Spat out the window.

He switched the radio back on.

"What about the Sheriff, now?"

"DU PREE, he's dead on the damn lawn. Look, I am sorry I yelled at you. Please go over there before somebody else gets killed. Please."

"OK." SHIT SHIT SHIT.

Du Pré thought maybe he'd drive over to Benetsee's hideout, stay drunk for a week. What's this all about, now? Huh?

He drove toward Fascelli's, the Crossed Eyes Ranch. I look at cow asses, I don't have to do this I don't have to do this.

But I do.

Shit. SHIT.

He could see the house, spotlighted. A helicopter circled over it.

The Sheriff was on his back on the lawn, his head all bloody. He was wearing a bulletproof vest.

Seven deputies were crouched around, some Highway Patrolmen, lots of assault rifles and shotguns.

"Now, what?" said Du Pré. He had decided to address this to a silver-haired Highway Patrolman who looked so disgusted he likely had a fair idea of what was really going on. Du Pré guessed.

"You Du Pré," said the HP. He had Scott Parsons on a nameplate above his left shirt pocket.

"Yes," said Du Pré.

"Well," said Parsons, "this guy keeps screaming that he won't come out unless you go in, he didn't shoot the Sheriff, and he also feels that we are a bunch of fucking assholes."

"No shit," said Du Pré.

"He's probably right on all counts," said Parsons.

"How many other people in there?"

"I don't know," said Parsons. "When I got here things were about like they are."

"OK," said Du Pré, "I go talk to him." He walked out across the lawn, hollering "BART BART! It's DU PRÉ." He walked out into the lights, holding his hands away from his sides.

"That is you, Du Pré," said Fascelli.

"I don't got a gun," said Du Pré. "Where's your sister, the maids and all?"

"In the swimming pool," said Bart. "It's empty. When these idiot assholes started shooting I had them get in there. I got in there, too. Where do they find these people, anyway?"

Du Pré looked down at the Sheriff. His face was gone. So he'd been shot in the back of the head.

"OK," said Du Pré, "I am coming up to the front door and I am arresting you and I am taking you to the jail. We do it fast, OK?"

"Sure," said Fascelli.

Du Pré went to the big ornate carved front door, it opened, Bart stepped out. Du Pré took his arm.

"I don't got no handcuffs," said Du Pré, "but we play I do."

"Hi, Mom," said Fascelli, smiling out at the floodlights. He clasped his hands behind his back while Du Pré pretended to clap cuffs on his wrists.

Du Pré and his prisoner walked out to the silver-haired Highway Patrolman.

"I arrest him," said Du Pré, "you drive us to the jail, huh?"

"You read him his rights?" said Parsons.

"Oh, yes, officer," said Fascelli.

Du Pré and Fascelli got in the back of the car. Du Pré left the door open.

"You got some handcuffs I can borrow," said Du Pré. "He ought to be wearing them we get to the jail."

Parsons unsnapped the case on his belt, unlocked the cuffs, and handed them to Du Pré.

"You don't have to do that," said Fascelli. "I won't give you any trouble."

"Look," said Du Pré, "you better be wearing these when we get there, these fools think you half-escaped or something." He looked at the shot-up house, the milling deputies, all armed, all looking very lost.

He snapped the cuffs on Bart's wrists.

Parsons drove fast all the way to Cooper.

The last sight Du Pré had of the scene of the siege was of four people standing around the body of the Sheriff.

But that Sheriff, he wasn't ever going to get up.

78

✦ CHAPTER 24 ✦

"D u Pré," said Madelaine, "you been having a rough time lately. Maybe you better go see Father Van Den Heuvel."

"I need to build up my sins," said Du Pré. "Big stack of them so that God handles this personally."

Madelaine threw up her hands. All this means, Du Pré, he has to blaspheme.

"So what did Foosli tell you?"

"He said he's inside the house, having drinks with his sister, the Sheriff is suddenly on the lawn with a bullhorn yelling for Bart to come out with his hands up. So he goes to the window, wondering who is playing this joke on him, and there is this shot, hits the Sheriff right in the back of the head, comes from behind the fence and the hedge. The other deputies go crazy, they shoot for a while or scream into the radio for a while, and Bart tells everybody in the house, get into the swimming pool—they got one there, middle of the house, cause they won't get shot there. They get in it."

Madelaine poured some more coffee for Du Pré.

"So then Bart say he shoot a few times over their heads, say he won't surrender to no one but me. 'They are stupid and crazy,' said Bart to me, 'so I know you at least.' He trusts me. I don't blame him, not wanting come out in front of them deputies."

"But who shoot the Sheriff?" said Madelaine.

79

Du Pré thought that he knew but he also thought he didn't give a rusty shit at this point. Also he wasn't going to tell anyone he damn well knew old Booger Tom had done it, see if he could get the cops so riled they kill everyone in the house.

"Whew," said Madelaine. "What the Sheriff going to arrest him for, anyway?"

"I don't know," said Du Pré.

"This very mysterious."

"This very stupid, what this is, I think. You seen Maria?"

"At the grocery store."

Du Pré nodded. "I better go out to the house, see if she is there, tell her I love her, case she's forgot."

"Du Pré," said Madelaine, "why don't you tell me you love me, case I forgot."

They held each other.

Du Pré went out, started up his old car, shifted into reverse.

Madelaine came after him.

"Du Pré," she said, "you got a dirty temper, you keep it close for me and Maria and Jacqueline and all. You don't got a mean bone in your body but you sure got lots of mad ones. Mad bones break pretty easy. All them cops, they are upset. One of them get shot dead, the others go crazy."

Du Pré nodded.

"Give my love to Maria," said Madelaine.

They all really take care of me, Du Pré thought. Now what I do for them? Really?

Maria was in the kitchen, cooking a goose. She'd washed the colored crap out of her hair and didn't have any makeup on. She had enormous black eyes, like her mama. She moved like her mama. Du Pré suddenly went very sad.

80

"Lots of calls on the phone, I told everybody you went to the dog races, Spokane," said Maria. She grinned.

Du Pré smiled. Maybe he would go to Spokane, hide out.

"Some lawyer for Fascelli called, wants you to call him. He's staying in Cooper, the little motel."

Du Pré grunted. Fascelli, he wasn't guilty of anything but a busted life, got to be cold as the moon. Back of the head, the slug that got the Sheriff. Booger Tom? Could the old fart still see that well? Or did one of the deputies get the twitch, all the wide world to hit and the bullet gets the Sheriff?

"I'm the head of the Honor Roll again," said Maria. "So I thought today, this morning, I'd wash my face and be a good little Catholic girl again."

Du Pré nodded. He'd never been fooled, but he had held his breath a few times.

"Also I don't think you need to talk to Bucky Dassault again. You got plenty on your plate, Papa. I won't let you down."

"You never have let me down, Maria," said Du Pré. "Maybe I let you down sometimes. I don't know what to do, you know."

"No, you love me good. You proud of me, proud of Jacqueline."

"Yes."

"Can I help you," Maria said, "I would, too."

Du Pré hugged her. Maria gave him a sunny wide smile.

Du Pré drove off to Cooper, see this attorney. Probably some expensive attorney from New York or something. Lizard briefcase. Manicure.

Platform shoes.

✦ CHAPTER 25 ✦

"This *farce*," said the attorney, "confirms what I always believed to be the case of Montana."

Young guy, lots of money, three-piece suit fit him so well he seemed to flow one place to another, like water. Long thin dark face. Deep, precise voice.

Probably never been on a dirt road before in his life.

"They don't do things like this, Dee-troyt?" said Du Pré. He sipped his coffee.

The lawyer regarded his with loathing, like it had dripped out of a sick bull.

"Did you know," said the attorney, "that Mr. Fascelli was holding the squadrons of the law at bay with a *starter pistol?* That there wasn't a live round of ammunition in the house, for obvious reasons. Barbara Fascelli is at the Betty Ford Center for the nth time. Bart will be out on bond this very day, and I will take him to a quiet place in Michigan. The maids left in a body, the masseur left with the hairdresser, the refrigerator is full of rotting caviar, and there is no case whatever. Thank you, by the way, for saving the life of my client. Each time one or another Fascelli dies there is a protracted struggle over the remaining millions. The money is excellent, but the work squalid."

Du Pré had never met a creature like this attorney, Foote. He thought about it. Probably didn't matter who got elected president, this was one of them as ran the country. Quietly.

"What do you think of all this?" said Foote, leaning forward. He seemed genuinely interested in Du Pré's thoughts.

"I don't know," said Du Pré. "I kind of like Bart. But he got not one chance in life he don't run away, take nothing of that damn money, spend his days washing dishes or something. He's not a bad guy, but he is in a very bad place."

"No," said Foote, "he is not a bad guy, and that is that."

"But who shot the Sheriff?" said Du Pré.

"One of the deputies, probably," said Foote. "I have yet to see the autopsy and ballistics report, but I would expect one or another of his faithful sidekicks misfired while loading one or another of the assault rifles."

Booger Tom probably can't see that well anyway, thought Du Pré, and I don't *care*.

"One thing I still don't know," said Du Pré. "What was the Sheriff going to arrest Bart for?"

"Um," said Foote, "you really don't know? He was going to arrest Bart for murdering his brother, Gianni, who disappeared nearly thirty years ago."

Du Pré nodded. "So the teeth match up?"

"Maybe they do, maybe they don't," said Foote. "Nothing back from the state lab. The Sheriff, mind you—he must have been pretty drunk—didn't even have a *warrant*."

Du Pré looked up, laughed. "You're shitting me."

"I am not. I suppose he spent a couple pleasant days at the jug, watching Clint Eastwood movies over and over. Like I said, I had always suspected Montana was a place chockful of people too stupid to walk downhill, which is where civilization is, if you are at all interested."

Du Pré nodded. He wasn't interested in civilization.

"Anyway," said Foote, "I bear thanks to you from Bart, who feels you probably saved his life. So do I."

Du Pré shrugged.

"Bart only understands giving money away to express gratitude. He is astute enough to realize that you do not need or want money, and he fervently wishes that he was the same. But he did think that an offer to send your daughter to any school she can get into, all expenses, all travel, everything, contingent upon her making good grades—he is not prepared to render another human being as worthless as he feels himself to be—might possibly not be offensive to you."

Du Pré's eyebrows shot up. He suddenly realized that Maria would have her dream, if she wanted it, and she might not know even that it was her dream. She wanted the best, would work hard for it.

Now, Du Pré, he thought, don't get the swelled head.

"Well," said Du Pré, "it's fine with me, but my opinion, it don't mean shit, really, so he would have to talk to my daughter."

Foote's eyes shot up. Sideways. He tipped his chair back and laughed.

"She is a minor, Mr. Du Pré," said Foote, "so your blessing is vital. I am to take it she is an independent girl."

"Her own damn country, she is," said Du Pré.

"Well," said Foote, "I have time enough to make the offer to her in person, if we can find her. Prior to taking Bart back East. I have a Learjet due in at five."

Du Pré shook his head. Bart was a nice man, should do something, anything, not die screaming in some alky hospital.

Du Pré drove Foote to the high school in Cooper, fetched Maria out of class, stuck her in the car with the young attorney, took a walk in the gray light so he didn't screw things up by hovering.

He came back in fifteen minutes, to find Foote and

Maria sitting on the dented hood of his old police cruiser. They were laughing.

Foote was smoking a long thin cheroot.

Maria was grinning like a mule eating chitlins.

Foote offered Du Pré a cigar.

Du Pré smoked it reverently. It was the best tobacco he had ever had.

Before Maria went back into the school, she kissed her father.

"See what happen," she said, "to a daughter of a good Métis man?"

Du Pré drove Foote to the courthouse.

They shook hands.

Foote's eyes crinkled with a kindly intelligence. He offered his hand again.

"That's for me," said Foote. "Bart's the only decent one of the bunch. Thanks. He deserves some help, not the twaddle they will give him at the place where I am taking him."

"He come back?" said Du Pré.

"Probably," said Foote.

"He ought to," said Du Pré.

"I think so too."

Du Pré drove off, wondering about a lot of things.

✤ CHAPTER 26 ✤

I ain't so smart but I'll do my best," said the acting sheriff, Benny Klein, former long-haul trucker and present little rancher. "I can't believe old Sheriff Johnson didn't have no warrant."

I can, thought Du Pré, that one dumb bastard. This Benny, he will do a pretty good job, if he don't die of terror when he has to speak to Kiwanis or something.

"So what do you think of all this, Du Pré?"

Benny held a report that said that the teeth could well have come from the jaw of Gianni Fascelli, or someone like him had those same holes in those same teeth. Lots of people got holes in those two teeth, nothing exclusive about it.

Du Pré shrugged.

"I got to go, inspect some cattle," he said. "I don't want any more of this mess. I am a simple cow-ass expert. I check to see them cows branded outside, not inside, them hides, I sign off. I have work to do on my one-horse ranch. I got two daughters. I am not a detective. Good thing, too. For everybody."

Klein nodded. It was about three in the afternoon. Lawyer Foote and a vodka-swilling Bart Fascelli had taken off in a prop plane, they would catch the Learjet in Miles City, a whole week ago.

Good luck to him, thought Du Pré, that lawyer, he don't need luck, he make his own.

Maria was bringing home six, eight library books a day and she was staying up till four in the morning reading them.

I got one married off, thought Du Pré, making babies and loving them and me, the other going to get a Nobel Prize in something, soon as she figure out what. Now I got to worry about Madelaine's four.

I got to take that oldest boy hunting, explain to him about rubbers.

The fire alarm sounded, Du Pré and Klein looked at each other. The county fire department was whoever happened to be in hearing of the alarm and near to the old fire truck, which had been bought in 1948 and used a lot. It was a pretty thing, faded red and lots of brass and gauges, but it wasn't much at putting out fires, which had mostly burned completely out before the truck lumbered up and the crew remembered just exactly how to hook up the hoses.

Du Pré and the Sheriff walked outside, looked up toward the Bench. There was a giant column of black smoke coming from the very place the Fascellis' huge ugly fat wet house was.

"Shit," said acting Sheriff Klein. He jumped in his car and drove off, without his hat. Du Pré followed him. The fire truck would get there by and by, in time to damp down the ashes.

God, Du Pré thought, looking at the blazing house. Flames were shooting a hundred feet in the air, glass was shattering, and the roof and some of the walls had already fallen in. You couldn't get closer than a couple hundred feet.

Booger Tom was sitting on the fence, working on a fifth of whiskey like he meant it.

"How the hell the fire start?" said the Sheriff to Booger Tom.

"Oh, that," said Booger Tom. "Well, Mr. Bart wrote me a letter, said he'd canceled the insurance, and to burn the place down. Sent five hundred bucks to buy gasoline and diesel fuel—told me to make sure—said he wasn't defrauding anyone and he would goddamned well burn down his own house if he wanted to."

"So I soaked the place down, opened the windows, tossed in a match, and there she is. Hah." *Glug glug.*

Du Pré laughed so hard he doubled up.

The new sheriff scratched his head.

"Well," he said, "people burn down old barns all the time. You get a burning permit?"

"No," said Booger Tom. "Piss on your damn burning permit."

"I'll have to write you a ticket," said Sheriff Klein.

Booger Tom nodded graciously. "Want a drink?" he said, offering the bottle to Klein.

"No," said the Sheriff, "I better not. I seem to remember that the fine is fifteen dollars or something. Just come in to the courthouse when you have a mind to."

Booger Tom nodded.

There was a towering column of flame rising up in the exact center of the burning house.

"That's the three hundred gallons of diesel in the swimming pool, said Booger Tom. "I thought of that my own self. *Belch.*"

The Sheriff left, Du Pré watched the fire.

"Hey, Du Pré," said Booger Tom, "there's a little note here for you from Fascelli."

Du Pré held it out at arm's length, squinted.

"Dear Du Pré"—the handwriting was pretty shaky and loopy, so Bart wasn't feeling so good when he wrote it—"I am coming back and when I do I am going to raise the cows myself, live in a sheepwagon, and make Booger Tom the foreman and me the hand. I promise, Bart."

"Hey, Tom," said Du Pré, "you know Fascelli says he is going to come back, make you the foreman, himself the hand?"

"Yup," said Booger Tom.

"What you think of that?"

"Well," said Booger Tom, "I think that if Mr. Bart will learn how to shovel shit and like it, or at least say that he does, he might do all right."

Du Pré nodded.

There was a God, maybe, time to time.

✤ CHAPTER 27 ✤

Benetsee motioned to Du Pré. I got to pee. The old man clambered out, stood swaying, pissed. It was dark out, cold with frost.

They were supposed to be hunting deer.

Which meant that maybe Du Pré would shoot a deer for the old man, but the drunken old fart's gun was going to stay locked in the trunk of the car. Argue all you want, old man, the answer is no.

"The hunter dream the deer and the deer come," said Benetsee.

"Shape you in, I don't want to see what you dream come at all," said Du Pré. The car smelled like the drunk tank. Benetsee belched, adding a little more to the stench.

"Park here," said Benetsee. Du Pré parked where he was

going to park anyway. The brush below hid a path deer used. Every day. Morning and evening.

It was a half hour or so till the light would begin to rise. Du Pré got his rifle from the trunk, came back to the warm seat in the wine fug.

He rolled a cigarette, handed it to Benetsee. The old man dug in his dirty jacket for matches, found some, lit it. Du Pré rolled himself another.

"So," said Benetsee. He took a pinch of tobacco, rolled down his window, muttered for a moment, dropped the wad to the ground.

An offering.

They sat, smoking.

Du Pré poured himself some coffee. He sipped it. The purls of steam rose and stuck to the windshield.

"Too much excitement lately," said Benetsee, "but I think things calm some now. People ought to go out, sit, wait for deer more. It is restful."

Smoke. Belch.

"Wonder who shot that fool Sheriff," said Du Pré. The FBI had finally been called in on some bullshit pretext, they were being snotty to everyone. The bullet that had gone through the Sheriff's head had gone right on into the house and maybe out the other side and maybe not. Anyway, now the house was a sump of smelly ashes. Who knows?

Du Pré had seen the report on the Sheriff. Death instantaneous. Since everybody started in firing like fools the moment after the Sheriff went splat on his back it was extremely hard to find out where anybody thought the first shot had come from.

What with everything, it was even impossible for the FBI to frame anybody, like they usually did.

Du Pré was finding the whole thing hilarious. The FBI

had interviewed all four of the Sheriff's deputies who had been crouched there in backup, and who had fired every round they had for the rifles within a couple minutes of the Sheriff's rapid shuffle off this here mortal coil.

The Highway Patrolmen had arrived a little later, and they hadn't fired a shot among them.

Du Pré never took a gun out of his car.

Booger Tom was not likely to confess in a fit of remorse, on account of Booger Tom was not the type to feel such a furrin emotion.

Talk all they want, them FBI, not much good, that.

There was a rattle of scree, flat little rocks racketing down a slide of stone. Something there had loosened them.

The trail led across the scree to the trail Du Pré would watch just as soon as it got light.

Du Pré got out, racked a shell into the chamber, took the caps off the lenses of the sight. The scope was light-gathering, and he could see well enough if the deer wasn't behind a bush. It would be another half hour before he could see a deer behind branches well.

Du Pré swung the rifle, looked out at the spot on the trail he'd shot maybe two dozen deer on in his life. Some even in season. In Montana, one out of five deer shot was taken legally. Since the cattle business in Montana had collapsed, the ranchers weren't even killing deer wholesale to keep them off the grass and out of the haystacks, so there were lots more deer now than when Du Pré was a boy.

Du Pré saw a nice six-point buck, swung the scope back, put the post and crosshair on the spot where the spine joined the skull.

POWWWWW . . . and the echoes, back and forth, back and forth.

The deer was flopping, just a little. Good place to aim for, since either the animal dropped in its tracks or Du Pré missed clean. He hurried down to the deer and slit its throat to drain it. If he shot the deer in the chest he didn't have to do that, but it messed up the ribs and organs, and the liver was the best part.

Du Pré walked back up to the car, jacking the shells out of the rifle. He put the rifle in the trunk and walked back, dragged the deer to a spot where it lay downhill, watched the bright blood plume from the throat.

Blood steamed on the stones.

Du Pré ringed the anus, tied it off, slit the deer open, jammed his hands into the chest cavity and grabbed hold of the windpipe, esophagus, and heart. He heaved. The viscera came free.

He pulled a plastic bag from his pocket, shook it open, set it beside the guts. He cut out the heart and liver, dropped them into the sack, reached into the abdomen and carved the kidneys out from their wads of backfat. He closed the bloody sack and stuck it in the game pouch of his coat.

Du Pré dragged the deer up to the car, his feet sometimes slipping on the wet stones. It was hard work, the animal weighed closer to three hundred pounds than two. Du Pré was running sweat by the time he had it on the ground behind the car.

He opened the trunk and heaved the deer in. He propped the trunk open so that the air would cool the carcass. He stuck sticks in the chest cavity to keep it open, cool that meat.

"Where's your tag?" said Du Pré to Benetsee.

"No," said Benetsee. He had some more wine.

Du Pré tagged the deer with his own tag.

This old fart got nerve.

I owe him one.

❧ CHAPTER 28 ❧

Got you good, didn't he?" said Madelaine. She was stuffing Du Pré's bloody clothes into her washing machine.

"No," said Du Pré. "I expected it."

"He's some old fart, eh?" she said, adding detergent to the wash.

Du Pré was rosining his bow, getting ready to fiddle for a ribbon. Blue. My favorite color.

Maria was coming to hear Du Pré fiddle, and Jacqueline, too. He had given Jacqueline money for a babysitter, so she and Raymond could have a little time away from the babies. Raymond worked like three men to keep them all, fine young man, perhaps in time he could fall into something paid better than jackknife carpentry, plumbing, the feed mill.

Du Pré heard the door. Maria, laughing, and so was Madelaine, both very gay. Like they had some secret, a happy one.

"Hey, Du Pré," Madelaine called. "Let go yourself, come out here, see how your women love you."

I know my women love me, thought Du Pré, now what is this?

The two women smiled at him. Jacqueline had come from somewhere and she, too, sat on the couch. Big white box on the coffee table, blue ribbon, little card in an envelope.

Du Pré raised an eyebrow. "Now what's this?

"So open it, see," said Jacqueline. All three giggled.

Du Pré took the little card out. To our good Métis man, love.

Du Pré opened the ribbon knots, let the blue ribbon fall to the table, fold it up, use it again, hardly wrinkled.

Tissue paper.

Du Pré folded it back. A vest on top, soft white leather, all worked with quills in patterns, hummingbirds and suns and teepees, animals. Beautiful. The quills were all dyed with the old dyes, from sunflowers, salmonberries, choke-cherry root, he hadn't seen those dyes in many years.

A soft cream silk shirt, full sleeves, tight cuffs.

Gaiters of soft white deerskin, quilled with beaver tails, the Pole Star and Big Dipper. Compasses.

A red velvet sash with black beads.

Moccasins with turquoise and yellow and red and black beadwork. Nez Percé that.

A little round Red River hat, soft black felt, with a beaded band and a hard narrow brim.

A bright turquoise silk scarf.

"My my," said Du Pré. "This is too fine stuff for me."

"We made the stuff from what we could see in that old picture of your great-grandfather," said Jacqueline. "Maria found them dyes, in a book, no one living we know knows them."

"So, you happy?" said Madelaine.

Du Pré's throat choked up. Such good people, his women. All this must have taken many hours.

He lifted the vest, looked at the tiny careful stitchings.

"My, my," he said, slipping it on, fit perfectly over his old stained blue work shirt.

"Papa," said Maria, "you put it all on, not one thing at a time."

Du Pré dressed in the bedroom, all the finery. He looked at himself in the big mirror, the dark skin, straight black Indian hair, black mustache. A Métis man, got a fiddle and a pipe.

"We take this fine-looking man to the fiddling contest," said Madelaine. She beamed at Du Pré.

I got me some beautiful women, I'm very lucky.

They all piled into Du Pré's old cruiser, went off to the old Toussaint Bar. It had another name many years ago but someone didn't like it and blew the sign off with a shotgun one very-drunk-out Saturday night. So it was the Toussaint Bar, no sign.

Du Pré was embarrassed when he walked through the door, he hoped he wouldn't have to shove anybody's teeth down his throat for insulting the beautiful handiwork of his women.

People whistled. A couple old grandmothers came to him and one got right down on the floor to look at the fine beaded moccasins. The other fingered the sash.

They rattled at Madelaine in Coyote French, waved their hands and beamed, their store-bought teeth too blue-white.

The fiddle contest began, and Du Pré blew everybody's hats in the creek. He pinned the blue ribbon to his Red River hat. He looked down at his moccasins, up at his women. He beamed.

He played a tune about the sounds the axles of the carts made when the people came down here to hunt the buffalo, make winter meat, do the hard dirty bloody work, sing while they did it. Get everybody set for that long cold Northern winter. Black ravens on white earth. Wolves howling in the river bottoms. The men wandering far on their long woodland snowshoes, Cree snowshoes, get those furs, buy calico and guns, kettles and rum, beads and medicine, brass tacks for the rifle stocks, salt and tea, dried fruit, maybe coffee.

"Good, Du Pré" cried the grandmothers, swaying.

Red River.

✤ CHAPTER 29 ✤

Thanksgiving. Du Pré and the priest went to fetch Benetsee. Back at Du Pré's house, three women, one kitchen. Jesus.

Du Pré parked out on the road by Benetsee's shack, saw the dirty white plume of the smoke from his fire, felt the acid bite of it in his nostrils, on his tongue.

Du Pré and the priest trudged to Benetsee's door, Du Pré tapped twice, turned the latch, let go when the old man swung the door open. A warm fetor poured out, stale food, stale wine, old man, tobacco, wet dogs. The two old dogs, heelers, left over from Benetsee's days in a sheepwagon, tending the woollies. They were nearly blind and so stiff they rocked from side to side when they walked. Wheezy woofs. Honor satisfied, they staggered back to bed beside the stove.

"Good day," said Benetsee. The old man was sober, clear-eyed, had combed his shock of white hair, black eyes glittered in his brown face. He'd dressed up, old necktie even, gravy stains and greasy spots. Mostly clean shirt. He shrugged into an old army greatcoat, picked up a bundle of brain-tanned deerhide.

"Good you come for me," he said, "long walk."

Du Pré looked out into the yard, two old trucks up on blocks, under the snow.

They walked to the car, the clumsy priest nearly fell.

Way things going, thought Du Pré, everybody have to stay at my house. I got plenty of blankets, lots of floors.

Nice soft floors, though.

"How have you been, Benetsee," said the priest. "I think of you often."

Benetsee thought for a moment. "Old," he said, "I been old."

They all laughed, got in Du Pré's car.

Sush sush sush went the tires in the deep snow. County plows wouldn't be out for a while, maybe not till tomorrow. Du Pré remembered riding in them with Catfoot, his father cursing and shifting gears. The trucks were old, Catfoot slammed them into drifted snow so hard sometimes the trucks slowed and stopped, went sideways.

Then the wind would put the snow back.

Catfoot got called out on bad nights, he had a couple old trucks and plows, not too much good, but anything helped when the blizzards came. Catfoot, the little rancher, brand inspector, roadman for the county, combiner of grain, good hand at poker. Did everything. Had to.

Du Pré shifted in his seat. His ass itched.

"Your women very kind," said Benetsee. "I don't hear from my sons and daughters any more."

Too much trouble to them, thought Du Pré, that's very sad. He thought more. Too much trouble to *me*, thinking about the deer hanging in Benetsee's meathouse with Du Pré's tag on its leg.

Old fart. Good old man, knows things.

Du Pré turned into the drive to his house. The snow and wind had erased his tracks. Raymond's pickup was there now, he'd been out fixing someone's plumbing. Hard-working man.

They struggled through the snow to the house. Du Pré walked behind, ready to grab the clumsy priest or the old man, but they made it to the door all right. The priest sort of fell into the house.

The house was hot and steamy from all the people sweating, the cooking, the old Peerless woodstove hot and covered in dishes.

Much laughter, whiskey and lemon and cinnamon. Father Van Den Heuvel and Benetsee had large glasses.

"Du Pré, said Benetsee, "you play fiddle, huh?"

"We got a half hour till we need you to carve," said Madelaine, "so you play the fiddle, I quiet these savages down." She looked at all the small children running, squirming, squealing.

Du Pré got his fiddle, tightened up the bow, tuned. He began to play, nothing in particular, make his fingers fly, they were a little cold. Du Pré played "Baptiste's Lament."

Benetsee pulled a willow flute from his coat, stuck it in the corner of his mouth, Métis way, so your pipe fit in the other.

The fiddle and the willow.

River bottoms, the wagons full of meat, new babies in the bellies of the women. The wind was from the north and smelled of snow. White owls scudded through storms. Coyotes sang, hunted rabbits in teams, the rabbits ran in circles. One lap, fresh coyote.

The old *chansons*.

Du Pré felt for a moment that he was floating through the roof and looking down. An orange county road truck bashed through the snow, little Gabriel laughing in excitement while Catfoot shifted the gears and cursed in Coyote French, some bad English.

Catfoot, he did everything, like a good Métis man.

He even mined for gold, had an ancient little dragline, pull up thirty feet of the old gravels, from the bed of the old Missouri, when it had flowed north to Hudson Bay. The gold was heavy, it sank to bedrock, right there on the bones of the earth, the gold was. Where the river couldn't dig any deeper.

Tens of thousands of years ago, maybe millions, when the Missouri flowed north and east, till the high white glaciers crept down and bulldozed berms to send it to the Gulf of Mexico.

But before that the strong brown waters roiled north. Red River.

✤ CHAPTER 30 ✤

Du Pré came back late, from having taken Madelaine and her kids home. The house was still hot and steaming. The women and Father Van Den Heuvel had washed every dish, wiped every surface. The house still throbbed from all the people.

Maria was running the vacuum over the worn old Sears, Roebuck carpet. She had a kerchief around her head, to soak up the sweat. Du Pré threw open the front and back doors. He turned the thermostat down. The windows had been sealed off for the winter, translucent plastic stapled to the frames.

Maria mopped at her throat with a paper towel. She went to the back door and stood in the cold, hands on her hips and her head back.

"Some fine Thanksgiving," she said, head turned to Du Pré. "Some fine fiddle, some fine Papa."

"Some fine daughter."

They held each other.

"I'm going to be a doctor," said Maria. Du Pré nodded. Last week she was going to business school, start her own company, make something, she hadn't said what.

Du Pré hugged her.

"Benetsee was very sweet," said Maria, "and the Father say a nice grace, remember all the people who are gone, couldn't be here."

Du Pré nodded. He had taken a heaping plate outside, left it on a fencepost for hungry ghosts, any passing by.

The clean cold air felt good. Du Pré looked up, the air from the house was rising out the doors, turning to frosty fog.

"Would it be all right with you I don't have any kids?" said Maria. "I don't think I'll have time, myself."

"You do what you want," said Du Pré. "Jacqueline tell me she just have litters every other year from now on, we're covered."

"Papa!" Laughter.

The house was getting cold. Du Pré shut the doors, turned the furnace back on.

"That old picture album," said Du Pré, "one got Grand-papa's picture in it, you know where it is?"

Maria nodded.

Du Pré had put it away when Catfoot and Maman had been killed. Hurt too much to look at it, Catfoot in his soldier's uniform, Maman in her wedding dress.

Aunty Pauline in her fringed leather dress, standing on a horse that was running very fast. The leather dress was very short. Aunty Pauline had long slender legs, long slender fingers, blond hair, big dark brown eyes, big tits.

Maria shuffled around in the closet a little and brought the book of photographs out. Red leather, black smudges on it, the leather had dried out and cracked a little. .

Du Pré opened it. His father's soldier medals were pinned inside the front cover. Nothing big time, Good Conduct Medal, the African Campaign Medal, Italian Campaign Medal. Expert Rifleman's badge. Honorable discharge paper folded and stapled to the cover.

Catfoot's high school graduation picture, breed face, white teeth, on the lawn in his silly gown with his beaming Papa and Mama. Catfoot as soldier boy, hat looked too big on him, he barely made the height for the army.

Catfoot and his bride, Heloise, big smiles, fun night ahead. Catfoot and his bride and the priest, Father Leblanc.

Little Gabriel du Pré, maybe two, fat little knees in short pants. Aunty Pauline behind, big smile, lots of dark lipstick, good-looking woman, holding little Gabriel, squirming.

She used to take me up on her horse, I'd sit between her and the saddlehorn while she made that damn horse fly. Hold on to the horn so hard I don't doubt there are little fingernail marks in the leather. Still got the saddle, maybe I should check.

Aunty Pauline in a white dress, so short it could have been a bathing suit, hair flying, hat on a string dancing behind her, a lariat looping above her, held in one hand, fringed glove on it.

Some fine-looking woman.

Aunty Pauline trick roping. Aunty Pauline in a line of pretty girls, Calgary Stampede, some of those girls no better than they should be, like Aunty Pauline.

Like my mother say that, go tch tch tch.

Aunty Pauline, three husbands, probably a few more by now.

101

"What you lookin' for there, Papa?" asked Maria.

"I think I know something I don't want to," said Du Pré.

Maria shook her head, went off.

Du Pré whistled, few bars from a portage song. Carry them big heavy packs of pelts, maybe carry two.

Soon, he would have to follow his blood north.

Red River.

✤ CHAPTER 31 ✤

B art Fascelli came back, and he called. Please come.

Du Pré drove out to the ranch. There was a big new double-wide trailer next to the well house. A new four-wheel-drive pickup, lot of lights on top of the cab. Dude wagon.

Bart Fascelli had aged ten years, and he trembled sometimes.

"First couple weeks I had bugs crawling underneath my skin," he said. He broke into a cold, greasy sweat, shivered.

"You all right to be out here alone," asked Du Pré. This man was sick, maybe have convulsions or something.

But Bart's eyes were clear and hard, whatever it was he wasn't afraid of it, death, too.

"Hospitals are very boring," said Bart. "I have been a piece of shit all my life. The dogfucker doctors told me I might die, but I don't care. I'm going to work hard, eat good. I can't sleep at night at all. Can't sleep period. I had a favor to ask of you, maybe you pass it around. Please don't come by if you have any booze on you or in you. Thing I want to do most in all the world is get drunk and sleep. I feel like hell. If I drank I'd feel a lot better. I could eat, I could sleep, I could be right back where I was, go through this shit again. I don't want to. I don't know if I can do this. But I'll try."

Du Pré nodded. "What about Booger Tom?" he said. "Old Booger Tom, he drinks some."

"I told him just please stay in his cabin if he's drinking. I am afraid right now to even smell the stuff."

Du Pré sipped his coffee. Bart Fascelli was drinking bottled mineral water. A lot of it. He seemed to be thirsty down to his soul.

Du Pré looked at the corner of the little living room. A prie-dieu, nice one, old, walnut, with a Bible open on it, couple votive candles. Good. Bart, here, calling on all his friends, help me.

Du Pré had seen a couple people die of the booze, livers gone, lot of pain at the end, painkillers didn't work, the liver couldn't send them into the bloodstream or something. Cirrhosis.

Bugs crawling under his skin. Jesus. Du Pré had had the roots of his hair hurt plenty times, sure enough, but nothing close to that.

"You know Father Van Den Heuvel?" said Du Pré.

Bart shook his head.

Of course, the priest for the poor people, he hate this rich bastard, that's what poor Bart think. Now, here, something I can do for him.

"You OK to drive?" said Du Pré.

Bart nodded, looked puzzled.

"What I want you to do, favor to me, is follow me over to the priest's. He's a very clumsy man, can't barely walk, shouldn't swing an ax, maybe hurt himself."

"I can swing an ax," Bart murmured. Du Pré had seen him ride, Bart had grace and power in him for physical things.

"You embarrassed to meet our poor priest. You think that he hate you. Well, I don't know, he got no reason to like you, probably he don't think about it one way or another. But I drop you off there, he's at church this afternoon, hearing confessions, or over at the hospital in Cooper. You split his wood for him, then maybe you talk, eh?"

"Hah," said Bart, "you're a good shrink. The shrink at the hospital told me I didn't ever think of anyone else. I didn't know how. Well, that's not really true, but you know what is?"

Du Pré waited, Bart was searching for the right words.

"I can give people money. I can send someone to help them. But I never have and don't really know how to give anything my own self. To go over to the clumsy priest's and split his wood for him. I can do that, he can help me bind up my soul. But I would never think of doing that, myself. Send money, send someone else. I don't think that I have any value, you know. That I myself with these two hands can do anything but sign a check, make a phone call."

Du Pré nodded, waited. I been sad, but this . . .

"The kind of money I have just poisons," said Bart. "Poisoned us all. Poisoned Gianni, he has been gone now for twenty-five years. Not a trace, not one. Flew to Denver, walked out of the airport, and no one ever heard anything again."

Du Pré nodded. Tell me about it.

"I want to get well. Find out what happened to my brother. My own self. Those teeth you found, they aren't sure. Not enough of them. I want to go back up there, sift that ground you took me to real carefully, see if I can maybe find more, lay poor Gianni to rest, lay me to rest, too."

His own self, thought Du Pré. He could hire specialists, do it right now, but he wants to get well, go up there, sift that earth and find his brother. Hear his brother speak out of the grave. This Bart, he will do all right, if he does it.

I'm pretty sure that I know already, Bart Fascelli, I will in a little while anyway. But I won't say that now.

Fascelli started up his fancy new pickup, followed Du Pré to the priest's. The woodpile was covered in snow. There was a foot of white stacked narrowly on the handle of the ax.

Du Pré got Bart a broom from the little entryway to the Rectory.

When he drove away, Bart was swinging the ax, an easy motion.

All them fencing lessons, thought Du Pré, probably that kung fu crap, too. All that time, tune your body, never play a tune on it worth dick.

Me, I got to go feed my cows.

✦ CHAPTER 32 ✦

Du Pré was shoveling hay into the feedrack. His cows were close around the pickup. He didn't even license the ancient IH truck any more, just used it to do chores on the ranch. The bed of the truck was icy. Du Pré's feet kept slipping when he shifted his weight.

Some of the cows were pulling at the wisps of hay sticking out of the feedrack. The others were bawling. They heaved against the pickup, trying to get at the feed.

When I move this pickup, thought Du Pré, the dummies will know where they are again and go around to the other side where there is plenty of room, but right now they are too confused to know where they are.

Sometimes I feel that stupid. Sometimes I wish I *was* that dumb.

Du Pré saw someone out of the corner of his eye, a man in a tan topcoat wearing cheap hiking boots. The waffle soles so well made to pick up a nice load of cowshit, get it all over your car's rugs.

"Mr. Du Pré?" said the man. "Jotila, FBI. I wondered if I could talk with you for a minute?"

Du Pré looked at him.

"Sure," said Du Pré. "We have coffee. I tell you what, you go to the back door of my house, to the kitchen. I don't got no Dobermans or anything, I got to get this truck out of here so these dumb cows can eat. I will be there in ten minutes."

"I'll just wait," said the FBI man.

So freeze your ass, thought Du Pré. Official business, stand around in the damn cold.

Du Pré forked off the last of the hay, dropped the pitch-fork on the hard icy truck bed, struggled over the side and got into the cab. He cranked the old engine, it wheezed to life, he backed it out the open gate. The cows wouldn't stray from the feedrack so long as there was any hay in it.

The FBI man walked behind the truck. When Du Pré looked back the man was straining against the gate, to drop the loop over the post. Well, good, he's ain't hopeless anyway.

Du Pré waited for him to trudge up, led him into the

back entryway of the house. Du Pré slipped off his packs. The FBI man struggled with the iced laces on his boots. He got one off, put his foot down in a puddle of icy water. He winced. He took off the other boot. Hit another puddle with that foot.

Du Pré went into the kitchen, the man followed.

"Put them socks on that radiator there," said Du Pré. It already held a couple of pairs, some gloves drying hard like boards.

Du Pré poured coffee. "You like a sandwich or some soup?" he said.

"No," said the agent, "I had a lousy hamburger in Toussaint."

"You still tryin' to find out who shot that fool Sheriff?" said Du Pré.

The agent nodded glumly. Interview everybody over and over, spread a lot of glue, maybe your fly steps in it. Maybe not even the right fly, but we always get our man, even if it's the wrong one. Ask Leonard Peltier.

"You went out there after you were called on the radio," said the agent. He was scribbling in his notebook.

"Yes," said Du Pré, "they been calling me a long time by then."

"Do you know why Fascelli wanted you?"

"Uh, he knew me some, I guess." Drunken asshole Sheriff shows up without a warrant, for Chrissakes, arrest the man, someone outside shoots the Sheriff in the back of the head, the deputies go apeshit and blaze away, you sitting in there with a starter pistol to protect yourself with, you'd want someone you knew, too. Jesus. Shit.

Jotila tapped his gold pencil on the table. Nice pencil, heavy gold, kind you get you want someone to know you own a nice pencil.

"That old cowboy, Booger Tom, he shot the Sheriff, didn't he?" said the agent.

Du Pré's eyebrows shot up.

"I don't know that," said Du Pré. "I didn't get there till it was all over. Long time."

The agent looked wearily at Du Pré. He shut his notebook.

"I have been an agent for fifteen years," he said, "and I have seen the police fuck up a lot, but this is world-class. When those asshole deputies opened up like they were storming a beach or something old Booger Tom must have blown them a kiss, walked away carrying a torch, mooning the dumb fuckers. Not a one of those nitwits looked *behind* them, for Chrissakes."

"They wouldn't," said Du Pré. The deputies, they were scared. They had assault rifles, pump shotguns, bang bang bang.

"Why do you say that they wouldn't?"

"Don't think they had ever been shot at before," said Du Pré. "Besides, when the Sheriff fell over *backwards*, they would have thought that the shot had to come from the house. They don't know much. Head shot, the body falls toward where the shot came from, if that bullet goes through the skull."

"How do you know that?"

"I shoot a lot of deer in the head," said Du Pré. This guy, maybe he wants me to be the killer now. Well, I got six witnesses I was fifteen miles away, so screw him.

"I think I'll ask Booger Tom to take a lie detector test," said the agent.

"He won't do it," said Du Pré. I'll tell him not to, Mr. FBI man. That asshole Sheriff killed his own self, far as I am concerned. You be dumb enough, you be dead. It's the law.

"The Bureau is burning my ass to get something on this case," said the agent Jotila. "I don't want to stay in Butte, Montana, the rest of my life."

Du Pré shrugged. Threaten Booger Tom to me, you prick, I got no use for you at all. I don't know that he did it, mind you, and I do not care to find out if he did.

"Just one of those things," said Du Pré.

The agent nodded glumly.

"I'll go back to beautiful Butte, now," he said.

He pulled on his socks.

✦ CHAPTER 33 ✦

It got to be Christmas. There was some heavy snow, a lot of wind. Du Pré heard the county road trucks going by. Raymond had got a job with them, the pay was good depending on how much it snowed. Du Pré slipped money to Jacqueline anyway, not in front of Raymond, few years he would have a handle on everything. Not that I ever have, Du Pré thought.

Jacqueline had been four months pregnant when she married her Raymond, girl in her position had to be sure that her man didn't shoot no blanks, just bullets, thank you. Lucky Raymond. He loved her, looked at her like a sick calf. He give her babies, she love him back. Get his balls shot off, he have to find a new home.

Du Pré grinned. I got me some strong women, here. The old saying, that the strength of the Métis was the men's humility, but the backbone of the tribe was the women, who gave life itself.

Jacqueline was pregnant again. She was set on having a baby every nine months and one day, as near as Du Pré could figure.

Du Pré heard a truck in his drive, looked out. It was Bart and Father Van Den Heuvel. Since Bart had taken on the task of splitting the priest's wood while the priest had taken on the task of sticking Bart's soul back together they had spent a lot of time together. Bart had his first chance at life and the priest wasn't going to die over some kindling. Lucky folks, Du Pré thought.

Two of them, maybe they ought to get married.

Du Pré opened the door and the two men came in, stamping the snow off as best they could.

Bart was looking much better. His face had lost watery flesh and now there were some lines that the weather had written, lines of age that had been there but stayed smooth because his body was so soaked in booze. Clear eyes, but very tired.

Can't sleep much yet. I've heard about that, worst thing about the booze, you can't even die at night a little, get some rest, stop things from running though your mind. Banging doors.

Du Pré caught himself. He was going to ask the priest if a hot toddy would go down good, cold day.

"Give the father a hot toddy," said Bart, "I'm better now."

The man needs you to do what he says, thought Du Pré. He made two stiff ones, a cup of strong tea for Bart. They sat, sipped, didn't say anything.

"Cards?" said Du Pré, finally, eyes twinkling.

"No," said Bart, "I have a favor to ask."

Bring the priest to back you up, must be a favor too big for the telephone to carry.

I know what it is.

"I have to find out what happened to my brother," said Bart. "I don't know how to go about it, though, and I was talking to Father Van Den Heuvel and he said you were a smart man and knew this place and you could find out if anyone could."

The priest was looking resolutely away. This was between Bart and Gabriel, he was just here for ballast.

"Why me?" said Du Pré. I know fucking well why me, fate, why me.

"You found the skull, which is probably Gianni's. The teeth. You must want to know."

I already know, I think, said Du Pré to himself, under his mustache. But this one, he's right, I have to know for sure.

Du Pré finished his toddy. He got up, made another one, get this cold out of my bones. He poured Bart some more boiling water, there was still lots of good in his teabag. The priest was only half through with his hot whiskey. Du Pré gave him a little more whiskey, hot water, dollop of lemon.

"I am no detective," said Du Pré.

"Please," said Bart. "I can't do it myself, I don't know how. I need to stay here, work my ass off with Booger Tom, pray. Sweat at night, take five showers a day. I'm still nearer dead than alive."

Du Pré looked at the priest. The big man was wiping his glasses so that he wouldn't have to look at anybody.

"What you want me to do?" said Du Pré.

Bart pulled a manila envelope out of the game pouch at the back of his expensive English hunting coat. Good waxed cotton, breathes, thornproof, keeps out the cold winds. Thousand dollars, probably.

"This is what the private detectives my family hired found. It isn't much. My brother flew to Denver. He stayed

111

one night at the Brown Palace. The next morning he bought an emerald necklace. He rented a car. And that was the last that anybody ever saw of him. He must have paid cash for the gas, there were no credit card slips from after the day he picked the car up in Denver. He had a lot of money on him. And a necklace worth seventy-four thousand dollars, 1967 dollars.''

"Plenty people kill your brother for that," said Du Pré.

"Whatever," said Bart. His hands started to shake, he trembled. His eyes rolled up in his head, *gaaaacking* sounds came from his throat. He was stiff and shaking.

Father Van Den Heuvel jammed a folded napkin in Bart's mouth. He grabbed Bart in his huge arms and held him till he quit convulsing. He helped him to the living room and laid him out on the couch.

Du Pré stood back, sipping his toddy.

"He'll be all right in a minute," said the priest.

Du Pré nodded. One sick man, this.

"Will you do it?" Father Van Den Heuvel asked, looking at Du Pré. "He'll pay you, give you money for expenses. It might help him."

Bart stirred weakly. His eyes opened.

"Seizure?" he whispered. He shook his head. "Sorry," he said.

"Yes," said the priest. "We don't mind, Bart."

"It's fine," said Du Pré, setting down his glass. "Even if you fuck up, get drunk or something it's fine. You got friends here, Bart, you don't know how to have them but you'll learn."

Bart stared up at the ceiling. His eyes filled with tears.

"I find out who killed your brother," said Du Pré.

Bart slid a black leather envelope out of his coat pocket. He handed it to Du Pré. "There's five thousand in there," he said. "More, any more you might need, call Lawyer Foote at this number." Little card, expensive paper.

"But when I find out," said Du Pré, "you do what I tell you to do about it, you hear? Do what I say."

"Yes," Bart whispered, nodding. "I just want to know."

✦ CHAPTER 34 ✦

Du Pré went to Raymond and Jacqueline's little house for Christmas dinner. Madelaine's people were in town and she didn't want to upset them, someone notice Du Pré knows his way around her house too good, and she an abandoned wife but still married in the eyes of God, and especially her relatives'.

"We all got them aunts," said Du Pré. " 'Cept me, my aunt, she a hooker on a horse, got a lariat, fer Chrissakes.

His third grandchild was so happy to see Grandpère Du Pré he pissed in Grandpère's lap. Thank you, little Dominick.

"I'm sorry," said Jacqueline, mopping Du Pré off. Lots of good that will do, thought Du Pré, sit through dinner now on my soaked nuts. This grandfather shit, well.

"You can wear some of Raymond's underwear, pair of his jeans," said Jacqueline. Raymond had one pair good pants, church pants, he was in them.

Du Pré changed in their bedroom. He rolled his soiled things together, stuck them in the game pouch of his old hunting coat. Benetsee's deer. Blood on the sleeve. He'd forgotten the old man, been too busy. Benetsee, he hadn't come round, either. Hadn't seen him three, four weeks? Thanksgiving? Damn me. I got to go check. Cow asses, where these days go.

"Hey," said Du Pré when he came out, "I better go see about Benetsee. I have forgot him."

"We didn't," said Jacqueline. "Father Van Den Heuvel took him to that Bart's. I would have them here, but . . ."

This tiny house. Even with just Du Pré and Maria extra it was stuffed to bursting. The three little ones slept in a big closet off the tiny bedroom.

When they ate today it would be on a kitchen table made of a full four-by-eight sheet of plywood sitting on the little kitchen table, chairs for four. Raymond had made a bench, too, for the little ones. Plenty of room for the people, plenty of room for the food. Bart, now, he had never had a meal like this one here. Poor bastard.

Raymond carved the turkey. A huge bird, Du Pré had driven all the way to Great Falls for it. Bought stuffing mix, chestnuts, and fresh oysters.

The Métis people had lots of goiter, no iodine. Big throats, till the oysters came. Eat oyster stew one Friday time to time after that. In the old days, the Métis traded for salmon, but the whites they stole the fish, too.

Du Pré wondered who the first Métis to see the ocean was. Most likely they saw Hudson Bay.

Red River.

Tomorrow, Du Pré would drive east and then north, back up the trail of the returning buffalo hunters, the noisy Red River carts. Supposed to be no snow for two days. Hah. This country, it sat out there, breathing, waiting for the winter, like a big white cat and you the mouse.

They ate. Du Pré's grandson added to his legend by throwing up over himself and much of the table. One glob stuck to the side of Du Pré's wineglass. Du Pré stuck out a finger, wiped it off, looked at the lump, smeared it on his napkin.

"Oh, poor baby," said Jacqueline, grabbing the boy.

"Good, strong Métis stomach," said Du Pré. "He throw it far, that little one."

"Papa!" said Jacqueline, laughing. She took her baby to the sink, put him in it, washed him while shushing his wails.

"So you go see Aunty Pauline," said Jacqueline, returning. Little Dominick, damp and streaked, much subdued. The boy pecked at a fresh plate of food, eyeing distances, computing trajectories.

"Yes," said Du Pré, "I haven't seen her in a long time. Got some time, travel a little." He'd given Jacqueline a thousand dollars, to keep against need. Hard-headed girl. Raymond wouldn't even know until they were up against it. Just keep them shots coming, Raymond. Got to make them babies, regular-like.

Raymond looked around the table with pride. Jacqueline loved him enough to let him keep that.

Jacqueline had made a wild plum pie. Gathered the fruit from the bushes that hugged the little creek that ran behind the house. Baby in the little carrier on her back. Rum in the pie. Nutmeg.

I should have brought my fiddle with me, thought Du Pré. Well, I am going to take it with me, see those fiddlers up there know what they are about. Yes.

Du Pré poured whiskey in his coffee. Raymond had a little. The boy hardly drank. Boy, hell, man, got more kids than I do. I was that young once, but I drank lots more whiskey.

Maria sat very quietly, in her sister's house. Jacqueline had the babies, had proved herself. Du Pré looked at Maria, felt a little sorry for the world, it didn't lie down, do like she said. He laughed, shook his head. My girls.

Tomorrow I go back up that trail, drive first to Pembina, over in North Dakota, then right up past the little Catholic churches every twenty miles on the prairie. Once the Church had railroad cars made up like chapels for weddings, baptisms, funerals. Park it on a siding of the Canadian Pacific, tend to business.

That night Du Pré slept badly, excited, things gnawing at his mind. He dreamed, bad confusing dreams.

He woke up choking, in this house he had been born and raised in.

He remembered being in the little bedroom, the one that Maria had now, one night a very long time ago.

His parents had been talking low, in bed.

His mother, she had been crying.

✤ CHAPTER 35 ✤

Just one more piece Métis trash headed north, Du Pré thought. Them English hate us Frenchies, hate the Indians, see what it is like to come from an island. Carry it with you in your soul.

North Dakota in winter. Bleak. Du Pré recalled the joke, the big North Dakota winter sport, get the neighbors to help push the house down the road, jump-start the furnace.

He stopped at a gas station for coffee.

Aunty Pauline was in the little Manitoba town of Boissevain, not so far over the border. Du Pré had called her. She had a wonderful voice, the voice you get from many years of cigarettes and whiskey and broken loves.

Du Pré couldn't remember if she sang or not. He hoped so.

He wondered what she looked like now, sixty-some, he remembered her blond and beautiful and very strong. How his mother looked at her, not liking her. Too wild. Bring that out in Catfoot, she'd have trouble, threaten my house, my little Gabriel, I don't like her.

Dangerous women, they scare women not so dangerous.

The border. The Canadian side, man leaned down, asked where Du Pré is going, how long he plans to stay. Du Pré said a week maybe. Then they toss the car, even took out the seats while Du Pré sat in the waiting room, looking at a bronze plaque which stated the stiff penalties for beating the shit out of a customs officer.

It took Du Pré two hours to put his car back together. They had left his fiddle case open on the hood in the bitter cold. The fiddle's varnish had begun to wrinkle.

Take that, you Frenchy Indian piece of shit, we don't care you call yourself American.

The Scots were the worst. Live in the mountains on an island, invent haggis, you'd have a sour view of the world, too.

Fuck you, Du Pré thought.

Gabriel Dumont. If poor mad Louis Riel had let him, little Gabriel would have killed your precious General Wolseley, your redcoat troops, left you dead there. Spit in your faces.

Du Pré spat on the asphalt, all rimed with salt. So many people from the cities, never saw ice on the road. Come

117

booming up here from Chicago, wherever, car set on cruise control, hit a patch of ice and that's that.

But he liked the country. It felt like home. Very big sky, this. The Scandinavians broke under it, often enough. The North Dakota State Motto: I bain don't tink dis luek like Norvay . . .

Manitoba. Good woodland Cree word, or was it Chippewa? No English word good enough to name this country, for sure. Red River, I piss here it goes to Hudson Bay.

The road went north, straight as a stretched string. Long, lone, and a little up, long, lone, and a little down.

Boissevain. Little Catholic town, Métis town, little white church, very big graveyard.

Du Pré went to the saloon. Remembered that in Canada, the bars were divided, men single in one end, couples in another. The Canadians, they didn't like fights.

Du Pré called his Aunty Pauline. Man answered, seemed about to hang up, but he called her to the phone instead.

"I'll come there," she said, voice deep and smoky. "I look a lot different. Do you?"

Du Pré said yes.

He had a Molson beer, squat bottle with scratches on it. All Canadian beer bottles were the same, so they could take them back to any brewery.

Du Pré rolled a cigarette, smoked, thought his aunt would be a little while, put on a face, must take longer these days, try to sketch in what had fallen off.

But she came right away. Wearing crimson buckskins, cigarette in a long holder. She smiled at the barman, who smiled back.

My Aunty Pauline, the character. Du Pré liked her.

She was still a good-looking woman. Silk shirt, soft around the throat. Hard face, thick coat of makeup. Brown eyes very big still, lots of green eye shadow.

"So, Du Pré," she said, sitting down. Cheap large stones on her hands, or maybe even expensive ones. Du Pré couldn't tell. The shoulders of her crimson leather jacket were damp from the wet snow falling outside.

They didn't hug, didn't kiss. Aunty Pauline looked down, the barman brought her a drink brown over ice. Brandy? Du Pré paid for it, left the change.

"What you want?" she said. "All these years you don't want to talk to your Aunty Pauline, now you do. Your mother never like me."

"I got a question," said Du Pré. "Then I'll leave you alone."

Pauline sipped her brandy.

"You have a lover once, man named Fascelli? Gianni Fascelli?"

Du Pré waited a moment.

"Aunty Pauline," said Du Pré, "you hear me?"

She had frozen. Drink in hand. Her hand shook. She set her drink down.

"No," she said finally.

"I think that I know better," said Du Pré, "you know?"

"Look," said Aunty Pauline. "This Fascelli man, he sees me ride in a show, OK? He fall in love with me, crazy love. He has lots of money, sends me gifts, follows me around the circuit. Miles City, he's in the stands, Havre, Calgary, Spokane, all around. But he scares me. He has crazy eyes, he's always drunk, he has so much damn money."

Du Pré nodded, sipped his beer.

"So I tell him to leave me alone."

Du Pré had another swallow.

"He gets mad with me one night, threatens me with all these gangster people in Chicago he knows. I don't go with him, he have me killed. So I meet him at a hotel, stay in his bed three days. I'm very scared."

Du Pré nodded.

"He pass out drunk, I get up, dress, grab my suitcase, run to Catfoot, hide."

"So he was looking for you?" And, thought Du Pré, the money in his wallet and left nut, most likely.

"He sent people to ask questions, sent gifts, too, said he would be by soon, and just take me with him."

Du Pré looked at her. We don't none of us got a straight story, he thought, but poor Aunty Pauline.

"So that's what you know now," she said. "I got a younger man now, he's very jealous, so I got to go."

Du Pré nodded.

He watched his aunt walk away. Still had a nice ass, must be she still ride some. Whatever.

✦ CHAPTER 36 ✦

Du Pré fiddled. He stood in his Métis finery out in front of the bandstand, lights on him, while the people clapped and danced and cheered. People mostly looked a lot like him, some few English.

The men wore a lot of white with red sashes, the women silks in brilliant colors, white teeth in brown faces.

A man bowed from a life on horseback, hands twice the size they should be for his height, he played the good ringing bones. Somebody had a washtub bass, they pulled on the string and broomstick and the bottom bowed up, slide that deep note.

Good people.

Du Pré fiddled till his fingers hurt, found himself scooting off from the playing of the others, dropping little clusters of icy notes back down on the melody.

He was knee-walking, grass-grabbing drunk. Couldn't lie on the floor without holding on.

Some people took him home with them, saying these Manitoba Provincial Police bad on drunk drivers, love to arrest people from the States.

Du Pré awoke the next morning, still pretty drunk. He was asleep in a cupboard bed, under a bunch of quilts. He sat up, and he smiled, thought about the night before.

The master of ceremonies had unfurled what he said was the new Canadian flag. A big green frog pissing on nine little beavers. Du Pré began laughing again, thinking about that flag.

Smell of smoked venison frying, slap of spoon mixing up the pancake batter.

Du Pré sat down at a long trestle table. He looked up, looked down, seemed like he was looking at a bunch of cousins.

"You got the big head, he?" said one man, about Du Pré's age. When he smiled, he had no upper front teeth. Oh. That man, one of the fiddlers from the night before.

"Oh," said a plump pretty woman, "you play that fiddle good." She set down a platter of venison, big platter of fry bread.

Peppersauce for the venison, chokecherry jam for the fry bread.

I feel like home here, thought Du Pré. Montana, it is home, I know, I like it, I will die there, but my people are up here too.

Du Pré was famished. He ate and ate till the hosts clapped and laughed at him.

"He need a good woman feed him more," said a man

121

at the other end of the table. "They got no good women down in them States, eh? You take one of ours back, eh?"

Du Pré blushed, he thought of Madelaine.

Now I got to go all the way over to Moose Jaw, the Oblate Fathers Home, see that old Father Leblanc.

He can't break the secrets of the confessional, but I have to know this.

I have to know all of this.

After the big breakfast, one of the men drove Du Pré back to his old cruiser. Du Pré felt a little dirty, he'd sweated a lot in the stage lights. He was still wearing all the fine clothes that his women had made for him, leggings, sash, silk shirt, kerchief, vest, hat, moccasins. He had a flight feather from a red hawk in his hat band now, someone had given it to him the night before.

Métis man with a hangover, fiddle on the seat beside him, smell of rum and cheap tobacco, going down the road in a old car with American license plates.

No one stopped him. He drove through the little towns, some English, some Métis, the old Red River country, must have been some fine country once, before the English.

This air, I know it, Du Pré thought, breathing deep. It was cold out, but he drove with the window down, to clear his head.

He stopped for lunch in a little Catholic town, asked the man at the garage where there was a good cheap little motel. The man at the motel looked like Du Pré and charged him fifteen dollars for the night.

He bathed and changed into jeans and boots and a sheepskin vest, waxed cotton coat, put on his battered Stetson. Packed the Métis finery away, he would take it out the next time he found a fiddling contest, here or back over the border.

Du Pré was in no real hurry.

The next morning he went to confession, went to Mass. He asked the priest where he could buy a pretty missal. He paid the priest a hundred dollars for one, a beautiful thing, cover by some Métis woman, soft white deerskin, beaded, quilled, the priest said it was a hundred years old. Some of the pages were stained, it looked like the marks of tears.

This book had lived some, that's for sure.

He found a quick dry-clean place, had his scarf and sash and shirt cleaned. Now I am ready for the next fiddling, yes.

Moose Jaw. It couldn't be any place else, this place that did need to be named Moose Jaw. He didn't care why it was named that.

The Oblate Fathers Home was a big old brick building, well kept, a lot of pretty junipers around it, the white trunks of birches. Chapel right off the entrance. Du Pré went in, crossed himself, and he prayed for a while.

He asked where Father Leblanc was. The attendant led him down a brightly polished hallway, floors and walls of maple and birch. He motioned Du Pré into a room, a small one with leaded windows and bright chintz curtains. A narrow bed, a desk, a prie-dieu. Father Leblanc was slumped, boneless, in a heavy old leather chair.

His old head and face were hairless, so wrinkled he looked like a ball of string. He wheezed and whistled, dreaming.

"I won't bother him now," said Du Pré. "I am one of his old flock. I will wait here till he wakes."

Du Pré took out the missal, opened it to the page marked by the faded blue silk ribbon, read.

Father Leblanc slept.

✦ CHAPTER 37 ✦

Du Pré's Latin wasn't so good, never had been.

He closed the missal, looked out the window at what was left of the day. Not too far back, it was the shortest day of the year. He was some farther north here, the shadows seemed longer, the blue in them colder.

Winters used to be much tougher, back in the time of the grandfathers. And there had not been so much to fight the winter with.

Or hunger.

Or cold.

Father Leblanc stirred. His sagging old eyelids lifted, he looked for a moment like a very old turtle.

Father Leblanc blessed Du Pré.

"You don't remember me," said Gabriel, pulling off his hat. He leaned close, put his face near to the old man's. "Can you hear me, Father Leblanc?"

"Yes," the old priest said, his voice a wet whisper, "I think I know you. Are you not the son of Guillaume du Pré?"

"That was my father, Catfoot," said Gabriel. "You know, you baptized me, gave me my first communion."

The old priest's eyes moved slowly to the gathering dark out his window. He pushed a little button on a cord pinned to the sleeve of his cassock.

The attendant came in a few minutes. Father Leblanc ordered some tea.

The old priest asked questions of the Toussaint people, who had married, who had babies, how was the youngster Van Den Heuvel?

Du Pré answered. They sipped tea.

"But I didn't come here for a simple visit," said Gabriel, "I have a question for you. So I must tell you what I know. Then I will ask you the question, and when I do, I will offer you the missal here . . ."

He let the old priest look at it. His eyes were infinitely sad. Du Pré took it back.

"My father, Catfoot, he killed a man named Gianni Fascelli, cut off his head and his hands and put them up in the mountains, next to an old plane wreck had a couple other skeletons. This man, this Fascelli, was an animal, my father killed him because he loved his sister, my aunt Pauline, and this man was threatening her. Us Métis, you don't mess with our women."

The old priest was still, looking out the window.

"So I know all that," said Du Pré, "figured out some more things, too, but they are not very important. But I need to know this, for my father's soul, and I don't want you to say anything. I need you to sin just a little for me, Father Leblanc."

Du Pré picked up the old man's hand, wrapped it around the missal.

"What I need to know is did my father feel bad about killing this man. Did Catfoot repent and ask God's mercy? That's all. I need to know that. So if he did, I want you to take this missal, and if he didn't, I want you to let it go. For the living, I want you to sin just a little."

The old priest looked at Gabriel with his sad patient eyes.

The old hand clamped shut on the missal. The old priest pulled the little book away.

Du Pré bowed his head and wept. The old priest reached

out, made the sign of the cross on Du Pré's forehead with his thumb, fingers light as smoke on Du Pré's skin.

Du Pré looked up, nodded.

"I thank you for the living, Father," said Du Pré.

The old man was looking out at the dark. He held the missal lightly in his hands, his lips moved.

Du Pré picked up his hat and left. Outside the cold winter air stung the tears on his cheeks.

He drove down into Moose Jaw, found a motel, put the fiddle in his room so it wouldn't get frozen. There were some restaurants close by, Du Pré ate a bad supper of overcooked beef and vegetables that had been simmered so long they were transparent mush.

He walked on, found a saloon, went in and had some whiskeys.

He went back to his motel, there was a stupid movie on the television, fine with Du Pré.

Well, Du Pré thought, I know it all but for that last thing with the priest before I come up here. But it was the only question that was important, can't bring the life back to any of them, can't pull the bullet out of time, can't do much. But Papa, he have hot blood and a lot of pride, and I am glad he apologized to God for his sin, there, that his pride didn't take and carry him all the way up to that damn train. Well, Catfoot, now I go and clean up the last of it. You old bastard.

He went to sleep and slept till midmorning, with his fiddle asleep on the table beside him.

Du Pré drove south the next day, down toward Montana, down the route that Gabriel Dumont had taken, thousands of English hunting him. The little man slipped through them all, drifted through the Cypress Hills, down to Montana forever.

Spent the rest of his days not talking to priests.

✤ CHAPTER 38 ✤

D u Pré," said Madelaine, when he stood in her doorway, tired from the road. "Du Pré, I think that you find everything that you were looking for, eh?" She kissed him.

Du Pré nodded. Well, not exactly, but he knew pretty much where everything was, pretty soon he'd have everything, everyone paid, the loose ends all knotted off. Then what? More grandkids, piss in my lap.

"You hungry, Du Pré?" Madelaine pushed a strand of dark hair back from her forehead. Little gray in it, looked very good. She was not a vain woman, dye her hair, look foolish. Du Pré smiled, loving her.

"Yes," said Du Pré, grabbing her, lifting her up, carrying her to the bedroom.

"Du Pré!"

After, they lay laughing for a while. Madelaine ran her finger over Du Pré's chest, nuzzled his ear.

"I miss you. You find your crazy aunt?"

"Yes," said Gabriel. "You know, I love my aunt, but I don't think she will have it. She got a young, jealous man, don't sound good."

"You got an old jealous woman here. You play your fiddle for them Red River women, eh? You forget your Madelaine?"

"Just the six times," said Du Pré, "I'm so drunk, maybe more."

Madelaine whacked him, not hard.

"You not like that," she said, propping herself up on her elbow. "Too good a man, hurt those who love you. Six, maybe more, some bullshit, Du Pré. Hah."

Du Pré looked at the ceiling. She got me there.

"That Bart working horses with Booger Tom, he get kicked, got his leg in a cast now," said Madelaine. "I don't think nothing else happened while you were gone. Maria comes by every day, we are going to be all right, now she got something to look after besides you."

"What?" said Du Pré, "she got a new boyfriend?"

"Oh, no," said Madelaine. "She got no time for a boyfriend. Now she is studying to be a senator, she says."

"Oh," said Du Pré. She go to Helena one time, but Washington? Never. Oh, God. Senator Du Pré, the one in the miniskirt. Don't you got to be old, like twenty-five or something?

"So what you find up there," said Madelaine.

Du Pré didn't say anything.

"Don't tell me, huh?"

"I don't tell anybody till I have it all right here, in my hand," said Du Pré. He closed his fist, gripped hard.

Madelaine grumbled about it a little.

"You see Benetsee?" said Du Pré.

Madelaine shook her head. The old man hadn't been in church this last Sunday, but then he often didn't come to church. But the smoke was coming up from his chimney, so he had to be all right.

They got dressed. Du Pré yawned, he was all off in his sleep, been making too much road, found out too much, he was worried about his aunt.

Write her? Say when your young man leave you you remember your nephew down here? She would hate him forever for his pity. What Pauline would do, get dead

128

drunk, drive her car very fast, point it into something big. *Waaahaaaaaaaaaaaaaaaa. Bam.*

She was plenty tough, all right. Tough herself to death, that girl.

I am glad that Maria doesn't much like horses, thought Du Pré, she's the same tough, but at least she have a chance. Pauline, there is just a poor girl with big tits and good legs.

"Well," said Du Pré, "I got to go now, see that Bart and the old man."

Madelaine nodded.

Du Pré's car smelled a little of garbage. He had a paper sack full of browning apple cores and sandwich wrappings. He drove to the Toussaint Bar, put the sack in the trash bin at the side of the place, along with the empty bottles and the soggy napkins and paper plates from their lousy hamburgers.

The Toussaint Bar, where love is suddenly taken drunk.

Pauline, you ought to come down here, not stay up there alone, down here you got family.

Old Benetsee, now he's family, too. Spooky old man, lived on nothing, people brought him food, fixed his window it got broken. Split his wood. Benetsee, wheezy old dogs, wheezy old man with his flute in the side of his mouth.

Thing is, thought Du Pré, since we invent writing we remember too much and forget the important things.

Du Pré drove away. The day was warm and overcast and there was a black smudgy line on the northern horizon, soon they would have an Alberta Clipper run down the front of the Rockies, make the windows rattle in their frames.

Glad I come down before that thing, thought Du Pré. Most storms came from the west, the ones from the north

129

were in a bigger hurry and they dumped a lot more snow.

Du Pré knocked on Benetsee's door. He heard a chair slip on dirty linoleum, the old man pushed back the faded calico curtain and peered out at Du Pré. He smiled, couple teeth here and there. Very yellow, brown at the roots.

"Du Pré!" said Benetsee, "good to see you! Some wine, you bring?"

Du Pré shook his head.

"You go get some then, or I don't talk to you," said Benetsee. He shut the door, real firm.

Du Pré did as he was told.

✦ CHAPTER 39 ✦

Benetsee, playing the flute, glass of cheap white on the table, stuck there among the crumpled papers and bread rinds, a cut of venison black and dried, some apples as wrinkled as the old man.

Benetsee, playing his flute, looping melodies, came from somewhere Du Pré had never been. Played until Du Pré fidgeted, then he stopped the tune. Chop.

"So," said Benetsee, "you find out some things, maybe too much?"

Du Pré nodded. He wasn't going to tell anyone anything until he had dug up the rest. Not Madelaine, not Maria, not Bart, and for sure not this old fart.

"That Red River country pretty good, huh?"

Du Pré nodded.

More flute. Was there a point to all this?

The old man stopped again. He got up, shuffled over to a shelf, took down his bundle of deerskin, brought it to the table. He undid the thongs, unrolled it.

Pipe bowls. Just some hunks of rock, some the rude shape hacked out, others smoothed down perfectly, ready for a willow stem. The red stone glowed, seemed to have some light within.

Benetsee poked around in the pipe bowls, picked up one, set it back down, picked up another.

"This one," he said. He belched, held out his glass. Du Pré unscrewed the cap of the jug, poured him more wine.

"This stuff kill you, you know," said Du Pré.

"I just die sometime," said Benetsee. "Nothing kill me. I just die when I want to."

OK. OK.

Benetsee reached down by the table, brought up a quiver, one full of willow pipe stems. He selected one, white as paper, pared the butt with his pocketknife, twisted and jammed it into the smokehole. Dug a little pipestone mouthpiece out of the rubble in the bundle. Carefully pulled off some strands of sinew from a smelly little bunch on the table. He lashed the sinew three places on the pipestem. Took a little leather pouch from his stained old coat, fished out a wad of feathers.

Red-shafted flicker. Bright crimson quills, soft black and gray barbules. He fixed the feathers to the sinew lashings, two, three, two.

"Here," said Benetsee, offering the pipe to Du Pré.

Du Pré took it, looked at it close, held it away from his eyes. Carving of a bobcat, back arched, paws on a grouse, grouse with feathered leggings, so it was winter. Not a bobcat, tufts on the ears, so it was a lynx.

"Pretty soon you smoke that," said Benetsee. "You know when and where and for which man. Smoke it,

131

watch the smoke rise, go to his tired soul on the Star Trail."

Du Pré rolled a cigarette, handed it to Benetsee, made himself another.

They smoked. The old man had pinched a little tobacco from the end of his cigarette, rubbed it in his fingers, dribbled the tiny flakes on the pipe bowls in the deerskin bundle.

Du Pré left, he drove away from the old man's with the pipe beside him on the seat.

Bart's truck was parked by his trailer, the curtains on the window were open. When Du Pré knocked he saw Bart through the window in the door. Bart struggled up from the couch and stumped on over.

He looked out at Du Pré and smiled.

Du Pré looked down. I got news, can't tell you yet, one last thing here before I do. So fire me.

"Du Pré!" said Bart. Each time Du Pré saw Bart's face he looked older but better, his face was running hard to catch up to time, even over sharp rocks.

Du Pré looked down at the walking cast, up to the knee, a rubber heelpiece.

"Booger Tom said I was only thirty breaks away from being some kind of horseman," said Bart, real proud, beaming. I got hurt and I didn't get drunk, I am winning big.

Du Pré came in. Bart hobbled to the little kitchen, made tea.

They sipped the tea, didn't speak for a while.

"Well?" said Bart finally.

"I got most of it," said Du Pré. "Just one or two more things, I think, then I will have the whole story." I got the whole damn story, I just need . . . the things that aren't just words.

"OK," said Bart.

132

"But I'm going to wait to tell you until I have those last one, two pieces, you don't mind." Even if you do mind.

Bart shook his head, smiled. Fine. You do what you have to.

"Here," said Du Pré, "is the rest of your money. It didn't cost that much." He pulled out a stained envelope, dropped it on the coffee table.

"Keep it," said Bart. "Give it to Van Den Heuvel if you don't want it. No, you keep it, you should be paid for your time. I insist."

Du Pré nodded. He took the money back. For the oatmeal for my grandchildren, soon we buy it by truckload.

"You want to help me find these last one, two pieces, eh?" said Du Pré.

"Of course," said Bart. "Is a pig's prick pork?"

Du Pré snorted. "We got to wait until there is some warm weather, spring most likely, then we will need a big diesel shovel."

Bart nodded.

"Just the two of us," said Du Pré. "We look for these things."

"I can order up any piece of equipment we need any time," said Bart.

Du Pré looked down at Fascelli's cast.

"That hurt a lot?"

"Some," said Bart, "but not too bad. I try to ignore it. Booger Tom would have ignored the broken leg altogether."

"Well," said Du Pré, "what I will need is a guy who knows how to run one of those big diesel shovels, see, we got to move a lot of gravel, thousands of tons, move it real carefully. So I need a real good guy, stir his coffee with the bucket on that shovel."

"I'll hire the best," said Bart.

"No," said Du Pré. "Just you and me, huh?"

"Oh," said Bart, "I become that real good guy with that shovel, stirring his coffee with the bucket?"

Du Pré nodded. I'll be down by that damn bucket, he thought, you better be good.

"I'll take care of it," said Bart.

Du Pré nodded.

"My own self," said Bart.

Du Pré nodded.

❖ CHAPTER 40 ❖

Bitter cold day, wind so cold that it burned.

Du Pré stood by the chute, looking hard through his frosted lashes at the steers' hides, the brands, some of them messed over with frozen shit. Messed over too damn artfully.

Days like this, I should have been a brain surgeon, thought Du Pré, indoor work anyway.

He reached out, rubbed hard on the green smears on a steer's rump. That one, that one is worked over, god damn it. This guy, I have been thinking of him like that for some time now.

Du Pré stepped down from the chute, his boots sliding on the welded pipe the thing was built of.

The rancher was huddled down against the cold.

"Mr. Higgins," said Du Pré, hard against the wind, "those brands are reworked. No way I sign off on this one. Your cattle here are impounded till we know who they belong to."

The man straightened right up.

"Bullshit," he screamed. He had two sons with him, they heard the noise, didn't know what it meant yet, but they started to walk over to Du Pré and their father.

Du Pré ran to his car, got in, started the engine, flicked on the radio. "Du Pré here," he said quickly. "Say, I got a bunch of bad brands, the Higgins place, you get someone out here, do it now."

"Got it," said the dispatcher.

Higgins smashed Du Pré's window with a crowbar. His sons were behind him. Everyone yelling but Du Pré.

Du Pré scrabbled in the glove box for his gun. Higgins had bashed the glass mostly in. Du Pré grabbed his .38, opened the far door, slid out and stood.

Higgins came at him around the car, screaming, crowbar in his hand.

Du Pré aimed low and shot him in the leg, aiming for the kneecap.

The man folded up. The sons were unbuttoning their coats.

"Shit shit shit shit," said Du Pré to himself, running toward the stock tank, good heavy-gauge metal, I hope.

He glanced back. Both sons were down on the ground with their father, one had a gun in his hand.

"You drop that!" Du Pré yelled. The son looked up, started to lift the pistol. Du Pré fired. The son slammed into the side of Du Pré's old cruiser.

Shit shit shit shit.

The second son looked over at Du Pré, terrified. Sirens down the road, coming on quick.

"Don't shoot! Don't shoot!"

He raised his hands. Higgins was on the ground, writhing, his leg clamped in his hands. The other son was against Du Pré's tire, and looking too damn still.

Sirens. Come on come ON.

The Sherrif's car was just a quarter-mile away and closing real fast. Du Pré thought the dispatcher might have heard the glass break when Higgins started in with the crowbar. Whatever.

Wonder if that guy knew what he was doing, when he lifted up that gun. I don't know. What else could I do but shoot? Not shoot. Shit.

Du Pré wished that he hadn't fired, probably would wish that for the rest of his life. Nothing clean about this at all.

The Sheriff's car came into the turnaround and slid sideways on the frozen mud. Deputy came out of the car with a pump shotgun in his hands, pointing it at Du Pré.

"No!" Du Pré screamed, standing up and dropping his gun. "Them! God damn it! Them!" He pointed over at the three by his car.

Higgins was flat on his back now, his forearms pointing straight up. The son that Du Pré had shot looked very dead. Bundle of dirty clothes. The other boy was on his knees, hands raised very high, screaming don't shoot don't shoot don't shoot.

Oh, God, thought Du Pré, how does all this happen over a little bad money? Things gone to hell, just like that.

The deputy was too lightly dressed for the wind. He walked forward, waving the shotgun. The son on his knees went flat on his face. The deputy went to him, handcuffed his wrists behind his back.

Higgins had passed out from the pain.

Du Pré knelt by the man that he had shot. He reached out his hand, pressed a thumb against the man's throat. Nothing.

Some fine day this. Du Pré's groin burned with cold. Pissed his pants.

136

"Du Pré," said the deputy, "you're bleeding, man."

Du Pré looked at his belly. Little blood running down his left pant leg. Big black scorch mark on his coat.

"God damn!" said Du Pré. "I am one fine law enforcement officer! I shot myself, I think!" I get a combat brand inspector's badge, sure enough. Ain't this some shit.

He looked up. It was quiet. High above, an eagle soared.

❧ CHAPTER 41 ❧

Du Pré sat on the examining table, looking incuriously at the furrow he had plowed in his belly, calculating an inch that way, two inches that way, hoo boy.

The doctor bent over, scrubbed at the wound. Du Pré winced, but didn't feel anything except the scrubbing noise through his flesh. *Scritch scritch scritch.*

"You're lucky," said the doctor. "Just a superficial skin tear. All stippled with powder, though, some of it will fester. The scar will look like some kid was stabbing you with a pencil."

Higgins had been flown out to Miles City, his knee was shattered. The son Du Pré had shot was dead, shot right through the heart.

" 'Scuse me," said Du Pré. He lurched over to the wastebasket and threw up. The doctor waited.

When Du Pré quit heaving he went back and sat on the table again.

The doctor finished sewing him up, put a bandage on the wound, gave him a shot.

"Just lie down for a while," said the doctor, going out the door.

The acting Sheriff Benny Klein came in.

"How you feel?" he said.

"Shit how I feel. I just kill somebody, shoot myself over some damn hamburger meat. I feel like shit, that's what."

Benny had a clipboard, a little tape recorder.

"Guy bashed in the window, I am scrambling out the other side, must have shot myself then, I run to the stock tank, shoot back . . . no, I shot Higgins in the leg, then I run to the stock tank, shoot back, guy falls over, other one sticks up his hands . . ."

How long all this death and pain take, ten seconds? Fifteen?

Du Pré did not mention how the deputy pointed the gun at him first. All in all, it was not a day to remember well.

"Yeah," said Benny, "things are always confused. Only time I was ever shot at was up at Fascellis, we all panicked and fired everything every which way like we was at Dien Bien Phu or something. And no one even fired at my ass, except the Sheriff was dead on his back on the lawn. You know how many times the four of us fired? Eighty-one. I never heard a one of them."

Du Pré felt weak and sick.

"OK," said the Sheriff, "I got to suspend you pending the investigation. Got to have you turn in your gun."

Du Pré didn't offhand know where his gun was. Pocket of my coat, maybe. And it is hanging right over there. Du Pré got up, went to it, fished around, brought out the old pistol. Cocked. Safety off, live rounds in it. Oh, god damn it all to three kinds of hell.

Du Pré let the hammer down, spun the cylinder, two rounds gone, three left.

"See," said Du Pré pointing, "here, this first one is

138

where I shot myself because I was behaving in a threatening manner, the second is where I killed Higgins's kid because he was behaving in a threatening manner."

"Hey, calm down," said Benny. "You seem to be in shock or something. We can do this later, you know, but I have to take the gun." He tugged the gun out of Du Pré's hand and dropped it into an evidence bag.

"You rest up, you hear?" said Benny.

"I'm sorry," said Du Pré.

There was someone screaming down the hall, probably Higgins's wife.

"Get drunk," said Benny. "Get drunk, rest up, back on the horse."

Us cowboys, thought Du Pré, we sure keep it simple, yes. He nodded, began pulling on his clothes.

A nurse stuck her head in the door. "We'd like you to stay tonight," she said. "You might be in shock."

"I just killed a man," said Du Pré, "and I am in shock, yes, but I will not stay here tonight."

"So," she said. "Well, you take care and we're here if you need us."

"Du Pré," said Madelaine from the doorway. Maria was looking in over her shoulder.

They had both been crying.

"Tell you two what," said Du Pre. "You are lookin' for a hero, I am not him. Me, I want to go home, start on the south end of a half-gallon of whiskey, go all the way to the North Pole."

Madelaine and Maria looked at him. They grinned. "Sure," they chorused. "Maybe we go along with you," said Maria.

Du Pré signed himself out of the hospital, against medical advice. Goddamned right. Lots of people, they die around these quacks. Happens all the time.

That other time, that guy was just reaching for a rifle, I shot him but he lived. Got a suspended sentence. This Higgins boy, he is dead. That old man Higgins, I hope that he gets gangrene in that knee, goes all the way up to his scalp. After it gets his balls.

Du Pré sat in Maria's car, between her and Madelaine.

"How come you got this car, you aren't old enough to get a driver's license yet without I sign for it, and I ain't signed for nothing," said Du Pré. "You just lucky I am one suspended law enforcement officer."

"Shut up, Papa," said Maria. She drove off. When she came to the stop sign at the parking lot entry to the street she put out an arm to keep Du Pré from slamming into the dash at half a mile an hour.

"OK," said Du Pré, "I let you take care of me, don't talk back."

"What you want to eat?" said Madelaine.

Du Pré said he didn't want to eat for a while, maybe a couple of years.

They dropped Madelaine at her house, her kids would be wondering where she was.

"I see you in a little while," she said, kissing Du Pré.

"Go to the bar," said Du Pré to Maria. "I get some whiskey."

He bought three bottles, opened one of them on the drive to his house, drank a big slug and felt very dizzy.

Du Pré barely made it into the house. He staggered to the bed and fell on it and slept.

✤ CHAPTER 42 ✤

We some fine pair, eh?" said Du Pré, looking at Bart's cast. Du Pré was walking comma-shaped, so as not to stretch his stitched stomach.

Bart had stuck his hand in something mean. It was bandaged, and he moved it very, very gingerly.

The chinook wind had come, warm from the north and west, most of the snow had melted off, there were pools of water on the frozen ground. Du Pré's soaked cows were pulling hay out of the feedrack, grimly chewing. No place to lie down, chew their cud. Soon it would get very cold again, and the world would be glazed hard and very difficult to stand on.

"Where do we need this big shovel, anyway," said Bart. Du Pré rolled a cigarette. He lit it.

"Oh," he said, " 'bout ten or twelve miles from here, old mining claim of my father's."

"Your father had a mine?" said Bart. That, too.

"Gold claim," said Du Pré. Probably an emerald necklace down there, few other things, like an old car. Under the gravels, in the old riverbed. The Red River.

Go all the way down to bedrock, then there is no more story. Just the old earth, keeping the rest of its secrets.

"You go to big diesel shovel school?" said Du Pré. He looked at Bart's cast hard.

"Correspondence course," said Bart. "Lotsa pictures."

Mail-order course. Shit shit shit.

"Yeah," said Bart, "I was reading this stupid magazine, found an ad, said make big money, learn to operate heavy equipment. So I sent off for the stuff."

"Oh," said Du Pré, looking at his cigarette.

"When I was a kid, I had a couple toys, one of them was a big diesel shovel. I loved it the most. I have a deep and heartfelt, spiritual understanding of big diesel shovels. Trust me."

"OK," said Du Pré. He started to laugh. Bart, here, he is learning a lot from old Booger Tom. Laugh at snakebite, broken bones and let's do something even if it's wrong. Horse throw you, get back on till one of you is dead or you are moving down the trail.

Du Pré hobbled over to the stove, poured more tea for the two of them. Set the cups back down on the table.

Bart also had a bandage over his eye. He's learning, he is learning.

"Tell you a secret?" said Bart, raising a conspiratorial eyebrow.

"Sure," said Du Pré.

"I just up and bought a big diesel shovel. I always wanted one but I never knew how bad. So I called the big shovel dealer, said tell me about big shovels. He had an especially nice one, not too big, since I am not too big a man. Big enough, though. Pretty, too, kinda pale green. Got a stereo in the cab. Lots of levers and fun buttons. Make a new man of me."

You are doin' fine there, Bart.

"Now, I was thinking on having it racing striped but I decided that that would be in poor taste. Didn't get the fake polar bear fur upholstery either."

Hee, thought Du Pré. "Now where is this big shovel you got?"

"Well," said Bart, scratching at his cast, "I think it

might be here within the hour, maybe two, they have to move an extra power line or something."

"What?" said Du Pré.

"It was just an impulse," said Bart, "but I suddenly just had to have that pretty pale green big diesel shovel. Here. Start it up, dig a lake or something for practice."

Du Pré looked out the window.

"The ground is pretty frozen," said Du Pré.

"The salesman assured me that this here big shovel would not notice whether the ground is frozen or not."

"How big is this sucker, anyway?" said Du Pré.

"Oh, that," said Bart. "Well, they do make bigger ones, or anyway one bigger one. What I wanted, see, was those real delicate controls. You could fill a dump truck with one bite, whirl around and crack open a poached egg that was sitting on someone's head."

Du Pré considered that.

"Whose head?" he said finally.

"Uh," said Bart, pausing tastefully, "it is after all, *my* pretty pale green big diesel shovel. It would not do to lend it out, any more than it does to lend out one's toothbrush. Very personal item, this here big diesel shovel."

"Tell you what," said Du Pré. "When this shovel comes, I am going to put an egg on a rock, and when you crack it just so nice . . ."

"Guaranteed," said Bart.

The telephone rang. Du Pré answered it. For Bart.

Yes. Yes? Yes. Yes! Be right there.

Bart put the phone down.

"Well," he said, "it is here and we need to lead them to wherever that big shovel needs to be."

"Oh, boy," said Du Pré. He liked toys.

✤ CHAPTER 43 ✤

W ell," said Du Pré, looking up at the pale fluorescent
green monster shovel, "how much you pay for this
thing?"

"I got it on time," said Bart. "I paid them just the one
time."

Well, all right.

Du Pré looked around at Catfoot's old claim, remembering. His father had worked here on and off for fifteen
years. There was the little dragline, looked like a damn
kid's toy next to Bart's big kid's toy. Little D2 cat, blade
resting on the ground, a couple of hydraulic lines broken
off. Rusting drums that Catfoot had filled with what he
hoped was paydirt to wash down and never got to. A
homemade grizzly rocker. The gold got caught in an old
piece of carpet, and when all the paydirt was run, Catfoot
burned the carpet and little globs of gold were left in the
big old frying pan. Some smelter. Not a lot of gold, ever,
but it kept Catfoot busy, and when the price of gold was
left float he made out pretty good.

Du Pré remembered his days here. The old equipment
was broken more often than not, his father would be
cursing it in Coyote French while he banged the offending
parts with wrenches.

What the West was built with, blasphemy.

Booger Tom, there, when he lost his temper and cussed
with a serious heart he revealed himself to be a poet.

144

"Wanna come up and look in the cab of Popsicle, here?" said Bart.

"Popsicle?" said Du Pré.

"Sure," said Bart. "Don't she look like the color of those awful popsicles you used to eat when you were a kid?"

Du Pré nodded. Yes, it did.

Over time, Catfoot had moved a lot of gravels. Down thirty feet to bedrock, old pumps straining, sometimes the old man had to pawn his guns to buy diesel to keep everything going. Du Pré looked down into the deep wide hole, water in it. The dragline bucket was down there, out of sight.

When Catfoot had got down to the bedrock, he would climb down in the hole and shovel the blue-gray paydirt into fifty-five-gallon drums, haul them up with the bucket.

Red River.

Maybe a quarter-mile of dredge spoil here, years and years of work for Catfoot. Du Pré tried to remember where things were what year. He couldn't. Had the old man started at the other end and just worked steady over here? Or had he jumped around? Being Catfoot, he would have jumped around. Shit.

"Du Pré, damn it," said Bart, "this is the only time you get to set foot in my pretty cab. Got a virgin on the dash. Hairy dice on the rearview mirror. Cassette recorder and player with monster ju-ju and bunga-bunga. This thing is pretty noisy. The speakers are three feet across."

Du Pré scrambled up into the cab. He felt some stitches in his belly tear. Well, god damn them, I got work to do.

Bart turned the key, let the headring heat till the light went off. Pressed the starter. The huge engine caught and rumbled, the cab shook. Sounded very businesslike.

Bart shoved a tape in the tape machine. Tammy Wy-nette.

Bart fiddled with a couple levers. The huge arm extended itself, and he fiddled with some others and the bucket waggled.

Bart pivoted the cab, the arm, the bucket. The controls were light and easy. He waggled the bucket in time to the music.

"I'm gonna pick up a couple of those old drums there," he yelled, pointing with the bucket at a few rusting fifty-fives.

Something went wrong. He smashed them flat. The bucket went three feet into the frozen gravels.

"Popsicle, you whore!" yelled Bart.

"That egg, now," said Du Pré.

"What fucking egg?" yelled Bart.

"This egg," said Du Pré, removing one from his coat pocket.

They were yelling. Bart motioned for him to pay attention, he scrabbled around in the jockey box, came up with a little radio had an earplug hanging out of it and a slender microphone with a headset. The microphone was a long thin tube of clear plastic with a thin wire in it.

Du Pré put it on. He adjusted the headset. Switched on the little radio.

"Earth to Du Pré," said Bart, softly.

Damn easy to hear, this, through the earplug.

"OK," said Du Pré. "You practice with old Popsicle here and I go out and walk around, see what I can remember."

"Do my best," said Bart. "Put that egg over there on top of that post, will you?"

"Oh, hell," said Du Pré. "You can't see a damn thing for that bucket, it is half the size of my house."

"Not true, my friend," said Bart, "I went first class. This sucker has a TV camera out there." He pointed to a little screen, pressed a button. The screen came on.

"Jesus," said Du Pré, "it is not even in color. How you going to enjoy watching my blood spurt all over it if it isn't a color camera?"

"Oh, ye of little faith," said Bart.

"Oh, me of no fucking faith at all," said Du Pré. "I go put that egg on the post now."

Bart nodded.

"Du Pré," said Bart, "we are looking for a Mercury, Colorado plates, been down there a long time, right."

Du Pré nodded.

"When we find it," Bart went on, "we got a couple Masses to pay for, go to."

Du Pré nodded.

"We both go to both of them," said Bart.

"Oh, yes," said Du Pré.

♣ CHAPTER 44 ♣

Du Pré and Bart Fascelli stood by the bucket, looking at the torn metal. Some pale green paint on it. A bumper. A smashed Colorado license plate on it, all the enamel gone. The numbers were in stamped red rust, the plate was bent in half.

They looked down into the water rising in the blackish gravels.

"Well," said Bart. "There it is. You were right."

Du Pré nodded. It gave him no pleasure.

"I'll get a chain around the car," said Du Pré. "The chassis should hold, I think."

147

He scrambled down the pit walls, gravels loosening under his feet, water percolating everywhere. The heavy chain on his shoulder fouled his balance and he fell and came up wet and freezing. Little determined snowflakes fell from a black sky. Maybe rain, then ice. The time of the bad cold was coming. It was up there north, crouched, dark, merciless.

The time of white owls, boiling hooves for soup, leaving the frozen winter dead in the trees.

Du Pré shivered.

He ran the chain around the frame of the car, bent from the years spent under the tons of shifting gravels. These stones were headed for the Gulf of Mexico. They flowed very slowly, but they did.

The mountains stand up to their waists in their own flesh, thought Du Pré, spalled off by ice and time.

Bart moved the bucket down slowly, to where Du Pré could put the chain through one of the eyes on the lip.

Du Pré fought his way back up. He raised his hand, palm up.

Lift lift lift he motioned.

The chain lost its slack. A couple of pebbles stirred near the buried car. The frame bent a little. And then the car came up, sheet metal tearing, stones clattering down. Smashed to a dented tangled mass a fourth the size it once was.

Bart lifted it up and swung it round, set it down on the spoil drift. Water ran out of the wreck.

He killed the engine of the big diesel shovel, opened the cab door and dropped down the ladder.

Four weeks we been doing this, thought Du Pré. He looked back at the gravels they had so carefully moved, knowing what was down there, wanting to find it and not wanting to find it but having to find it all the same.

148

And, well, boys, there you have it.

"Not much of a Grail," said Bart.

"Have to do for the likes of us," said Du Pré. Now we can let the sad past sleep, and be maimed by it forever.

Muddy water dripped out of the wreck. A few shreds of upholstery gone mud-colored, gobs of muck stuck out of the car. The glass was all long ground to powder.

They took a spud bar and tried to pry the wreck apart. No good. Bart went back up into the cab of the shovel and fired it up again, lifted the wreck and lumbered back to the old dragline. The weight of the dead machine was enough. Du Pré chained the old Mercury to the old dragline and Bart pulled the wreck apart.

They sorted through the wreck, ran hoses on the parts. No emeralds and gold, no money, nothing.

"And no fucking map to the Lost Bullfrog Mine," said Du Pré.

Not that it mattered.

A car horn sounded. Madelaine and Maria, worried, had come out to see if Du Pré and Bart had killed themselves yet.

They brought sandwiches and hot coffee. It was mostly dark now and soon to be dark all the rest of the way.

"We have to report this," said Du Pré. "Just as soon as we god damned well feel like it."

Bart was eating a sandwich. "Sometimes after I have busted hump all day I feel like I have never tasted food before," he said. "Good sandwich."

"Come to supper tomorrow," said Maria to Bart.

Bart nodded. "Guy could do worse than be a shovel man," he said. "I have."

Du Pré, Madelaine, and Maria left then, leaving Bart to his Popsicle, thoughts, and prayers.

At the house, Du Pré drank some whiskey, didn't say much.

"You find everything that you are looking for maybe you can go back to being Du Pré now," said Madelaine, going out the door to her children. "You maybe want I leave my address with you, describe the house?"

Du Pré laughed. Madelaine, she wasn't laughing.

"See you tomorrow," said Du Pré to Maria.

He drove behind Madelaine to her home.

✦ CHAPTER 45 ✦

Du Pré drove through a strong May blizzard out to his house, wondered if this heavy snow would crush the old shed he had been meaning to shore up for the last ten years or so. He only remembered it when he couldn't do it, like the leak in the roof.

Maria was in the kitchen, baking bread. The table was piled with books and there was a new computer, too, one Bart said he could not possibly use because he was just a simple shovel operator. The computer still had the warranty card on it.

"Papa," said Maria, "there is something funny hanging in the tree back there." She leaned over the sink and pointed out the window to the willow by the little creek.

Du Pré squinted. Something white, had a couple birds on it.

"Looks like a piece of suet," said Du Pré.

"Well," said Maria, "I didn't hang it up there, pretty high."

A good eight feet off the ground. There was a path through the snow to it, from the yard, the trail went out across the white field beyond the creek.

"That's funny," said Du Pré.

The suet was hung over the stobs of the lilac Catfoot du Pré and his young bride had planted so long ago. The lilac had died, the leaves had turned yellow a couple of years ago. Du Pré had cut the dead trunks away and he had meant to grub up the roots but he had forgotten to do that.

Like hell, I hate digging up roots.

Du Pré looked down at the tracks in the snow. Coyote. The animal had stood beneath the suet, tried to leap up and get it and couldn't. When the birds pecked the slab of fat some chunks broke off and fell down into the snow. The coyote had scratched around a lot, for the good fat after this hard winter.

"OK," said Du Pré, "you old fucker."

He went to the shed, got a spud bar and a shovel. The ground was thawed, it always did under the snow. He slammed the spud into the earth, grabbed the shovel, and down about a foot and a half he hit something hard but not like a rock is hard.

Little brass box, size of a Bible.

All green, been here a while, thought Du Pré.

He took it to the house, put it in the sink and washed the dirt off. A little box, well-brazed seams all around. Du Pré looked at the bead.

Catfoot's bead, that, as much his as his handwriting.

"What you got there?" said Maria.

"Something I think belongs to Bart," said Du Pré.

He went back out to the shed, got a cold chisel and a hammer. Cut the top off the box on the kitchen floor.

Nice and dry in the box. Catfoot lay up good tight bead, there.

A suede envelope, black. A flat packet wrapped in foil. Du Pré pulled them both out. Nothing else.

"See this, now," said Du Pré to Maria. He opened the suede envelope. He lifted out the necklace, green gems and gold, all brilliant in the light.

"Oooohhhh," said Maria. She reached for the necklace. Du Pré let her have it.

Du Pré peeled back the foil. Thick packet of hundred-dollar bills.

"What's this?" said Maria. "What is all this?"

Du Pré told her all of it.

She sat at the table, looking out the window, at the failing light.

Du Pré reached across the table, took her hand, squeezed it.

"I got to go up to Bart's a minute," he said. "Talk to him about a couple Masses."

✦ CHAPTER 46 ✦

Bart looked at the money and the brilliant necklace. His whole face twitched.

"What a bunch of shit," he said. "My family. A bunch of money and a bunch of shit. We hated each other. I loved Gianni. You know why? He was gone before I was old enough to know him. He must have been a prize asshole. Oh, God. I spent all my time waiting for Gianni to come back. At least he was my goddamned brother."

Du Pré rubbed his eyes.

Bart sipped his tea. He wanted a drink, bad.

"I didn't want to know, either," said Du Pré.

Bart poked the necklace like it was a prize snake that had died just to be rude.

Bart took a pouch of cheap tobacco out of his bathrobe and rolled a cigarette. He lit it. He sucked the smoke in hard and blew it out. He shook his head again.

"You people," he said.

Du Pré looked up. What?

Bart began to cry, softly.

"Us?" said Du Pré. He didn't know what us Bart meant.

"I spent all of my time whining," said Bart. "Well, boys, there you have it."

Du Pré didn't know what the fuck Bart was talking about.

Bart wailed. It was the cry of some creature wounded to death and the killers closing.

"I can't stand this," said Bart.

I can't either, thought Du Pré. So get drunk.

Bart went to the cupboard and took out the whiskey and had a lake of it.

"You people," he said again.

"What goddamned people?" said Du Pré. "You tell me that. My father killed Gianni. Well, you stupid asshole, I would have too."

Bart nodded.

"He needed killing," said Du Pré.

Bart sat back down, calm. He poked the necklace again.

"What did Gianni do to make Catfoot so mad?" said Bart.

Du Pré lit a cigarette.

"Pauline asked him to kill Gianni," said Du Pré, "and Gianni was some asshole, so Catfoot just killed him. Cat-

153

foot was a careful guy, you know, it's hard to find a body you take care. So I think he just did it.''

"You people," said Bart.

"I don't know what *you people* means," said Du Pré.

"You're killers."

"Oh," said Du Pré. That.

Bart sat back hard in his chair and looked at the ceiling.

"Festerfuck," he said.

Du Pré sat and rubbed his mustache.

"Hey," he said, "what about these Masses."

"We need 'em for our souls," said Bart.

Du Pré waited. He yawned.

"How the hell could Catfoot just kill my brother and bury him and go on with his life?" said Bart.

"I got to go home," said Du Pré.

"Answer me, goddamnit," said Bart. He was starting to cry again.

"Your brother was a piece of shit," said Du Pré, "and your brother was a bad man to one of Catfoot's women. Catfoot didn't even know you lived, but he would have killed you too, he was so tired of Pauline's goddamned bitching. You don't push people so far, you know."

"You people," said Bart, again. He started another ciga-rette.

"My father a murderer and your brother needed killing and I am very tired of this," said Du Pré.

"I want to give this necklace to Maria," said Bart.

"She's down at the church," said Du Pré, "so we can go now."

He walked out. He whistled "Baptiste's Lament."

Many stars above.

Specimen Song

✤

For Tim Gable,
bookseller, wry raconteur, and grouch

✦ CHAPTER 1 ✦

Du Pré had never sweated like he was sweating in all his life. The air flowed in and out of his lungs like honey. The strings of his fiddle were greasy.

This Washington, D.C., he thought, now I know why everything comes out of it is so fucked up. People live here too long, say a month, it poaches their brains. I feel sorry for them, where I just used to hate them. Thank you, Jesus.

He put his fiddle in the old rawhide case his grandfather had made and he walked down through the crowds flowing slowly from one stage to another of the Folk Life Festival.

Least all these pretty girls hardly wearing anything, Du Pré thought. Thank you, Jesus.

Du Pré stood at the back of a crowd watching an old black man play a battered guitar, had a neck of a wine bottle on his finger. Du Pré nodded at the rhythms, the lonesome heartbreak of the glass sliding on the high strings. Some good music this. But the man's accent was thick and Du Pré couldn't make out very many of the words. He didn't have to. Bad luck and hard women.

Du Pré sucked in another lungful of honey flavored with car exhaust and city smells. He thought of how he had come to be here.

Three months ago, in a bitter Montana March, winter hanging on late and the mud yet to come, he and Madelaine had gone over to a fiddling contest in the college town of Bozeman. Du Pré hadn't won anything at the contest, all the prizes went to youngsters, who, Du Pré had to admit, played lots more notes than he did, even if they weren't the right or even reasonable ones. And afterward, some bearded man in a down jacket had come up to him and intro-

159

duced himself as one of the directors of the Folk Life Festival at the Smithsonian, and said how he would like Du Pré to come in late June and play at it. The festival would pay his travel, put him up, and pay him five hundred dollars.

Du Pré had looked at the guy.

"Why you want me?" he said finally. "I didn't even win a ribbon. You sure you don't want that guy over there won the first place?"

"Hardly," said the man in the down jacket. His name was Paul Chase.

"Washington, D.C.," said Du Pré, "I have never been there. So I guess I would go."

Paul Chase offered Du Pré a notebook and felt-tip pen. Du Pré scribbled his address in it.

"You'll get a letter in a couple of weeks," said Paul Chase.

They shook hands.

Madelaine had gone to the bar to get some of the sweet, bubbly pink wine she liked and a soda for Du Pré. The place was crowded with young people. They were forming little knots here and there and fiddling while some other young folks played guitars or banjos. One guy had a dobro strapped on, and he slid the steel expertly up and down. Du Pré took his soda and Madelaine's arm and pulled her over closer to the dobro player.

Du Pré had never been close to anyone playing one of the strange-looking guitars with the perforated tin pie plate in the top. He liked the sound. The dobro player glanced up at Du Pré briefly and then looked down to his work again. Another wailing shimmer sliding.

In the car, headed out of town, Du Pré told Madelaine about his invitation to Washington, D. C.

"All people do in Washington, D.C., is shoot each other," said Madelaine. "I saw that on the TV."

They stopped at an old hotel in Lewistown and then drove on home the next day.

The letter came a couple weeks later, and the days went by, and then Madelaine drove Du Pré down to Billings to take his first long air ride since he was in the army.

Du Pré looked out at the runway and the whooshing jets.

"The hell with it," he said, "I think I won't go."

Madelaine laughed.

Du Pré got on the plane. He hated every minute of the trip, and now here he was in Washington, D.C., sweating.

I don't do this again, thought Du Pré. I am too old to be a rock-and-roll star.

Du Pré heard an eerie, trilling ululation. He walked toward the soundstage it came from. There were six Indians onstage, singing. Their voices were weaving in and out of one another like smoky flutes. The hair on the back of Du Pré's neck stood up. The music spoke to his soul. It was music of ice and seal hunting, nights a month long, deserts of ice broken and twisted, and the endless, screaming polar wind.

Du Pré picked up a program from the trampled grass, looked through it. Inuit throat singers from Canada. Whew.

The Inuit trailed off. They were followed by a Cajun band. Du Pré found his foot tapping to the music, accordion, washboard, some little guitar, fiddle, and a man playing bones.

The band finished the number and the bones player talked a moment about how you had to get just these sections of two ribs on the cow. Those sections rang best, he said. He started to play a solo on them, and Du Pré took out his fiddle and played it damped at the back of the crowd.

The crowd parted, some people looking back at Du Pré.

Du Pré stopped. He felt bad, like he'd stolen the bones player's audience. Hadn't meant to, but there it was.

"Hey!" the bones player called. "You come on up here, play something."

I got to, thought Du Pré. He was running sweat.

I make a fool of myself maybe.

Du Pré made his way to the stage. He clomped up the folding steps and out to a microphone. The rest of the band smiled and nodded.

The bones player laid down a rhythm and Du Pré fiddled off it, some notes here and there, little riffs, longer passages. He'd been playing the fiddle long enough, he could sometimes reach for things and his fingers would get them almost before his mind thought of them.

Du Pré heard a couple women scream off to his left. He looked over and saw a horse dancing with a pancake saddle off on its left side. The crowd was afraid of the horse and the horse was afraid of the crowd. They were trying to pull away from each other, but the crowd was thick and everywhere the horse turned, he saw people and it frightened him more.

Du Pré went off the stage on one hand, leaving his fiddle lying by the microphone. He threaded his way through the crowd, and when he popped out into the space the horse had made around itself, he began to talk to the horse in Coyote French, making soothing sounds.

The horse stood still, grateful that here was a human who seemed to know him. Du Pré got hold of the bridle.

Du Pré led the horse away from the crowds. He saw some ambulance lights off by a jumble of portable outhouses, and a couple of police cars there, too.

"Well," said Du Pré to the horse, "now what about this? Huh?"

The horse whiffled. Du Pré rubbed the gelding's soft nose.

❖ CHAPTER 2 ❖

The big cop had sweated his linen sport coat dark under the arms and down his spine. He sweated so much that he messed up the notes he was trying to take.

"Fuckin' heat," said the cop. "So you caught this horse. You're one a the performers here?"

"Uh-huh," said Du Pré.

"Why you catch the horse?"

"I know horses pretty good," said Du Pré. "This horse, he was some scared, and all he wanted was someone around who seemed to know horses. So I just walked up to him and grabbed his bridle."

The detective waved to a uniformed patrolman. The patrolman came over slowly.

"I need to have you hold on to this horse," said the detective.

The cop looked at the horse, the horse looked at the cop. Neither was favorably impressed. The cop moved a hand slowly toward the bridle.

The horse's eyes got big.

"Look," said Du Pré, "this will not work. This horse, he needs someone who talks horse. I don't think you can talk horse. So, I maybe hold him till you find the owner or something."

Du Pré saw a young man in jeans and boots and a sleeveless T-shirt coming toward them. Kid had on a straw cowboy hat that had seen hard use.

"Jerry!" said the young man. He had a blond ponytail and a woven horsehair belt buckle. The horse shuffled a little and tossed his head. This was someone he knew.

"Thanks," said the kid. He took the horse's bridle from Du Pré and he stroked the animal's neck. "Got to get you to some water," he said to the horse.

"Whose horse's this?" said the detective.

"Van Orden Stables," said the handler. He pulled a sweated wad of business cards from the hip pocket of his jeans and offered the detective one. "Miss Price called from the hospital."

"Lady who found the body," said the detective.

The handler nodded.

"Christ," said Du Pré. "A *body?*"

The detective nodded. "You'll be here for the festival?" he said to Du Pré.

"Yeah," said Du Pré. "You need me, the office is in that striped tent over there. They will know where I am playing. I don't hardly

163

go to the hotel, you know. We sit here after dark and play music. Too hot to sleep, anyway, and I hate air conditioning."

"Thanks for catchin' old Jerry," said the handler. "He musta been some lonely."

"Where you from?" said Du Pré.

"West Texas," said the young man. "Can I please take him? He needs water real bad."

The detective nodded; the handler led the horse away.

"What is this about now?" said Du Pré.

"If I need to talk to you, I'll find you," said the detective. He tucked his notebook into his sweaty linen coat. Du Pré got a glimpse of the butt of a gun under the man's arm. He nodded to Du Pré and walked away.

Du Pré made his way back to the stage. He saw his rawhide fiddle case against the back curtain, near the cables snaking under toward the sound booth out front. There was a band playing old-time music at the microphones. Du Pré waited until they finished their piece and the applause started, then he went as quickly as he could to his fiddle, popped the case open to make sure the instrument was in it, went to the side of the stage, and dropped down to the grass. There were sandwich wrappers and empty Styrofoam cups everywhere about. The grounds had garbage cans every few yards, but some people just would not use them.

Du Pré went to the festival offices in the striped tent. It was little more than a phone-and-message bank for the performers. Three young women wearing as little as they could sat wearily on folding chairs, sipping huge glasses of iced tea.

"You know where Paul Chase is?" said Du Pré.

The women glanced at one another. "He's . . . at an appointment," she said finally.

"I know the police found a body," said Du Pré. "Is he talking to them?"

More glances. Finally, one nodded.

"Do you know when he will be back?"

164

More glances. Then the women looked past Du Pré. Du Pré turned, to see Paul Chase, looking like he was making his face brave, coming toward the tent.

Chase nodded to Du Pré and went on to the three young women and spoke in a low voice, Du Pré couldn't hear the words. They looked hot and weary and frightened.

Chase turned. His face was gray.

"I found some horse," said Du Pré, "so I had the police talking to me, too."

Chase nodded. "Woman who discovered the body was on a bridle path over that way"—he waved his hand—"wouldn't have seen it if she had been walking. The extra height, you know. She got down and looked in the shrubbery, and then she screamed and the horse panicked. So did she. She had a terrible asthma attack."

"Okay," said Du Pré. "So who was killed?" Madelaine was right about this Washington, D.C.

"A young Cree woman from Canada," said Chase. "She was here as part of a singing group. Someone stabbed her to death. It's just terrible."

A telephone rang; one of the women answered.

Chase stood still, shaking his head after a minute.

"I don't need this," he said suddenly, his voice savage.

First they get shocked, then they either choke up or get mad, Du Pré thought.

"I needed to talk to you about another matter, anyway, Mr. Du Pré," said Chase. "I need to think about another matter. Any other matter. We here at the Smithsonian would like very much to tape your versions of some of the old voyageur ballads, the ones you play and sing so competently. Could you possibly stay over a few days after the festival?"

"No," said Du Pré. "I don't like this place much. So I will be happy to tape what you want, but I do it at home. My daughter, she has a tape recorder."

"Uh," said Chase, smiling, "I hardly think that will do. We will

165

need a studio, you see. Recording is very difficult."

"Okay," said Du Pré. "We got recording studios in Montana. Maybe not so fancy as you got here, I don't know. But we got them and they have to do. I stay here till my plane out Sunday night, but I sweat enough for the rest of my life."

Chase nodded. "The land upon which Washington, D.C., is built was largely swamp when the sundry states donated it. Since then, the swamp has risen, I often think."

"Besides," said Du Pré, "I got to go to a powwow, been planned long time."

"Play fiddle?" said Chase.

Du Pré shook his head. "No," he said, "both my father and grandfather were canoe builders, and I still got some of their tools. I am not all that good, but lots of that stuff got forgotten, so I try to remember."

"Canoes," said Chase. "What sort of canoes?"

"What the voyageurs called 'big bellies,' " said Du Pré. "They were kind of little freighters for the fur trade. They had a couple funny things about them—you know, way the struts and braces were fitted. Used bone joints where things were twisted a lot, like that. I have made a couple since for a museum up in Calgary, but they weren't very good. You know how you got to do something a lot before you know it."

Chase was thinking.

"So you give me a list of these songs you want, you get hold of a recording studio—there are several in Montana—pay them, I go in and make that music for you," said Du Pré. He felt a little proud. Besides, once the music was safely here at the Smithsonian, it maybe wouldn't get lost.

"You'll hear from us," said Chase.

The telephones started ringing. Du Pré looked out in front of the tent. There were a bunch of reporters headed their way.

Du Pré slid out the back way, through a slit provided for ventilation.

Some damn thing, he thought. Always.

✤ CHAPTER 3 ✤

Madelaine was waiting for Du Pré at the bottom of the elevator stairs in the airport. Du Pré was carrying his fiddle. They went to the baggage carousel and soon his battered old leather suitcase crashed out onto it from the cargo room.

Du Pré had bought the suitcase in a pawnshop for ten dollars. It was covered in stickers from ocean liners. The ocean liners were all gone now, but the leather suitcase remained.

Like out in my shed, I got these brass tacks from the stock of a black powder rifle I found in the attic of an abandoned cabin, thought Du Pré. The steel was all rust and borers had eaten all the wood, but that brass stayed on. The gun had been so badly rusted that it didn't even clean up enough to tell what it was.

"So you get the clap, all those groupies in Washington, D.C.?" said Madelaine.

"Probably won't know for a while," said Du Pré. "That clap, it takes some time to come on, you know."

Madelaine kissed him. She was wearing some faint perfume—violets. She had rubbed the flowers behind her ears, he guessed. Sometimes she made tea. Du Pré thought of cool June mornings and the scent of violets and Madelaine. He was very glad to be back.

"So I see a girl singer got stabbed there," said Madelaine. "I told you they kill each other a lot there in Washington, D.C." She grabbed Du Pré's arm. She had about worried herself sick, Du Pré knew. He should have tried to call her, but it was hard to find a telephone.

"It was hot and wet," said Du Pré. "I don't think I do that again. I like this dry Montana air."

167

They walked out to the parking lot. Madelaine had brought Du Pré's old sheriff's cruiser with the patches on the doors where the decals had been. Good road car, though. On those long, straight stretches of Montana road, Du Pré drove maybe 120. Had to slow down for some towns. Once a highway patrolman had stopped him, but Du Pré said call the sheriff in his home county of Charbonneau, told him he was on an errand and needed to make time. When the cop went back to his car, Du Pré smoked it, getting back up to speed. He never heard anything more about it.

Du Pré tossed his suitcase and fiddle in the backseat. He felt dirty from the city air and all the miles of flight. He itched.

He held Madelaine for a moment. Murmuring.

"We go home and in a while we both find out I got the clap or not," said Du Pré. She looked shocked—for a moment.

"So everybody is all right?" said Du Pré. It seemed he'd been gone a long time, but it'd been only five days.

"Yeah," said Madelaine. "That Bart, he is working so hard on his house and that ranch. Old Booger Tom run him around and Bart don't say nothing to the old bastard, and Bart owns that place. Booger Tom, I saw him in the bar the other night and he say he try every way to make Bart blow up or quit or whine and Bart just won't do it. I think that Booger Tom kind of likes Bart for that."

So do I, Du Pré thought. Poor Bart Fascelli, rich boy, horrible family, then he is in his late forties and suddenly realizes that though he owns that ranch, Booger Tom owns himself. Bart, he wants to own himself, too. I like that man. Hope he don't never drink again.

"Bart is so very nice to Jacqueline and Maria," Madelaine went on. "Like a good uncle, you know. He is always very correct." Jacqueline and Maria were Du Pré's daughters. Bart had helped out Maria a lot and was going to pay for a college education for her. Since Du Pré's father had murdered Bart's brother, Du Pré thought that was pretty tough of Bart. He's probably a pretty tough man, don't know how much yet.

168

They were headed east to pick up the two-lane north to Toussaint. Du Pré looked down at the speedometer. Ninety. He slowed to seventy. Can't go fast on the expressway, he thought, but I want to get home. Take a long hot shower. Feels like my soul and half of my ass is still in Washington, D.C.

That detective, he never came to ask me more questions, Du Pré thought. I only caught the horse. Don't even know the name of the woman who was killed. Cree, though, like some of my people.

Madeleine fiddled around in a little cooler and brought out a can of beer for Du Pré and a wine cooler for herself. She popped the can open and handed it to him. Du Pré took a long swallow.

"That's pretty good," he said.

He saw the exit north up ahead. Get off this four-lane mess and back on a two-lane road. I am a two-lane man in a four-lane age. And they are welcome to it.

Du Pré glanced up at the bluffs above the Yellowstone as he turned round the exit ramp. The Roche Jaune of the voyageurs. They had been here so long ago, no one really knew how long. Tough men, could cover some country.

A huge hawk flapped up from a kill in a field across the highway. It held something small in one talon. Du Pré couldn't see what it was. The big bird turned in the air and locked its wings and floated on. Du Pré grinned. Home, it sure felt good.

"So, this Washington D.C., what was it like?" said Madeleine.

"Hot and sticky," said Du Pré. "But I met some nice people, some Cajun people from Louisiana. They talk some French like ours, only some different. Call it Coonass French." Du Pré spoke Coyote French. Well, those Cajuns had been descended from Quebecois deported by the English over two centuries ago to Louisiana. And we didn't talk so much after that. Du Pré's people were Métis——French, Cree, Chippewa, and some little English no one wanted to admit to——who were the voyageurs and trappers of the Company of Gentlemen Adventurers of Hudson's Bay. Or the Hudson's Bay Company. Or the Here Before Christ.

"They invite us down some winter to get away from the cold, Du Pré went on. "They play some fine music, accordion, fiddle, washboard. Call it zydeco."

"What they do with this washboard?" said Madelaine.

"Guy plays it; he puts big thimbles on his fingers, brushes them over that washboard," said Du Pré. "It sounds good. Anyway, they say we come down eat crawfish, drink orange wine."

"Orange wine sounds good," said Madelaine.

Du Pré looked at his watch. His sense of time was off. It must be the middle of the afternoon. Of course it was; his plane hadn't got to Billings until 2:30. Four o'clock and change. Du Pré was starving of a sudden.

"This next roadhouse, we get a cheeseburger," said Du Pré. "I am hungry enough to have supper with a coyote now."

It was still close to the longest day of the year, a little over a week ago. The light would remain past ten o'clock, and Du Pré figured if he pushed the old Plymouth, he could make Toussaint before sundown.

Up ahead, he saw a crossroads and the peeling white sign of a roadhouse that he knew and liked. He turned into the parking lot.

Christ, I am hungry, he thought.

✦ CHAPTER 4 ✦

Old Benetsee showed up the next evening, carrying some herbs he had gathered for Madelaine. She used them to scent the shampoo she used. Madelaine took the little bundles off to hang them in a sunny window before she ground them in the old brass mortar and pestle she kept on the sink board. Du Pré wondered about that old mortar and pestle, it was a pretty crude casting and probably pretty old. Maybe Hudson's Bay trade goods. He sometimes wondered how many pelts of beaver or mink or fisher cat or bobcat or fox the thing had cost. It might be the oldest thing in Toussaint, come to think on it.

"So you like them Cajun?" said Benetsee.

Du Pré nodded. He hadn't spoken to anyone about the Cajuns except Madelaine, and she hadn't been six inches away from him since he got back. But Du Pré was long past wondering how the old man knew things. He just did. When Du Pré listened to Benetsee tell stories or ask questions he had no way of knowing to ask, he believed in magic.

"I brought you this," said Benetsee. He fumbled around in his pockets for something and then found it in the lining of his coat. Benetsee wore his clothes until they turned to mostly holes. Madelaine had to fight him to get him to wear something that at least would keep out the wind.

"You goddamned old fool," she had yelled at him once, "you give me that mess of rags and put these things on! They are nice and dirty and you will like them fine! Hah!"

Benetsee brought forth a strange knife, one shaped like a hook, but the bend of the hook went along the axis of the knife blade. It was just a ribbon of steel bent back upon itself. The handle was a finely worked green stone, it felt a little greasy to the touch. Soapstone. Du Pré took the knife and looked at it. The blackish steel had a bright rim along the bottom where Benetsee had sharpened it.

"That's a pull knife," said Benetsee. "You can do some fine carvings those canoe parts with that."

Jesus Christ, thought Du Pré, I have *forgotten* this powwow. But it is not for four, five days. I suppose this old fart will wish to go, gamble some money. Probably my money.

Madelaine returned with a glass of wine for Benetsee, a big glass. The old man loved to drink a lot of wine.

"You maybe want a bourbon," said Madelaine. "I get you one."

Du Pré shook his head. He smiled at her.

Benetsee downed his big glass of wine, just poured it down his throat. Madelaine shook her head and smiled at him, then took the glass and walked back toward the house.

"You pull that knife to you, you know," said Benetsee, "for the fine shavings." He was digging around in his coat. "I got something else." Finally, he took the tattered cloth off and squeezed it till he found it hidden somewhere in the tangled folds.

Madelaine came back. Benetsee struggled for several minutes and finally he pulled a little canoe out of the crumpled cloth of his coat.

It was a carving, in some fine-grained wood. All the struts and braces and thwarts and ribs were carved in, too, and the outside of the canoe carved like birch bark. Du Pré could see some stains on the carving—on the seams, where the pitch went. Ah.

It was the carving of the *bâteau gros ventre*—the big-bellied boat. These canoes had been made up to thirty feet long and eight feet wide. They could carry a heavy load. A thirty foot canoe would take six men to portage it around a falls or rapids, maybe eight men; those bark canoes were heavy. Then the voyageurs would move the heavy packs of furs. They would load one another with as many packs as a man could stagger with and then they would bull up or down the trail around the river. There were many songs about especially tough voyageurs and how many packs of furs they could carry.

Du Pré thought a man might take two, three if he was very strong, but any song that said a man carried more than that was just a song. The packs of furs weighed over a hundred pounds apiece.

"You see this here?" said Benetsee, pointing to a thwart. The thwart curved in a lot, giving the canoe a waist. "Easier to paddle." He lifted the canoe carving and pointed to the stern, which was undercut with a roll on the bottom.

"They hang a piece of birch right there off its ass, make it go in the water better," said Benetsee. A birch round with rounded ends. Du Pré had never seen anything like this.

This old goat never tell me he know about canoes, Du Pré thought, though he seem to know everything somehow.

172

Benetsee drained the big glass of wine Madelaine had brought. He got to his feet.

"I go see now," he said, moving off toward the little creek that wound through Du Pré's backyard. There was a path there, older than the house, probably there before the whites came.

"I go see now"—Du Pré had heard that so many times over the years.

The old man hopped across the creek; the tag alders on the far side swallowed him up. A squirrel chirred angrily. Du Pré heard the scrawk of a blue jay.

But he was gone, like smoke on a summer morning.

Du Pré turned the model around in his hands. He thought of his people paddling one of these, pulling out at the portage, reaching into the pouch at the end of their red sashes for pipe and tobacco. Jokes. Thinking about their women at the end of the journey.

"Du Pré!" Madelaine called from the back door. "You have a telephone! Sound like someone from far away."

Who the hell be calling me from far away? Du Pré thought. I don't know anybody from far away. He put the canoe model down on the grass next to the pull knife.

It was Paul Chase. He wanted to know if Du Pré would want to go on a journey—paid, of course—by canoe over a portion of the old fur-trade route. Starting on the first of August.

"We thought we'd try for the best weather," said Chase. "We have a grant and can pay you, oh, four hundred a week plus your expenses."

"Where is this route you want to take, there?" said Du Pré.

Saskatchewan and Manitoba, the route home, through chain lakes and down little rivers between them. On the way, they would come to a falls where archaeologists were recovering a mass of trade goods from the pool beneath left by voyageurs who had miscalculated and wrecked. Du Pré should bring his fiddle.

"How long this take?" asked Du Pré.

"Six weeks."

"I don't think that I want to," said Du Pré.

"Just think about it," said Chase.

Du Pré said he would, but he wouldn't change his mind.

❖ CHAPTER 5 ❖

Du Pré finished "Baptiste's Lament." He let the last note fade off and he stood still till the man in the sound booth pointed his thumb up. Du Pré sighed. He had never worked so hard at his music in all his life. The recording engineer and producer were competent and relentless.

"Very nice. Great version. I'd like to maybe try it again in a little while, though. Maybe reach in there for something . . . darker."

The engineer and producer would exchange a meaningful glance.

"Yeah. Darker. Exactly," the engineer would say.

They had an uncanny ability to sense when Du Pré was just about to tell them to go piss up ropes and then stand under them while they dried. Then they'd break and wander out to a nearby saloon had good cheeseburgers.

Du Pré felt handled, like a cow in a chute. But the joke was on him, so he had to do his best. And maybe the Métis music would stay some alive. His daughter Maria was going off to some tony eastern school on Bart's money and a little of Du Pré's, and she would be a little Métis girl from Montana with a good education and the whole world before her. Her kids wouldn't be Métis, they'd be out in that English world there.

But the music wouldn't go on with Maria, anyway. She had a voice when she sang that would take baked enamel off cast iron.

Jacqueline sang beautifully, alto, *a cappella* ballads she had learned here and there.

So this music maybe live in some vault in Washington, D. C., Du Pré thought. Freeze-dried. Like them college kids come to the fiddling contests can play every note just right but it still don't work.

I am sounding like some old fart. I am getting close to being some old fart. Be fifty in three weeks. Shit.

Du Pré stuffed his fiddle in the case and then remembered his rosin, there on the floor by the chair. He picked it up, opened the case again, and tucked it under the neck.

I got everything. He looked at his watch. Six o'clock of a July evening. Sun should be down far enough, it won't hurt my eyes too much when I go out in it. Du Pré had been snow-blinded twice and he couldn't take too much sun without dark glasses.

A door opened into the sound room and Paul Chase came through it. He was dressed in the sort of outdoor stuff you got from expensive mail-order houses. The clothes were good and the boots were good; they had been designed by hardworking dilettantes for moneyed novices.

Du Pré thought of his father, Catfoot, going over the Wolf Mountains in the dead of winter, fifty below, with nothing but a pack on his back, snowshoes, to check that trapline. The trapped animals deserved a quick death, and anyway, it was hard to skin them frozen. Catfoot could cover his line in two days.

Carried some jerky, salt, and tea, a little chocolate. Find a fir tree and burrow down under the thick branches; the smoke from his little fire would go up through the dark green needles. Carried the same old pocketknife, a few matches.

"Du Pré!" said Paul Chase, "we thank you."

Now he will ask me if I go on his canoe trip, Du Pré thought.

"Say," said Chase, "have you given any more thought to perhaps going on this canoe trip with us?"

Du Pré nodded. Chase deflated a little behind the smile.

Them fucking boots he got on, they got buttons you press for maybe a beach umbrella or rockets take you up the rising trail. Du

Pré thought for a moment why this stuff irritated him. It allowed people who didn't know the country to go out in it. They could buy these keys that worked till they got in some trouble. Paper keys. Fill this out, send in a check, this stuff comes, the wilderness is yours.

"Yeah," said Du Pré, "I will go with you."

Chase looked surprised, but he caught himself.

"Oh, really?"

Du Pré nodded.

"Well. Wonderful. We will gather at Lac La Ronge and go by canoe down to York Factory."

That's right, Du Pré thought. He hadn't known till he'd read a book on the Hudson's Bay Company that the managers of the little fur-buying outposts were called factors. Then he asked Maria for her dictionary, but she had one in her computer. She punched a few keys and said it was someone who acted for someone else.

Du Pré had nodded and decided that he was glad his daughter liked this computer and the twentieth century, but Du Pré, him, he didn't much care for either of them.

"We won't be working as hard as the voyageurs," said Chase cheerily.

Du Pré looked at his space-age boots and the well-cut shirt with all the pockets and little epaulets to hold maybe the camera strap.

"Halfway through the trip, we will stop for a few days and stay at a hotel, rest up," said Chase. "But it should be interesting."

Du Pré was very tired and he wanted to go next door to the saloon and get a good drink and a cheeseburger, maybe drive partway home tonight, or just sleep for a few hours and then go on so he was in his own country early in the morning.

"What made you change your mind?" said Chase.

Du Pré shrugged. I am a cowboy; we shrug when we don't want to say nothing. It is not that we don't have anything to say.

Benetsee had changed Du Pré's mind for him.

"Something very bad going on up there," said Benetsee one summer evening just before Du Pré had to drive over to Kalispell to make this recording. Benetsee had drawn a map in some detail of

176

Hudson Bay. He had quickly sketched in some rivers on the great jutting peninsula on the east side of it.

"These people down here be killing this," said Benetsee, putting a hasty X roughly where New York and New England were. "And this is where some of the great songs come from."

"Killing how?" said Du Pré.

"These people want to build many dams on these rivers up here," said Benetsee, "and that will poison the waters and kill the fish and everything else that lives on them. Some Cree and some Chippewa, you know, they still live the old ways. But there are not very many of them, and these people they want that electricity."

Benetsee stabbed at the X.

"So this man ask you go along on that canoe trip, you ought to go," said Benetsee.

"I don't want to be slapping those blackflies and mosquitoes for six weeks, have to play my fiddle each night for these people like I am some tape recorder or something. Why I want to go across that country with a bunch of people don't belong there anyway, want to think that they know what it was like back then couple hundred years ago, huh?"

"Some of the people are coming from here," said Benetsee, "to go on this trip which is here." He sketched a route on the west side of the bay. "But they will bring couple *bâteau gros ventre*. They from over there on the other side."

"Why I want to leave Madelaine for six weeks, huh?" said Du Pré.

Benetsee looked at Du Pré with patience and contempt.

"There are these people come along with you there are our people," he said. "They got a whole bunch of songs—you know, songs you never heard."

"Okay," said Du Pré. "I still will not go."

Benetsee drank some more wine. He had his eyelids patiently down; he was nodding and his lips moved.

Du Pré looked over at the tag alder on the far side of the little stream that ran through his horse pasture.

There was a coyote sitting there, in the daylight. Du Pré had never seen a coyote this close or in the daylight.

The coyote had something in its mouth. The animal leapt over the little stream, came trotting up to Benetsee, dropped what he was carrying, ran back, and jumped the creek again, and he was gone.

Benetsee opened his eyes. He reached down and lifted the little black thing that the coyote had brought him.

It was an amulet, a carving in a black stone with rust red streaks in it. Du Pré looked at it. The carving was of a dog or a wolf, one just rising from the ground. The carver had used the rust lines for the animal's outline, the shape of the bones underneath the skin. It was perfect; there was nothing there that did not need to be and everything that had to be. A dog or a wolf getting up from the ground.

"Them coyote carry this all the way from where the dead are," said Benetsee, pointing at the black carving. "Our dead. This is very old, you know. The songs I am talking about, they come after this, but you know after the priests come, we speak them French some everywhere. So you go and get those songs; there is one for you."

Well. My son-in-law Raymond can fill in for me, inspect those cows, since he is through the paperwork for brand inspector. Not that the cow business is much left.

Benetsee was walking back along the path the coyote had taken. The conversation was over, Du Pré was going, and that was that.

Buy me few extra sets fiddle strings, Du Pré thought. Buy me a lot of insect dope, scare off them blackfly, too.

❧ CHAPTER 6 ❧

The cattle were jamming up in the chute. Du Pré and Raymond had already checked the brands and Du Pré had Raymond sign off on them.

"Way this cow business is, I don't know they need brand inspectors much longer," said Du Pré.

"Some people say they will raise buffalo," said Raymond.

"Oh sure," said Du Pré. "They say that, they don't know buffalo. I went out to South Dakota once, help some people round up buffalo. They don't round up. They tore up the corrals like so much wet paper and then they tore up the trucks and a lot of them got out. Buffalo. Bah. You know them things pivot on their front feet? They change directions so fast, while a horse, he has to take this wide circle he moving any fast."

"I guess they still have to be branded and inspected," said Raymond. He liked this better than hanging sheetrock or plumbing. Du Pré could not blame him for that.

"Madelaine said you were going to drive all those miles to Lac La Ronge," said Raymond.

"Fuckin' A I am," said Du Pré. "I fly to that Washington, D.C.; I will not do that again. Moves too fast and I am too old. Whoosh. Makes my head ache. Scares me shitless, too."

They got into Du Pré's old Plymouth cruiser. Du Pré's car was badly dented on the passenger's door where he had slid into a fence post on a road mudded up good. Corner fence post, railroad tie stuck down in some concrete. Crunch. Railroad tie hadn't moved much.

"How come you aren't taking Bart?" said Raymond. Kid was worried about something, asking a lot of questions. Shut up, Du Pré thought. Go on home and make me another grandbaby.

"That Bart is so rich, he would sort of buy the trip up," said Du Pré. "We would be out in the bushes there, and a helicopter with a big dinner and a chamber-music group would show up." Also, if he got drunk and off his head back there, he could be a real problem.

They drove on the wet yellow road back toward town. It had rained hard the last two days, unusual for late July. The weather seemed to be changing.

Du Pré had read somewhere that the big volcano that blew off in

179

the East Indies had caused this. But Du Pré also remembered some old songs about much rain and cold winters, so maybe the weather just did this, but over a long time, time greater than one human life. Pretty big world there, and those stars are very far away.

When Du Pré and Raymond got to Du Pré's house, there were people there already putting up trestle tables and stapling table-cloths to them, against the wind that would come up late in the afternoon. Always did, blew out of the west hard for maybe a quarter of an hour and then either kept up if there was rain coming in a day or quit if there wasn't.

Jacqueline's babies were toddling around the lawn. Madelaine's and some of their friends were playing volleyball in the pasture over the creek.

Du Pré showered and put on fresh clothes. His suitcase was packed—or, rather, a nylon duffel bag Bart had given him, along with a sackful of crap to survive on in the wilderness. Best way to survive in the wilderness is stay warm and dry and fed and don't get lost, but you make those arrangements before you go there.

Du Pré sat on his porch, watching the hummingbirds at the flowers along the creek. Summer ended when those whirring little birds left—usually about the middle of August. The Métis had known that, and when the English had come and put out little feeders for the hummingbirds, the Métis protested and said it made the birds stay around too long, so that there were not enough flowers to the south of them to feed them on their long journey. The English looked down their long noses and left the feeders up, and each year there had been fewer birds, until some English newspaper had said the same thing the Métis had. Du Pré knew some songs that weren't complimentary to the English. They did that sort of thing a lot.

People began to arrive, bringing hot dishes and salads and jugs of wine or big plastic thermoses of iced tea. Father Van den Heuvel came with Bart. The big, clumsy priest with the sweet smile and the former rich drunk who was now for some time just rich. Bart had bought a huge dragline some time ago and had found he sort of liked moving earth, and he had a little business digging stock ponds. He had a backhoe, too, and he dug basements, though there weren't many new houses going up. Not like in the western part of the state, which was turning into one big suburban resort.

"You didn't get Benetsee?" said Du Pré to Bart. "I will go and get him, then."

"He wasn't there," said Bart. He looked past Du Pré to the knots of people milling around the tables. "But he's here. Maybe he changes himself into a bird and flies here and then ducks behind a bush and changes back."

"No bird could carry all that bullshit," said Du Pré. They laughed. Sometimes Benetsee was an eerie singer and prophet, and sometimes they had to make bail for him when he got too drunk and did something foolish. Once the sheriff, Benny Klein, had tried to take the old man home, but all Benetsee did was fumble a minute at his flies and then piss all over the sheriff's new boots, which was more than even patient Benny Klein could stand.

Another time he had swiped the sheriff's car and spent a pleasant fifteen minutes weaving down the county road with the lights flashing and the siren going. He put the car off a steep bank and Bart had to buy the sheriff a new one.

Benny Klein tried hard to like Benetsee, but he found it tough going.

"I don't guess jail would do him any good or anything else," Benny had said mournfully, looking at Bart's check, "but, goddamn it, I am supposed to enforce the law, and he broke about six of them."

But nothing had come of that. Once, though, years before, Benetsee had been arrested in Miles City and jailed. And the story went, the old man howled out the barred window of his cell. There was an answer. And soon coyotes began to come into town, a lot of them, and the police were getting a lot of calls. The coyotes collected beneath the window of the jail and they howled back.

A couple cops took shots at the coyotes, but the coyotes didn't notice. This was strange.

The judge was old and smart. When they called him at home, he said to take the old man a few miles west of town and let him go. They did, and the coyotes left, too.

So Du Pré had heard.

The party picked up some speed early on. Most of these folks were little ranchers and this was a busy time, so it wouldn't go on too late. Du Pré fiddled some and there was some dancing and the food was hot and good and plentiful.

Du Pré was taking a leak out behind the lilacs when old Benetsee shuffled up to him. The old man took a little bundle out of his rags and pressed it into Du Pré's hand.

Leather. Du Pré unrolled it. A slingshot. Two long, thin straps of deer skin with a pouch in the middle for a rock. The Métis had used them to hunt birds, Du Pré knew.

"Learn how to use this sling here," said the old man. Then he took it back, put a stone in the pocket, wrapped the thongs around his right hand. He swung the slingshot around his head. It whirred.

Benetsee let go of one thong and the rock shot straight and true toward a magpie perched on a branch in the tag alder. The stone slammed into the bird, which crumpled. Benetsee went to the dead bird and pulled some feathers out of the tail.

"Nothing on these," the old man mumbled. He acted drunk. "Ah, here," he said, holding a tail feather like all the others up.

"See?" said Benetsee.

✤ CHAPTER 7 ✤

The canoe party was put up at a hotel in Lac La Ronge, which was a damn long way north. Du Pré had driven through miles of dark forest, here and there clear-cut to feed pulp mills. He thought of the voyageurs toiling through here in the fine misting rain. It must have been hard. Some men would have gone mad. No wonder when they finally made it home they celebrated so hard.

The forest would be a great weight. Du Pré saw very few birds. It seemed that there was little life here. Perhaps it came out at night. Then not. There wasn't much to eat in an old forest, the trees held it all.

Once, he got out and walked along the verge of the road, looking for animal tracks. He walked a mile without seeing anything but the skittering prints of a shrew in some very fine mud at the edge of a little puddle.

Mean little bastards, those shrews, had to eat their own body weight each day. So tiny, big mouths and lots of teeth. He'd watched one kill a grasshopper once, still remembered the crunching, tearing noises. It was over very quickly and the tiny silver-gray shrew was gone. Du Pré had picked up the husk of the grasshopper. The shrew had more or less unzipped the grasshopper's skin, gobbled up the fat, and gone on for another.

Them shrew weigh maybe three hundred pounds, they eat everything on the whole earth, Du Pré thought.

It was raining again by the time he pulled into Lac La Ronge. He found the hotel and parked his old cruiser across the street in a lot that had the hotel's name on it.

The young woman at the desk directed Du Pré to the dining room. It was early evening and the party had recently gone in for some supper. Du Pré saw Paul Chase slumped in a chair at the head of a long table. There were some young people sitting near him, rich kids, looked like, and then some Indians in jeans and wool shirts. Six of them, four men and two women, all with their black hair in long braids.

Du Pré walked up to the table. Paul Chase put on a sunny smile and welcomed him and bade him sit.

Du Pré found a chair down past the Indians. They all looked at him a moment and then they smiled, and those on the other side of the table smiled, too.

183

One of the men rattled at Du Pré in Chippewa, but the dialect was so far from Du Pré's little knowledge that he could only smile and shrug and say he was sorry but that the Coyote French was all he had.

Then they all rattled at him in their Bush patois. Du Pré could understand that.

"Them priests, they get around about everywhere," said Du Pré. They all laughed and the waitress came.

The food was superb. Whoever the chef was did what he could with what he could get that was fresh, and Du Pré had some lake trout with local wild mushrooms and a berry sauce that he thought was juniper. The trout was flaky and perfectly cooked. The butter it had been grilled in was dilled.

The table was so long that Du Pré hardly joined in the talk. The six Indians from Quebec kept slipping into that dialect he couldn't follow, and they were between him and Chase and his assistants—two young men and two young women, expensive clothes. Chase was wearing one of those jackets Du Pré had seen in photographs of people on safari in Africa. About a hundred pockets. Looked like it was cotton and not at all treated against the wet.

Du Pré looked off, suddenly dreaming, thought of a great weight of furs on his back, a muddy trail, a branch let go by the man ahead swinging back and hitting him, the water dripping and flying.

This was some wet country. Du Pré had driven through a swamp that smelled of cedar. The water, when he stopped to look, was as dark as strong tea.

Paul Chase finished a story, which everyone up there with him at his end of the table found terribly funny. Chase looked modestly pleased with himself.

This Chase is an asshole, Du Pré thought, and there better be some one knows this country, better two someones, or I maybe just get in my car and go back home. These Indians know theirs, but they are a long way from it.

Du Pré had once gotten into some trouble down in southern

184

Utah, a long way out in country that looked sort of like the kind he knew but turned out not to be like it at all. He hadn't come close to dying of thirst, but he was plenty scared. He hadn't forgotten that.

Well, I see what's what, but maybe I not get in these canoes at all.

One of the younger Indian men on the other side of the table came over and sat by Du Pré.

"You are the Gabriel Du Pré I saw the video of, shaping the thwarts for the canoe?" he said.

"Yeah," said Du Pré, puzzled. That video had been made only a month ago, and so fast it makes its way to Canada? Well, things did move fast these times. Too damn fast.

"I am the canoe builder," the young man said. "My name is Henri, but everybody has always called me Lucky. Anyway, I did the best on that pair of bateaux, best that I could. You gave me some good ideas."

Du Pré smiled. I drown now, it's my fault. Made a bad video.

"I saw you fiddle at the festival in June, too," Lucky went on. "You are very good. You bring your fiddle?"

"Yeah," said Du Pré. He'd thought of buying a cheap one to bring, but he sometimes believed his fiddle was a living thing and it might get pissed off being left back on an adventure like this one, grow sulky, not play so good after that.

So he had brought it. The slingshot was in the case, under the neck, with the cube of rosin and the extra strings and bridges.

If I go, Du Pré thought, which I am not till I see maybe we got a couple people look like they grew up on deer meat they poached right around here. I will know them when I see them. I had better see them.

Chase was looking over toward the door that led from the bar to the dining room.

There was a man standing in it, a very dark man, in a red-and-black-checked wool jacket and heavy canvas pants and high boots with rubber bottoms. He had a wool cap on his head, one with a round tassel on the end of it. The man had a large glass of something brown in his left hand. The hand was missing two fingers entirely and some parts of the others. He looked for a moment at Paul Chase, then he walked toward their table. Another man looking just like the first, only twenty years or more younger, followed him. He seemed to have all of his fingers.

When they passed Du Pré, he caught an odor of woodsmoke and fish and dogs.

This is looking some better, Du Pré thought.

Paul Chase introduced the two as Nappy Florissant and his son Felix. They were guides. They would be with the expedition throughout the journey.

The Florissants eventually shook hands with everybody, smiled, and showed that they both were missing a few front teeth. They went back to the bar, and eventually Du Pré followed.

He spoke to them in Coyote French. They liked Du Pré for that, bought him a drink.

"So you been down to York Factory?" Du Pré asked casually, sipping.

"Oh, yes," said Nappy, "I have been there. Him, too." He jerked his head at his son.

They had another drink.

"Yes," said Felix, "we have been to York Factory some, the both of us."

"They fly us there to fight a big forest fire once," said Nappy, "burning some bad, that one, couldn't see the ground from the plane. Lots of smoke."

"Then they fly us back Lac La Ronge. Made good money," said Felix.

"So we both been to York Factory," said Felix, eyes twinkling.

Du Pré laughed. These men would do, as they say in Montana, to ride with.

Or float with up here in the endless black-green forest, in the rain.

✦ CHAPTER 8 ✦

The mass of gear was monstrous. Du Pré walked around it, looked at the canoes, some fiberglass and the others bark, the big freighters. They looked crude, and they were. Bark and pitch, fir for struts and thwarts and ribs, laced with woven spruce roots.

Oddly beautiful. Even had the roll of birch under the stern.

"Got maybe a disco in here, roller rink?" said Nappy. He was used to greenhorns; they always brought ten times as much stuff as they needed, and the wrong stuff at that. "Maybe this big tent has a hot tub, maybe a nice deck." He kicked a huge bag.

"Papa, he has the big head this morning," said Felix. He looked at the piles of duffel and laughed.

"Where's yours?" said Nappy.

Du Pré pointed to his sleeping bag—a cheap Dacron one, but if it got wet, you could wring it out and still be a little warm—and two duffels with his clothes and few possibles in it.

Compass—didn't need one of those in Montana, since the mountains stuck up so high—some fruit leather and jerky; clothes, jacket and dew pants and rubber-bottomed boots, plenty of wool socks; some detergent and salt and tea; aspirin; six bottles of Canadian whiskey, full liters, none of this dinky little fifth business.

Du Pré had poured the whiskey into a six-liter gasoline can, a plastic one. Had a neat little spout you could unscrew. It had been made to hold gasoline for chain saws, but Du Pré had seen its other possibilities.

A knot of people was headed their way. Some TV camera people and a couple reporters. Paul Chase was in the center. One of the

187

reporters broke off and trotted over to Du Pré and the Florissants.

"Mr. Chase said to ask you when you would embark."

"Soon as we get all this shit loaded," said Nappy. "I say maybe two weeks."

The pile wasn't that bad, though, everything had been duffeled or put in dry bags. Du Pré asked about food, and Nappy said the Smithsonian had a whole department got good food together for expeditions.

"Somehow that don't make me feel much better," said Du Pré.

"We got a whole bunch in our two canoes, too," said Felix, laughing, "and there's plenty fish and a couple rifles. Deer and moose along the river and not too many them game wardens, you know. Lots of porcupines."

Du Pré had eaten porcupine. The meat was horrible, what there was of it. The flabby animals moved slowly and didn't need much muscle. But the liver, which was large, was delicious.

The gear was laid in the canoes; the members of the expedition got in and paddled off before noon. The day was calm. Lac La Ronge was big enough to have good-sized waves on it. They would hug the shore for the first couple of days, until they came to the lake's outlet and went down the river to the next lake.

Du Pré asked Nappy what river. He was riding in Nappy's canoe and helping the man paddle.

"All Red River," said Nappy. There were a lot of local names for the little stretches—had to be so the voyageurs would know where they were and what they were talking about. Du Pré took out a notebook and began to list them. The first was a twelve-mile stretch between Lac La Ronge and a small and unnamed lake called the Le Vieux.

They were paddling in to shore to make the first camp when Du Pré had a thought, one coming out of his buried mind into the light. He had once heard a song that went "La Ronge, Le Vieux . . ." but he couldn't remember the rest. A lot of the voyageurs' songs must have been *maps*. They were illiterate. They had to move through a flattish country that had no high, unmistakable landmarks. Songs were easy to remember. So somewhere there was or had been some songs which described the landscape the entire length and breadth of the fur trade, all of it.

"How much miles you make in a day, average?" said Du Pré to Nappy.

"We do maybe twenty. Long river stretch, maybe more. Takes a long time put up and take down these camps. Just you and me, we could maybe do sixty, even mostly paddling. That's hard work, though."

The shore was coming up. Du Pré thought he could see clouds of bloodthirsty mosquitoes banked up, waiting.

He could. The canoes were drawn up and people cursed and slapped and smeared themselves with repellent.

Nappy walked off toward a little sluggish feeder brook. He pulled up some bushy plant and stripped it of leaves. He pounded the leaves with the handle of his knife and then rubbed them on his face.

"What plant is this?" said Du Pré.

"Bug plant," said Felix. "It works better than them creams, keeps the blackflies and no-see-ums off, too. Them no-see-um, can't get people to bite they eat rotten fish or meat. So when they bite you, you get a little bad spot where they bite."

"Yeah," said Nappy. "These pretty girls, they look like they kissing porcupines before we get to York Factory. Shame, lose them nice complexions they got."

Chase and his assistants were setting up a big wall tent and laughing too hard about it.

I am not thinking this expedition will make it, thought Du Pré.

The Indians were putting up tattered and stained pup tents, three of them, and they already had a little fire going.

Paul Chase opened one of the big food bags and found "Food— 15 people. Supper."

We got thirteen here, Du Pré thought suddenly. No, we got fourteen, I guess. I am not superstitious. Like hell. I still go to that Catholic Church, yes.

The food the Smithsonian had sent was freeze-dried, everything from chow mein to pork chops to Irish stew.

Nappy and Felix had built a big fire. People sat on logs or duffel and poured boiling water on their plates and then they ate.

This is pretty good, Du Pré thought.

The firelight danced on the dark faces of the Indians and the bright faces of Chase and his young people. After a time, Chase rose and made the same introductions that he had the night before.

The two blond young men were Tim and Sean, the women, one redheaded and one brunette, were Hilary and Susan.

The Indian women from Quebec were Françoise and Eloise. The men were Lucky, Hervé, Guillaume, and Herbert.

Du Pré, Nappy, and Felix sat pretty much to themselves, the Indians pretty much to theirs, Chase and his four young assistants to themselves.

Du Pré got out his fiddle; the Indians dug out a couple of drums and an old flute, a plain silver one.

The mosquitoes whined and the smoke drifted up to the stars.

Du Pré fiddled for a while, then he listened to the Crees.

He wondered who would crack first.

First night out and this thing is already coming to pieces, thought Du Pré. I am here because of Benetsee. Chase and his people are here because it is their job to do fool things like this.

The Cree are here . . . . I don't know why. They got rivers where they live.

He wondered about that.

Nappy and Felix are here because they are paid to be here.

So I will trust them the most.

Suddenly Du Pré wished, without knowing why, that he had his gun with him.

These Canadians didn't like pistols, though, at all. They had gone through Du Pré's car with tweezers. Asked him flat out. Told him how long he'd be in prison if he did manage to smuggle one in.

For some reason, I had a nine-millimeter and a couple clips, I'd like this better, Du Pré thought.

The mosquitoes whined in front of his face, furiously. They couldn't stand the bug plant's juices and they couldn't land, but they smelled blood.

Du Pré heard an eerie, lilting cry.

A loon.

It sounded beautiful and quite insane.

✦ CHAPTER 9 ✦

They plowed on through the clear waters; the dark forest spilled down to the shore. The ravens sat in the tops of the trees, a pair every few miles, silent.

Make this country bloom, it needs to burn, Du Pré thought. My people used fire to bring up the grass and the game. But the paper companies see all that money on fire, they put it out pretty quick.

At midday, they heard the throb of diesel engines, came on a survey camp. A tall yellow derrick stuck above the dark trees. A big well-drill whirled.

"Lookin' for that nickel," said Nappy, "like the big mines down in Sudbury. For a long time there, the rainfall, it eat the clothes off the kids playing outside, eat the paint off the cars. Lots of people got the cancer. They are looking for another nickel mine."

They paddled on until the late afternoon.

A little river came into the bigger one at the campsite, and the bars in the little river were covered with wild strawberries. Du Pré and the others gathered fresh fruit, enough to feed everyone all they could eat. Once, Du Pré bent over to pluck the berries from a runner and he looked off maybe three feet to his left and saw a fawn lying motionless, still spotted this late in the year.

Du Pré mentioned the fawn to Nappy, who said it was a too-late one and wouldn't be strong enough to make it through the winter. The deer weren't numerous, and something seemed wrong with the ones Nappy killed. He didn't know what. They seemed weaker.

"Got some cousins, Wood Crees, say the deer will soon be gone; they can see it in their dreams. But they don't know why, either," said Nappy.

They were far off and away from the rest of the party.

"I don't think that Chase and his friends stay," said Nappy, "so I guess I don't get all my money."

Du Pré had thought the same thing. The whites barely spoke to Du Pré and the Florissants, and never to the Quebec Indians. They moved along each day, set up camps, Du Pré and the Quebec Indians made some music, and then they slept and broke camp and went on.

Du Pré was hard put to see a point to this expedition.

The next night, Du Pré took the slingshot from his violin case and walked down the lakeshore to a gravel bar. He picked up a rounded stone and put it in the pouch and whirled the thing like he'd seen Benetsee do. The rock crashed into the water at his feet. Du Pré frowned. He fiddled with the thongs for a while and tried again.

He stood there for an hour, practicing. The rocks began to go more or less in the direction he wished, but accuracy would take some time. Amazing, though, the extra velocity you could get from this. One awfully fortunate throw went four times as far as Du Pré could have managed by hand.

Du Pré rolled the slingshot up and headed back to camp. He found Nappy sitting on a log, smoking a little curved meerschaum pipe. The fingernails he had left were flat black under the tips.

"Had me an uncle used one of those," said Nappy. "Knock a duck right out of the air with it, he could."

"I feel pretty good, I can hit Canada," said Du Pré.

"Got some weather coming in," said Nappy. He was looking toward the west. The sky had been cloudless and pale blue all day. There was no wind.

192

Different country and I cannot read it, Du Pré thought. At home, I can tell you when a blizzard is three hundred miles away. I just *know*. But this country, it is different; I can't read it.

Pretty boring, too.

All that dark green forest. See a few ducks, hear a loon, see a raven once in a while.

Du Pré didn't feel like fiddling that night. He went for a walk in the moonlight on the lakeshore. The rocks were slick and large. After kneeling in the canoe all day, his legs ached, and once he had a bad charley-horse in his left calf. He had to rub it hard for several minutes before it loosened.

Goddamn, Du Pré thought before he drifted off to sleep, canoeloads of trade goods out and furs back in this country, take you six months to get to the other end of it and back, pretty crazy-making. But if that was all you knew, maybe not.

Du Pré was wakened by screams and yells, a crash of cooking utensils, and a sound like a hog rooting. Bear. He slipped out of his bedroll, pulled on his boots, took his big flashlight out, and shone it toward the noise.

Chase, wearing only underwear, was trying to climb a small tree.

The brunette woman, Susan, was screaming and holding her forehead. Blood welled out between her fingers.

Nappy and Felix were banging some pots together.

There was a little black bear sitting in the scattered contents of one of the food sacks, looking surprised. Bears can look more surprised than anything.

The bear didn't even weigh a hundred pounds, Du Pré thought. I have shot a lot of bears and that is a very small bear there.

The bear stuck his head down in the food and hiked up his rear end. Du Pré took a few strides, like a football placekicker, and kicked the bear's ass. The startled animal bawled, rolled a little, and took off at top speed for the night.

Everybody shut up. The hurt woman turned out to have stumbled and fallen on a protruding stob on a log lying near her tent.

193

Chase was up in the little tree, blinking. He began to descend, making loud noises of pain.

Ain't this some chickenshit, Du Pré thought.

Du Pré got his little first-aid kit and cleaned the woman's wound. Nappy appeared with a few mashed leaves in his grubby hand.

"Have her chew these and then smear this on," he said. "It will stop the bleeding and help keep the skin from scarring."

The woman shook her head no.

Nappy shrugged. Du Pré waited a little till the wound quit dribbling blood and then he closed the cut with butterfly stitches. Not a bad cut, but these head wounds always bled a lot. She would have a scar there among all those insect bites.

She had shaken her head no at the bug plant Nappy had offered her, too. A couple of the bites had festered badly enough that they would be pits on what had once been a creamy forehead.

Chase was cursing, or, rather, whining.

That man, he think only about himself, Du Pré thought. I don't like him, the Florissants, they despise him, the Quebec Indians don't like him. But he got these fool white kids need him for something, I guess.

Du Pré wished he hadn't come. But he had.

He would see this through to York Factory.

Maybe finally that dark forest would speak to him.

Ravens.

✤ CHAPTER 10 ✤

The bad weather Nappy had smelled coming came on late in the day, when the canoe party was rounding a headland with a long tongue of gravel snaking off it out into the lake. The canoes

194

were a good half mile from shore when the wind came spanking over the water from the west. Dark clouds had suddenly piled up and the lake bloomed with a quick chop that quickly swelled to small waves.

Nappy motioned to everyone to paddle for shore in the straightest line they could.

The Indians from Quebec had the worst job. Their canoes were big and heavy and hard to move, as laden as they were. But they dug in their paddles and the heavy boats made good way.

Felix had the girl with the cut head in his canoe. Du Pré and Nappy hung back. Chase, the two men, and the other woman were in two slender canoes, and they should have been all right. But Chase seemed to panic; he lost his rhythm and more or less fought his partner.

Nappy let loose a string of curses.

Chase's canoe hit something in the water—maybe a tree so waterlogged, it floated barely beneath the surface. They never did find out.

The canoe swung broadside to the wind, Chase actually stood up in the tippy craft, and over it went, foundered. Dunnage floated for a moment and then sank. Chase was wearing a life vest, but the other man wasn't and he couldn't swim very well.

Nappy and Du Pré came alongside the wreck, and Du Pré actually had to crack Chase's hands with the canoe paddle or he would have pulled them over, too. They managed finally to get the other man into their canoe. Chase was screaming something, but no one paid any attention. The waves were not very big and Chase was in no danger, so they left him shrieking and drove for shore while sleet pelted them, the front behind the wind was wet and cold.

They let the man wade in to the others, who were setting up tents, and went back out for Chase. He was clinging to the floundered canoe, red-eyed and out of breath. Du Pré was beginning to dislike this Chase a lot.

They finally got the man into the boat and ran in. The wind was screaming at the west end of the little lake and just as they pulled

195

the canoe out, a rolling front hit, the booms of thunder felt as if they were right overhead. Hail bashed down, some as big as eggs. Big enough to hurt you bad. They all huddled in the tents.

Chase had been a long time in cold water and he was shivering too much to speak.

The storm passed. Du Pré went out to the beach and saw Chase's canoe, and a lot of the waterlogged dunnage he had been carrying, had been driven in toward shore. He waded out and grabbed the canoe and dragged it in.

Felix saw him and came to help.

They turned the canoe over to drain and waited a minute, smoking, for some of the water to seep out of the bags.

Chase had recovered enough to start screaming at Nappy.

Nappy walked out to Felix and Du Pré, calmly lighting his pipe.

"Would that God had let him drown," said Nappy.

They nodded.

The man Du Pré and Nappy had rescued came over to them and thanked them.

"I think Paul forgot to take his medication," the man said. Du Pré thought his name was Tim, but not for sure. Weeks on this trip and I don't even know his name for sure. We are one tight team, Du Pré thought.

"We are two, three days from that archaeological place," said Nappy. "I think that we have to get there before Chase can get a plane to get him out of here."

"Leave?" said Tim. "He hasn't said anything about that."

"He will," said Du Pré.

They carried the bags up to the camp. Chase started scrabbling in them. He took a vial of pills out and swallowed two.

"We'll break this expedition off at the dig," he said after a minute.

"We'll go on," said the canoe builder. The rest of the Quebec Indians nodded in agreement.

"So will I," said Du Pré.

"I am in command!" Chase screamed.

"No," said Nappy, "I am. You are not shit, Chase."

"You won't be paid!" Chase screamed.

Nappy shrugged and walked away. Chase jumped after him and grabbed his shoulder.

Nappy punched him expertly. Chase folded up like a wet bag dropped. His assistants looked startled, then they started to laugh.

They all laughed. Chase was out cold.

"I don't work for him no more, he should not grab my shoulder, eh?" said Nappy.

More laughter.

Du Pré thought he heard the sound of an airplane. Engines snarling out there to the west. He saw a glint in the livid blue behind the storm front.

In twenty minutes, the clouds overhead had gone on, leaving a bright, washed sky.

The airplane came down from the north and roared overhead. The pilot wiggled the wings.

"One them de Havilland Otters," said Nappy. "What the hell he want here, anyway?"

Du Pré started to laugh.

The plane floated over the trees at the far side of the lake and slid into the water. The pilot throttled back. The plane roared on toward them. The pilot turned the plane broadside a hundred yards offshore and stopped engines.

The door opened. Big sunburned face in it. Big red hand waving.

Bart, the idiot.

A raft plopped out on the water. Bart lowered himself into it, screwed the paddles together, and began to row in, sort of—he wasn't very good at it.

"I got worried," he said to Du Pré, "And so did Madelaine, so I said, 'Hell, I'll go see.' "

Du Pré introduced Bart.

"So how's it going?" said Bart.

Du Pré shrugged.

Bart described the goings-on in Toussaint. Not much. Jacqueline was pregnant again.

Du Pré shrugged. Jacqueline was always pregnant. One more grandchild. Du Pré needed to write down their names, carry a card.

"Well," said Bart finally, "you need anything?"

Du Pré looked at Paul Chase, who was sitting up now, looking at some blood in his hand.

"Yeah," said Du Pré. "You could do us all this big favor. . . ."

✦ CHAPTER 11 ✦

While Bart flew off with Chase and his assistants and to pick up a few odds and ends he might need for the balance of the trip, Du Pré and the Quebecois and Nappy and Felix rested and dried out sodden stuffs and gathered wild berries.

After a decent interval, the canoe builder voiced a complaint. The expedition had been mercifully free of these idiot whites, but now Bart was coming back, and he was white. Frenchy Canucks and Indians were all right, but . . .

Du Pré thought about that for a long time, smoking his cigarette and sipping some whiskey and lake water.

"Bart ain't white," he finally said. "He's Italian."

Nappy roared with laughter, roared till his eyes ran tears. Felix smiled and shook.

The Cree looked dubious.

"Bart, he is a good man," Du Pré said. "Not like those others there. You are here why? The dams are to go on the other side of the bay, and let me tell you, this Bart, he has some real power and maybe could help you. I mean, he chartered that airplane for a whole week. His credit cards are maybe made out of some metal I don't know about. They are too heavy, those cards, for me to lift. But Bart, he is okay. Used to be a bad drunk, but not anymore."

After some talk among themselves, the canoe builder said that they liked Du Pré and if he liked Bart, then it would be fine. It was their law, anyway.

Nappy and Felix had shrugged when Bart offered them a flight home.

"We said we do this, so we better do it," said Nappy, looking at the places where the fingers on his right hand used to be. "Otherwise, it would maybe bother us."

So when Bart was dropped off early the next morning, the pilot rowing the raft to shore, they were ready to move. There was one paddler for each of the small canoes and three each for the freighters.

They made good time, Du Pré and Nappy slicing on ahead a half mile or so to give plenty of time to warn the freighters of coming portages or the shoals of broken rocks that sometimes rose to within a few inches of the surface.

They didn't halt for lunch, just chewed trail food and kept going. In the middle of the afternoon, Du Pré squinted hard and saw the boil of a rapids. He sent Nappy back to slow the others, beached his canoe, and walked down by the rushing water.

It was really a long waterfall set at a shallow angle, with a lot of velocity in the water. A well-trodden portage trail went through the trees and down. Du Pré walked for a few minutes. He saw a cluster of tents through the trees.

The archaeologists. The long, looping fall ended in a deep, long pool.

Du Pré thought of the voyageurs who said, "Well, we try it." He wondered how many had drowned. A lightly laden canoe could make it if the paddlers knew what they were doing. If nothing happened. The pool was mean-looking, swirls of water rising up beside the main current. Water was running around all over the place down there.

Du Pré saw someone in a frogman suit and mask rise up in the middle of one of the great, greasy boils, raise a hand, and sink back down. Then there were two black flippers in the air for a moment.

He heard a winch whine, a diesel engine speed up.

Du Pré walked on down. There were several people in stained, wet clothes guiding the cable. Others stood at tall tables, running water over piles of what looked like globs of rust.

Du Pré asked the first man he came to who was running this dig. The man said a name hurriedly and pointed to a tall gray-haired man with a clipboard who was standing on top of an old cedar stump, one hand on his hip.

"Dr. Pearse!" Du Pré said loudly.

"Yes," the man said mildly, "speaking."

"I am Gabriel Du Pré, part of that expedition from Lac La Ronge to York Factory."

Pearse looked down at Du Pré for a moment.

"Chase's expedition?" he said sourly.

"Chase left," said Du Pré.

"Now I must talk to you," said Pearse, clambering down from his perch. "Little Paul Chase left the expedition?"

"Yes," said Du Pré.

Pearse was humming, he was so happy.

Du Pré told Pearse the tale of Chase's departure.

"That little prick," said Pearse. "I have been stewing about having to be civil to him for weeks. And he's not coming. Thank you."

"He is pretty bad," said Du Pré.

Du Pré lingered for a few minutes, walking by the scrubbing tables, where people were knocking the worst of the sand and rust off the ax heads and bar lead, the kettles and frying pans, the fused masses of smaller metal objects.

The chunks were then carried to a spray booth, where a woman wearing a breather mask sprayed them with clear plastic.

Du Pré walked down by the pool. There were lines snaking out into it, tied to a cable that ran across the pool from shore to shore

200

coiled around huge trees on each side. The cable was high above, maybe ten feet. A kingfisher sat on it, head turning.

He glanced at the tidy little tent village. This was a well-run, clean, orderly camp.

He thought of the expedition, how disorderly it was till Chase had left.

Lot of wrecks here over the years, pile up that much trade goods. Damn furs would have floated off or rotted, bones ground to powder by the shifting gravels. The pool was big and mean *now;* when the snows melted and the spring runoff hit, it must be awesome.

Pearse wandered over to Du Pré.

"I . . ." he started, but then there was a shout from the shore down by the pool. People were pointing and yelling at the long falls.

Du Pré started to run to them.

He looked back up the long tongue of fast green water. One of the big freighters was coming down it, paddlers front and back digging to keep the big canoe lined right with the current.

Lucky, the canoe builder, was standing in the middle of the big canoe, holding a staff. Feathers fluttered from the tip.

The freighter shot across the foaming boil where the green tongue of the river dove into the pool. The paddlers dug in and the canoe went free into the green waters. The rear paddler dug his paddle in the water at the canoe's side and the freighter turned to the shore.

Lucky was still standing.

The canoe ground up over the gravels.

"Pretty nice canoe," said Du Pré to Lucky.

Pearse was smiling. "I guess some of the time it worked," he said. "You gave us quite a fright."

"Yeah, that's a strong canoe," said Lucky. "You got to hit the water right, though."

"Whew," said Pearse. "Who built it?"

"I did," said Lucky.

"I wonder," said Pearse, "if a lot of the deposits on the pool bottom are there because of bad design or flaws in the canoes. Interesting."

Lucky nodded.

"See if the other one works," said Lucky. "It don't got that birch roll in the back there."

"What other one?" snapped Pearse.

"That one," said Lucky, pointing back up the river.

Du Pré looked, winced.

The other big freighter was coming down, the women paddling this time. They were keeping the canoe lined well.

The big canoe shot down the tongue and across the foaming boil.

But Bart Fascelli lost his balance.

He'd been standing up like Lucky.

He shot off to the side and sank.

A thwart broke and the canoe hogged and the birch bark ripped down the side at the seams.

The canoe broached to and the women went in and the gear went over. The canoe swamped.

The hydraulics dragged everything and everyone under.

Du Pré glanced to his left, at Lucky, who was laughing.

"Oh, Jesus Christ," Du Pré screamed, running.

Before Gabriel Du Pré could prove how well he could swim (not very), the frogman came up, though, with Bart in hand. The frogman hauled poor Bart to shore, where he vomited a lot of water.

"You dumb shit," said Du Pré sympathetically.

"We knew that," Bart wheezed.

Du Pré went back up to help carry the smaller canoes down.

That pool, it eat one of these just fast like that, he thought, looking down at the path pounded two feet deep over the centuries.

✤ CHAPTER 12 ✤

The Crees sang as they paddled. They hadn't before. The songs were sad, the melodies on a strange tonal scale.

Early one morning, as they were loading the canoes, the Crees began a ballad, one in English, the words so burred Du Pré couldn't make them out. The song was about the burning of the Highlands.

"Where you learn that?" he asked Lucky.

Lucky shrugged. One of the Cree women, Françoise, said that the Hudson's Bay factors were usually Highland Scots. Their blood was commingled with that of the Cree/Chippewa, and many of the people scattered across the length and breadth of the Canadian fur trade had Scottish surnames.

"Mine's Routledge," said Françoise. She was a pretty woman. The light of the fire shone red in her black hair.

The Scots and the French, Du Pré thought. Them Jesuits must have been the hell and gone to the Rockies before we lost the war with the English. The one in the 1760s.

"Do you know 'Brave Wolfe'?" Du Pré said.

They nodded and sang it. Brave Wolfe dying on the Plains of Abraham. But the English took Quebec. And the Cajuns were removed to Louisiana.

The day was blustery, with high stratocirrus cloud and vees of geese flying in huge circles, to toughen the young birds for flying over half the continent to winter in the swamps of the Gulf Coast. They passed a flock feeding on wild rice in a shallow backwater. An old admiral goose honked contemptuously at them, bidding them be gone, and soon.

Fall came early this far north. Already a few times, there had been a thin skim of ice on the shores. The insects had pretty well died off, all but the infernal no-see-ums. Bart had brought along a cure for them; he said he had gotten it on a fishing trip to Alaska. White tequila rubbed on the face kept the fierce, tiny insects at bay. He would not use it himself.

That night, the Quebec Indians talked sorrowfully of their homes, how a few thousand of them had gone back to the old ways in the vast forests far from the whites and alcohol, one as disorienting as the other. They tried to live as their ancestors had done before the whites came, but that was impossible.

"It's hard to give up nails and twist drills and tea," Lucky said, laughing, "and why spend a day braiding spruce roots when you can pay a dollar for a big ball of twine?"

The Jesuits and Anglicans still moved among them, welcomed by most.

There were those, however, who would destroy everything they had. New York in its hunger for electricity and Hydro-Quebec, the giant electrical-generation company, proposed $20 billion worth of dams in the far north country.

Cities, they are vampires with very long fangs, Du Pré thought.

Bart shyly brought forth a harmonica one night and added lonesome notes to a slow sad song Du Pré was fiddling. Du Pré looked at him in surprise.

"When you learn to do that?" he said.

"Uh," said Bart, "Booger Tom. He told me I was shoveling shit so good, I'd probably make a mouth-harp player, and he showed me a few things. It's pretty simple, really." He slapped the harmonica against his palm to clear it of spittle and put it back in his duffel.

"If it is your country," said Bart, "and I seem to remember that the Canadians gave it back to you, why can't you just say no?"

Lucky explained that the long legal process hadn't extinguished rights and interests and there were so many that the courts would be full for a century. The government of Canada was treacherous about its gifts. After all, they were English.

Yeah, Du Pré thought, I hear that joke once, Frenchman going to kill you, he explains it logically; the German weeps a lot; and the Englishman just does it and says, "What knife?"

A crowded world growing more hungry and cold.

Du Pré was beginning to like this long, dark wood, though, the loon cries, the water everywhere. Montana was a tough desert till you got to the mountains. It was the winter that made things bloom.

"How far is York Factory?" Du Pré asked Nappy.

"Two days," said Nappy. "We make good time without those others."

They stopped the next evening at an Indian camp, a dreary place. The people were living in tents; several bearskins ripe and unscraped hung in stretchers. The men were off fishing or cutting pulp. The traplines had yielded poorly these last few years.

That night, the expedition was startled to see two brusque Scotswomen at the head of a procession of everyone else in camp, bringing gifts of berries and smoked fish. There was so much food left in the dry bags that they didn't need Nappy and Du Pré, and Françoise handed out hundreds of pounds of tinned goods and dried fruit.

They sang some songs around the fire. The Scotswomen were on a tour, taking notes and making sketches, for some book.

They went on in the morning. In the afternoon, a light plane flew high overhead, banked, turned, and came over the expedition, then went on east, toward where York Factory must be.

The plane came over the next morning, too, and then the party saw the signs of the town, trees cut, a road along the river. The water in the river deepened and slowed, here and there a plastic bottle drifted on the water, pushed about by the winds and chop.

They rounded a short headland and saw the little village spilling down to the water. Du Pré idly looked behind him. Something wasn't right.

He looked again. There was an extra canoe, and it was moving as fast as the paddlers could make it go.

In ten minutes, it passed Du Pré and Nappy.

Paul Chase was in it, of course.

Du Pré looked up toward the town, and he whistled to Nappy.

"So that Chase, he talk to those newspeople up there, you bet," said Du Pré, laughing. "That guy, he should be a politician."

The people in the freighters were pointing and laughing.

When Du Pré and Nappy pulled their canoes out, Chase was rattling away into a tape recorder while some TV cameraman sprawled out on the ground. Chase hadn't shaved in a few days and he was daubed here and there with soot.

"Excuse me," said a young woman with a notebook, "were you with the expedition?"

"Yes." Du Pré nodded.

She asked some questions about the trip, then one about the leadership of Dr. Chase.

"Oh," said Du Pré, "he was not there, you know. He left the expedition a few days out from Lac La Ronge."

"What?" she said.

"You see that man over there?" said Du Pré, pointing to Bart. "He came to see me in a chartered plane and he flew Chase and his people out."

Chase was looking over at Du Pré, his eyes narrow. He pushed his way through the reporters and toward the dock area. A little floatplane was tethered there.

The reporters gave up on him and scattered for the telephones or ran toward another plane farther down toward the bay.

The woman with the notebook was talking to Bart and taking notes furiously.

Du Pré laughed.

Chase's floatplane racketed to life and taxied away from the dock.

Some of these people, they take your breath away, Du Pré thought.

✤ CHAPTER 13 ✤

Du Pré and Bart had been home about a week, still chuckling over their journey. Madelaine had taken to yawning wide when they would begin to speak of it. Little boys, her eyes said, exchanging code words in a tree fort.

Jacqueline's husband, Raymond, had got a bid job on plumbing two homes over at the county seat of Cooper, so Du Pré got to go look at cow asses a couple of times. They hadn't changed. He checked the brands and signed off on the loaded cattle.

One evening, Benetsee appeared, looking ragged and, because it was late summer, dustier than usual. He smiled widely and grabbed Du Pré's hand in his old claw. The old man's grip was hard; his tendons pushed up against his weathered skin like wires pulled very tightly.

"So," said Benetsee, "I have been up through the Cypress Hills and some other places."

Du Pré nodded. The Cypress Hills were way the hell up in Canada. He wondered just where old Benetsee had gone, where he'd come from. How far? No use in asking the old man directly, anyway; Du Pré would never get a straight answer. He had yet to get one, anyway.

Might as well bet on the curls of rising smoke.

"You ever learn that sling rock thrower?" said Benetsee. "Takes some brains to use it. I will help you; you need it."

Du Pré had forgotten about the slingshot. He fetched it from his fiddle case. They wandered down to a little gravel bar in the stream. Benetsee peered for a moment and then plucked six rounded stones the size of small plums from beneath the clear water.

"You got to wrap this thong on your palm first," he said. "You see, it is cut longer, and then you hold the end of the short one so it is balanced."

He whirled the shot around his head and sent a stone eighty yards to knock a bottle off a fence post. Du Pré had found the empty pint bottle near the fence post just this morning and set it up. Stock stepped on that and it broke wrong, they could hurt themselves.

The bottle shattered into little shards.

They spent an hour, Benetsee sighing wearily each time Du Pré let a rock go. Du Pré could pretty well hit one of the four directions and not much better.

"Since these whites came, nobody can do nothing anymore," Benetsee grumbled. "Listen, you practice with this. I try you again. Maybe I go and pray for you now."

Benetsee left, muttering.

Like always, he would get up to some bushes and stoop and be gone. The bushes wouldn't wave. The most Du Pré ever knew of his passage was a bird or animal complaining. If they were complaining about Benetsee. Who knew?

Du Pré tried the slingshot a few more times. It was one of those things you had to do a lot and then it would make sense. Seemed simple. Like tying knots, it wouldn't work right until he didn't have to think about it anymore.

Du Pré wandered back to his house. He sat on the stump of a box elder he'd been meaning to grub out for the last ten years. Big black ants had chewed holes in the gray wood. Du Pré looked at them and decided he would let them win this race. He hated digging holes, gardening, and the like.

Madelaine came out with some lemonade. The summer had gone on hot right into the first part of September. Her children were in school, and after school they would wander back on their own time. The boys played softball and the girls visited friends.

Du Pré got off the stump and offered it to her. She sat down and handed him his lemonade.

"Some nice weather," she said, looking up at the snow-capped

Wolf Mountains. Up there, it could snow anytime and always did in mid-August. The peaks were clear only from the middle of July to the middle of August, and in the winter the snows could pile forty feet deep above ten thousand feet.

Du Pré heard the telephone ring. Maria was off somewhere. He got up and trotted to the open back door of the house.

He picked up the phone, heard the long-distance hum.

"Uh, Gabriel Du Pré," said a woman's voice he couldn't place.

"This is me," said Du Pré.

"You probably don't remember me," she said. "My name is Samantha Ford. I was the reporter who talked to you at York Factory?"

"Oh, yeah," said Du Pré, "when that Paul Chase slipped in like he'd been on the trip all along."

"Yes. He kept denying that he hadn't and called you all 'disgruntled employees.' The TV people had jumped the gun and didn't want to eat crow. But they finally had to."

"Well, he is a strange man," said Du Pré.

"Uh-huh. What I'm calling about is this. I moved from the Toronto paper down here."

"Uh," said Du Pré.

"I'm in Washington, D.C., not the state."

"Okay," said Du Pré. So what.

"The Cree woman, Annie McRae, who was murdered last June at the festival?"

"Uh," said Du Pré.

"Well, one of the Indians on your expedition had been there, and she said Chase had been dating Annie."

Du Pré straightened up.

"So I asked the cops here, and they didn't know anything about it. You know cops. They nod and chew and look bored."

"Yeah," said Du Pré. "Now, which one of those Quebec Indians tell you this?"

"Lucky."

"He say anything else?"

"He said Annie was a simple girl from the bush and she didn't know what to do about Chase. But she was . . . Lucky thought she was afraid of him. He's white; he's powerful; he's rich. Anyway, Chase brought her down to D.C. before the festival to tape some songs, even though Annie wasn't a solo performer, wasn't, in fact, very good. Then when Lucky and some others got there, she wouldn't ever leave them. Even insisted on sleeping on the floor of the room with the most men in it. When Chase tried to get her alone, she'd almost tie herself to Lucky."

"You tell the cops this?" said Du Pré.

"Some of it," said Samantha Ford.

"So why you call me?"

"I called Chase," she went on, "called him late at night; sometimes you can get someone off balance. He had been drinking or whatever. He was foggy. It seemed to take him a moment to understand my question. Then he blew up."

Du Pré waited.

"He said Annie had been sleeping with you, Mr. Du Pré."

"Christ," said Du Pré, "I don't even know what she looked like."

"So you weren't?"

"No," said Du Pré. That son of a bitch.

"Thank you," said Samantha Ford. She hung up.

Du Pré walked back outside. He leaned over and kissed Madelaine.

"Who was that?" she said.

"Woman reporter I talked to in York Factory," said Du Pré. "She call to ask me about that murdered girl I told you about at the festival."

Madelaine looked up at him.

"Well," said Du Pré, "this Paul Chase, what a weasel. She calls him because one of the Quebec Indians says Chase was after this murdered girl. He says the girl was sleeping with me."

Madelaine laughed. She laughed very hard.

"That's funny, Du Pré," she said. "Were you?" And she laughed again.

"No, I wasn't," said Du Pré.

"My Gabriel screwing teenyboppers," said Madelaine, "I don't think so."

"You ever talk to one of them?" said Du Pré.

"I have to," said Madelaine, "I'm their mother."

She sighed.

✦ CHAPTER 14 ✦

The little private jet shot across the sky. Du Pré watched the Midwest's patchwork of fields move beneath the wings. He toyed with a glass of bourbon.

Lawyer Foote sat in one of the other chairs, Bart in the third.

Bart was enraged.

Du Pré was both angry and bewildered.

Foote, the elegant attorney from Chicago's Gold Coast, looked bored.

"You two calm down," Foote said finally. "This is a farce. I don't even think it is necessary for us to *go* there. A deposition would have sufficed. It is up to them to find some *evidence*, for Chrissakes. I would bet things are closing in on Chase."

"I am just sick of that lying little prick," said Bart.

Foote sighed, picked up a book, and went back to reading.

"Do I have to cage the pair of you?" he said, offhandedly.

Bart and Du Pré sank back in their chairs for a minute. Then they tensed up and began to lean forward again.

"You are to keep your tempers, gentlemen," said Foote. "An

211

attack on Chase would not be worth it, to put it mildly." He did not look up from his book.

The plane got to Washington and circled just once before shrieking in to land. A limousine moved slowly out to the plane. The ramp went down. Foote got off first, carrying a slim attaché case and glancing grimly at his watch. Du Pré and Bart had no luggage. The black driver got in and drove off. He was separated from them by a glass panel.

The police station was new, in the late seventies architecture best called inhumane.

Foote spoke briefly to the desk officer. The man picked up a telephone. He talked for a moment and then pointed down the hall to the right. They began to walk toward it.

The big, rumpled detective whom Du Pré had spoken to in June, while he held the frightened horse, came out of a doorway and stood there waiting for them, hands in pockets.

They got closer. The detective stared at Foote with distaste.

"Just a few questions," said the cop.

"If I think the questions reasonable, I shall instruct my client to answer," said Foote. His disdain chilled the hall.

They all took seats at the conference table. There was a voice-activated miniature tape recorder sitting on it. No ashtrays. A sign on the wall thanked them for not smoking.

The detective rattled the case number into the recorder. Foote had scribbled a short note. He pushed it over to the detective, who looked sourly at it and then spoke the names of Bart, Du Pré, and the lawyer.

"You ever date this Annie McCrae?" said the detective.

"No," said Du Pré. "I don't even know what she looked like."

The detective rattled off questions; Du Pré looked at Foote before answering each one. Foote nodded; Du Pré spoke.

"But Paul Chase says you did," the detective said finally.

"Paul Chase is a liar," said Du Pré. He recounted the story of the expedition and Chase's grandstanding at the end of it. Told him to contact Samantha Ford at the Post.

"Thanks," said the detective suddenly. He waved to someone behind the mirrored wall. A door opened in the hallway. Heels clicked on the tiles. A tall, pretty woman came in the door.

"This is my partner," said the detective, "Detective Sgt. Michelle Leuci."

Bart was staring at her, and not just because she was Italian.

"You dragged their asses all the way here from fucking Montana?" said the lovely woman. "Rollie, you are an asshole. He could have been deposed there. For Christ sweet sakes."

Rollie shrugged.

Foote stood up. "We came to assist," he said.

Du Pré was looking at the beauty with the foul mouth. She had thick dark red hair, bright sapphire eyes, and a stainless steel 9mm automatic pistol in a holster in the small of her back, so her suit coat would cover it.

"This guy Chase has some connections," she said, "but they won't help if we can build a case. But what's he like? You said he cut in on you at the end of the expedition. Why'd he leave in the first place?"

Du Pré told them about the bear, Chase climbing the tree in a panic, the canoe capsizing the next day, and Chase's hysterics. How one of the assistants had said he wasn't taking his medication.

"So, what was he like?" Detective Leuci repeated. She sat down, lit up, and gave the bird to the thank-you sign.

"A little spoiled kid," said Du Pré. "Seemed like he couldn't think of anyone but himself. I began to have this bad feeling about him at the festival. . . ."

"Bad feeling?"

"I don't like him, you know. Hard at first to put a finger on it, but he smiles too quickly, says too many right things. I don't trust him. I wasn't going to come at all, because I didn't really want to. . . ."

"Why did you?"

Benetsee, Du Pré thought. He looked at Foote, who smiled.

213

"This old man I respect told me to," said Du Pré. "It's hard to explain."

Detective Sergeant Leuci leaned forward, eager to be explained to.

"He's an old man I know since I am a child," said Du Pré. "He sees farther than the rest of us can."

"A medicine man?"

Du Pré didn't know what to say. He thought.

"He just seems to know a lot of things there doesn't seem to be a way for him to know," Du Pré said finally. "When he tells me I ought to do something, he has always been right."

"A psychic?"

"He has visions, I think," said Du Pré lamely.

"Indian?"

"Some," said Du Pré.

"You have visions?"

Du Pré sighed. "Only when I am fucking drunk."

Detective Michelle Leuci roared with laughter. She had a big, honest, booming laugh.

"So," she said, still shaking. "My partner here finds you holding on to a horse, belonging to the rider who spotted Annie McRae's body. Where were you when you saw the horse?"

"I am onstage, playing with a Cajun band," said Du Pré.

"Before that?"

"I am onstage, playing my Métis music."

"What's a Métis?"

"Red River breeds," said Du Pré. "We are mostly Canadian. Voyageurs were Métis. Cree, Chippewa, Ojibwa, French, some little English. We come down to Montana after the second rebellion, in 1886."

"Fascinating."

She stood up.

"Thank you," she said. "We'll look hard at this Chase character. Get hold of Samantha Ford." She glanced at Rollie, who went out of the room.

214

"We're going to get some dinner," said Bart, standing up. He bowed to Detective Sergeant Leuci. "Would you care to join us?"

"Who're you?" said Leuci.

"Bart Fascelli," said Bart, "and please go get your fucking coat."

Leuci stared at him for a minute, she shrugged.

She nodded. She went out into the hall, in the next door, and came back.

"No place too fancy," she said, "or folks might think I'm corrupt."

Bart offered her his arm gallantly. She took it and they went out the door.

"We have been abandoned and forgotten," said Lawyer Foote. "They will go to some nice place. It's McDonald's for the help."

"We could catch them," said Du Pré.

Foote shook his head. Then he shook his finger.

They both laughed.

When they got out of the building, the limousine was gone. Foote waved down a cab.

They had barely enough money between them to pay the cabbie off when they got to the hotel.

Midway through dinner, the hotel manager sidled up to Foote and gave him a plain white envelope. Foote thanked the man, getting up to do so. He sat back down, peered into the envelope, and counted out three thousand dollars in hundreds. He handed them to Du Pré.

"Well," said Foote, "I think we should go. The plane can always come back for Bart when Bart surfaces."

"Why all this money?" said Du Pré.

"The rude prick pays," said Foote, taking a bite of his fish.

215

✦ CHAPTER 15 ✦

That would be the best thing for Bart," said Madelaine when Du
Pré described his disappearance. "Kinda rude for him to go off
like that, though."

"He's handicapped," said Du Pré.

"Huh?" said Madelaine.

"He's a rich kid," said Du Pré. "They are handicapped. People
always do for them, you know. Some of their wires never get
hooked up."

"I think I chew his ass hard he get back here," said Madelaine.

Du Pré grinned. Poor Bart. Madelaine's ass-chewings were artful.
As a mother, she got lots of practice. She was fond of Bart, so she
would do a good job, too.

It had frosted hard and the trees and bushes had started to turn.
The wind smelled of fall, late in coming this year.

Du Pré heard the distant boom of a shotgun. The grouse season
was open. Couple weeks, the season would open for pheasants and
ducks. The wild turkeys in the river bottoms. Du Pré thought
maybe he'd hunt for a turkey this year. He'd written off and gotten
a turkey call from some fellow in New Hampshire. Beautiful thing,
in an oiled leather case, Du Pré had played with it. You scraped a
dingus on the side of the call and the thing scrawked and gobbled.

I hope Benetsee don't see this, Du Pré had thought. He put the
call away.

Something nagged at the back of Du Pré's mind, nibbled in the
shadow––on that long trip through the dark green forest, over
the clear water, on the route of Du Pré's blood, one stream of
which ran all the way to France. Something. Once when he was

young, he had shot a bear. He'd been too excited and he'd wounded the animal, not killed it. When his father, Catfoot, shot something, it dropped, and he had told Du Pré to wound an animal was not to respect it.

Du Pré had been alone. He waited for the animal's wound to stiffen and then he tracked the bear, a good-sized black one. He came to a small glade. The glade was quiet, too quiet. He walked softly out on the path, past a big old ponderosa pine. Too quiet. He felt sudden fear and he turned, pointing the gun back the way he had come.

There was nothing there.

Du Pré stood there frozen for some time—he never knew how long.

A single drop of something fell on his hand.

He looked up. The wounded bear was directly above him, perhaps twenty feet up, clinging to the tree.

Spend a lot of time looking in the wrong place because I am thinking I am looking in the right one, Du Pré thought. I got to learn to look everywhere, see everything. Like Benetsee.

That man don't have visions, Du Pré thought. He just pays real close attention.

Or maybe he does have visions.

He remembered the coyote pawing for the lumps of fat in the snow directly over the brass box that held the story complete of the murder of Bart's brother by Du Pré's father, Catfoot. Someone had hung that piece of fat up there. Indeed, had known the story all along, it seemed. But, like any good storyteller, hadn't told it too rapidly. Benetsee hang that fat, yes.

Du Pré went into the house. He got his shotgun from the closet, put a few shells in the pocket of his jacket. There was always jerky, fruit leather, a plastic space blanket, and fatwood splinters to make a fire with in the game pouch in back.

"I drop you off and go shoot a grouse maybe," said Du Pré to Madelaine. It was getting close to time to take her home, anyway.

Du Pré barely saw his daughter Maria, a senior in high school.

Since Bart had offered to send her to any college she could get in, she had washed the dye out of her hair, quit wearing clothes that looked like they had been taken from the bodies of car-bombing victims, and spent her time studying with the same ferocity she had once devoted to driving her father up the wall.

Du Pré walked Madelaine to her front door—he always did—and then he got in his old cruiser and drove off toward the Wolf Mountains. The grouse would begin to come down to the logging roads to pick up gravel for their crops in an hour or so, and Du Pré, without a gundog, would pretty well have to stick to beating the bushes near the roads. Not that he cared if he shot a grouse or not, he liked being out in the bright fall air, liked the smell of the forest.

When Du Pré turned off the county road and entered the trees, he drove slowly on the left side of the road, glancing down at the verge for the tracks he might see—elk, mule deer, a mountain lion.

Must be that lion lives up by Belker Ridge, he thought. See a few more tracks, we had better trim them on back.

Mountain lions were simple killing machines. If their numbers grew, their solitary ways would bring them down near people, where they would feed on dogs and, eventually, small children.

The Montana newcomers would scream about killing such nice big puddy-tats.

We have always had dudes out here, Du Pré thought, but this last bunch think they know things.

Du Pré saw a couple ruffed grouse up ahead taking dust baths and scratching in the fine gravel at the road's edge. He pulled the car off as far as he could go and stopped it, pulled the shotgun out of the case, got out, racked a couple shells in, and began to walk casually toward the grouse.

They looked at him and took less time to dust and peck.

Du Pré got closer.

The grouse became nervous and dashed off into the woods. Du Pré ran after them. They were fast runners. Du Pré was a little faster. He pounded over the thick needles. The grouse took flight, their wings booming. Du Pré threw the shotgun to his shoulder and fired.

218

The grouse kept right on going.

I ought to shoot the bastards on the ground, Du Pré thought. It pissed him off to miss a shot.

He walked back to the car, stuffing another shell in the shotgun.

Just as he stepped out of the woods, four grouse boomed up from across the road, wings whirring, heading straight up. Du Pré shot twice and two birds folded up and fell.

I am some hot shit, Du Pré thought. He walked into the trees and picked the birds up, crumpled on the ground, the little wind ruffling their soft feathers.

He drove on to the end of the road and saw no more birds. He backed and filled at the Kelly hump that blocked the road and then headed back down, in no particular hurry. He got back home with an hour of sunlight to spare. He cleaned the birds, shucked their skins, and put the carcasses in salty water. He would bake them in aspic and then chill them overnight and they would be tender then, make wonderful sandwiches.

Shadows.

He went to the violin case and got out the slingshot.

He went down to the creek.

What about this, now? he thought, sending a stone in flight.

What about this?

Blood dropping from the sky? Long time ago.

✤ CHAPTER 16 ✤

Bart showed up, looking chastened. Du Pré drove him home from the airstrip in Cooper, and Bart stared out the window. Once, Du Pré looked over, to see him wiping his eyes.

Du Pré was a good friend; he kept his mouth shut and waited.

"She didn't tell me to go," he said. "I suddenly realized I was acting like Gianni. So I told her about that. She just smiled at me and said she was a simple girl, really. So I took back most of the stuff. Said I'd go home for a while and think, I hadn't had a lot of practice in being human."

Du Pré laughed. After a while, Bart did, too.

"She has a week of vacation the second week of October and she's going to come out here. At least I can send a plane for her."

"Yeah," said Du Pré. "Anytime you can avoid the Denver airport is better than a time you can't."

"I love her."

This was not news to Du Pré. Under the embarrassment, Bart was very happy. He would go on being very happy till Madelaine lit into him ever so sweetly. But Madelaine was very smart about people. She'd fry Bart good but not burn him.

He is trying very hard, Du Pré thought. I am proud of my friend here.

Bart was building a modest log home with the help of Booger Tom and such ranch hands as were between tasks. The ranch had been running as a tax write-off for years; there were more hands than the place needed, but Bart refused to fire or lay anyone off. He had said time would shrink the crew.

But if a cowboy broke down within a hundred miles, they knew they could come here and work up a stake to go on.

Bart was well thought of among the cowboys.

"I will be glad when I can get that trailer out of here," said Bart.

Most of the logs were stacked for the house's sides. Then the rafters and rooftree had to be set and the place sealed off before the winter. Bart's big dragline had been pressed into service to lift the logs, the bucket replaced with a ball, hook, and choker chain.

Booger Tom was sitting on the log pile, whittling and spitting tobacco. The old goat was out of another time, still wore the checked pants and custom high-topped boots and gigantic pure silk scarf—so dirty, it was hard to discern the pattern in it, true, but pure silk nonetheless.

"Shit," said Bart, "I thought it'd all be done by now."

"We wuz all too ignorant," said Booger Tom. "We need a leader."

Bart grinned and so did Booger Tom.

"The hands is all off working," said Booger Tom, "but I expect a couple could come help tomorrow."

"She is lookin' good," said Du Pré. He suddenly thought of the money of Bart's he had. He fumbled for his wallet.

"Bart," he said, "that lawyer, Foote there, he give me all this cash—I don't know what for."

Bart looked at the thick green wad.

"Oh, that," he said finally, as though it took him a few moments to think up what it was.

"Yeah, this," said Du Pré. He got annoyed when Bart did this, and then annoyed with himself for getting petty with Bart when the big man was just generously trying to help.

"I need some help here," Bart said, groping. "You know I got to get this closed off before winter. So say thirty dollars an hour?"

Du Pré started to say that was more than double the going price for a tradesman around here, but he caught himself and nodded.

"I will go get my tools," said Du Pré. "Or are you tired, maybe want to start in the morning?"

"Might snow tonight," said Bart, looking at a pure blue sky.

Du Pré nodded and drove home. He dug out his belt and hammers and some huge chisels Catfoot had made out of old lumbermill band-saw blades—called slicks—and his big chain saw, a line level, and some big pencils.

Bart probably had three of everything they needed, anyway.

They worked till very late, setting logs. Tomorrow they could put the last course up and peg it in, then begin to set the end rafters and the rooftree.

"You know, Bart," said Du Pré, "with that big-ass dragline we could just build it down here and lift the whole thing up."

Booger Tom snorted. He'd never seen it done that way, so it ought not to. Booger Tom knew what he knew, and what he didn't know, he'd rather not, like most old cowboys.

"Thanks," said Bart. "That's the way to do it. Of course. We'd better measure the damn thing ten times before we start, though. If we lift it up there and it don't fit . . . think of the shame."

Du Pré was whipped when he got home.

This middle age, he thought. Catfoot never let it get to him. If I had to be a voyageur, I'd die. Paddle all the time, then carry everything on the portages, running from the snows, or running from the spring melt.

Life, she was very hard then.

Madelaine called. It was Friday night and she wanted to dance a little to the jukebox at the Toussaint bar.

Du Pré said sure. He felt like falling into bed.

He awoke next morning with a small hangover, a warm place in the bed where Madelaine had just been. He could hear her feeding her brood. They got up early even on a Saturday.

Bart would be working, for sure.

Du Pré pulled on his clothes and boots.

"You going to work for that Bart," said Madelaine, not turning from what she was making on the stove, "so I come out maybe lunchtime and I give him a good bite on the ass, yes?"

Du Pré grunted noncommittally. Best not get in the way of fate, especially Bart's.

He ate some bacon and eggs, filled a big jug with water, and went off. He sat in the car, letting the engine warm up, rolled a cigarette, and smoked. There was thick frost on the glass. The heater was good. When he finished the cigarette, he switched on the wipers, and the frost slid off. He got out and scraped the back window.

He drove out to Bart's, parked and fished his toolset out of the big locking gang box.

Bart had rolled the last course of logs around and formed a rectangle with them. Then he and Du Pré took measurements several times and called them down to Booger Tom. Sides and then diagonals to make sure the thing was square.

They pinned the logs together with big steel bolts and lengths of

222

pipe. After the thing was set, they would heat the green-ash pegs and drive them on in; the dried ash would take on water and swell and hold tight.

Madelaine showed up a little after lunch with a hot pan of rich lamb stew, a big jug of iced tea, and two loaves of the wonderful bread she made every Saturday morning. Good butter from the neighbor's cows.

"Mmmm," said Bart, savoring a mouthful of the stew. "How many bushels of garlic does this have in it?"

"Just a half," said Madelaine. "You work my man too hard."

"Huh?" said Bart.

"Yah," said Madelaine. "You leave him in D.C. He has no money, has to walk the whole way back to the hotel."

"Oh, god," said Bart. "Just shoot me."

"Eat more stew," said Madelaine, "and shut up."

On the way home, Du Pré saw old Benetsee walking down the road toward Toussaint. He stopped and the old man got in, and Du Pré handed over his tobacco pouch and papers to him.

He dropped Benetsee at the bar. Benetsee leaned back in the window and Du Pré just held up his hand and fished twenty dollars out of his jeans and gave it to him.

He will be asleep in Madelaine's garden shed in the morning, Du Pré thought.

I will check the cot and blankets and pillow.

❧ CHAPTER 17 ❧

Du Pré looked at the letter again. It was still there.

The letter was from Lucky, the canoe builder, and it asked Du Pré to please come in the spring, along with Bart, to go on a trip down the Rivière de la Baleine. This was one of the rivers to be dammed.

They go and dam the River of the Whale, Du Pré thought. Well, that is about right.

Do this next late June, as soon as the ice is off the river. There were few settlements of Indians along the river, and no whites. They would have to either be flown out or spend a lot more time going around the shore, including James Bay, but they asked Du Pré to come and bring his fiddle.

"This is for us," Lucky said at the end, "nothing to do with that bastard Chase. Just us bastards."

Du Pré shrugged and got up. He didn't have to decide right now. Maybe he had given enough blood to the insects of Canada. Maybe his head hurt too much.

I mention this to Bart, I end up going. I have to mention this to Bart, they asked me to. I could *forget* to mention it to Bart. No, I could not forget. I wish I was more of a bastard.

Du Pré reached for his coffee cup and winced. He'd driven one of the big chisels into the fork of his left hand. Fifty-two stitches. It was a dumb thing to have done and that hurt more. Never look *away* when you are using a sharp chisel.

Four days before, they had hooked the dragline's cables to a cable cradle and lifted the roof, completely sheathed and shingled, onto the big log house. Bart held his breath. Du Pré held his breath.

"Won't fit," said Booger Tom sourly.

After a little banging and cussing, it fit, and they pegged the top course of logs in.

Bart took everyone out to dinner and gave everybody three days off.

"When something goes that well," he explained, "I think we should stay away for a while and not piss off the spirits. This is big bunga-bunga."

Shaping a joint, the last one that day, Du Pré had hit his hand.

Blood everywhere.

"Don't *bleed* on my house!" Bart had yelled.

Du Pré laughed and made it down the ladder without fainting, which was the point.

On the way to get stitched up, Du Pré vomited.

"Eat another piece of that prime rib there," Bart had said at the table, "fulla red blood cells."

Du Pré had smiled wanly.

But this business on the Rivière de la Baleine, now, Du Pré wanted to go. He liked the name. He had liked Lucky and the other Quebec Indians. Shy people, people of the woods and shadows, who walked pigeon-toed and were only as Catholic as they had to be.

Du Pré drove out to Bart's. Bunga-bunga or not, Bart was busy cleaning the place up. He'd built the rough casing frames for the windows and doors and chain-sawed through the logs. Roofed and with the holes cut the place was looking very good.

There were masons at work inside, laying up stone for the chimney and kitchen exhaust fan and services to go up through, the huge fireplace with the glass front and heat unit. It wasn't a huge house, but it would be very comfortable.

Bart looked tanned and lean. He'd lost the watery alcoholic flesh he had carried for years. His eyes were bright. He smiled easily. Du Pré would catch a flicker of his old sadness sometimes, in the back of his eyes, but never for very long. Maybe it was something he *should* be sad for. He had lost a lot.

"The beautiful and wondrous Michelle Leuci arrives tomorrow afternoon," said Bart.

"You have this done by then?" said Du Pré.

Bart ignored him, thinking of the beautiful Michelle Leuci.

"There is no place near here to get decent flowers," Bart said suddenly.

"Bart," said Du Pré, "you go and get Madelaine and she will find you some things from around here for a bouquet."

Bart looked at Du Pré for a moment, uncomprehending, then he got it and smiled.

Jesus Christ, Du Pré thought, he has got it very bad over that

225

lady. She seems like a nice lady but I think she must be very tough to do what she does and still be very beautiful.

My friend here has been lonely so long, he doesn't know what it's like not to be.

"Just don't buy her the fucking county, Bart," said Du Pré. "She want some of you, I think."

Du Pré saw the sadness flicker, a black flame in the back of Bart, one faint ripple of pain behind his eyes.

"You are some nice guy," said Du Pré. "Just you don't start spending tons of money on her, act like that's all you know how to do. Take her for a horseback ride."

Bart was a very good horseman.

"Take her up on the bench, look for petrified wood."

Du Pré rattled off a list of things the poorest person in Toussaint could do. Bart listened carefully.

"Yeah," he said finally, "I don't know a lot of things, Gabriel. I missed out on them, you know. Other people did them for me. You keep telling me what to do, okay? This is some woman, and I'm not any prize."

Du Pré snorted.

"You are a kind man, Bart," he said finally. "These days, that's a prize. Any day."

Bart walked off and conferred with the masons for a moment, and then he waved to Du Pré and headed off toward the barn. Booger Tom was working a young colt in the round corral.

Bart climbed up on the fence and talked to Booger Tom, who seemed to ignore him. Actually he was just watching the colt.

Bart came back, rubbing his hands hard. Both he and Du Pré got cramps from gripping handles all day, even though they took calcium tabs and ate a lot of cheese.

"I got this letter from Lucky," Du Pré said, remembering. "He wants us to go on a canoe trip next June. Down one of the rivers that this Hydro-Quebec wants to dam, over on the east side of Hudson Bay. The river is called the Rivière de la Baleine.

"The River of the Whale," said Bart softly.

226

"Yeah," said Du Pré.

Bart looked over at him, waiting.

"I will go, I think," said Du Pré. "I think I say no, Benetsee come and tell me to go."

"We will go."

Du Pré nodded.

Bart turned back to his house.

"What color should I paint the door?" he said.

"Red," said Du Pré.

"Red?"

"So ask this Michelle Leuci."

"Michelle . . ." said Bart, savoring the delicious syllables.

"Jesus," said Du Pré, "I can't take more of this. You say hi to her. You act like you been hit between the eyes with a poleaxe."

"I have," said Bart.

"So has she," said Du Pré.

"How so?"

"She is not coming here for the sights," said Du Pré. "You bring her down to the Toussaint bar tonight. I will fiddle, get a few other people. You won't have to talk so much."

"Thanks," said Bart.

Du Pré didn't say anything more.

He went back to his car, trying not to laugh out loud.

✤ CHAPTER 18 ✤

Bart brought Michelle Leuci down to the Toussaint bar about ten. It was good that they had found the bar. Since they were so lost in each other they kept tripping over chairs and knocking over glasses.

Du Pré played the fiddle, someone played the piano, and a guitarist no one knew but who was damn good kept picking icy little bunches of notes in the background. Du Pré didn't much like electric guitars or, for that matter, electricity, but this guy . . .

Madelaine laughed behind her hand at the lovers. She was very happy for Bart, whom she treated with the loving disdain big sisters bestow on their little brothers.

The evening was pleasant. No one got drunk.

Benetsee came in just a half hour before closing, shuffling along, bright black eyes flicking here and there like a smart old bird's.

"Who is that?" said Michelle, leaning over to Du Pré and putting her hand on his.

"That is old Benetsee," said Du Pré. "You remember you asked me about him when I talked to you in Washington?"

"He's the seer, the medicine man," she said. "I need to talk to him."

"Buy him a jug of wine, he talk to you," said Du Pré. The old goat talk to you in riddles and parts of sentences, stories don't make any sense till things happen to you. Let him drive you nuts for a while.

"Bart is going to work a little on the house in the morning," said Detective Leuci, "and I have to talk to you for a while. I would like to talk to him, too."

"Okay," said Du Pré, "I will be at Madelaine's. I will get a jug of that bubble-gum wine he likes."

"Will he be at Madelaine's?"

"He will probably sleep in the garden shed like usually," said Du Pré. "If he doesn't, I know where he lives."

If he ain't either place, ask the fucking coyotes.

Du Pré bought a big jug of cheap wine to go.

Bart and Michelle went off into the night. Pretty soon, Du Pré and Madelaine left, too. Benetsee hadn't said anything to them, he just stood at the back wall, glass in hand, nodding his head to the music, or, when the music stopped, just nodding his head.

Michelle Leuci came rolling up the next morning at nine in Bart's

Land Rover. She was dressed in new outdoor clothing from one of the mail-order houses. She greeted Du Pré and Madelaine with a jar of marmalade made in England.

"I've eaten," she said to Madelaine's offer.

After breakfast, Madelaine started cleaning up. Her children were all off visiting friends or, since the older boys were now pretty damn independent, off hunting. Du Pré took Michelle Leuci to the living room. They carried mugs of coffee.

Du Pré rolled and lit a cigarette, and Michelle pulled a long filter tip from a silver case—Ah, that's Bart there, Du Pré thought—and they smoked for a moment.

"This asshole Chase," said Michelle, "we have nothing on him we can use for a decent case. I am sure in my gut he did it. But we got nothing. We dug around in his past. Rich kid, private schools that he kept getting thrown out of. Tried to burn one down, I understand. Another place he was expelled for killing animals slowly and painfully—dogs and cats. That's two on the sociopath's list of lovely childhood qualities."

"What's a sociopath?" said Du Pré. He didn't know the exact meaning of the word.

"Smarter than hell but cannot grasp that there is anyone in the world but them. No conscience. No empathy with anything. But they are smart, and hard to spot. They *act* human, most of the time, but they aren't."

"They killers?" said Du Pré.

"Sometimes. What I wanted to pump you about was, exactly what was he like on the trip? Starting from day one. What exactly did he do and how did he do it?"

Du Pré recounted the journey. How Chase and his assistants had pretty well retreated into a shell, except for setting up camp and doling out food. How Chase had acted the night the little bear wandered into camp.

"He's a real asshole," said Du Pré.

"Wonder what made him drop the mask," said Leuci, knuckles to mouth.

229

"You know about how he cut in at the end of the trip," said Du Pré. "I told you."

"Was it just him?"

Du Pré thought back.

"The paddlers looked like locals," said Du Pré. "He didn't bring the assistants back with him."

Leuci shook her head. She shut off the little tape recorder and closed her notebook.

"That poor girl," she said, "Annie McRae. Never been in a town of more than a few hundred people. Murdered in Washington, D.C. I am going to nail that bastard's ass to the wall."

Du Pré got up. "You want to see if Benetsee is here?" he said.

"Sure do."

They walked out back to the garden shed. The door was halfway open. Du Pré looked in. The bed had been slept in, but the old man was gone.

"We go out to his place, then," said Du Pré.

Since it was on the way to Bart's, she followed in the Range Rover. She ground the gears a little, not used to a stick shift.

Du Pré parked in front of the old man's shack. No smoke from the chimney. No old fart came to the door, but the old dogs came round the house and wheezed at them till honor was satisfied and they could go lie down someplace warm again.

Du Pré put the jug of wine just inside the front door and closed it.

"I don't know where he would be," Du Pré said. "Listen, if I see him, I tell him that you want to see him."

Detective Sergeant Leuci was looking around the shabby, littered place curiously. She began to walk around back.

Du Pré waited.

"Du Pré!" she called, loud, not frightened.

Du Pré walked round toward her voice.

There was a small stand of apple trees in back of Benetsee's shack, planted there many years ago, not for the apples but to attract deer, who love such fruit. So you could shoot them out the

230

back window. Not so much work then, carrying meat home. The trees were twisted and ill cared for. Their apples were small and wormy.

There was a big black feather twisting on a length of black thread tied to a tree branch. The feather had been painted some.

Oh Christ, Du Pré thought, here we go.

Du Pré caught the feather and jerked, breaking the thread.

There were some tiny daubs of paint bright on the vulture's pinion feather.

Six canoes, four small and two large.

Stick figures, fifteen of them.

Du Pré with his fiddle, Bart bigger than anyone, six Indians with headbands, Chase with his spade beard, the two white women, red hair and brunette. The assistants who were male weren't pictured as human, though.

One was a dog, the other some bird Du Pré had never seen.

"What is it?" said Leuci.

"I don't know," said Du Pré.

✤ CHAPTER 19 ✤

Du Pré followed Michelle toward Bart's log house. He had the painted feather in the inside pocket of his jacket.

That old fart and his damn riddles. But. Perhaps he only knows the riddles, not the answers? I don't want to do so much of the old man's thinking for him, Du Pré thought. I can barely do my own.

The Rover turned off on to the rutted road to the rising house. The heavy trucks had torn the roadbed up and Bart hadn't got round to grading it. Du Pré's car lurched and creaked as he tried to thread his way past any number of places he could high-center on the transmission.

Bart had fixed an aromatic cedar bush to the highest point on the double-pitched roof.

A saw whined inside. A hammer bashed.

Michelle Leuci went on in.

Du Pré finished his smoke, got up, and stumped over the torn earth to a window hole. He leaned in and whistled.

Bart was putting treated-oak brackets on the rafter joints.

"Hey," said Du Pré, "the union says that you got to stop and pay some close attention to pretty ladies."

"Down tools," said Bart, coming down the ladder. He unbuckled his carpenter's belt and dropped it. "Find anything?" he said.

Michelle Leuci nodded her head yes. "But we don't know what."

"You know old Benetsee," said Du Pré. "Drive you crazy, like trying to nail smoke to the wall."

"Would mamselle care to go riding?" said Bart, bowing.

"Only if it is an old and very polite horse," said Michelle Leuci. "I am a city girl. I, uh, have never . . ."

"Oh," said Bart.

"Riding lessons were offered by my parents," Michelle went on solemnly, "but all they could afford was a merry-go-round ticket once in a while.

"Ol' Trapper, do you think, Gabriel?" said Bart. Booger Tom was nowhere in sight, so Bart was really asking a question.

"Oh, yeah," said Du Pré. Trapper was a fine old gentleman of great patience and good manners.

Bart brushed sawdust off his arms, chest, and stomach and then he hugged Michelle.

They went off arm in arm toward the stables.

Du Pré grinned.

He went back to his car and sat there for a moment, turning the black feather with the crude paintings on it this way and that. There is something here that I am not seeing, Du Pré thought. This is what Benetsee sees.

The strange bird. Dogs were a cheerful part of Cree life, but this bird . . . the beak had two deep notches in it. It looked like a mean bird. And long talons.

And a bent neck. Was the bird a killer, or an eater of carrion? Du Pré shook his head. It didn't look like any symbol he knew of, not that he knew that many.

Du Pré walked over toward the horse barn. He knocked loudly on the sliding doors. Maybe Bart and Michelle had hit the hay, real hay.

"Yo," Bart called.

"Michelle," said Du Pré, "I need to maybe sketch part of that feather there, write to Lucky, ask him if it means anything to him."

"Good," she said. "I was going to do the same thing. Normally, I'd take it to the Smithsonian. . . ."

"Yeah," said Du Pré. "Well, every time I talk to an expert, I end up knowing less than I do when I talk to someone who does it."

They laughed. Du Pré went off to his old cruiser. He sat in it a minute while it warmed up and he watched Bart and Michelle ride out. Well, Bart was riding. Michelle, she was having an ass-and-saddle fight like any other novice tight with fear. Trapper glanced back at her and then Du Pré swore the big old bay gelding shrugged.

I've had worse, if you could read horse talk.

When they were perhaps two hundred yards away from the barn, old Booger Tom came out, shaking a little with laughter. The old goat rolled a cigarette. He looked over at Du Pré and nodded.

Du Pré put the cruiser in gear and backed round. He drove forward and lurched and dodged out to the county road through the crater field Bart's service road had become.

High fall. This was the best time of the year, except that the fat-assed drunks from the flat would show up for the opening of the big-game season next Sunday. This was Sunday, so it was two weeks. Well, two weeks was two weeks.

Du Pré despised the out-of-state hunters, like every native.

When he turned on the road leading toward his place, he saw the slumped, boneless shape of Benetsee walking very quickly toward town. The old man could cover country, for sure. He walked pigeon-toed a little, like Catfoot.

Things are looking up, Du Pré thought sourly. First murder I get in my life happened a long time ago and everybody's dead who had much to do with it. Now I got one happens while I am fiddling in front of thousands of people. The woman could have been knifed by anyone who was there and who could now be three thousand miles away.

Du Pré slowed and opened his window.

"Hey," said Du Pré, "you want a ride to somewhere?"

Benetsee slowed and came over to the car. He leaned down. His breath was rosy with alcohol. Sickening.

Du Pré looked up at him. He almost started.

The old man had smeared charcoal in his eye pits.

"Hey," said Du Pré, "you will not go snow-blind now. You have to have snow and a bright day."

Benetsee started.

Du Pré had never seen him off balance.

"Unh," the old man grunted. He was pointing to a wad of bar napkins jammed in Du Pré's diddy box, a weighted tub that fit over the transom.

Du Pré handed him a couple.

Benetsee spat into one and rubbed his eye pits.

"Good," said Du Pré. "Now you just look dirty like usual."

Benetsee went round to the other side of the car, opened the door, and flopped in. He had to slam the door twice to latch it.

"Take me to Stuart's Rock," he said. He seemed to be wheezing, it was hard for him to breathe.

Du Pré drove him there. Stuart's Rock was a chunk of Canada that the glaciers had brought down and dumped on the east side of the Wolf Mountains. It was a pale red and didn't look like the rocks here. It wasn't even that big, just about the size of half a house trailer.

Du Pré pulled off on the verge.

The rock was out in a pasture.

234

Benetsee slipped through the sagging barbed wire and walked over to the rock and climbed up on it. He pulled something from his pocket or maybe the lining of his coat. Du Pré couldn't see what it was.

The old man dropped the thing and then began to whirl it round and round.

Whirrrrrrrrr. Rooaaar.

Bullroarer. Flat piece of wood on a thong.

What's this? Du Pré thought.

The old man kept whirling it, facing to the east.

✦ CHAPTER 20 ✦

Du Pré woke up smelling Madelaine's hair. The phone. The damned telephone was ringing.

Maria, my daughter who lives in the library and I only see by the light of her computer screen? A beer bust? I don't think so.

Du Pré fumbled for the light, got out of bed, went round to the other side, and lifted the receiver. Madelaine stirred.

" 'Lo," he said.

"Du Pré?" It was Michelle Leuci's voice.

"Yes, it is me," said Du Pré.

"Rollie just called," she said. "Another one."

"What other one?" said Du Pré.

"Another murder," said Michelle. "A young woman, an anthropologist from Canada."

"Oh," said Du Pré.

"She was strangled. She had been working late, researching in one of the collections. Now, the security there is tight, so whoever did it had to have the right ID and code cards—if I have that story right."

Du Pré was thinking of Benetsee standing on the Canadian rock with the bullroarer thundering.

"Okay," said Du Pré, "so where was Chase?"

"They're looking for him."

"When did this happen?"

"Sometime early evening," said Michelle. "She was last seen alive about six P.M. The ME's report will take a day or so."

Six would be . . . four here. Jesus Christ.

Du Pré remembered the angle of the sunlight. Benetsee had been there close to four, on that rock.

Goddamn that old man.

"I will try to call Lucky in the morning," Du Pré said. There was a phone number in that letter, he thought.

"Where was she found?"

"Rest room. Apparently the killer was just waiting behind the door. Strangled her with some piece of rawhide."

"Rawhide?" said Du Pré. That stuff was usually pretty stiff.

Michelle said, "Bart's flying me back. . . . Just a minute. He wants to talk to you."

The phone was shuffled.

"Yo," said Bart. "Listen, Gabriel . . ."

"I get your house buttoned up for you," said Du Pré before Bart had a chance to ask. "The doors and windows come, I put the doors on backward and the windows in upside down," said Du Pré.

"Thanks," said Bart, hanging up.

The telephone rang again.

"Yo," said Du Pré.

"Papa," said Maria, "did Bart's lady find you okay?"

"Yes," said Du Pré. "Hey, how come I never see you anymore?"

"I'm sorry, Papa," said Maria. "You know I want to do well there. There will be all of these people went to really good schools, you know, and . . ."

"Yeah," said Du Pré. She will not be a little Métis girl much longer, my Maria. What she wants is not here now. But she will come back.

"Why don't we go on a picnic for lunch, just you and me, eh?" said Maria.

"Yes," said Du Pré. "I miss you."

"I'm sorry, Papa," said Maria softly. She hung up.

Madelaine was sitting up in the bed, mussed and beautiful.

"Who was those?" she asked.

Du Pré told her.

"Lots of nuts in Washington, D.C.," said Madelaine.

At midday, Du Pré pulled up to his house. Maria was sitting on the porch. She had a big hamper, and she was smiling widely. She walked to the car and got in and leaned over and kissed Du Pré on the cheek.

The day was warming. This late in the year, it took some time to get past the night's frost and then the sun was golden. The grasshoppers had died, the mosquitoes, too.

They drove for an hour, all the way to a favorite place, where a spring bubbled up from below a gray-yellow scarp near the barely traveled road. There was a pool there, thick with willows and small, darting trout. Indians centuries ago had carved pictographs in the soft limestone. Vanished peoples, no one knew who they were. There was one worn, dark carving that looked sort of like a Viking ship, but it had been dismissed as a fraud by experts. Still, it looked older than all of the other carvings.

Maria had made tuna salad and a bowl of crudité and had brought some pop for herself and some whiskey for Du Pré.

"It is a lovely day, Papa," said Maria.

He looked at his pretty daughter. I don't understand any of my women, but I am glad they like me, Du Pré thought.

"I know you are working very hard," said Du Pré.

Maria sighed. "I am scared," she said, "I think when I get to the college in the East, I will fail, you know. I hardly know anything."

Du Pré laughed. Maria could read a book and then, months later, tell you what page and paragraph held some obscure bit of information you might have expressed an interest in. Get out of the way, you Muffies and Hilaries, you have little moccasin tracks right up your backs. Not that my daughter will wear moccasins, or has since she was twelve. That was when she tired of going to powwows. Indian bullshit, she had said. Du Pré's eyes opened wide and his brows rose. He was supposed to wash her mouth out with soap, but all he could do was laugh.

Then a couple years later, she had decided to be a badass, wearing torn clothes and boots and chewing gum so loudly she rattled the windows. Got caught with a bunch of kids drinking, maybe doping. Let her schoolwork slide. Ran around with guys so dumb, they'd be in Deer Lodge Prison as soon as the courts could arrange it. A month after their eighteenth birthday, for their thirtieth stolen car.

But that had all changed. When Du Pré was figuring out, slow, since he was so dumb, who had killed Bart Fascelli's long-vanished brother Gianni, Maria had changed. Perhaps she saw the hurt Du Pré had at finding that his father, Catfoot, had done it. Catfoot was dead more than twenty-five years, but it still hurt.

And then Bart had said he'd pay to send her to any school she could get into for as long as she cared to go and kept her grades up.

A straight, bright road from nowhere to the big world.

The dumb boys, the gum, the insolence evaporated. Maria's face was pressed to her computer screen, keyboard, books.

Bart had more money than all but a handful of countries, as nearly as Du Pré could figure it. Almost killed him, but he was doing well.

"What's Bart's girlfriend like?" said Maria.

"I think she is a tough cop with a heart of butter," said Du Pré. "I hope Bart don't fuck it up."

"He will if he starts thinking he's not good enough for her."

"Yes," said Du Pré.

They drove on back home.

Du Pré walked past the living room a couple of hours later. Maria was on the telephone, practically yelling.

"I tell you, you deaf bastard," she said, "you screw this up—I know you, you start to think that you are not good enough for her—*I won't go to college!*"

She slammed the phone down. Du Pré looked at her in awe. He grinned.

"Bart's the kind of guy needs a good woman," said Maria, "so I was just telling him what to do and seeing that he does it."

"Oh," said Du Pré.

"I read his label pretty well," said Maria, "all the fine print, too."

"Oh," said Du Pré again.

Du Pré turned to go.

"Papa," said Maria.

Du Pré halted.

"I read yours well, too. You are both nice men. I love you."

She smiled sunnily.

Du Pré nodded and walked away without saying anything, but he was feeling very lucky.

✤ CHAPTER 21 ✤

I don't know what it s'posed to mean," said Lucky. The phone connection was bad, crackling and hissing.

Du Pré thanked him. He put down the receiver.

I either got no answer or no for an answer, he thought. The Cree and Chippewa do not allow publication of their religious beliefs. Maybe the Black Robes drove them underground.

Du Pré sighed and dialed Michelle Leuci's office number in D.C. She wasn't in. He left a short message. No fish on the line.

Du Pré slapped his palms against his thighs, frustrated.

He took some bourbon out on the porch and sat in the collapsing rocker, staring off across the fields. A red fox came up out of an irrigation ditch, carrying a hen mallard in its mouth.

Probably one wounded by a hunter, Du Pré thought. He wondered if the duck season was open. Then he thought about the news that in Montana, only one deer out of six was shot legally. A Montanan will obey any law he thinks is a good one, when it's convenient to do so.

The telephone rang. Du Pré got up and went inside. It was Michelle.

"No luck," she said. "Well, shit. Frustrating. You know, the woman killed at the festival was killed with a stone knife. Found the tip in one of the wounds. Broke off on a rib."

"What?" said Du Pré.

"What what?"

"What stone knife? What tip?" said Du Pré.

"Lessee," said Michelle. Someone coughed near her phone in passing. "Yeah. Recovered a triangular chunk of obsidian thirty millimeters on a side, approximately."

"You never found the knife," said Du Pré.

"No," said Michelle. "Obviously, it came from one of the collections, but they have so much stuff. Nothing has turned up missing."

"Listen," said Du Pré, "I have this idea. Now, can you find this piece of obsidian?"

"ME's office can, I'm sure."

"I want to know if there is—it should be shaped on two sides. One side will have the broken place on it. What I am saying is that the tip of that knife was *made* to break off. I think it is a *bakihon* knife, Yankton Sioux."

Michelle didn't answer for a moment. Scribbling her notes.

240

"That rawhide the second victim was strangled with?" said Michelle. "Strange stuff. It's made of eelskin."

"Eel skin."

"Could you ask that old man to paint another feather with a few more details in it this time?" said Michelle.

"Uh," said Du Pré. "How is that Bart?"

"Fine," said Michelle. "Listen, we'll call you later."

She hung up.

Du Pré went out again to his rocker and his bourbon.

I am being drawn into this now, Du Pré thought. I feel like I did driving up to Manitoba to get the rest of the story from my Aunty Pauline. Feeling the Red River, down there in the deep gravels. Deep in my blood, too.

Du Pré drove back out to the log house. He'd put in the windows. He put on his belt and grabbed a four-foot level and took the claws of his hammer and broke the metal banding around the prehung doors. Not much to hanging a door if you built everything right, level and plumb. Don't do it right, you had your errors chase you through the house. But the place had been well-found.

Du Pré fiddled with the door's framing for a moment. He walked the door in its finish frame over to one of the exterior openings and wiggled it in.

He pulled shims through to back where he would drive the heavy, small-headed casing nails. He tapped them in till they grabbed a bit of the heavy, rough framing, checked everything for plumb, took a shim, and lifted the latch side of the finish door frame up so there was an even clearance all the way round. He banged the nails home. He set the heads in an eighth of an inch.

Pretty damn good, Du Pré thought. He had a swallow of bourbon and a smoke. It was getting dark. He fired up the motley of photographer's spots on their chrome stands that Bart was using for construction light.

The knife, the knife, the garrote. Obsidian and eelskin.

241

The notch-beaked bird. Old Benetsee with his bullroarer, trying to fend off evil in the east.

The second exterior door took longer, little things, and Du Pré left a dent in the casing. He cursed for a moment, then reflected that the humiliating black dent would fit under the doorstops when he placed the finish mouldings on. Whew.

"Working pretty damn hard for a Sunday evening," said Booger Tom, walking on the booming plywood subfloor in his high-topped boots, custom-made by Wilson's in Livingston.

"Christ," said Du Pré. He'd lost track of the days. So Michelle was working today, and usually he took Madelaine out for some pink wine she liked.

One more door to go.

"Well," said Booger Tom, "just wondered if the lights got left on. I believe I'll go watch a movie and have some drinks."

The old cowboy went out.

The wind rose up like it usually did in the evening. The doors that Du Pré had put up began to rattle and bang. He nailed them shut good and tight, that wind could get maybe eighty miles an hour here real quick, blow the hair off the dogs and the bark off the trees.

One more door to go.

The damn thing was possessed by evil spirits. First Du Pré had to shave a bad spot the planer had missed in the mill where the framing lumber had been sawn. He got the door in finally, but the rough framing was a little off and he had to pull it back out and beat the heavy two-by stock back with a sledge. That fixed that. He set the door.

The wind rattled the door.

Du Pré nailed it shut.

He turned out the lights everywhere but the room where the tools were stored and the table saw sat. He put his belt down on the floor, rolled a smoke, had a pull of bourbon, put on his hat, shrugged into his jacket, and walked toward the front of the log house.

I hope Madelaine isn't too hurt or angry, Du Pré thought.

He pushed on the door. It didn't move.

Du Pré stood back.

Jesus Christ, he thought, I have nailed myself in. All of the doors are nailed shut and all the windows have stops in them to keep them from being left open and then jammed when the house shifts.

Du Pré snorted. He went back to the tool room and got a hacksaw blade. He sawed slowly through the nails, which were hard to reach. The blade kept jamming.

Finally he wore through the last one. He put his fingers in the hole where the doorknob would go and pulled, and it swung open.

He went back and got three nails and a hammer and dragged a bag of concrete over and set it where it would catch the door if it blew open, so the hinges wouldn't get sprung.

Du Pré nailed the front door shut from the outside. He took the hammer with him to the old cruiser. He got in and rolled down the window and spat out on to the yellow earth.

He fumbled for his keys.

A great horned owl hooted from a branch that seemed to be right overhead.

They hoot that close, somebody's gonna die, Catfoot used to say.

Who? Who who who?

✤ CHAPTER 22 ✤

Du Pré banged away on Bart's house for three days, putting down thick pine flooring with long, tempered screws in deep countersunk holes. Later he would tap birch dowels in and cut them off flush. The pine was pitchy and yellow. Bart had had it custom-milled down in Georgia. Du Pré looked at the bill and smiled. The flooring cost more than Du Pré had paid—was still paying—on his house and land.

But it would be pretty.

The thick scent of pine in the house was almost cloying. Du Pré unpinned the windows and propped them open. Add a lot of cedar and you wouldn't need a refrigerator; nothing would ever rot.

From time to time, Du Pré wondered about Michelle and Bart and the big, quiet detective Rollie and the murders and when the next one would be. Where it would be. Who it would be. There would be one, for sure. He had called and warned Michelle, who agreed, frustration rasping the edges of her speech.

"These guys, these serial killers," she said, "it tears you up because they are crafty, and until he makes a mistake, we haven't got much of a chance of connecting. So I wait here or at home for a call telling me another woman has been murdered. And I wonder how many calls like that I am going to get before I find anything. He's right here, in this city, and someone's going to die, and I can't do one fucking thing."

The best they could do was keep a close watch on Paul Chase. But they couldn't get an agent on Chase's turf. The staff had been there a long time. Once Chase went into the building, their only hope was to watch all the exits, but they couldn't. There were too many and some were tunnels underground.

They didn't even have enough on the man to demand a look at his medical records. A call to his shrink was received frostily.

"I don't think that it is Chase," Du Pré had said. "I don't think he got the balls for it."

"It doesn't take balls," said Michelle, "and it's always someone so damned unlikely, no one can believe it when they're caught."

So Du Pré pounded nails and felt like an idiot. He was almost used to it, but sometimes it bothered him, like now.

If I was any dumber, all I'd need would be regular watering and a little shit once in a while, Du Pré thought.

He spent a full day leveling and sanding the high spots on the floor. He vacuumed up the sawdust, covered a dust mop with tack

244

cloths, and made a final pass. He stapled plastic over all the windows and vent holes and went home.

The next morning, he mopped off the last of the dust and rollered the whole floor with expensive epoxy resin. The ventilation was bad and by the time he was through, he was light-headed. He knocked off for the day. At home, he drank one beer, staggered to the kitchen sink, and threw up. He drank as much water as he could stand and spent the rest of the day either guzzling or pissing. By early evening, he felt better.

Oh my God, Du Pré thought, if Bart had done that . . . it might have set him off. I got to talk to him about that.

Bart had gone a long time without going on a tear and he was trying his damnedest. If he does go on one, I will watch over him and not nag, either, Du Pré thought. But I hope that he don't.

He took a long shower, but his skin still reeked of epoxy. So it was in his system. He took Madelaine to the Toussaint bar for her pink wine and some dancing to the jukebox, but he stuck to water. He felt better with each passing moment.

The bar had a lot of people in it; the full moon was up and that seemed to bring people out, brighten them. There were dances and time to time a fight out front in the dusty street, drunks throwing haymakers and falling over.

They went home under the moon in a clear sky. Far from the cities, the air was clear and the sky a velvet blue-black. Some stars burned in bright colors, looked very, very close. They sat on the front porch at Madelaine's for a moment. Suddenly all the coyotes began to sing, arching warbling howls, a language that Du Pré was sure Benetsee spoke as well as he spoke any other.

The howls fell off.

The telephone rang.

Madelaine got up.

Du Pré grabbed her hand.

"That is for me," he said.

"You expecting a call this late?" said Madelaine, smiling.

"Yes," said Du Pré, his stomach clenching, "I guess I am."

"Du Pré," he said as soon as he had the telephone up to his mouth.

"Another," said Michelle. "This time, a secretary who had been working late. She talked a moment with the security guard in the parking structure. He went to the john. He came back. Her car didn't come out, so he went to look. She was lying beside it, with her keys in her hand."

Christ, thought Du Pré. If it was here, I would just shoot this Paul Chase and see if the murders stopped. Even if the murders kept on, we can spare Paul Chase.

"Massive skull fracture, literally popped her eyes out of her head. Left the weapon—a war club, I guess you'd call it."

"You see it?"

"Yeah. ME's got it. It was a round rock like you'd find in a riverbed. Had a handle of something wrapped in rawhide, with a loop at the butt for your wrist. Not your wrist, I'm sorry."

"Yeah," said Du Pré. "I think that's called a *watunk*."

"You know what I'm talking about?"

"Yes," said Du Pré.

"We still have a full tail on Chase, but not only can he slip out of his office, he lives over in Virginia on an estate, complete with wrought-iron fence and rottweilers and electronic security. So I think that's a waste of time and a lot of manpower."

"This secretary wasn't Indian?"

"No," said Michelle. There was a pause. "Right," she said, "I don't know."

"Listen," said Du Pré, "I think maybe I will go and look for Benetsee and talk with him. Last murder, he was here and made me drive him to a medicine place, and he was waving a bullroarer just before the last woman was killed."

"What's a bullroarer?" said Michelle.

"A piece of wood shaped like a narrow shingle, on a thong. You whirl it around and it makes a big noise."

"Never heard of it."

"Maybe Benetsee saw something in his dreams," said Du Pré.

246

"I wish he would just tell us," said Michelle. "People are getting killed here, you know."

"I don't think he can," said Du Pré. "I think maybe he sees the riddle but not the answer. The answer's always there when you look back. But I don't think he is not telling us. I think he is telling us all he knows."

"I'm sorry," said Michelle, "I'm just frustrated."

"Me, too," said Du Pré. "How is Bart?"

"Fine," said Bart.

He's with Michelle, he's fine, Du Pré thought.

"I will go try to find Benetsee," said Du Pré.

"Bring him here," said Michelle.

"He wouldn't go," said Du Pré.

"I thought not," said Michelle.

Du Pré hung up. Madelaine had come in. She was yawning and looking at Du Pré with her eyes half-closed.

"I got to go find Benetsee," he said.

"You got to find me right now," she said, taking his hand. "You can go look for that old goat later."

✤ CHAPTER 23 ✤

Du Pré drove toward Benetsee's shack. The moon washed things white or black. The landscape was ghostly and unmoving.

The old man wasn't there. Du Pré went in, moving gently through the four old dogs, who wheezed in his way. They got his scent and went back to bed. Du Pré felt the stove. It was cold.

That damn old man, Du Pré thought, he always knows when I am coming and plays these games with me.

There is always a point to the games.

So. Where is the old bastard?

The moon is washing him.

The coyotes. Du Pré went to his old cruiser and dug his fiddle out of the trunk and tuned up. The sudden cold skew-jawed the strings. He tuned three times before the strings quit warping off.

Du Pré played his coyote song. He played howls on his fiddle and then he would stop-time and howl. It was a song from the Red River cart days, when the Métis came down from Canada to hunt the buffalo, driving the carts with their big wheels. Drive them buffalo into long, blind corrals and kill them with spears to save the gunpowder for them Sioux. Flesh out the buffalo, hang the sheets of meat on racks made of willow, dry them with fires made of red alder. Fold up the dried meat in rawhide parfleches, go north again, ready for winter.

Du Pré finished and waited.

The coyotes burst into chorus, crescendoed, stopped.

One howl kept going. It came from a cliff a mile or so away, a low one, perhaps fifty feet high. It wavered and sank.

The coyotes sang again, softer this time.

The lone coyote on the cliff howled.

Du Pré walked toward the cliff where Benetsee was. He stopped. Shit. He had forgotten to bring wine. Well, the old man would have to make do with water. Then Du Pré remembered he had a bottle of bourbon in the trunk. He went back and got it. Fiddle in one hand and whiskey in the other. Tobacco. Questions.

The land was stark, the trail a ribbon of pale gold across the white. Sagebrush stood gray, bark white and silver. The grass was dead and it waited for the winter.

Coyotes.

A jackrabbit, coat already going patchy white, dashed in front of Du Pré, a coyote twenty feet behind.

Another coyote be waiting ahead, spell the first one, and that damn rabbit run in a circle till he drop and get eaten, Du Pré thought. He remembered the first time he had seen that story in tracks in the snow.

The trail went to the right of the cliff, up through jumbled slabs of stone. The rattlesnakes would be chilled and sleeping, in huge balls of hundreds in the caves.

Du Pré's head rose above the cliff top. He looked over and saw a bush near the edge of the cliff. The bush stood up.

Du Pré walked toward the old man.

"Ho," said Benetsee. "Long way for a polite young man to come bring an old man some whiskey," he said.

Du Pré shook his head.

"The bottle is too small to be wine," said Benetsee. "So since you are a polite young man and not a cheap one, it must be whiskey, no?"

He took the bottle, cracked the seal, and drank deeply. Du Pré took out his tobacco pouch and rolled them cigarettes.

"This evil man, he don't like the Cree," said Benetsee.

"He only kill the one Cree," said Du Pré.

"Three," said Benetsee. "The woman from the Canada school was half-blood, a Métis. The last one was Métis, too. Red River Breed woman from North Dakota."

No telephone out here in the sagebrush, Du Pré thought. No telephone in his house. I am the second person in Montana to know about this last killing.

Du Pré waited. Benetsee would tell him what he wished to when he wished to. Du Pré went over to the edge of the cliff and slid to the earth in the cross-legged set of the Indian.

They looked out at the sere landscape. A coyote trotted across the field, up to Du Pré's parked car, pissed on a tire, ambled on.

A vee of geese crossed the moon, high up and headed for the Gulf of Mexico.

"I cannot see his face," said Benetsee. "But these women, they pass by me on the way to the Star Trail, and they are weeping. Most of the dead are happy, but they are not."

But the Star Trail isn't Cree, Du Pré thought. I don't know what the Cree think about that. Us Métis, the Jesuits got to us so long ago, we've lost some of our poetry forever.

249

"*Babiche, bakihonnik, watunk*," said Benetsee. Choked, stabbed, and crushed.

"Could you maybe tell me how to find him?" asked Du Pré.

Benetsee sat silently. He lifted chaff between forefinger and thumb and let it dribble, to see what way the imperceptible wind was blowing.

"Used to be an ocean here," said Benetsee, "long time ago."

Du Pré nodded. Yes. Eighty million years ago.

"Métis used to camp over there," he said, pointing to a big stand of willows around a spring that ran clear, sweet water. "You go there and stand sometimes, you can see where the corrals were for the horses. You go in the early spring, you can see where they drove the buffalo. Grass comes up greener where the posts were."

"I can't see him," said Benetsee. "He is in the dark there, hole in the mountain. I can't see him, just I maybe see him when he starts to move, see his eyes gleam. See him rising up, stirring, little bits of shadow. Then the women pass me when they are dead."

Du Pré waited.

"He hates Indians," said Benetsee.

Du Pré nodded. He took the bourbon from Benetsee and had a swig. The burn felt good. It was flat cold out.

"I try to scare him back," Benetsee went on. "Maybe there's another way out of the mountain."

Du Pré waited.

"Maybe that's just where he sleeps," said Benetsee.

Okay.

"How big is the mountain?" said Du Pré.

"Can't tell," said Benetsee.

Okay.

They sat silently.

"You come over to Madelaine's with me, huh?" said Du Pré.

Benetsee didn't say anything. He didn't move.

Du Pré got up, a little stiff.

"I am very tired," he said. "I will go to sleep now, grandfather."

"You going to go there?" said Benetsee.

"I don't know," said Du Pré.

"He just quit till you leave," said Benetsee.

Shit shit shit, Du Pré thought. Now I got to worry I don't go there the bastard be killing Indians because I stay here where I'd rather. Shit shit shit.

"Maybe he don't quit," said Benetsee. "I can't see."

Whew, Du Pré thought. Fucking Washington, D.C. Thank you, you old prick.

"When he's ready again, I'll know," said Benetsee.

"You let me know?" asked Du Pré.

Benetsee shrugged.

Du Pré started to walk away.

"Gabriel!" Benetsee said loudly, his voice young and crisp. If it was *his* voice.

"Yes," said Du Pré.

"He will come looking for you when he's ready," said Benetsee.

Okay, thought Du Pré.

Benetsee tossed something to Du Pré. A smooth round black stone the size of a small plum.

Du Pré wrapped his hand around it. He opened his fingers and looked at it for a moment. He put the stone in his pocket.

Christ, I am tired, he thought.

✤ CHAPTER 24 ✤

Du Pré turned the painted feather in his fingers. Canoes, Indians, a bearded white man, a dog, a bird with a notched beak and talons. He slipped the black steatite carving of the rising wolf from his pocket. The stone was warm from his body and slick as soap.

The jet flew east swiftly. He would land in D.C. in a couple of hours.

Du Pré thought he would rather have come on a horse, but things did not move reasonably this late in the century he had been wrongly born in. Zoom. Flash. TV, movies, computers. Zoom. Shit.

Well, Du Pré had thought, if he is going to come after me, then I will go and spit in his face, maybe he come after me before he kills anybody else—which is fine. I am a good hunter, too. Maybe write a little ballad about it, "The Indian Killer and Catfoot's Son." The asshole wants to play, we'll play.

At least I stir the shit.

Du Pré was unused to such cold anger in himself. He hadn't had a reason to know it was in him till now. D.C. had very tough gun laws, which didn't work except to keep the good people unarmed, so the bad ones had an easier time of it. So Du Pré had no gun, no knife.

I got moccasins and shadows, though.

Benetsee had brought him a pair, plain, all soft leather, unlike the stiff-soled Plains moccasins. The pair Benetsee had given him would wear out walking to the outhouse in Montana. Die of the rocks and cactus. But they were very quiet.

Benetsee had also given Du Pré a little obsidian knife, a ceremonial one, a hole drilled through the handle. It was on a thong around Du Pré's neck.

I am going to a strange land to hunt someone dangerous and all I got is what little I know and some magic an old drunk gave me.

Fair enough.

The plane suddenly lost a lot of altitude and Du Pré's stomach rose up right between his ears. The plane quit plummeting and Du Pré's stomach sank slowly back home.

Horses are mostly nice people and a good way to travel, doesn't put your fucking stomach up between your ears.

Du Pré was going to the capital of the twentieth century and he didn't like either of 'em.

252

Du Pré sipped a little bourbon. He rolled a cigarette. He looked down at the clouds.

The plane made its approach and Du Pré watched the ground rush up, the runway flash by. The engines screamed in reverse. He was there. Stopped. He promised himself he would go home on the train. He was never getting on one of these goddamned things again. His mind was plumb fixed on the subject.

The limousine rolled across the runway to the door. Du Pré came down the stairs, determined never to go up them again. He got in the door the black driver opened for him, feeling embarrassed. He was not comfortable with servants, with being cosseted.

Bart was in the back. He looked great. Du Pré shook his hand as the car pulled away. Bart stared steadily at Du Pré. Du Pré couldn't see that black pain flitting in the back of Bart's eyes.

"You sure this is a good idea?" said Bart.

"Hey," said Du Pré, "you ever round up cattle? Foreman always says the same thing in the dark when you got to get up. Let's do something even if it's wrong."

"Michelle's worried," said Bart.

"Worst thing happens, the world will go on fine without a dumb-ass Red River Breed plays the fiddle some," said Du Pré. "World always goes on fine; it's the only thing it knows how to do. Tears dry up, people forget. So."

"Well," said Bart, "she is at work, wanted to see you as soon as you came in. Officially, she doesn't know about you, understand."

"I walk in her office, she knows," said Du Pré.

"We're having dinner in Norfolk," said Bart. "You ever eat oysters?"

"Plenty times," said Du Pré. He loved oysters.

Du Pré showered at the hotel while Bart spoke softly into the telephone. They got into the limousine and took off, picking up Michelle Leuci in the parking lot of a shopping center several miles away.

She kissed Du Pré on the cheek and squeezed his hand.

"It will be all right," said Gabriel. "Benetsee said so." Not too much of a lie, since Du Pré had no idea what Benetsee thought all right was; the old man's mind and speech were as hard to separate as strands of smoke or the words from a coyote's howl.

"What are you going to do?" said Michelle.

Du Pré just looked at her.

"I maybe commit harassment," said Du Pré. "I'm very ugly in the face, you know, so when I hang it in front of someone else's, it is maybe more than just impolite."

Bart roared with laughter.

Michelle sank back in the seat. After a while, she laughed, too.

"You aren't carrying any gun, are you?" she said suddenly.

Du Pré shook his head. "It is against the law here," he said. "I got a pocketknife my papa made." Du Pré slid the little knife with the blade set in a brass fitting that you unscrewed from the handle and turned around so the blade was out and screwed it back in. The brass came off an old gasoline stove, the steel from a saw blade, and the handle was a hollow tube of Osage orange, the magnificent bow wood that the Plains Indians used. A recurved bow made of this tough wood could send an arrow through a buffalo's chest and clear out the other side.

Michelle looked out the window.

Bart put his arm around her shoulders.

Du Pré wished to Christ they'd get wherever, because he could use a smoke. God meant me to fly, He'd have given me a rocket up my ass. I *hate* this twentieth century, bah.

The limousine stopped in front of a dimly lit restaurant in the old part of the downtown.

"Smoke now," said Michelle. "This place has gone granola on us."

She lit up. Du Pré rolled a smoke and lit it.

"My vices," said Michelle, "are all that separate me from beasts."

Du Pré laughed. They smoked, finished, stepped on the butts.

They went in. It was a place that Du Pré liked, shabby, worn decor that had once been pretty elaborate, a spanking stainless-steel

254

kitchen smack in the middle of the room. The tables were black Formica, and the waiters spread worn, starched tablecloths over them as they seated the customers.

It smelled wonderful.

They ate oysters and crayfish, lobster and cod, peppery coleslaw, and drank lots of iced tea.

"Oh damn," said Du Pré, leaning back, "this is the first thing I have liked about this Washington, D. C."

"I don't know if I could stand all the quiet out there," said Michelle.

"It's actually kinda noisy," said Bart, "just different noises. Not so many bodies hitting the pavement, splat. Automatic gunfire, no."

Bullshit, no automatic-weapons fire, Du Pré thought. I know there is a guy has a P-51 Mustang fighter plane everything works on, including the 20mm cannon. Don't know who he is. Course, schoolkids there don't own machine guns like here. Hmmm. Well, some of them do, but they don't *use* them.

They left. The limousine dropped them in front of the big, expensive hotel that Bart was staying at. Du Pré had a room across the hall.

Late that night, Du Pré slipped out, walked casually through the lobby, nodded at the doorman. He had his old leather suitcase and his old denim jacket over his arm. He walked a mile before he got a cab. He let the cabbie take him to a cheap hotel. He rented a room, listened to the drunk on the crying jag through the thin wall.

The next day, he bought a cheap light blue suit and a silly fedora.

I hate to shave off my mustache, Du Pré thought.

He shaved it off and walked outside.

The wind tickled his upper lip.

✤ CHAPTER 25 ✤

Du Pré walked into the big, gawky building, and he studied the directory until he found Chase's name. The guard directed him down a long corridor.

I am a simple man, Du Pré thought, opening the door to Chase's office, so I will just do a simple thing.

The office was opulent, refurbished with Chase's money, no doubt. An elegant young woman sat at an antique desk. She looked up slowly and smiled.

"May I help you?" she said.

"Paul Chase," said Du Pré.

"He is in a conference at the moment," she said. "And you are . . . ?"

"I am in a hurry at the moment," said Du Pré. He went past her quickly and opened the door wide. Chase wasn't behind his desk. Du Pré stepped inside, hearing the secretary moving behind him.

Chase was on a couch near the wall, screwing one of the women from the summer's expedition.

"Hey, Chase," said Du Pré, "I got something for you. Didn't bring my fiddle, you know."

Du Pré slid the little sculpture of the rising wolf from his pants pocket.

The woman was frantically putting on her clothes.

Chase was thunderstruck, mouth open.

"You see him here?" said Du Pré, advancing. "You see this little sculpture? Means something, yes, Chase?"

Chase slumped momentarily.

The woman ran out the door, buttoning.

The secretary was screaming into her telephone.

Chase had a seizure. His eyes rolled back in his head, his tongue wriggled wildly out of his mouth, his arms and legs jerked.

Du Pré walked out, through the anteroom, opened the door, saw a men's room door across the hall, and went into it. Feet pounded down the hallway, a long run. As soon as they went into the office and were silenced by the thick carpeting, Du Pré stepped back out, jacket over his arm, and went swiftly out a side entrance. The fall air here was crisp and the leaves on the maples yellow and red.

At the hotel, he changed back into his Levi's and boots and left the cheap suit and shoes on the bed.

"What the fuck happened to you?" said Bart, a little angry, when Du Pré came in the door of the hotel suite.

"I . . ." Du Pré said, feeling his naked upper lip, "I got drunk. I shave off my mustache. I got this nice tattoo. . . ."

Bart shook his head.

Du Pré called room service and ordered some cheese and a double bourbon, a few crackers.

He went to a little ice cream table with filigree chairs by the bay window and sat there. The bellboy brought a tray, set it down. Bart handed the youngster a bill and the bellboy left.

Du Pré sat, nibbling and sipping.

"You know, Bart," said Du Pré, "I didn't need to shave off my mustache. I was too hasty there."

I didn't know it would be so simple. Now I got to take shit for it till it grows back out. But my beard, it grows like I use chicken shit for soap. That is my French blood there.

The telephone rang. Bart picked it up and got an earful. He was holding the receiver a good two feet from him. Once in a while, he winced.

"It's for you," Bart said sweetly when whoever was on the other end paused for breath.

Du Pré took it. "Hello, Michelle," he said.

"What the fuck did you do?" she yelled. "You bastard. I had people who were supposed to be watching you!"

257

"Well, yeah," said Du Pré, "but I am a shy man and I don't like to be stared at, you know."

"The paramedics hauled Chase off in straps," she said. "What the fuck did you *do?*"

"I don't think he likes me," said Du Pré. "When he figured out who I was, his eyes rolled up in his head. He foamed."

"Christ," said Michelle Leuci, sounding more like a detective. "I'm sorry."

"It is okay," said Du Pré.

"Well," she said, "don't do that again. Next time, stay where we can see you."

"I will go back to Montana now," said Du Pré.

"What?"

"I am going home," said Du Pré. "It isn't Chase. He was biting his tongue and blood was shooting out of his mouth. It isn't him."

Detective Leuci was silent.

"I'm sorry," said Du Pré.

"He was taken to a private hospital in Virginia," said Michelle.

As long as he was there, nothing would happen, Du Pré thought. Poor Chase, used like a coyote uses a bush. "This guy, I wonder if I have ever seen him. I know that he has seen me."

"What do you mean he has seen you?" said Michelle.

Du Pré had been talking to himself, the mark of people who work alone.

"I have to think some," he said, "and I can't think in cities."

"Nobody can think in cities—just look at the fucking newspaper," said Michelle.

"So I will go home. What I meant was, Benetsee said this evil man would come after me, and I was just wondering if I have ever seen him. Then I thought he must have seen me."

"Why?"

"He was at the festival and I was playing," said Du Pré, "so he has seen me. I don't know him, but he knows me."

"Okay," said Michelle.

"I am pretty blind here," said Du Pré, "like you don't see what there is to see there."

"There?" said Michelle. "There's nothing there but a long view."

"Yes," said Du Pré.

She laughed. "Well," she said, "it's a jumble, for sure."

Du Pré handed the phone back to Bart. He went back to his seat by the window. He looked out at the city street. Panhandlers worked the crowds, who lurched away from them like minnows shying from a turtle. A couple homeless folks, shapeless masses of layered rags, slept off their drunks in the day's dying heat. Papers and plastic cups danced in the breeze. The air felt used.

An ambulance screeched past.

This city is not fun, thought Du Pré. Life could be very terrible here.

He sipped his bourbon. He ate some cheese.

Down below, two cops hauled a ragged, screeching woman toward a car. They held her as far away from them as they could.

Du Pré could hear her screaming, even up this high.

"Michelle said you were planning on going back," said Bart.

Du Pré nodded.

"I'll go, too," said Bart.

"I was going to take the train," said Du Pré.

"Oh bullshit," said Bart. "We can be home in a few hours."

"That's your home, isn't it, now?" said Du Pré. He had a sip of bourbon.

Bart scratched his chin.

"Okay," said Du Pré.

"Let's go," said Bart. He picked up the telephone, dialed.

They were over Kentucky by dark.

When the plane landed in Billings, Bart turned his sad face to Du Pré.

"I've got to go back," he said. "*She's* there, you know."

Du Pré nodded.

❧ CHAPTER 26 ❧

Winter.

Every twenty-five years or so, we get one of these, Du Pré thought. He was standing outside at high noon, in minus-forty cold, the sun pale, watching the column of smoke from his woodstove go straight up for many hundreds of feet.

Second time in my life I have seen sun dogs, Du Pré thought. The sun with its two outriders. The name is nice, sundogs, but they mean weather that kills.

Three of his cattle had died. Frozen, legs locked. They had been seeming just fine, but the black night took them. There was room with the other cattle in the loafing shed, but these chose to wander out to the farthest corner of the field and die on their feet.

Maybe by late March, they'd be thawed enough to skin.

Or maybe just get them into a truck and take them to the landfill.

The coyotes were feeding on the dead cattle a little. But the meat was frozen so hard, even they had trouble with it. Well, if this weather gives the coyotes trouble, it is bad, Du Pré thought, and I have to see if that old fart Benetsee is all right. I am sure that he is, but I have to go see.

He opened the door of his old cruiser. The metal scrawked and the hinges made a sound like fingernails on a blackboard.

Winter is always tough here, but then every once in a while you get one like this and it is an evil god.

One morning Du Pré had gone outdoors, and when he looked at a fencepost, a huge white owl had spread its wings in the pale sun. An Arctic owl, round of head, wings nearly six feet from tip to tip. Du Pré had seen them before, but not very often.

He turned the ignition key and the engine caught at once. He, like everyone else here, had a head-bolt heater plugged into the engine to keep it warm and some heat tape wrapped around the battery.

He set the heater on high and got back out; the exhaust was a needling icy stink in his nostrils. He unplugged the heater and hung the stiff extension cord on a post. He went back inside. No use in even trying to drive the car until it was good and warm. The tires would be frozen hard to the ground.

Du Pré listened to the radio. The schools were all closed. A family over by Harlowton had died when their trailer caught fire. Too many electric heaters on old wiring.

The telephone rang. Du Pré hesitated. Maybe I have already left, he thought.

He picked it up. Goddamned altar boy.

"Christ," said Bart, sounding like he was in the other room, "it is tit cold out there."

"It is that," said Du Pré. "How is that D.C.?"

"Well, about zero," said Bart. "But it's that wet cold goes right through you."

Du Pré thought about the ragged people sleeping outside in their little houses of cheap wine. Jesus.

"I will be out when this breaks," said Bart. "I'm afraid the jet would swoop in for a landing and the wings would break off."

"Yeah," said Du Pré.

"Michelle wanted me to call you and tell you that Chase is still in that hospital. Looks like hell, lost a lot of weight. She doesn't want to call herself. Some sort of political bullshit in the department. So she can say, no, she isn't talking to that asshole out in Montana. And the investigation of the three murders is stalled. But at least we are not asking for help from outsiders. We can fuck this up and do nothing right here in the DCPD."

"Yeah, well," said Du Pré, "like I said I don't think the guy will move till he has Chase to screen him."

"Cold bastard."

"Yeah," said Du Pré. Well, stab, club, strangle are not hobbies for your warmhearted people.

"How's . . ." said Bart, launching into a list of inquiries on the health and well-being of everyone he knew in Montana. He was obviously very lonely. What life he had ever had was here and he was in love with a city girl.

Du Pré hoped it wouldn't tear him up too much.

"Look," said Du Pré, "I am going to check out old Benetsee, so why don't I maybe call you tonight, after I see him. Also, Maria, she asks after you."

"Is she there?" said Bart.

"Sort of," said Du Pré. "She is in front of that computer you gave her. Maybe she has been dead for weeks, all I know. Just a minute."

"Hey," Du Pré yelled at his daughter, who was staring hard at the computer screen, "Maria."

She stirred a little. Du Pré stuck the back of his hand under her nose.

"Remember my smell?" said Du Pré. "I am your friend."

"Christ," said Maria, looking up, eyes narrowing but mouth smiling.

"That Bart, he wants to talk to you. He is lonely and living in a madhouse, so you be nice to him."

When Du Pré shut the door on his way out, she was laughing hard, so Bart must be laughing, too. Good.

The car lurched free, lumps of ice annealed to the tires. Du Pré thumped down the driveway and up the road at a crawl. Until the tires shed their shacklings, he couldn't go more than a few miles an hour for fear of shattering the cold, fragile steel of his tie-rods and steering gears.

A song ran through Du Pré's mind, a song about the cold, clear black nights that came just before the arctic air mass bellied down over the land. The Métis knew what that meant; the song was a prayer, a begging to be spared.

Do not linger too long, oh cruel white queen.

The car jumped. The ice had fallen off the tires. Du Pré sped up. The traction was excellent. It was too cold for a film of water to form between tread and snow. The car held better on this than it did on the rolling gravel of summer.

But this was no time to go in the ditch.

Benetsee's shack sat back in undisturbed snow—no tire tracks or beaten paths, just the little meanderings of winter creatures. Du Pré left his old cruiser running, pulled as far off the road as he could get, and swung his booted feet through the light, crisp snow, rolling like a sailor unused to shore.

The old man opened the door before Du Pré got there. He had a big glass of wine in his hand.

Since he hadn't gone out in three weeks and the whole shack would not hold enough wine to last him for three weeks, Du Pré wondered if the owls were fetching it for him.

Benetsee's four ancient dogs crowded in the door to woof at Du Pré.

The ancient fug in the cabin was chthonic.

Du Pré cleared a pile of old clothes and newspapers yellow with age off a rickety chair and sat down.

"Old man," said Du Pré, "I was worried about you."

Benetsee grinned. He had a few teeth left, randomly protruding from his old bluish gums.

"You know I see my own death, and you aren't in it," said Benetsee. "But it is good to see you. You ought to practice walking."

Riddles again.

"Can you hit a flying bat with a stone from the sling?" asked Benetsee.

Du Pré had forgotten the sling. It was still in his violin case.

Benetsee dug around in a rubbled pile of unrelated junk. He found a deerskin bag. He grunted with pleasure or relief.

"You save these," he said, "for that day."

Du Pré opened the string tie at the top of the bag. He tipped it and six black stone balls a bit more than an inch across rolled out into his palm. The balls had simple incised patterns, no images.

After awhile, Du Pré left.

On the drive to Madelaine's, he wondered if he were falling back in time, like someone going over backward off a steep ladder.

✤ CHAPTER 27 ✤

Bart stumped through the slop. The Black Wind, the Chinook, had come, warm with the Pacific Ocean's heat, and it had hammered down the snow to a thick, wet crust and swelled the streams till they jammed with ice and pooled and flooded the pastures. The cattle were soaked. If another hard arctic cold air mass descended, they'd die, glazed, standing, with grass in their mouths.

He stopped by one of the big picture windows. A dead magpie lay in the mud. It had flown into the window in a high wind and the smash had left a patch of blood and feathers on the unyielding glass.

"If I landscape now," Bart grumbled, "I'll have to use a spoon."

Du Pré nodded. In some places, the county roads were washed out. Over by Miles City, the freeway was closed because an ice dam on the Yellowstone had backed water over it.

"Jesus Christ," said Michelle Leuci, lifting one foot as she leaned against a door frame. She was looking, in some awe, at six inches of gumbo that had attached itself tenaciously to the sole of her boot. The mud was the consistency of peanut butter. It looked like peanut butter made from bleached peanuts.

"We'd best take our boots off inside," said Bart.

"Splinters," said Du Pré.

"You finished the fucking floor," said Bart. "So not a splinter in sight."

They took their boots off and stepped in. Bart picked up a long, sharp splinter immediately. He yelped and sat and peeled off his sock and pulled it out, wincing.

"Good help is hard to find," said Du Pré.

"You're fired," said Bart.

"Poor darling," said Michelle. "You dumb shit."

True love, Du Pré thought. He remembered Bart's swollen, alcohol-bloated face the first time that he saw him. Good going, Bart.

"I still can't get over how right you were," said Michelle, looking at Du Pré. "Chase has been in that loony bin for four months going on five; nothing happens at all. I gather they raked him off the ceiling finally. Drugs. Fried mind. The killer must hate him a lot."

"His money protected him," said Bart. "I know quite a bit about that."

Michelle went to him and put her hand on his shoulder.

"This Lucky says while we have been frozen so bad, they have had the mildest winter anyone ever heard of," said Du Pré. "So I will go when he says, I guess. Runoff in April maybe, instead of June."

"The weather's changing," said Bart.

"Yeah," said Michelle. "You got ten months of it here, and two more of real bad sledding."

"City girl," said Bart.

"I remember the perfume of bus exhaust on summer mornings," said Michelle, "and the muggers hatching in the twilight."

They had come just for the weekend. Michelle was to be on duty first thing Monday morning, two thousand miles away.

"What about your brand work?" said Bart.

"My son-in-law, Raymond, will do that," said Du Pré. "If it is someplace I know funny things happen, I will go with him."

"So you want to do this?" said Bart.

"Sure," said Du Pré. Lot of finish carpentry on this log house. I like the smell of the wood and the way it comes up in your eye when you rub the oil of tung on the finished piece. Catfoot liked making things with his hands—knives, guns, strange machines, fiddles, headless corpses. Oh, fuck it, that shit brother of Bart's *needed* killing. Had me pretty lost there for a while, Bart, too.

"I want some arrows in the roof," said Michelle.

"Huh?" said Bart. Du Pré looked at her.

"I want some fucking arrows in the roof," she said, "or the cops I work with won't believe it is still Montana. They won't believe I ever *came* here. They think the Little Bighorn was last week and you folks beat off Indian attacks every few nights."

"I got drunk in Fort Belknap and got attacked by Indians," said Bart.

"Can't blame them," said Michelle. "I have heard some stories of you drunk."

The telephone rang in the empty house.

Bart went and got it. He pointed to Michelle and held the receiver out to her.

"Leuci," she said. She listened, frowning, her teeth holding her lower lip.

"Jesus Christ," she said, "a whole fucking *week.*"

She listened some more, looking worried.

"Rollie," she said, "unless we have a lot more folks and luck, there's no way we can keep track of him. His estate has too many ways out of it. Look, I'll . . ." She listened again, interrupted.

"You're right," she said. "Okay." She hung up.

"Chase was released a week ago," she said, "been at home. We just found out that he was out. You know how? An announcement in the Smithsonian's newsletter. After an extended illness, Dr. Paul Chase will resume his duties. On Monday."

Du Pré sighed.

"What time does that thing start?" said Bart.

"Four," said Du Pré. He was fiddling in a contest at the Toussaint bar, the long contest ended at the summer all-Montana fiddler's contest in Polson. Du Pré didn't go to Polson anymore, since he'd won twice. It seemed unfair.

Bart pulled a check out of his shirt pocket and gave it to Du Pré.

266

Thirty thousand dollars. Well, he'd have to pay some other subcontractors out of it and who knew what else.

"I am going to set up an account with this," said Du Pré.

"Set up an account, set up three mistresses," said Bart, "I don't give a shit."

"Big talk," said Michelle, "Biiig talk. Madelaine would stop that. Most interestingly."

"I see you there," said Du Pré, turning and walking to his boots. He sat on the doorsill and pulled them on. When he stood up and tried to walk, the heavy mud off-balanced him and he fell back into the door.

"Drunk again," said Bart. "Dock him."

Du Pré made the universal sign for eat shit and die.

He picked up a shingle scrap and scraped. The mud hung on. Finally, it tore free, making a gross sucking sound. The other was easier. He stood up and walked toward his car, platforms rapidly building.

He slumped into the seat and pulled the clabbered boots off. He started the car and drove. Mud stuck to the tires slammed hard against the wheel wells.

This goddamned country, Du Pré thought. It is a *person*.

He got to Madelaine's and parked so he could step out on the grass in his stocking feet.

She met him at the door.

"You have to leap out a window, Du Pré" she said. "Some jealous husband, eh?"

"Gumbo," said Du Pré.

"His name was *Gumbo?*"

"I am wet and tired," said Du Pré. "I want to take a nap and then I got to go fiddle."

"No nap," said Madelaine, taking his hand. "I'll think about maybe you fiddle."

✤ CHAPTER 28 ✤

The Toussaint bar was jammed with people mostly smoking. A blue cloud hung down from the ceiling to the top of the bar. It rasped the lungs and throat and gave the light shape and changings.

Du Pré fiddled. The place grew quiet save for heads nodding in time, feet tapping, and the coughs of the college kids who had made the long journey, only to have their unpolluted lungs and tender little throats seared. Du Pré could see them standing in back as near the open door as they could get. He couldn't laugh; it would make him drop the beat.

One of the Norwegian ranchers from up on the bench played the spoons, clacking and rippling. Du Pré wished for a Cajun with those good ringing rib bones.

He finished. He was sweating from the hard playing and the close, wet air. He went to Madelaine, sitting at a little shelf table built into the wall. He put his fiddle in the case and tried to close it. Something was jammed in the seal where the two halves met. The slingshot. He pulled it out and recoiled it, placed it under the fiddle's neck.

He'd been practicing some, and he was good now some of the time. Then he'd do whatever he thought he'd been doing with it and the stone would fly off forty-five degrees away from whatever he was aiming at. He was trying now to forget the thing in his hand and just look at what he was trying to hit, like a good shot with a rifle. The brain knows more than the mind does.

"You fiddle good, Du Pré," said Madelaine. She turned and looked behind her toward the door. It had opened and a shaft of bright light stabbed through the fug until the door swung to again.

Bart and Michelle were standing there. Michelle had on a simple rough-out leather jacket, jeans, and blue rubber-bottomed boots. She looked stunning. The men in the place gaped just long enough to piss off their women.

Bart and Michelle just stood for a few minutes. They couldn't see. When their eyes adjusted, they looked over and saw Du Pré and Madelaine and moved toward them. Du Pré got up and motioned Michelle to his seat. He and Bart stood.

The college boys were playing some lousy version of "The Red-haired Boy," the beat scotched up by their periodic coughing fits. The crowd went from quietly respectful to telling very loud jokes in two minutes. The kids slunk off, cased their instruments, and left. Du Pré watched in sympathy. They didn't live, the poor things; they only studied on it.

"We have to go in an hour or two," said Bart, "but Michelle wanted to listen to you play."

"I will be playing in maybe ten minutes," said Du Pré.

Bart went off through the crowd and came back with four drinks in his huge hands—bourbon, vodka, sweet pink wine, and club soda for himself.

He looks like he is getting younger, Du Pré thought, maybe growing back through the time that he missed. He is a good man.

Du Pré sipped slowly, and by the time that he finished his drink, the crowd was calling for him. The old Norweigan rancher got out his spoons. Du Pré took out his fiddle and checked the tuning. It was fine. He put rosin on the horsehairs of his bow. He tucked the fiddle under his chin.

Du Pré thought of his blood, the voyageurs, in the dark green wilderness, in canoes. Dark waters, dark songs. Long hard days and bitter weather. One's wages were all too often death. Dark waters flowing past deep green-black stands of trees, packs of furs. He played. He thought of the voyageurs and he let his fingers and bow describe them.

He let the music fade, one long, lonesome note, in the distance of the past.

The crowd did not move or clap. They sat transfixed. Du Pré looked over at Madelaine. Michelle was staring at him wide-eyed, her hand to her mouth.

Entertaining is simple. One up tune, one medium, one down, one up, and so forth. Du Pré played a reel, a dance tune, the happy music that was played at the weddings where the couple jumped over a broom. The priest would be along someday to bless it. No reason to hurt the feelings of God.

The crowd cheered and clapped. Du Pré bowed. He launched into a lament, a song of men homesick for their houses, lovesick for their women, tormented by not knowing if they were still remembered and still loved. When the wind was against the canoes on the homeward voyage, the men said that their girls weren't pulling on the rope to bring them home, they were playing around with the loafers at the home post. Men away from home are all Ulysses hoping for a Penelope.

The rancher with the spoons sat quietly through the sad song. Du Pré held a note and then began to shiver the bow and spark the tempo and he then shot into a fast-tempoed question song, where the fiddle was two people asking sassy questions and giving sassy answers. People began to beat out the time on glasses.

Du Pré looked around the room at his friends and neighbors— young and old, weathered and pale, few teeth or gleaming rows, well-off and poor, faithful or weak. He felt fondness for them all.

I live in a place where you can have personal enemies, Du Pré thought. Sometimes they are more use than your friends.

The door of the bar opened, but Du Pré's eyes were too used to the dark to see who it was. He kept playing. The door closed. He looked down at the floor, bobbing with the rhythm. He closed his eyes and pushed the music hard. He glanced over toward the little table where Madelaine and Bart and Michelle were sitting.

Maria was leaning over, talking to Michelle, who was stuffing her cigarettes into her pocket and looking up at Bart. She looked stricken and angry. Maria stood back.

Michelle practically ran out the door of the saloon. Bart was right behind her.

Du Pré broke off in midstride. He put the fiddle on top of the rickety old piano and rushed toward the door, shoving people out of the way.

Someone else was dead. But who and where?

Du Pré caught up with them at Bart's Rover. Michelle had the cellular telephone in her hand and she was punching frantically at the buttons. She had an unlit cigarette in her mouth and her lighter lit in her moving hand.

"Rollie!" she screamed. "What the fuck . . ."

She listened. Her face crawled and twisted. She put the lighter down on the seat. She bit her lip.

"Shit, Rollie," she said. "Shit."

She listened some more.

"Right now," she said. She turned off the phone.

"Two more," she said. She sounded as if she were speaking underwater.

Du Pré looked down at the mud between his boots.

"Little girls," she said. "Little Indian girls. One eight and one nine."

"I come with you," said Du Pré.

"The fuck you do, Du Pré," said Detective Leuci. "I know how you think. I like it. But you stay right here. You come to D.C. and I will arrest you."

"I didn't say nothing," said Du Pré, angry.

"You didn't have to," said Michelle softly. She got out of the Rover and went to Du Pré and put a hand on his cheek and turned his face to hers. "I know you, Gabriel. No. No. You stay here. Find Benetsee. Stay here. No."

271

Du Pré looked at her, his black eyes burning.

"Bart," said Michelle. "Let's go."

They drove away.

She's right, Du Pré thought as they pulled away.

We both are.

✣ CHAPTER 29 ✣

Benetsee and his dogs were gone. The spring weather was terrible. Every year, it killed flatlanders dressed too lightly. Hypothermia set in, they got disoriented, and they died trying to make fires after they had forgotten how to strike a match.

Only thing to be afraid of here is a cold wind, thought Du Pré.

And other people—some of the time.

He opened the door of Benetsee's stove and thrust a finger down in the ashes. Cold. Settled. So he'd been gone at least three days. Maybe five. It didn't matter. The old man would be fine, wherever he was. He'd come round when he wished to.

I wonder if the Prophets were as much of a pain in the ass, Du Pré thought. Must have been. People killed them for a little peace and quiet.

Du Pré left the jug of wine on the table. He unscrewed the top so that if it froze pink ice would ooze out and the jug wouldn't burst. He rolled a cigarette out of the wind and smoked. He went back out to his tired old cruiser and got in and sat, looking up at the surging sky. The weather was high up. A few mackerel clouds.

He looked at the side of the road. The little pasqueflowers were up. Boil the bulbs down, you got a thick green gum that made a good arrow poison. The first flowers of spring are death. This country is a person.

He drove on toward Bart's new house. The weather had been dry and windy and the mud didn't cling so much. Few more days of wind and sun, it would be dust. Snow, mud, and dust, the three seasons of Montana.

The front door was standing ajar. Du Pré looked at it a moment and wondered if Bart and Michelle had left it so. He took his 9mm from the glove box and racked a round into the chamber. He circled the house, looking for tracks, but all he found were old ones.

He still pushed the door open and went in gun-first. He checked the place out.

All I know about this is from watching cop movies, Du Pré thought. Hope the guy I'm looking for only watches cop movies, too. Even odds.

This is silly, he thought, straightening up.

The air inside the log house was cold and smelled of pitch. Du Pré fired up the rocket heater to take the chill off. He looked at the muddy footprints on the floor. Mine. Bart's big feet. Michelle's. It seemed a long time ago.

The place heated up rapidly. The rocket heater, designed to dry topping compound on sheetrock, threw out a vast amount of heat in very short order. By the time that Du Pré had gotten his tool belt on, the chill was gone, and by the time he had swept the place out, it was getting too warm.

A ton of work—build cabinets, case things out, trim. Won't be able to finish before I got to go with Lucky and them down the River of the Whales.

But I think that it will take a long time for Bart to talk Michelle into leaving her pavement and muggers for sagebrush and coyotes. So I wonder now if Bart will ever live in this house. Play with his dragline again. Maybe he doesn't really like it here, just needed a far place to get well in.

Du Pré switched on the planer and started to feed the pine through, taking it down so he could fair off the window casings. He stared at the blades intently. They could take off the tips of fingers faster than the eye could follow.

The planer screamed.

Someone tapped him on the shoulder. Du Pré whirled, and the piece of wood he let go shot through the planer and slammed through the lower glass of a window before sailing out into the mud. Du Pré was scrabbling for his 9mm.

"Yer phone's ringin'!" yelled Booger Tom. He was looking at Du Pré like Du Pré had three noses. Du Pré remembered he'd laid the 9mm down over by the toolboxes.

Du Pré shut off the planer.

Booger Tom walked out the door, shaking his head and muttering.

Du Pré lifted the phone. He pressed the button.

"Du Pré!" said Michelle. "Christ, I must have let it ring forty times."

"I got to hook a light up to it," said Du Pré. "I was running the planer and I couldn't hear anything." Wouldn't have heard a bear if it walked up and commenced taking a chunk out of my ass.

"Chase has split. We can't find him," said Michelle. "We are going henshit here."

"Oh," said Du Pré.

"Just oh?" said Michelle.

"I don't think it is him," said Du Pré. "The killer, he just uses Chase for cover. Maybe he follows Chase, though. I don't know."

"The little girls were visiting with a school group, both of them were Ojibwa. The teachers and parents who came kept a close eye on them. We still don't know how they got separated, or if one was snatched and then the other."

Du Pré didn't say anything.

"Knife," said Michelle. "The bodies were shoved in a cabinet, a guard noticed blood seeping out the door."

"I can't find Benetsee," said Du Pré. "His dogs are gone, too. He travels, I don't know how. Maybe the trains."

"Is he Métis?" asked Michelle.

"I don't know," said Du Pré. "Sometimes I think he was here before God. He's . . . I don't know."

274

"Chase wouldn't go out there, would he?"

"I don't think so," said Du Pré. "I don't think that he likes me very much. Also, he is a coward, you know. He may be crazy, but he is still a coward. So, no . . ."

"When do you go to Canada?" asked Michelle.

"I go maybe three weeks," said Du Pré. "Whenever I am going, I think I go earlier than I say."

"Good," said Michelle. "Wait a minute." She put her hand over the mouthpiece of the telephone.

"Sorry," she said. "Well, let me know when you do go."

"Sure," said Du Pré.

Du Pré turned the telephone back off. He rolled a cigarette and smoked. He nodded.

He unplugged all the extension cords and dropped his tools in the box. He shrugged into his jacket and tucked the 9mm in the waistband of his pants.

He went out, shutting the door and slipping the wooden block into the hole in the doorframe to block it shut.

He walked over to the bunkhouse and banged on the door. Booger Tom came finally, yawning.

"I have to go away for a while," said Du Pré.

Booger Tom nodded and shut the door.

Du Pré went home and packed. He didn't need a lot. He put the duffel in the trunk of his car. He locked the 9mm in his little gun room off the bedroom.

He drove over to Madelaine's.

The next morning before daylight he drove off. She stood in the doorway in her white nightdress, one hand upraised.

✤ CHAPTER 30 ✤

Du Pré smelled the cedars in the bog. A little stream cut through pale gold sands. He watched a blue jay bright as silks peck at something in the duff.

He reached in his pocket for a rock, put it in the slingshot, whirled it round and let it fly at the ripple of water in the stream, the only disturbance on its surface. The stone sent up a column of water a few inches high. But it had gone where he wished it to.

He was tired. He had been driving for twenty-six hours. He had stopped to practice with the sling. He was too tired to think. A good time to practice, since thinking was unhelpful. He took a few more shots and missed just one, when he began to think about letting go.

He got back in the car and drove on. The road was gravel. He had a case of liquid-rubber repair tubes in the back and four other tires mounted on rims. The snowplows kept the road open year around, but the blades of the plows left steel splinters. He'd had five flat tires since he'd begun.

All this trouble to slip away and travel in shadows, Du Pré thought. But all anyone has to do is wait at the end, for they know where I am going and who with.

But they don't know where I am now. I want them to think I am in D.C. I want whoever it is just not to know where I am. I want them to worry.

He came to an Indian village, a reservation. It was the same. The ramshackle shacks and broken cars, the packs of starving dogs, the little children wild as lynxes, running for cover and looking back with their beautiful ancient black eyes. Fish drying on smoke racks. A huge bearskin on a stretching frame, the rounded-end cordwood

276

tossed onto the stretched skin to stretch it further. Whites paid for big. They were very strange.

Du Pré parked, then got out and stretched, rolled a cigarette. An old person—he couldn't tell man or woman—looked out from the tumbled folds of a filthy blanket with eyes of such deep contempt, Du Pré cast his down.

I am somewhere in Quebec and I don't really know where, Du Pré thought. I know what kind of Quebec I am in, though. The forgotten part and the forgotten people. A quarter of the inmates in Canadian prisons were Indian. Two percent of Canadians were Indian.

And this old person despises breeds, too, Du Pré thought, turning away. I cannot blame them.

He drove on to a roadhouse, where he had a hamburger and fries, malt vinegar to cut the grease. The white owner looked at him, indifferent. Du Pré paid and left.

Lucky's village was another hundred and fifty miles, at the uttermost end of the road—if there was a road. Some of the potholes on this one could swallow a car. The highway funds obviously went to roads the whites had more use for.

Maybe those wrecked cars, they bought them south and drove home once.

Du Pré slept by the road, in a turnout. He woke before dawn with his bladder full. He pissed and steam rose. There were no insects yet. The car was covered in a thick frost. Fogs boiled out of the cedar bogs. This country had been two miles under the ice not so long ago. Lakes and bogs, the leavings of glaciers.

Du Pré liked it. It was thicker with life than his country, but just as tough. The sky hung down here. Out there, it vaulted and one could get crushed under the weight of heaven.

He heard geese overhead, above the mist. Big flights passed, the honking calls swelled and faded. He looked at the shadowed woods. Easy to lie awake at night afraid here, to think of the loup-garou, fell creatures in their inhuman strength, hungry for blood fresh from the throat.

He lit the little gasoline stove, made coffee, heated a can of pork and beans. By the time he was through, the sun was stabbing through the mist. Golden slanting columns. He heard a woodpecker hammering on a dead tree. The eerie rasp of a deadfall stirred by the wind, rubbing on another tree, the noise sharpened by the rosin in the live one. Like the fiddle's bow. *Screeeee*.

Du Pré started the old cruiser and went. He drove slowly, there could well be logging trucks coming.

He came to a crossroads, or rather three-fourths of one. The road he was on dead-ended in it. He turned to the north. Lucky was up there maybe a hundred miles—if the map was okay. He had twenty gallons of gas in jerricans in the trunk. Spare fan belts. A lot of hope.

A huge orange logging truck burst out of a foggy tunnel of trees. The monster was square in the center of the road. The driver made no move to get over. Du Pré looked off to his right. The verge was almost nonexistent. He got as far over as he could and stopped. He slid over and opened the far door and scrambled out and moved down the side of the road toward the implacable barreling truck so that if it did hit his car, it wouldn't push it onto him.

The truck missed Du Pré's old cruiser by inches. The draft of its passing made the old car dance on its springs.

Du Pré ripped off a string of names of no pleasure and gave the trucker the finger. The truck went on and vanished into mist.

The last part of the journey is always the worst, thought Du Pré. And maybe I am going to find this guy who kills Indians at the end of it, and he will maybe try to kill me. I am afraid now, but when I see him before me, I will be angry. Cold and angry. Rage is a binding net.

He carefully got the car back up on the road. The outer tires had begun to knock the lightly packed sand down. Over another foot and he'd have to hitchhike.

Another truck came thundering out of the lightening mist. This driver got as far over on his side as he could. There was plenty of room.

Du Pré wondered if the first guy had eaten too many pocket rockets. Maybe he was just an asshole.

Du Pré was starting up a longish, smooth grade when the top of his fuel pump blew off. The gasoline in the engine compartment flamed up and rubber burned. Du Pré stopped the engine and the car, then grabbed his fire extinguisher and popped the hood open. He had to use a stick to lift the hood. The fire burned low by then, and a shot from the extinguisher put it out.

There, Du Pré thought. Ass fucking end of nowhere in Quebec, where the Indians hate me, the English hate me, and the French think I am a mix of both of the ones *they* hate.

The fire was out. Du Pré stood in the stink, wondering how he'd get to Lucky's village.

He heard a big truck coming from behind him, the orange one. Du Pré cursed and ran for cover.

The truck slowed.

It stopped.

The driver climbed down from the cab.

"Bad," said the man, a stocky French-Canadian with a pock-marked face and a cigarette hanging off his lower lip.

"Could I hitch a ride?" said Du Pré. "Take me just a minute to get what I need."

"We just take the whole thing," said the driver. He clambered up on the trailer and switched on the hydraulic self-loader. He twiddled some levers and the huge steel jaws spread and the boom swung and he grabbed Du Pré's car around the middle, diddled a moment till the tops of the jaws found the frame, and lifted the cruiser up and set it on the trailer.

"Nice paint job there," said the driver. "I was afraid I would maybe scratch it."

Du Pré helped set the chains and boomers.

"How far are you going?" said Du Pré.

"End of the fucking road," said the driver. "If you had looked some English, I would have left you there."

They smoked and didn't talk.

279

✤ CHAPTER 31 ✤

Yeah," said Lucky, "I tried to call you, but your Madelaine, she said that you had already gone. Good that you are here. I need some help to finish this last canoe."

He was helping Du Pré set up a tent. The village was poor and the shacks were crowded.

Far off in the woods, someone was playing a flute.

Grave children watched them put up the tent.

Du Pré felt at home.

It was like this around the fur posts, he thought. God, people must have been poor back then. We can't imagine.

Eloise, Lucky's wife, brought them coffee, hot and thick with sugar. She laughed.

Lucky looked at her.

"I am just happy," she said.

"She's like that," said Lucky.

Du Pré pounded in a stake.

He ate with them that night, some good white fish and vegetables, homemade bread and preserves. He rolled a smoke.

Lucky took Du Pré's pouch and made himself a cigarette.

"We got the same people we had last time 'cept for Françoise, who is going to have this baby."

Du Pré nodded. Women did that.

"Also this Bart," said Lucky, "he called and said he would be here in a week or ten days."

"Good," said Du Pré.

"It's such a bad thing Hydro-Quebec wants to do," said Lucky. "The young people have worked hard to set up their little communities, ban drugs and alcohol, go back to the old ways that were good and use the new ones that are good. Now these dams could destroy that all.''

"The mercury will kill off Hudson Bay," said Eloise. She had lost the hesitant bad grammar of the poor Indian. Du Pré could hear much education in her voice. Poor little Indian girl, indeed.

"There's too much brush where the water backs up," said Lucky, "too expensive to grub out. So they flood it, and the brush chemically will fix mercury into methylmercury compounds. Very lethal, and they concentrate in the food chain. In us. You know about the stuff?''

"Yeah," said Du Pré. He remembered he'd read something. Heavy metals. Mercury was very poisonous.

"New York City needs electrical power," said Lucky. "So they are happy to take our land and lives for it.''

"How did you meet Chase?" said Du Pré suddenly.

"Him." Lucky laughed. "Oh, you know us Chippewa don't allow any publication of our religious beliefs, sue you right now, but we get these people want to find out things. So we tell them a lot of shit, but they can't get any two Chippewa to tell them the same stuff, and if they say anything, we say, That's right, and we sue.''

"Anthropologists," said Lucky. Same tone of voice a housewife uses with the word cockroaches. "When I was a kid, they came to dig up an old burial ground, so old, we didn't know who was in it. What kind of Indians, you know. We think we have been here forever, but our history is brief, if not short. Not much to write in it, you know. My committee at Brown was even half-hoping I'd tell them true Chippewa religious tales.''

Okay, Du Pré thought, Brown is one of the places Maria is thinking of going. Backwoods canoe builder. Sure.

"These anthros dug it up. End of the season, they had a party. All of them wore a human vertebra on a ribbon in their lapel or pinned to their dresses. Disgusting. So they left. So we dug up all the bones and moved them. Buried them simply out of sight.''

"They came back and had a fit," said Eloise, "but no one knew anything. We didn't know if they were Mishtawayawiniwak or not, but they deserved to sleep."

"What's Mishtawa . . . um?" said Du Pré.

"Canadian Chippewa, Cree, Ojibwa," said Lucky. "Our American cousins get pissed off, think we look at them as second-class."

"So we are going down the Rivière de la Baleine," said Lucky. "Brave Indians going up against powerful interests. Actually, Hydro-Quebec is so scared, they have tried to buy us off. They don't want us asking why screw up the River of the Whale? Very bad publicity."

"Asking it sadly from bark canoes," said Eloise. "In good sound bites."

Du Pré howled with laughter.

"You remember when Chase rejoined the expedition for the last mile?" said Lucky. "And we didn't do anything?"

"Not much, anyway," said Eloise.

"We got a couple of reporters really curious," said Lucky.

"We talk to them once in a while."

"They smell a story," said Lucky.

"We only waved it under their noses a little," said Eloise.

"And Bart has helped a lot," said Lucky.

Oh, Du Pré thought, so he is not sitting half-dead with love all of the time. Good.

"He owns some TV stations," said Eloise.

No fucking doubt, thought Du Pré. He has been sober now for a few years and I bet he is just finding out what all he owns. Michelle says, yes, he will own heaven, too.

Which he deserves.

"That Bart, he is something," said Du Pré.

"Come on," said Lucky, "I will show you these canoes. They got left out by mistake and the porcupines chewed them so bad I had to build new ones."

Lucky led Du Pré to a huge wall tent set on a puncheon floor, up on pilings. He fiddled with the tent ties and went inside. Du Pré waited until a gasoline lantern flared. He stepped in. The two big freighters were up on forms, struts and braces pinned and partly lashed. Long coils of braided spruce roots hung from the side poles. Birch bark was stacked cup-down at the far end.

Toolboxes filled with carefully organized shaves and chisels and drawknives. Expensive tools, all with beechwood handles and precise bright grindings on the cutting edges—well-used and well-kept.

"We got about three weeks, and this lacing and steaming the bark takes time," said Lucky. "I could sure use some help."

"You know these murders?" said Du Pré.

Lucky nodded.

"The police think it is Chase. I don't think so. I think that it is someone uses Chase, only strikes when Chase is around."

Lucky looked at Du Pré. He seemed very sad.

"He may come after me," said Du Pré.

I hope he does anyway.

"Well," said Lucky, "don't worry about here. We know everything. Who said he would come after you?"

"Old man I know sees things," said Du Pré. "He's never been wrong."

"I would like to meet him," said Lucky.

Du Pré nodded. Me, I would just like to know where the old bastard is.

Lucky turned down the lantern and they left as the light died.

Du Pré slept deep.

He dreamed of owls and fire, black waters and endless ice, great bears and white wolves, piles of soft furs.

Some fiddle music.

A mountain with a hole in it, like the eyesocket of a skull, something moving back in the mountain, a flash of black eyes in black.

283

♣ CHAPTER 32 ♣

Du Pré spent his days in the pale light and cedar smoke, helping Lucky pitch and fit and lace the canoe skins together. The village pulsed around them. Children stuck their heads under the tent wall to stare solemnly, flitting away like chipmunks at any glance from Du Pré. Lucky could look at them directly, but Du Pré was alien and alarming.

They worked well together, so well that they could ask questions of one another merely by holding up a piece. The other would look at it and nod, or perhaps walk over and point at some confusion.

They ate fish and drank clear water tart with cedar. No alcohol was allowed in the village, but sometimes a drunk would come back from his sad journey to a roadhouse, reeking and eventually ashamed. The people said nothing to the offender. They didn't have to.

Lucky showed Du Pré how to carve the breaker rolls from birch logs, to fit under the scalloped stern. He wouldn't say where he had come upon this design. Du Pré thought it might lessen drag. It might not, too. He didn't know. The freighters were big and clumsy and it was likely enough the breaker rolls were merely cosmetic, but if Lucky's ancestors used them, well, that was a pretty good reason.

Me, I bake my own rosin from spruce pitch from a tree on the south slope. That tree is smart enough to find a spring or it couldn't live. Same way to look for music.

Du Pré liked the fish. The Chippewa were a fishing and trapping culture. They needed vast lands and good waters. He liked the people. They walked pigeon-toed. Some unfortunates were crippled by hip dysplasia. They lived in another time.

Rain. It began as a patter of sleet and little pellets of ice, then rain. Du Pré lay curled in his sleeping bag, the hypnotic sound of the drops on the cloth lulling and gentle.

He woke. He had heard something.

Light danced through the wall of the tent.

The canoe shop was on fire.

Du Pré struggled into his pants and pulled on his pacs and he ran out, shirtless. The cold rain stung his skin.

Flames boiled twenty feet in the air for just a moment, then fell, and the tent cloth was gone. The canoes burned brightly for a while, shed slabs of burning bark, the struts weakened and the canoes fell flaming into the burning floor.

Nothing to do.

Du Pré tried to remember the sound, a whoosh or a whump.

Someone had poured gasoline in there. The fire went up too fast for anything else.

He went back to his tent and got dressed, put on his jacket and hat. He took a good flashlight and started casting about beyond the circle of footprints made by the people who had come to watch helplessly.

"The bastards," said Lucky, "those rotten sons of bitches." He sounded plenty Anglo-Saxon when he was mad.

Du Pré didn't wait to find out who Lucky thought had done it. He moved off into the trees on a trail, stabbing the beam at the bushes to see if anyone had moved through them. He found where a man had come through the brush to the trail and moved off toward the big lake to the east. Du Pré followed the footprints. The man wasn't running, just striding purposefully down to the water. The rain had masked the boat's engine. There would have to have been a plane over there somewhere out of sight, and now it was above these leaking clouds, heading back.

Somebody with a lot of money didn't want this trip to happen.

Du Pré wondered if the Hydro-Quebec people could be such fools. Or had their dealings with the quiet and seemingly despairing Indians given them blinders of contempt?

Lucky and Eloise would go down that damn river on logs and Du Pré on an inner tube if they had to.

Nothing to be done right now, Du Pré thought. I don't got a plane in my backpack, and anyway, I hate to fly.

Lucky and Eloise were smiling, happy, whistling when Du Pré got back. They couldn't have been more joyful.

"We are getting to them," said Lucky. "We are getting to them real good, you bet."

Du Pré squatted on his wet heels. He felt the cold on his ass. He wiped his hands on his shirt, got out his makings, and rolled a cigarette.

"Okay," said Du Pré. "So I guess you had made these canoes to be burned, yes? And you got others?"

Lucky grinned.

"You sure it was them?" said Du Pré.

Lucky's face got hard and then bewildered.

"Who the fuck else would it be?" he said.

"Chase," said Du Pré, "maybe. Maybe someone you haven't thought of."

Lucky looked down, lost.

"You got people, you got politics," said Du Pré. "What are your Chippewa politics?"

"We got some traitors want to sell this place, all of our land," said Lucky, "but they don't live here. They are apples—red out, white in—but I don't think they would do it now. Wait till later. This maybe jacks up the price, you know."

Du Pré nodded.

"The canoes are hidden a few miles downriver from where we take off," said Lucky, "hidden well. Hervé and Guillaume are there and they are armed and very good in the woods. They seem to be fishing, drying fish, anybody sees them. All winter, they were there trapping. We fly to where the canoes are, you see. We won't be stopped."

Du Pré sighed. He thought he should have been told, then he thought it didn't matter. Or was he here because of Bart and Bart's power?

Hmm, Du Pré thought, am I being used or being spared?

Either way, I don't much like it.

Lucky stood up. He peeled off his leather gloves and dropped them carelessly on the big round of wood the maul was buried in. He turned and walked away toward the outhouse.

One glove fell off.

Du Pré picked it up and tossed it on its mate.

He rolled a smoke.

When he lifted the match to his cigarette, he smelled gasoline, very faintly, and the tobacco bloomed with smoke.

❖ CHAPTER 33 ❖

Lucky looked haggard in the TV light. Cameramen elbowed one another viciously for prime shots. Reporters yelled questions.

Burn two canoes in the Canadian bush and you'd think a rock band's plane crashed here or something, Du Pré thought.

Lucky said the expedition would proceed as planned.

Some RCMPs were around, asking questions headed toward blaming the fire on a drunken Indian.

Bart had showed up.

And, while Lucky was being pestered by the reporters, so had Paul Chase.

Du Pré had seen two floatplanes come in and had assumed that they bore more reporters.

287

" 'Lo bro," said Bart, behind him.

They stood watching Lucky. The guy was good. He managed to look both oppressed and fearfully determined.

The other woman from the first trip Du Pré had been on, Françoise, had showed up with the newspeople. She spent her time speaking softly into a small tape recorder.

Bart looked up and stiffened, like a dog at the sight of another on its turf.

Paul Chase was walking toward them, wearing a gleaming white smile nicely set off by his UV parlor tan.

"Hi," he said.

Du Pré wanted to strangle him.

"You're wrong about me," said Chase. He smiled again. It was a smile blank as a clouded moon. His eyes were open too wide.

Bart and Du Pré just stared at him till his smile shriveled and he walked dejectedly away, one more little man cruelly misunderstood by everyone.

Lucky quit talking. The reporters fanned out and began jabbering at anyone who'd stand still for it.

The young woman from the paper who had talked to Du Pré the last time came stalking.

"Who did this?" she said.

Du Pré shrugged.

"Someone who doesn't want this trip to succeed," said Bart.

"Hydro-Quebec?" she asked.

Bart and Du Pré looked at something very interesting very far off.

"Thanks," she said, leaving to grasp more garrulous prey.

"This trip, it will be wet and cold," said Du Pré.

"Yes," said Bart.

"Why are we doing this?" asked Du Pré.

"Yes," said Bart.

"Why are you saying yes yes?" said Du Pré.

"Yes yes," said Bart.

They walked over toward Lucky, who was talking earnestly to the woman from the newspaper. He had a long braided thong in his hands, one with a piece of antler at each end. The leather was smooth and a deep red. He kept running the thong through his hands.

Du Pré and Bart stopped and waited.

"What is that cord made of?" said the reporter.

"Eel skin," said Lucky, "best kind of *babiche*. Very strong."

"Shit," said Bart, whispering, "that's the stuff the killer used on the second victim."

Du Pré nodded. His people hadn't made eel-skin *babiche*. They were a long damn way from eels. He remembered stretching the rawhide and slicing the reims from the hide, lacing up the snowshoes Catfoot made. Varnishing the *babiche* so that it wouldn't get wet and stretch.

I wonder that shit Chase is going to follow along, Du Pré thought.

Probably.

"Did Hydro-Quebec do this?" said the reporter.

"Ask the mountains," said Lucky dryly.

"Why did you choose the Rivière de la Baleine?" said the reporter.

"It's very important to my people," said Lucky.

"Do your people worship whales?" she said.

Lucky stood silent.

"Do they?"

Lucky didn't move.

She scribbled something.

"Du Pré, Bart," said Lucky, suddenly smiling, "let's go get something to eat."

"I have a couple more questions," said the reporter, as though Lucky owed answers to her.

Lucky walked round her. She did not exist.

The three of them headed away from the ruck of people, heads down, each with his own thoughts. The reporter asked a couple more questions, but she got no answers and she gave up.

"Very smart," said Bart. "The River of the Whale. Isn't there a

289

way you could get baby harp seals and the rain forest in on this, too?"

"I don't know what you are talking about," said Lucky. "And I never saw a harp seal in a rain forest on a whale's back. I'd like to."

"Among the primitives," said Bart.

"Chase isn't competent enough to follow us," said Lucky, "so he'd have to hire paddlers, have to have flunkies. What a strange man."

"He may have killed several of your people," said Bart.

Lucky shook his head.

"No," he said. "He is too weak, too frightened."

Du Pré pulled out his pouch. The slingshot came with it. He wadded the thongs and pocket back up and stuck them in his jacket. I must practice where no one can see me, he thought.

Eloise was sitting in the front of the shack. She looked very angry.

Lucky went to her. He put his hand on her shoulder and she covered it with hers.

They murmured in Cree.

Bart and Du Pré walked away.

"We can carry rifles, at least," said Bart. He was always ready to go to war.

Du Pré nodded.

"Michelle sends her best and says if you drown me, she won't have you to supper for at least a month," said Bart, "and she means it."

"What if I pick another way?" said Du Pré.

"I'd have to check," said Bart.

"These Hydro-Quebec people are to spend twenty billion dollars on these dams," said Du Pré, "so I think they plan to make more than that. So with so much money in it I don't think they play fair."

"Capitalism and its absolutes," said Bart.

"Just a bunch of poor Indians," said Du Pré, "who would care?"

"A lot of people would," said Bart, "if they knew about it. That Lucky is one smart man."

The murmuring from the crowd of reporters and cops and Indians changed a little—a different rhythm, different notes. A woman screamed.

Du Pré looked at Bart. They began to walk fast, then ran.

The crowd was standing in a circle, looking down at something on the ground. A Mountie was moving around something, his hat in his hand.

Bart and Du Pré bulled their way through the crowd.

There was a big black raven on the ground, wings flapping.

It had two bleeding notches in its upper beak and one wing was injured.

The Mountie put his hat over the bird and tried to grab it. The bird scratched hard with its feet and the Mountie cursed and dropped it.

The crowd stood and stared.

The bird quit struggling and stared back.

Little ropy crimson strands of blood hung down from the deep notches.

Du Pré picked up a stick, stepped forward, and crushed the bird's skull.

The Mountie opened his mouth. He shut it.

Du Pré picked up the dead raven and looked at the beak.

He was angry, breathing hard, his eyes seeing red.

He heard wings. Night.

Owls.

❖ CHAPTER 34 ❖

Du Pré looked at the little telephone Bart could call anywhere in the world on from anywhere at all in the world.

This twentieth century is a goddamned terminal disease, Du Pré thought. It is getting into every little corner of the world. We left beer cans on the moon. There's no place to run.

Bart handed the little black folding phone to Du Pré.

"Hi," said Detective Leuci. "I bet you hate this thing."

"Yeah," said Du Pré.

"At least you can check in on your trip," she said.

"Yes, Mama," said Du Pré.

"We didn't even know where Chase was," said Michelle. "Aren't we good cops? Guy's like water, any little hole. What do you make of the bird?"

"I don't know," said Du Pré.

"Is Chase going to follow you?"

"I ask him, call you back," said Du Pré.

"We're talking to the Mounties," said Michelle.

Du Pré said nothing. So what the fuck some dumb cops from Montreal or Ottawa going to do for us? This guy is here somewhere, he knows us, and we don't know him. How did Benetsee know about the bird? The bird is not a person, it is a sign, a badge, a calling card, a warning.

One guy with a rifle take us all out sitting on the water like them ducks. We can't get in the water, it will be so cold, we will die in a few minutes. This guy, he knows the bush. This guy is a fox.

"You check out those two guys who were with Chase last summer?" said Du Pré.

"Of course," said Michelle. "Sean St. George and Tim Charteris. Both working on doctorates. Both absolutely clean. Good students, good family, good this, good that. Chase has a lot of weird stuff in his past, but no prosecutions."

"These guys, what are they working on for this doctorate thing?" asked Du Pré.

"Anthropology," said Michelle.

"I didn't think it was rocket science," said Du Pré, and then he felt bad, having been snotty.

"I am sorry," said Du Pré. "I just wondered what exactly they are writing these things on."

Michelle called over to someone, waited.

Du Pré could hear someone reading painfully, limping along a sentence full of words that were beyond his pronunciations.

"Tim Charteris is writing something on the Basque penetration—doo wah—of the Canadian wild. There were Basques there a long time ago."

Du Pré had heard some stories about that, knew a couple of fiddle tunes. The Basques had been killing whales off Newfoundland and Nova Scotia centuries before Columbus had stumbled ashore in Dominica. Very clannish and closemouthed were the Basques. They would set sail from Bilbao and come back with barrels of whale oil and never a word where they got it.

"And St. George is doing something on . . ." She paused, struggling with the word in front of her. "Hungwitching shamanism."

"Hungwitchin," said Du Pré. The People of the Deer. Far, far to the north, in the forests. "Michelle, could you maybe do me a favor? You find out what those Hungwitchin believe in, you know, what they got for a religion, maybe?"

"Okay," said Michelle.

"Also, you could maybe call Madelaine, have her see that old fart Benetsee is around," said Du Pré, wishing to Christ the old fart was right here. Even some of his riddles would help.

Du Pré handed the nasty little black magic object back to Bart, who murmured into it for a while and then folded the talking piece back into it and stuck it in the pocket of his vest, which had about forty, the kind photographers wear to announce that they are photographers. If you filled each pocket, you probably couldn't stand up.

Du Pré was happier in other times. Maybe a rifle, some salt and tea, a horse. Eat your way along. No telephones. You die, you are a skeleton long time before they find you. Now you can't even die, they airlift you out, plug you full of tubes, give you a full set of new organs.

Twentieth century. Bah.

The air still smelled sour. Burned cloth.

293

A few people milled around down by the water. The Mounties were gone. They had taken the bird as evidence.

Maybe it's got microfilm in its gizzard, Du Pré thought, a little videotape. Computer chips.

Shit.

Chase was off by a copse of old spruces, talking earnestly to the woman reporter, who was taking notes, and waving his hands a lot. He saw Du Pré and his speech stumbled. He turned away.

I scare him, thought Du Pré. Good.

But what about his Charteris and St. George? They are not here.

No, I just haven't seen them.

Du Pré rolled a smoke, lit it, and went looking for Lucky.

Lucky and Eloise were in their cabin, going over the checklists of supplies for the trip, arguing in soft voices.

Du Pré found a box and sat on it.

"Anybody camp around here you wouldn't know about it?" said Du Pré.

Lucky shook his head no.

"You *sure?*" said Du Pré.

Lucky shook his head yes.

Du Pré took out one of the soapstone balls and twirled it in his fingers.

A plane? He threw the bird out of a *plane*, Du Pré thought. Shit. So much coming and going.

And I am off and don't look up.

Du Pré went looking for Bart. He left so quickly, Eloise came after him to see what was wrong, followed a ways, shrugged, and went back to the lists.

He couldn't find Bart. Chase was still talking to the woman reporter. Du Pré's eyes locked on him and he started running and so did Chase, leaving the woman shouting a question, pencil poised over paper.

Chase was fast, wearing running shoes and desperation. Du Pré's rubber-soled boots were heavy and not made for such work. Chase made the mistake of looking back and tripped over a downed sapling and crashed into the brush. Du Pré was on him before he could struggle up and get to speed.

Du Pré lifted Chase clear of the ground, rage swelling his strength.

"I am tired of this shit," said Du Pré. "So I tell you, you cock-sucker, anything more happens I come after you, and not to tell you a funny story. I don't care you got anything to do with it or not."

Chase wriggled; his tongue crawled out of his mouth.

Du Pré just held him for a moment and then set him down.

Chase was wheezing hard, like he had asthma.

"DU PRÉ!" Bart yelled, "Goddamn it. Quit!"

Du Pré turned. Bart was standing there, looking stricken.

"I thought you were going to kill him," said Bart, shaking.

"I might," said Du Pré.

Chase ran.

They heard him fall again, hard.

They walked back to the village.

✤ CHAPTER 35 ✤

It took two de Havilland Otters to ferry the gear and the people to the canoes waiting in the malevolent forest along the Rivière de la Baleine. One whale, not two, or many.

The forest below was the color of dark dreams, the kind you rise through to a grateful waking.

The river was past spate, dropping, milky with soil and glacial dust. Du Pré shuddered. The water was cold, cold, cold.

Black soggy trees floated on, barely breaking the surface.

There would be logjams. There would be ice jams.

I live in a goddamned desert, Du Pré fumed. I am never going to go anywhere again that don't have prickly pear cactus in sight.

Lucky was riding up with the pilot. Suddenly, they banked and dropped, flew over a long lake, turned once more, and set down. Du Pré flopped against the belts when the Otter eased down in the water. Waves raced to the shore.

There were three Indians standing on it, their clothes so stained with wood smoke that they were the color of old bark.

Du Pré helped shove the two canoes out of the Otter's belly, one fiberglass freighter, one fiberglass half-ton, and he got down in the big canoe and caught the duffel Lucky tossed to him.

The plane with Bart and Eloise on it set down and taxied to a stop.

Lucky tossed bags swiftly. There was a lot of gear, broken down into fifty-pound nylon bags. Du Pré moved to the smaller canoe. When it was full, he caught the paddle from Lucky and dug for shore. The day was windless. The water was clear. He saw a pike in the weeds on the bottom, broad head pointed toward a school of minnows.

The three Indians waded out till the water got up to their ankles. One caught the painter Du Pré tossed, and pulled the canoe over the gravel and duff till it halted. They unloaded the gear. Lucky nosed in to shore and the other two helped him. By the time they were through, Bart had landed.

Du Pré looked up and saw a dark figure with a rifle behind a bush. Felix. He waved but didn't take his eyes off the far shore or the sky. So Nappy would be with the birch-bark canoes.

An hour later, the Otters were gone and the lake was settling back to glassy smoothness.

They began to portage the gear over a rise to the river's banks. The river had cut down into the rock and soil. The two big bark canoes were moored bow and stern, and a linked boom of logs curved round them.

Du Pré hadn't seen Nappy yet, which was fine.

I don't see him and I know that he is here.

"Any other planes, they come by?" said Du Pré to Felix.

Felix shook his head. "Up thirty thousand feet, maybe," he said. He kept flicking his eyes here and there. "But all they got to do is wait. We just got the one river, you know, goes the one way. So."

Logjams, ice, cold, wet, rain, freeze-dried food, snipers, thought Du Pré. I am not an adventurous man. But I will be one. He thought of the two little girls dead and bleeding in the cabinet.

By sundown, they had the gear and canoes down to the water. They set up a camp. Lucky and Du Pré got the early watch, two to sunrise. They were tired from the flying and the lifting and hauling. Du Pré ate a can of tuna and gnawed at a roll of fruit leather and didn't bother to find any of the Canadian whiskey he had somewhere in the mound of duffel.

He crawled into the tent and slipped off his boots and stuck them outside upside down on the boot stakes. He slid into the bag and after it warmed a little he slipped off his pants and heavy shirt and piled them under the bag's flap for a pillow. The air was damp and close and smoke from the fire wandered in. He woke up sneezing once, then didn't wake until Lucky pulled his foot.

Du Pré went up the river a quarter mile to a sort of blind Nappy had built, a place where he could see a long stretch of water. Lucky was over by the big lake and Guillaume was downstream, high up in a tree so he could actually see the campsite if anyone came into it. Not a really tight arrangement.

This Hydro-Quebec, they probably hire retired commandos, thought Du Pré, shivering in the frost. Why worry, I'll be dead before I know it. He opened the bolt of the hunting rifle and checked the shell in the chamber and the safety.

Benetsee. Benetsee. I need to talk to him, even on Bart's magic telephone. The old man would hate that thing. Any shithead can talk on it from anywhere. Don't need the coyotes and ravens.

Nothing happened all night except that it got damned cold, and when the sun gleamed up in the east and the air inversion began, it sucked all the heat out of Du Pré's body. He was shivering when he walked back to the camp.

They had a hot breakfast of oatmeal and raisins and coffee.

They began to sort and load.

A dead caribou floated past, bloated enough to ride high in the water.

Like the last time, Du Pré and Nappy would ride point and Bart and Bart's magic telephone would ride in the rear. The only person who was on this trip who was inexperienced, Bart could be expected to float past the others if anything happened.

"We dig you a nice grave," said Du Pré.

"Fuck you," said Bart.

Du Pré and Nappy shoved off and floated out to the fastest current. They swung to and headed downriver, getting perhaps a mile ahead of the others, so that if there was a bad spot and they dumped, one or another dripping scout could make it back upriver to warn the rest of the party.

"Let's not go over," said Du Pré to Nappy. "I don't want to do this whole trip with my nuts up between my lungs."

"Yo," said Nappy.

The river was straight and smooth. It cut some, but not much, into the shield rock of eastern Canada, tough granite. The soil was not all that deep and the trees were not as large and more closely bunched than in the great forests to the west.

Hunters would starve here, Du Pré thought. This is some tough country, green or not.

Rafts of slush bobbed in the calmer waters toward the shore.

The forest was silent—no birds, no squirrels chirring indignantly at invaders. The sun rose higher and the fog rose, tendrils and tentacles writhing in the sun.

They hove to at the end of a long, calm stretch and waited till the first of the freighters came into view. The paddlers didn't wave, so everything was all right.

Du Pré's hands were stiff and he had a cramp in the left one, a knotting charley-horse. He pressed hard against the thwart to stretch the muscles.

They ate a little while paddling. When the sun was two hours from setting, Nappy pointed to a flattish meadowland with a couple sand eskers running at the far side. They were even and looked like berms.

"What did these?" said Du Pré to Nappy.

"Old riverbeds used to run on top of the ice," said Nappy.

Tough country, Du Pré thought.

By the time he had finished his cigarette, the other canoes were nosing in.

He went down to help off-load.

He looked at the sky, hoping for ravens.

✤ CHAPTER 36 ✤

They approached the great bay. Two weeks on the river and they had not seen anything threatening. A TV crew had descended once, planes flopping down, but the weather turned nasty and the pilots took off, with the cameramen shooting and cursing.

Du Pré stood up and dropped his pants and mooned them.

"They don't use that on the five o'clock news," said Du Pré.

Nappy nodded; he was giving them the finger.

No nothing. Not a trapper or a fisherman. The season was too late for good fur and too icy for good fishing. The bugs were just beginning to bloom in numbers.

Lucky fretted. He had expected more coverage—more TV crews, more ink, more everything.

"If there is no one there, we did this for nothing," Lucky said. He was so upset, his cup of coffee lopped over the rim.

Maybe this Hydro-Quebec bought everybody off, Du Pré thought. They probably do that sort of thing, they planning to spend $20 billion. Also New York, they need those hot tubs and lights.

Bart was talking to Michelle. Every time they stopped, he punched in a number and there she was, usually. She could call back, too.

No Benetsee, no nothing in Washington, no Paul Chase, who for all they knew was a day behind them or something.

Maybe Chase come busting out of the side waters near the river's mouth, Du Pré thought, but I think they will be waiting for him this time. That woman reporter is nobody's fool.

What a world, this twentieth century. Du Pré tried to think of something he liked about it. He thought of duct tape and the penicillin, since he had gotten a good case of clap once. He couldn't think of anything else right offhand.

There was a town, Kuujjuarapik, just north of the river's mouth.

Maybe two days down the river to the bay, Hudson Bay, shallow and mean with storms and shoal waters.

And then the skies were full of helicopters and little floatplanes and Lucky quit spilling his coffee.

Reporters paddled out in little rafts, helicopters flew down close enough to nearly capsize the canoes.

The party paddled past, smiling. When they pulled into the last camp before the bay, the newspeople converged like flies on a nice cat turd.

A couple of the smarter crews brought food—fresh fruits and vegetables and ice cream, steaks, booze. Bribes.

Du Pré and Nappy still stood watch.

Much easier now for something to happen, maybe, or maybe it would happen down at the bay, or not here in Canada at all. Maybe, Du Pré thought, I am wrong about everything.

Bart wandered out to where Du Pré was sitting, rifle across his knees, with half a bottle of whiskey and a plate of food. He let Du Pré eat and have a couple snorts and then he dialed Madelaine.

"Du Pré!" said Madelaine, "You forget what your Madelaine look like. I see you on the TV! Your clothes need a wash."

"So do I," said Du Pré.

"I can't find Benetsee and no one else can, either," she said.

300

Maybe the old bastard was dead and the coyotes had dragged him to a den and he was just a few stumps of bones. Could be.

But he could have said good-bye somehow. He die, his own time.

What am I doing here?

"Damn," said Du Pré. "I miss you."

"Yeah," said Madelaine. "Since I see you so long ago, my hair gone all white, my tits down to my knees, and I got no teeth."

"My dick fell off," said Du Pré. "I got this fungus."

"You come right home, Du Pré," said Madelaine. "Them Quebec girls can't last."

She hung up.

Du Pré had a tight feeling in his chest.

"Mr. Du Pré," said a woman's voice behind him, "I need to talk to you. We met in York Factory, remember?"

The woman reporter who'd stayed to get the story on Chase.

"Why did you come on this trip?" she asked.

See if I can kill some bastard killed some people, Du Pré thought.

"I wanted to see this country," said Du Pré. "Pretty fine country to drown, you know."

The reporter looked at him.

"What do you think of Hydro-Quebec's plan?" she said.

"I think we have destroyed enough of the world," said Du Pré. "We maybe ought to take better care of it."

"Are you part Indian, Mr. Du Pré?" she asked.

"I am Métis," said Du Pré, "Red River Breed. Twice we rebel against them English. My people came down to Montana from Canada after the second one. Lots of distant relatives up there."

"Is the Métis a tribe?"

Du Pré thought.

"I guess so," he said. "We fight them Sioux and Assiniboine and Gros Ventre pretty good."

"Where is Paul Chase?" she said. "I thought he'd be here at least by now."

So did I.

"I have not seen him," said Du Pré.

301

"You sitting out here with a rifle because of Chase?" she said. "Guy's got no more guts than a Junebug."

"Lots of people don't want us to be doing this," said Du Pré. "There is a lot of money here."

"Tell me about it," she said.

Du Pré rolled a smoke. He felt like a fucking fool.

"I am going back, get some whiskey," said Du Pré.

They walked back toward his tent. The light was bright and the evening cool hadn't started, but it felt like it would frost good tonight.

The reporter took a tin cup of whiskey, nodding at Du Pré.

"What about the murders?" she said.

"Police are working on them," said Du Pré.

"So are you," said the reporter.

"I am just here paddling."

"I come from California," she said. "On the back side of Shasta. Cattle and sheep country. Isn't like California at all. Not many people. My daddy once killed somebody. For trying to molest me when I was a kid."

Du Pré waited.

"He didn't say anything about it and no one pinned it on him and he died without telling me he'd done it. But he had this look in his eyes, Mr. Du Pré. He was out of another time and he had killed someone and he would again and ask no one's leave if he felt it right. You have that same look, Mr. Du Pré."

"I am tired," said Du Pré.

"My card," said the reporter.

Anybody turned up dead, I'd best call, I guess, Du Pré thought.

"I'll see you tomorrow," said the reporter. She was a very pretty woman with very hard green eyes. Laugh lines.

She walked off.

Du Pré stared at the card in his hand.

Helicopters. Lights.

Bullshit.

Frost.

✤ CHAPTER 37 ✤

Lucky had thought only as far as descending the river. When Du Pré asked him what arrangements there were for getting back out, Lucky smiled sunnily and shrugged.

Du Pré was enraged. He went down to the shingle and walked along, kicking stones. Bart came up behind him, laughing.

"It's all right," he said. "I called, they'll be here for us tomorrow. Calm down. Lucky put all his thoughts into the trip and nothing more."

"His goddamn antenna fell down," said Du Pré. He was out of bourbon, too, and there was nothing available in the settlement. The Inuit forbade alcohol.

All the newspeople were gone. There wasn't anything to do.

There is something not right about all of this, Du Pré thought. I am tired and disgusted and I just wish that I was moving somewhere. Just moving.

What's not right? I need Benetsee.

He thought of the mangled, tortured bird. Some sick bastard did that.

That woman reporter, she was right—it is not Chase. He is sick and treacherous, but he is weak.

Du Pré and Bart stood there, smoking. After a while, Bart left Du Pré alone.

Du Pré stared out over the bay; the sun was beginning to set. A flock of ducks in the light, white wing patches flashing. A lone blue heron flapping, long legs dangling behind.

There was some weather coming, low dark cloud on the far horizon.

Du Pré reached in his jacket pocket and found the slingshot. He bent to the shingle and picked up a rounded stone and slung it out over the water. The stone was not balanced, and it curved off to the left before sending up a little tower of water.

His mind was full. He kept slinging stones, kept looking down. Kept thinking but could make no sense of it.

As he began to put the sling away, his hand touched a stone in his pocket. It was almost perfectly spherical, he had found it upriver, drawn to its perfection for the slingshot.

He got off the shingle and began to move through the low shrubs, toward the trees.

A Canada jay sat on the top of a willow.

Du Pré whirled the slingshot.

The bird flew. Du Pré put some arm into the last whirl and popped the thong.

The bird flew and the stone flew, drawn to the same point. A puff of gray and white feathers.

Du Pré's belly sank. The last thing he had thought possible was that he would hit the jay. Now he'd killed something for not one good reason. He poked around in the tree line till he found the crushed bird, blood running from its beak, eyes glazed, skeleton crushed from the rock.

He put the bird up in the fork of a tree so something would find and eat it.

You practice this till you snap like a bow made of bois d'arc, old Benetsee had said. Osage orange, the finest bow wood in North America. Old times, a Sioux would trade a horse and a blanket for a bow of Osage orange. They could drive a killing arrow into the chest of a buffalo or a bear up to the feathers, the nock, sometimes clear on through.

He'd just done that. He remembered the spring, how a ripple of force seemed to have begun at the soles of his feet and flashed to the pocket of the shot fast as an arc of light.

So it was like that. Du Pré had begun to hunt when he was seven, with his father, Catfoot, who started him with a BB gun and worked him up to a .25-20. To this day, Du Pré did not sight a rifle. He just looked with both eyes open at what he was trying to hit and swung and squeezed the trigger. He'd shot antelope at four hundred yards, the good shot which clips the spine from the skull. Running antelope.

What had foxed him was that he was the force behind the stone, his muscles, not the tamped charge of guncotton that pushed a bullet. But it was in a way the same.

I just step back in time ten thousand years, Du Pré thought. This white time, it is very new and not much good for anything but pissing you off. Here I worry about I got to wait a day for a ride out of here. I don't think a thousand years ago I would have been so upset.

He headed back toward the little village and the piles of duffel. He still had some tobacco somewhere in one of his bags.

Bart was sitting on a stump near the pile of duffel, talking and laughing. Must be Michelle. He waved Du Pré over. He handed the phone to him.

"Hello, Gabriel," said Michelle. She sounded clear and crisp. These phones were some sort of magic.

" 'Lo," said Du Pré.

"So you guys made it down all right."

"Yes," said Du Pré. He didn't tell her his thoughts.

"Everything has been mercifully quiet around here," she said. "Oh, the usual ruck of drive-by shootings and all, but I guess that's just a part of American life now."

Yours maybe, Du Pré thought. You drive by and shoot in Montana, you have people shoot back. They got better aim, too, since they aren't moving.

"Will you come here with Bart?" said Michelle.

"I need to get home," said Du Pré. "I got a car parked over at the end of a road. So maybe they drop me off, I don't know."

See my Madelaine. See my home.

He gave the telephone back to Bart and walked away to give Bart some privacy. Though you could hear the big man laughing and talking a long ways off. Well, he was happier than Du Pré had ever seen him.

Du Pré dug around in the duffel till he found the bag with his tobacco in it. He was shoving his hand around the bottom when he hit a flannel shirt with something hand-sized and long in it . . . a bottle of whiskey he had missed.

"There is a God," said Du Pré aloud. I get home, I go to Mass a few times; it will make Madelaine feel better.

Nappy and Felix were putting up a tent. Du Pré went to help them and shared his find with them. They were laughing and tired. It had been a tense trip, wondering about who was off in those dark trees with a scoped rifle maybe.

"This time, each time, I feel like my own shadow," said Nappy. "Wonder why I came on this trip. It does not seem real to me now. I will not remember it until later."

"Uh," Felix added, "Ever' time I go out in that forest, I am some scare, you know, and I go out there all my life."

Du Pré sipped his whiskey, they ate some cold beans and turned in. The trip was over and they were tired because of it.

Just before Du Pré dropped off, he wondered where Lucky and the others were.

Talking with the Inuit, he decided.

✦ CHAPTER 38 ✦

Du Pré looked around Madelaine's kitchen, not quite believing that he was in it.

She stood by the stove in her robe, her hair undone. They'd damn near broken the door to the house down in their haste to get to bed.

She was frying some bacon and eggs for Gabriel.

She turned and smiled at him.

Du Pré couldn't quite believe she was standing right there, either.

My eyes are here in Toussaint, Montana, he thought, and my ass isn't even across the Canadian line.

He looked outside. It was high Montana spring, when the snow turns to mud and the wildflowers erupt.

Benetsee's head went past the window over the kitchen sink.

"Jesus Christ!" said Du Pré. He ran to the back door in his bare feet.

"You old bastard!" Du Pré yelled. "You come in here now. I got to talk with you some now!"

Benetsee stood by a stone planter filled with prickly pear cactus all in blooms of primary colors. He was rocking on his heels and looking at the flowers.

He turned. His eyes looked very sad and old and deep in his head.

"Du Pré," he said. He rocked on his heels. "Du Pré," he said again.

Benetsee followed Du Pré into the kitchen. Madelaine had already poured him a big glass of pink wine. She dished up Du Pré's eggs and then she began to cook some for the old man.

"I need to talk to you and no one can find you," said Du Pré.

Benetsee nodded. He seemed quite unconcerned that no one had been able to find him. He looked off out the window, thinking of something else.

"Pretty bad thing that was done to that raven," said Benetsee.

Du Pré nodded and ate his eggs. He was past wondering how Benetsee knew things he couldn't possibly know. He just did.

And when he didn't, he wouldn't say anything, nothing at all. Not being coy, just not saying anything.

"I saw that man," said Benetsee, "but I couldn't see who it was, it was so dark."

Du Pré ate his eggs. The bird had been mutilated in broad day-

307

light, damn near high noon. But what kind of darkness was he talking about?

Madelaine poured Benetsee some more wine and set the eggs in front of him. Benetsee ate hungrily. He drank the second glass of wine. Madelaine poured him another.

Benetsee looked at Du Pré, unblinking. Du Pré fetched his tobacco pouch and watched the old man roll a smoke.

"I thank you, Madelaine," said Benetsee. She smiled at him.

"I am lost in this," said Du Pré. "I was pretty sure I knew who does these things, but it isn't him, so I don't know. I'm pretty mad."

Benetsee nodded. He stood up.

"He wears funny moccasins," said Benetsee, "they have a soft sole like coat leather maybe."

Du Pré thought on that, but it didn't mean anything to him. Catfoot had worn moccasins a lot. He got them from some relations in Canada. Du Pré tried to remember what they were like and couldn't. So maybe there was a pair or part of one at his house, maybe in the attic or the workshop. Old pieces of leather had uses, if you could get to them before the pack rats did.

Benetsee went outside. Du Pré kissed Madelaine, pulled on his socks and boots, and went after him. The sun was good and warm. He saw a male mountain bluebird flash past, brighter than a clear sky after a rain.

Benetsee was standing by the house, looking at the new leaves on the lilacs. The flower cases would open in a week or so and then the place would be perfumed and the bees would come in numbers.

"You going to play at that music party they have out east?" said Benetsee.

"Guy who runs it don't like me," said Du Pré.

Benetsee nodded.

"This man who kills Indians will be there," said Benetsee.

Christ, Du Pré thought. And fifty thousand other people.

Benetsee put out a gnarled, dirty hand and felt the bark of the lilac. He ran his thumbnail on it and squinted at the spot he'd rubbed.

"I be home now," he said to Du Pré.

"You want a ride?" asked Du Pré.

But Benetsee was walking away, off toward his house maybe, or maybe he would detour a thousand miles, talk to the coyotes.

Du Pré went back inside, feeling tired.

"Du Pré," said Madelaine, "you are a long ways from your Madelaine. Now, you want to find this evil person, I think that you had better, Du Pré. It seems he is owning you some. That is what hate does, Du Pré."

Du Pré started to apologize, but shut up when he realized she wasn't complaining, just stating simple truths.

I want that bastard dead, Du Pré thought.

Rage burned up in him.

We walk under the same sun and share the same night and it's too close.

"I am going to go to that music thing," said Du Pré.

Madelaine nodded.

She had her arms crossed and she was looking down at the floor.

Du Pré went to her and hugged her.

"Thank you," he said.

"So I pray some more for you, Du Pré," she said. "I do that a lot, since you don't pray so much."

Du Pré nodded, holding her.

"I want to go for a drive and see the wildflowers," said Madelaine, "I will leave a note for my kids." Her children, even the younger ones just started in high school, could come home and fix themselves something to eat and do their little chores. Madelaine wouldn't be back very late anyway, but if she was, they'd be fine. The neighbors watched, too. One of the good things about a tiny town. The only unforgivable sin was making too much money.

They drove off toward the Wolf Mountains. The flowers were coming up, not too many blooms yet. The great fields of clover that would splash yellow and red and lavender across the foothills were a couple of weeks from blooming. But the prickly pear had their waxy flowers popped, sometimes five different bright colors in a single patch.

This was the only time of year when there was a lot of water.

Ducks paddled in ponds near the road. Teal, mallards, wood ducks, and the coots ran over the dead mats of vegetation from last year. Geese honked and flew high overhead.

They saw a peregrine drop on a pair of mallards and clobber the male, who fell down a couple hundred feet and was dead long before he hit the earth. The falcon swept in and landed on its prey.

The wind came up and the dead grass danced.

They drove back to Madelaine's.

When Du Pré came in after Madelaine, he took one look at little Suzanne's face and knew.

"This lady called for you," said Suzanne, handing Du Pré a scrap of paper.

Du Pré looked down at Michelle's number.

✤ CHAPTER 39 ✤

Y ou look funny in this rich man's car," said Madelaine. "Too bad about the old police car."

"Yah," said Du Pré, "well, it was gone when I checked and Bart got me home, you know. Then he buys me this thing, I don't want it but maybe I will not hurt his feelings."

"How much this cost?" asked Maria.

"I don't know," said Du Pré. "I think maybe I buy some penny loafers, drive with them on."

"You better be gone now," said Madelaine. "The train is on time you bet."

Maria was off to her summer tutorial before entering college. She had told Bart that she wanted to take the train because she had never been out of Montana and she wanted to see the Midwest. Ride the train through New York and on to Massachusetts.

"Bye, Madelaine," said Maria, leaning over and looking across Du Pré, who was giving Madelaine's hand a squeeze.

"Oh, yah," said Madelaine. "I forgot, I got to talk to you a minute, Du Pré, won't take long. Leave this silly thing running and you come here a minute."

Du Pré got out and he walked to the back of the Rover. Madelaine grabbed his left ear and pulled hard so the ear was down near her mouth.

"I gon' tell you something," she said. "You pay attention some, yes? You go that damn Washingtondeecee. You go play little boy, them canoe up in Canada. You come back. You want to know what happen you are gone?"

"Ah," said Du Pré. "Let go my ear, please."

"Fuck your please," said Madelaine. "I hold on to your ear so you will listen. Now you go off, I get ver' horny you know. It is a sin I know but I get horny and I like to screw and this one, God can keep his opinions himself. Ver' horny. I think about your nice dick and I miss it."

She gave Du Pré's ear a twist.

"Hey!" said Du Pré, "that hurt!"

"Good," said Madelaine. "I want you remember this. So you are gone, Du Pré and I am ver' lonely and I miss you a lot and I love you and I will not fuck nobody else 'cause of that. So where that leave me?"

"I am paying attention," said Du Pré. "Now let go my ear or I stomp on your arch there, your foot."

Madelaine let go of his ear.

"Where that leave me is this," said Madelaine. "I go to Cooper and I go the grocery store and I pick the potatoes over and I find a couple right ones and I come back home and I carve a dick out of them, pretty much like yours. I know your dick pretty good, and I put a nice head on it and everything. Works pretty good you know, but it don't smell right and of course you are not there to tell me funny stories. Breathe in my ear."

Du Pré nodded.

"That Potato Dick best on the second day, it is having some give to it a little, second day is the best, third day it is not smelling so good and out it goes, I got to carve another one."

"Okay," said Du Pré. "I find this bastard I stay here in Montana for a long time."

"You don't belong any other place," said Madelaine. "I worry about you, you come back you got a bad look in your eye."

"Okay," said Du Pré.

"Okay," said Madelaine. "I love you but you are an asshole."

"Okay," said Du Pré.

"Go on now," said Madelaine.

Du Pré got back in the Rover. The rear of it was stacked with Maria's luggage. A lot of her other stuff had already been shipped by parcel carrier.

He turned the Rover around and drove off toward the county road, which would take them north and west so Maria could catch the train in Malta. The southern train through Billings had been shoved off the tracks, long time ago, real stupid thing to do.

"I will miss you, Jacqueline, everybody a lot," said Maria, "I will miss this. I will get very homesick. Real different place, isn't it?"

"Oh, yeah," said Du Pré.

"It is very nice of that Bart do this for me," said Maria. "I won't let him down."

"He wanted to do too much for you," said Du Pré. "But this is good. Now when you get there, you please remember who you are, who your people are now."

"Yes, Papa," said Maria.

"Us Métis we here before anybody," said Du Pré, "long time before that Champlain. We come here a long time gone," said Du Pré, "to be free. We are here before that Champlain, before them

Vikings, too, probably, long time before that Columbus."

"Why?" asked Maria.

"Get away them tax people, them priests," said Du Pré. "They always come along, though."

They rounded the western edge of the Wolf Mountains and looked out on the high rolling plains, big and tough and open. The highway went on straight to the west, miles ahead, they would crest a long grade and see another rising and the horizon twenty miles away.

Red cedars in the draws and clinging to the rocks, cattle grazing, the quick flash of white from the rumps of antelope headed for safety. Buzzards circled over north, lowering down on a dead animal out of sight in the folded land.

"I got to go," said Maria, "but I know I will sometimes be on my bed back there crying. It is different, huh? Everything close together and a lot of people."

"Oh, yes," said Du Pré. "Every breath of air been used five, six times before you get it."

"Oh, Papa."

"Pretty dangerous, too, you be careful where you go. It is not like here, someone watching you all the time."

"I like that," said Maria. "You know here I get in trouble because I am standing next to a guy drinking beer, I got to go talk to that puke Bucky Dassault, there."

"Well," said Du Pré, "not any fun but you don't do it again."

"I don't get *caught* again?" said Maria.

I cannot ask no more, Du Pré thought, my beautiful young daughter here is going off to that fancy school and she will come back to visit sure enough but I won't see her again. This is pretty bad, I got a lump in my throat like the one the day I drop her off at her first kindergarten school.

She run home from that. I ask her, you scared, she say, no, I am some *bored*. She already knew how to read. I take her back she bite that little Gary Klein so they have to send her home. I give up, send her to the first grade. The next year.

I am all my life being a father cutting deals with my daughters. They always win. I am glad they like me all right, they didn't I would be long *dead*.

My wife died such a long time ago, but I can see her in their faces and I had my great luck, Madelaine.

I don't understand any of my women.

They passed several cattle herds being moved down the verge of the road, to new pastures. The cowboys waved and the heeler dogs scuttled round, nipping at the hooves of the laggards, barking and jumping.

One of them gave Du Pré and Maria the finger.

"Why he do that, Papa?" asked Maria.

"Oh," said Du Pré, "it is this dumb silly Rover that Bart bought for me, it looks like a car those flatlanders with a lot of money buy, move here, screw everything up. We lucky he don't shoot at us."

"All changing," said Maria.

"Always does," said Du Pré.

"I wonder what will be left when I come back," said Maria.

"Land, it always stays the same," said Du Pré. "Not much that we can do about it, bad as we get. But the people on it and their hearts, they change a lot, this is a bad time, now."

They drove a while, silent. Magpies lifted up from the carcasses of squashed rabbits and then settled when the Rover passed. Once a huge porcupine stopped them dead in the road, the ancient animal waddling across the asphalt. He was headed for the trees down by a little pond below the road grade.

They passed through a cut in the yellow-gray limestone, the bed of the sea which had run from the Gulf of Mexico to the Arctic Ocean so long ago, and now was mountains, some rising even beneath the plains.

There was a flat pan of sagebrush and scrubgrass ahead. The road ran straight as a taut string.

There were four animals on the right side of the road, each about a hundred yards apart from the others. One two three four.

Coyotes.

314

"Damn," said Maria, "I have never seen that in the daylight for sure!"

Du Pré slowed. They passed the first coyote and as soon as they did the animal turned and trotted out of sight. So did the next three.

"Benetsee", said Du Pre, "I think he say so long to you."

"Ah," said Maria. "But I will be back."

He knows more than you, my child, thought Du Pré, you will visit but you will never return.

They got to the train station a couple hours later. The train was on time and Du Pré loaded Maria up and he kissed her and it pulled away, Maria waving till Du Pré couldn't see her any more.

He drove back home.

He stopped in Cooper and bought Madelaine three big very long potatoes.

✤ CHAPTER 40 ✤

The phone rang at Bart's house. Du Pré knew. He swore and picked it up.

"He was strangled," said Michelle. "Guy named David Ross, a linguist. Specialized in the dialects of Cree and Chippewa, and he was working on some rare dialect when this happened."

"Where did it happen?" asked Du Pré. He remembered the smell of the halls in the Smithsonian.

"In the parking garage under Ross's apartment," said Michelle. "At about two A.M. We think that the killer was waiting for him. He was found about six by another tenant. Lying right by his car. The keys were on the floor nearby."

"Why do you think he was waiting?"

"There's a good place nearby," said Michelle. "The door is electronic and quick. Good lighting. No place outside to hide near enough to dash in in time."

"I am coming to that music festival," said Du Pré.

"I thought you would," said Detective Leuci. "Remember how strict our gun laws are. Also remember that D.C. isn't fucking Tombstone."

"Yeah," said Du Pré.

"If you can find him, I'll take care of the rest," said Michelle.

"I am very confused," said Du Pré, "which is a good sign."

"Yeah?"

"Uh-huh," said Du Pré. "It means maybe Benetsee will help me out." He didn't mention anything that Benetsee had already told him.

"Well," said Du Pré, "how is that Bart?"

"He," said Detective Leuci, "is a sweet man."

"You let me know anything else?" said Du Pré.

"If you will do the same," said Michelle. She was reading him.

"Okay," said Du Pré. "Benetsee said he saw the man who mangled that bird. He wore moccasins."

Detective Leuci was very silent.

"I have been thinking it is not Chase," said Du Pré. "He is too weak."

More silence.

"So you are not telling me everything, either," said Du Pré.

"I can't," said Michelle.

"Okay," said Du Pré. "But if you don't tell me and it puts my people here in danger, I will be very angry."

"Call me at home after eleven my time," said Detective Leuci.

She hung up.

Du Pré walked out to the kitchen.

"I got to go to my place a little while, look for something," he said, "You feed your kids and I take you out, big fun, a cheeseburger and some pink wine, maybe french fries."

"It is Friday, Du Pré," said Madelaine. "Tonight they have some fish and the prime rib, you know."

316

Du Pré had forgotten what day of the week it was.

"Okay," he said. "You can be Catholic and have the fish and I will have the prime rib."

"I am not that kind of Catholic," said Madelaine. "My God don't worry about what you eat, just what's in your heart." She was chopping cabbage for coleslaw.

Du Pré went out to his old car and started it and drove out to his place. He hadn't been there in over six weeks, but it was spruce and well tended, his daughter Jacqueline and her man, Raymond, watched it. There was a light burning inside.

Jesus, Du Pré thought, even the windows have been washed.

And I need to talk to my Maria, too, I have forgot her off at that fancy college.

On Friday night, Maria would be off having some good time, Du Pré thought. I tell myself that, anyway.

He walked round back and opened up the long shed where the tools and workbench were. The doors slid open easily—that Raymond had oiled the tracks, too. The workbench was covered in dust marked with pack rat tracks.

The joists overhead were holding a bunch of slowly rotting wood crates. Du Pré couldn't remember if they'd ever been moved since his parents had been killed by the train thirty years ago almost.

He dug round under the bench for a moment, but all he found were boxes full of little scraps of wood and cans of nails.

He went outside to the overhang and lifted a stepladder down and dragged it back in and unfolded it. The ladder was so old and the joints so weak, it was like trying to climb a staggering drunk. Du Pré caught hold of a joist and pulled himself up. He reached up and felt for the top of the box. There wasn't one.

He hauled himself up farther and then he swung up on the joists. It was cramped against the shed roof. He started digging around in the boxes, which were dusty, an inch of dust, and crosshatched with old cobwebs.

The last box held what he was looking for. Well, it's always the last box, yes?

317

Du Pré was sneezing from the dust. But he'd spotted Catfoot's old leather-working kit, a sheet-metal box with a leather handle now completely gnawed away. He tried to haul the box back to the ladder, thought about it, and then just jimmied it till it fell through and crashed on the floor.

Dust blew up like the thing had a powder charge in it.

Du Pré swung down, held onto the joist till he leveled, and dropped the two feet to the floor. He went outside, sneezing, then back in and dragged the box out onto the ground. The air in the shed was half earth.

The fall had shaken things loose. Du Pré saw some rat-gnawed coils of old dried *babiche*, a folded half hide of reddish brown leather cracked with age, and the metal kit. He poked around in the withered scraps and couldn't find anything like what he was looking for. The old shoes and boots and moccasins . . . had he given them to the church for the poor? It was so damn long ago.

I must have, he thought. I gave all the clothes to the church.

He remembered Catfoot making moccasin soles from the neck hide of bulls. Thick stuff, he cured it some way, not the *babiche* way, some other way.

There is something here.

Nothing.

Du Pré fiddled with the trunk latches Catfoot had brazed onto the sheet-metal box. He lifted the lid.

There was a pair of moccasin soles, grayish white and half an inch thick, already buck-punched off at an angle all the way around, ready to lace the uppers to.

The bottom of the box was a welter of leather-working tools, hole punches and needles and little knives and awls.

Du Pré piled all the old leather back in the box and took out the leather-working kit and then put the box in the shed and took the kit to his house. He went to the bathroom and looked in the mirror.

He was all-over gunmetal and ocher from the dust.

He stripped and showered and found some clean clothes in his bedroom. Everything smelled a little musty and unused.

"I will drive fast and blow off the stink," he said aloud as he got into his car, after putting the leather kit in the trunk. Madelaine was waiting, all pretty, wearing her red silk dress. They went down to the Toussaint bar and had supper. Madelaine drank some pink wine and Du Pré sipped bourbon. He was beginning to feel maybe half-way home.

❧ CHAPTER 41 ❧

Well, the libraries around here are not too good," said Du Pré to Maria. She sounded as if she was in the next room—miracles of modern electronics.

"Okay Papa," she said happily, "now what exactly do you need to know?"

"The moccasins your grandpapa made, they are a Plains mocca-sin," said Du Pré, "and I think maybe the moccasins that the Woodland peoples make are different. I seem to remember some-thing, but I don't know how and why they are different."

"Which Woodland peoples?" said Maria.

"Cree, Chippewa, Ojibwa," said Du Pré.

"I could send these by computer," said Maria.

"Just tell me over the telephone," said Du Pré, "and quit your messing with your old father. I don't like those computers. It is so no one can even use a summer name anymore."

"What's a summer name?" said Maria.

"It is the name a cowboy uses when he doesn't want folks to find him," said Du Pré.

"Okay," said Maria, "I will go find out. I'll call you at Made-laine's if you are not at home. How is Jacqueline, my nieces and nephews?"

"There are two more of each since you left," said Du Pré.

"Papa!"

"Okay." He hung up.

Computers. Christ.

He went outside and stared at his four horses in the pasture.

I don't even like *cars*, Du Pré thought. You can't talk to them when you ride somewhere.

But he got in his and drove out toward Benetsee's. He parked and got out and went to the front door of the old man's shack and knocked. No answer. He went around back.

Benetsee was digging a grave for one of his old dogs. The dead animal was on the ground, near a bull pine. The old man was chiseling away at the hard soil.

"Hey," said Du Pré, "I am sorry about old . . .". He couldn't remember the old dog's name.

"He was a good dog," said Benetsee, "but he got old and died."

"You want some help there?" said Du Pré.

Benetsee stopped digging and put both his hands on the end of the shovel handle.

"When I get old and die, then you can help," he said.

Du Pré looked at Benetsee; the old man looked back. Then they laughed.

Du Pré smoked while Benetsee dug a hole for his dog.

"All that matters, those moccasins," said Benetsee, "is that they are very quiet, you know."

What I get for thinking it is complicated, Du Pré thought.

"This man," said Benetsee, "he walks like an Indian—toes in, you know."

"He Indian?" said Du Pré.

"He walks like one," said Benetsee. He slid the body of his dog into the grave and pushed earth on top of it. Then he began to pile rocks over the turned earth. When Du Pré helped, he didn't say anything.

The rocks would keep out the skunks and coyotes.

Benetsee whistled something in a pentatonic scale. He put out a hand and Du Pré gave him his tobacco pouch. The old man took four pinches and dribbled them over the grave while he muttered under his breath.

"He was some good dog, yes," said Benetsee as they walked back to the front of the shack. Du Pré carried the shovel. He saw two nails on the siding about the right height and he hung the shovel up.

"I show you how this man move," said Benetsee.

And he changed. The old man became coiled and supple. He moved across the littered yard like a stalking fox or bobcat. One foot reached out and gently took the earth, then the other; the old man crouched and his hands were out in front and loose.

He did not spring; he rushed smoothly forward and grabbed his prey rising.

Benetsee had something in his hand—a thong, weighted at the end with a stone.

A garrote.

Benetsee moved his hands a little and a knife appeared in the right one.

"You see?" said Benetsee.

Du Pré nodded. I see plenty good now.

Benetsee walked to Du Pré, like the fox, like the cat. His left hand shot out and grabbed Du Pré's wrist; his grip was hard, his palm callused.

"You know him now when you see him," said Benetsee. "Maybe not the first time, but you suddenly know. He will know you know. You better kill him then quick. He sure gonna try to kill you."

"I hope so," said Du Pré. He was very angry.

"Don't be brave talker," said Benetsee. "You better ask for some help right then."

"What kind of help?"

"Help for your heart," said Benetsee. "When fox hunt a mouse, he don't get mad about it."

Du Pré nodded.

Benetsee took Du Pré's arm, led him to his shack, went in, came out with a bundle. He unwrapped the dark brown deerskin. A pair of moccasins with soft, high leggins, soft soles.

"This all I can help you. On that day I sing for you, listen," said Benetsee.

And then Benetsee was an old man again, bent and weary from digging the dog's grave.

Du Pré left. He drove back to his house and opened all the windows to air the musty smells out. He found a big can of cinnamon in the cabinet over the stove and put a pile of it in a glass dish and set it alight. The cinnamon smoldered; the smoke curled through the house.

The telephone rang. It was Maria. She bubbled with excitement.

"I got all sorts of stuff on moccasins," she said.

"I don't need it now," said Du Pré.

"Oh," she said.

"I am so dumb," Du Pré said. "I had my answer long time ago, but I couldn't see it. It is just that the sole is soft."

"It is that," said Maria. "Did you know that some Cree use a thong to crisscross-wrap their leggins, that they wore a kind of . . . bandage of leather from the moccasin top to some way up their calf?"

Du Pré stiffened.

"You find anything maybe they use a little piece of stone on the end of that thong for something?"

"Oh, yes," said Maria, "a knot stone. The weight kept the knot tight. It had a hole in the middle and the thong was pulled through and then wrapped around to hold."

"Thank you," said Du Pré.

"What is this about?" asked Maria.

"Those murders in Washington," said Du Pré, "I am thinking now that I maybe know who did them."

"Who?" said Maria.

"I tell you when I really know," said Du Pré.

"Okay, Papa," said Maria.

322

"How you like it there?" said Du Pré.

"I got some way to catch up," said Maria, "but they have this program, and it's good. I was whining about how bad the schools were out there and my tutor smiled at me and said maybe I got a lot of something else."

Du Pré laughed.

"So it will be fine. I am just a little Métis girl from Montana."

"You are a good Métis woman and smarter than hell," said Du Pré.

"I love you, Papa," said Maria. "Be careful."

They talked a little more and then Du Pré hung up and drove over to Madelaine's.

✦ CHAPTER 42 ✦

I've been trying," said Michelle Leuci, "but the phone's out up there. The mail plane is going to check, but that isn't for another week."

"I am worried about Lucky and them," said Du Pré.

"The Mounties don't care to be bothered," said Michelle.

"It's just Indians with a broken telephone," said Du Pré, "so, no, I don't think that they would care."

Du Pré sighed.

"Are you okay?" said Michelle.

"Yes," said Du Pré. "No."

"I get to where I can't sleep," said Michelle, "thinking about bad guys. They rob everybody."

"Uh-huh," said Du Pré.

"So you'll be here in two weeks for the festival?" said Michelle.

"Yeah," said Du Pré.

"The old man told you the killer would be there?"

"Benetsee," said Du Pré, "yes, that is what he said. But you have to watch what he says real close, you know. He says what he means exactly."

"That'd be enough to confuse about anybody," said Michelle.

"Yeah," said Du Pré. "You tell that Bart it is pretty out here now and his house is coming along good."

"His house at the end of the world," said Michelle.

They said good-bye.

Bart may never have that much to do with his house, Du Pré thought, but then, he was always just hiding out here; his life now that he has one is somewhere else.

Du Pré took his fiddle and drove over to Jacqueline's, mumbling the names of his grandchildren over and over and hoping he could get them right this time. Jacqueline had wanted to be a mother and she had started very young. There were five now, and she wouldn't even be twenty-one for a couple of months. She'd married a nice young man, Raymond, who loved kids, and Raymond was coming along, learning how to be a brand inspector like Du Pré, just when the cattle business was about done for.

Jacqueline was frying chicken while Raymond and Father Van den Heuvel rode herd on the brood of kids, the youngest still rocking the crib as hard as he could and Jacqueline pregnant again.

The big blond priest and Du Pré were good friends, even though Du Pré seldom went to church and almost never to confession. Du Pré sat on an old chair on the front porch and fiddled. The little children came and listened for a while and then, bored, began to tussle with one another.

Du Pré watched them getting their clothes dirty and was thankful he'd had just the two girls to raise, though they had pretty much raised him, too, after Du Pré's wife died so suddenly.

"How was your trip on the river?" said Father Van den Heuvel.

"That is some cold black country," said Du Pré. "I see pretty much how they think those woods hold the loup-garou up there."

"You learn any new songs?" said Father Van den Heuvel.

Du Pré shook his head.

"No," he said finally. "I am not sure now what the point was in going. You know that Hydro-Quebec wants to build a bunch of damns up there, ruin the country, kill the fish. I had thought that there was a good reason, maybe get some publicity, it is so far away from anything, but now I have gone down that River of the Whale, I don't know if anything will come of it."

"I saw you on television," said Father Van den Heuvel. "Just for a second. You were standing with Bart off to the side while one of the Indians spoke."

Du Pré nodded.

"What have the murders to do with that?" asked the priest.

"I don't know," said Du Pré. He fiddled for a moment and then let the notes die away.

"You know the story about the various nationalities committing murder," said the priest. "The Frenchman will explain logically why he has to kill you, the German will weep copiously, and the Englishman will say, 'Uh, what knife?' "

Du Pré laughed. Well, that was how the English were remembered by the older Métis.

Madelaine arrived bearing potato salad and a huge jug of iced tea. She took the salad inside and left the tea on the porch. There was a big chunk of ice in the jar.

"I just wonder who would profit from killing those unfortunate people," said Father Van den Heuvel.

"I can't think of anyone," said Du Pré. "There was this bad, weak, rich man we thought was the one, but there is no reason for him to do it, and he is just crazy and weak, too."

Madelaine came out and greeted the priest. She kissed Du Pré and then she sat on the porch steps.

"Hydro-Quebec isn't foolish enough to make martyrs," said Du Pré. "And to be killing people in America, it's too risky. They are mean bastards and twenty billion dollars is a lot of money, but there is too much at stake to risk all that."

"What are we talking?" said Madelaine.

"Trying to think who wins with these murders," said Du Pré.

"It is some crazy person," said Madelaine. "Anybody who would kill anyone else is a crazy person."

Du Pré nodded. He'd once killed a man who was trying to kill him and it was a very crazy few seconds. It still made Du Pré want to puke.

They ate chicken and potato salad and made small talk and then it was time for Jacqueline's children to nap. Du Pré and Madelaine left, Du Pré dropping the priest off at the little Catholic church, and then Du Pré went over to Madelaine's. They sat in the soft May sun. The lilacs dripped heavy perfume.

There were heavy black rain clouds in the west.

Her children were all off doing adolescent things. They went to bed in the late afternoon and fell asleep after lovemaking and didn't wake until dark. The light stayed late now, a little more than a month away from the summer solstice.

The storm struck just at sunset, the wind came up and lightning stabbed down on the plains to the west. Pinkish black clouds roiled around the peaks of the Wolf Mountains to the north. They watched the clouds seethe.

"Come on," said Du Pré, "I will take you down to the bar, buy you some pink wine."

Madelaine checked her children. They were all home but the oldest boy, who had a girl and so was hardly ever around, anyway.

"Pretty good kids," said Du Pré.

"They are that," said Madelaine. He had seen her be stern with them. Then the kid would slouch off and Madelaine's face would break out in smiles. So they got instructed but not hurt.

The rain pounded down. Du Pré let Madelaine off right at the front door and he parked a little bit away and ran to the bar, with huge drops slapping his hat.

The place was crowded. Country music on the jukebox and a few couples dancing tightly on the tiny dance floor.

They stayed late.

326

That night, Du Pré woke up in the deep dark. He could still smell the storm, which had passed.

Who gets what from these murders? Some crazy person.

Who?

What do they want?

He got up and went out on the porch and smoked. He flicked his cigarette butt onto the lawn.

They do it because they like it.

That's all.

✤ CHAPTER 43 ✤

Bart's plane flashed down out of the blue sky and onto the runway at the Billings airport.

Du Pré was standing with Madelaine, holding a bag and his fiddle case.

"Pret' good for some ol' cowboy from a place in Montana so far from anywhere, we got to pipe in the daylight," said Du Pré.

They kissed. Du Pré walked toward the plane, which had turned around and was moving rapidly toward the terminal.

The steps came down and Du Pré went up. There would be a few minutes delay, but the pilot had an errand in Rapid City and would refuel there.

Du Pré was alone in the cabin. The furnishings were leather and expensive woods. There was a bank of telephones on one wall and a few complicated machines Du Pré didn't recognize and wouldn't care to.

One phone rang. Du Pré picked it up.

"Good afternoon," said Bart, "I hope you have a pleasant flight."

"I could have driven," said Du Pré.

"I'd worry," said Bart.

"Well, I thank you."

"I bought a house," said Bart.

Okay, Du Pré thought. Maybe the White House?

"It's a nice house, not very big."

"Servants."

"Just one," said Bart.

"A butler?"

"No, asshole, a housekeeper. I never learned to wash dishes. How's Booger Tom?"

"Haven't seen him," said Du Pré. Which was strange, but then, Tom could get an itch and decide he'd like to be an old cowboy in Texas and that would be the last anyone heard of him.

"Is that Paul Chase around?" asked Du Pré.

"Yeah, I guess. They pulled the tails off him, you know. The guy is a crazy weasel, but, hell, not capable of murder."

"He will be the next one killed, I think," said Du Pré.

"Good," said Bart. "Now I must ask why?"

"I just got this feeling."

"Benetsee give you that feeling?"

"Yes, sort of," said Du Pré. "I don't know."

"I'll pass it along."

"I suppose I got to stay in your house there," said Du Pré.

"Of course," said Bart. "The hotels are all full of crack dealers and lobbyists. Very noisy. I have a very quiet house."

The plane's engines began to whine. They said good-bye and Du Pré braced himself for the takeoff. The little jet was quick and fast and in moments they were at altitude and cruising. In the time that it took Du Pré to roll and smoke two cigarettes and look out the window a little, they were descending to Rapid City.

The pilot and copilot came back through the cabin and said that it would take about an hour. Du Pré followed them down the stairs. He found a bar and had a couple drinks and went back and waited for ten minutes. He was paged. He went to the gate and down to the plane and they were soon off.

Du Pré fiddled thirty thousand feet over America. Bart met him at the D.C. airport. He was driving a Land Rover. He was wearing a jacket and a tie.

Detective Leuci waved from inside the Land Rover.

Du Pré went with them to dinner to a very fancy place, so fancy that no one paid any attention to his jeans and boots and worn denim shirt.

"This place costs so much, they figure you have to be a rich eccentric to dress like that," Bart explained.

"I am just an eccentric," said Du Pré.

They ate good French food in tiny portions. Bart drank mineral water. The two of them looked happy.

"So," said Michelle over coffee, "why Chase?"

"I just have this feeling," said Du Pré lamely. He didn't know why except he knew it was going to happen. Like he could tell from the air when a storm was coming even though the western sky was clear.

"It was Benetsee," Du Pré went on. "He said I was looking in the wrong place. Not exactly said that . . . but . . ." But the old man had changed to a fox, a cat, a hunter coiled and stalking.

They left. The night was thick, the syrupy air clogged Du Pré's lungs, made his skin feel oily.

Bart had bought a modest house in Georgetown, one with a high brick and iron fence around it. The gate opened when Bart pressed a button on the dash of the Rover. They drove into a spotless garage with a crimson floor. There were no signs at all that anyone lived there. No lawn chairs hanging, no stuff.

The house was spare and bleak, wood floors drummed, without carpets and furniture to damp them.

"I'm getting some more stuff soon," said Bart, leading Du Pré through the downstairs. "I just bought it four days ago."

Probably a half million, Du Pré thought. House here can cost two ranches where I am, I bet, maybe four.

They went into the living room, which had a sofa and a couple heavy stuffed chairs and a thick glass coffee table. Bart went to a pantry and made drinks.

Du Pré rolled a cigarette.

"Why exactly do you think Chase is in danger now?" asked Michelle.

Du Pré squirmed.

"Dreams," he said finally.

"You have been having dreams about Chase being killed?"

Du Pré shook his head and cleared his throat. "No. When I am out hunting sometimes, I will . . . I always dream the deer before the deer comes a little. I can't explain it very well."

Michelle lit a cigarette. Bart brought a couple soda cans to use as ashtrays.

"I'm . . . I don't understand," said Michelle.

"I know that I know the killer," said Du Pré. "I know him if I see him. I will know him when he moves. I won't till then. It is many things. When you go to track something, you are not just looking for footprints or the marks of hooves. You look at the country and see what isn't right about it, something; sometimes you stare for an hour without moving. You try to see everything."

"The killer was in . . . whatever that unpronounceable village was where you came out of the forest to the bay."

Du Pré nodded. Benetsee had said so, he had felt it himself, and then there was the mutilated raven. He had gone over and over that scene in his mind and he couldn't see what must be there.

Raven. Dead soul.

"I am very tired," Du Pré said. Bart showed him to a bedroom. Du Pré undressed and crawled between the cool sheets. The air smelled canned from the air conditioner.

In the middle of the night, Bart came and shook him awake.

"They just found Chase," Bart said. "Come on."

Du Pré rubbed his eyes and willed his mind to rise.

✤ CHAPTER 44 ✤

Chase was facedown in the ornamental pool. The cops had brought lights and photographers were clicking away. An ambulance sat off a little ways, lights slowly revolving. Three cop cars doing the same.

It was after four in the morning and some workmen were still on the job. The music festival began the next morning. Du Pré walked away from the revolving lights. The sidewalks were well away from any cover and Chase was a good hundred feet from the nearest shadow, and it wasn't large.

A big man in white coveralls carrying a tool kit walked past.

"Hey," said Du Pré, "did these lights go out ever tonight?"

"Oh yeah," the man said. "Somebody shorted everything out real good. Took us half an hour to get the damn things back on. I been here since seven yesterday morning. All so a bunch of goddamned hippies can listen to their fucking music."

Du Pré laughed. Well, boys, there you have it.

He walked back over to the pool and the dead Chase and the cops.

Some ambulance attendants were lifting the body. They carried it to the edge of the shallow pool and set it down carefully on a black body bag. They climbed out, zipped up the bag, lifted it to a gurney, and wheeled it away.

An owlish-looking woman, huge glasses with pinkish frames and hair in a severe knot at the back of her head, scribbled notes in a small black notebook. She had a microphone attached to the lapel of her blouse and she was talking to it while she wrote.

Detective Leuci stood, her arms around her chest. It was hot. She wasn't cold from the weather.

Michelle came over to Du Pré.

"It seems he was stabbed," she said. "There's a hole in his shirt, on the back, where the heart is. The ME waded out and poked it and she said the blade was still in him. Could feel the broken end, real narrow."

Killing blade, Du Pré thought. You grind away where the blade meets the tang so when you stick the thing in somebody, you can break off the handle and leave the blade in and nothing to grab to pull it out.

"Guy said the lights were out for half an hour," said Du Pré.

Michelle nodded.

"It's the same man killed the others," said Du Pré. "He was hunting Chase, then it got dark, and in he came. I wonder if Chase was running?"

"The building lights stayed on," said Michelle. "The circuits out here were tripped and a big fuse fried. Why it took so long for them to get the lights back on, finding another fuse that fit."

"Well," said Michelle, after a moment. "We know where he is, sort of."

They walked back to the parking structure. Bart was sitting in the Rover. Too smart to follow Michelle around while she did her job. Du Pré nodded at him, half-smiling.

"I will know him this time when I see him," Du Pré said.

I will know him when he moves. What Benetsee gave me is as good as a photograph of someone you have never seen. He will know me, too. Will he have a gun? So far, he has not used one. So far.

Thousands of people here. Wonder if my chanky-chank band will be here.

Least Chase can't run me off.

He must not have had much of a life. Didn't deserve one, either.

"Du Pré," said Michelle, "You *worry* me. You can't just kill this guy and scalp him. Then I'd have to arrest *you*. Christ, you people out there watch *High Noon* three times a week till you believe it?"

Du Pré looked at her a long time. He shrugged.

"This guy is crazy," said Du Pré. "How many more dead people do you want, eh? You can have them, you know. When I find him, he will do something."

"You don't have a gun, do you?" said Michelle.

"No," said Du Pré.

"We haven't got enough to arrest anyone or we would have," she said.

"When I find him," said Du Pré, "I am going to crowd him till he jumps. That's all. He will jump."

"Let's go get some breakfast," Bart said, sensibly.

They went to a twenty-four-hour franchise and ate horrible food and drank weak coffee. The sun was coming up by the time they finished.

"I think I go and sleep for a while," said Du Pré, "go over to the festival later."

Bart dropped him off and he and Michelle headed back down to her office.

Du Pré crawled back in bed and fell into a rolling sleep. Dreams rose and sank. He tossed and writhed and the covers wrapped around him. Nonsense dreams full of dread he could not fathom.

He woke. He was on his back, looking at the ceiling, the last ephemeral scene clear in his mind. Benetsee and his bullroarer, on the rock.

Du Pré showered and put on fresh clothes. A linen shirt Madelaine had made for him, cool in this weather, cool as anything.

He called a cab and went out to wait for it. It was two in the afternoon. The heat and humidity pressed down on him. He was running sweat.

The cabbie dropped him near the festival. Du Pré walked to a ticket booth, paid, and went in, carrying his fiddle case.

He heard zydeco, began to move through the knots of people toward the sound. He couldn't tell if it was the band he had played with last year.

333

It wasn't.

He wandered on.

He heard the eerie trilling of the Inuit throat singers and went toward the band shell it came from. The crowd was small but marveling.

Du Pré found some shade but not any breeze. He squatted on his heels and waited.

The singers paused.

A man vaulted up on the stage, smooth as water flowing—flowing back uphill. Smooth as a cat gaining a ledge.

Du Pré sat, hunting.

The man was carrying a big bottle of mineral water. The Inuit passed it round. How miserable they must be in this heat.

Du Pré waited.

The man flowed back down to the ground.

He was wearing soft, high moccasins with a crosshatch lace.

Du Pré stood up and began to move toward him casually. He moved in spurts and jerks, from one knot of people to another.

The man was hunkered down, butt on his heels. He was with several Indians.

Du Pré knew all of them.

Du Pré slid up behind the little half-moon of people looking up at the Inuit.

"Hey, Lucky," said Du Pré, face next to Lucky's ear, "that Hydro-Quebec, they pay you kill those two little Indian girls, too?"

Lucky turned slowly.

Du Pré saw something red pass behind Lucky's eyes, like a curtain drawn.

Lucky turned slowly on his bent toes.

He looked at Du Pré and his eyes were sleepy.

Then his hand moved and Du Pré felt something slice across his forehead. He flinched.

Lucky jammed a knuckle into Du Pré's windpipe.

Someone screamed.

334

Du Pré couldn't see. Blood was welling down over his eyes.

He stood up, trying to protect his throat.

People were yelling.

But he couldn't see a fucking thing.

♣ CHAPTER 45 ♣

Du Pré felt the prick of the needle and the scritch of the suture being drawn through.

"You want something for the pain yet?" said the doctor.

"No," said Du Pré.

The doctor shrugged and went on with his tapestry work.

Well, I was right, Du Pré thought. And Lucky saved me some trouble there. If he had just asked me what the fuck I was talking about, I wouldn't have known what to say.

The doctor finished stitching.

Du Pré stood up. He was just a little light-headed, maybe from the pain. He still had some blood stuck to his eyelashes.

He felt like an asshole.

"Thank you," he said to the physician. But the man was hurrying off to another patient. There had been the approaching wail of an ambulance while Du Pré was on the table.

He looked down at his bloody linen shirt.

Damn head wounds bleed some quick, he thought. So much for Madelaine's nice shirt that she made for me.

Bart was waiting in the lobby. He had his hands shoved in his hip pockets and he was looking at the ceiling, maybe counting the holes in the acoustical tile.

"I am all embroidered," said Du Pré.

335

Bart looked at him. "I can't tell," he said. "You got a bandage on it."

They went out to the Rover.

"Lucky took off like a streak of shit," said Bart, "and they are after him for assaulting you. But they don't have enough to get a warrant for anything else."

"I won't press charges," said Du Pré.

Bart nodded. "I told Michelle I thought you might not."

"She pissed?"

"Uh," said Bart, "I wouldn't, you know, ask her for a kiss for a couple days."

"Maybe it wasn't even Lucky," said Du Pré. "Maybe it was someone who was behind me and I didn't know it."

I barely saw Lucky move, Du Pré thought. He is very fast.

"Are you sure it is Lucky?" said Bart suddenly. "Absolutely sure?"

"Yes," said Du Pré.

"Well," said Bart, "what are you going to do about it?"

"I don't know," said Du Pré.

"You won't just kill him?" said Bart. He was remembering how Du Pré's father had killed Gianni Fascelli, Bart's brother. He was a little bit afraid of these Montana people.

"I don't know," said Du Pré.

The telephone in the car chirred. Bart picked it up and listened for a moment.

"Well," he said, "I told you I thought probably he wouldn't."

He listened.

Du Pré could hear Detective Michelle Leuci yelling on the other end.

"You might as well yell at a stump," said Bart. "Yes, you can."

Bart handed the telephone to Du Pré and changed lanes.

"Goddamn it," said Michelle, "at least we could hold him and grill him."

"I don't think that would do any good," said Du Pré, trying to sound apologetic.

336

"Goddamn you," she said.

"You catch him or something?" said Du Pré.

Silence.

"He will go back home," said Du Pré. "He will go back home and he will wait. You can't arrest him. You can't hold him if you do."

"The Mounties are checking up on his movements," said Michelle.

"Big shit," said Du Pré. "They are going to run into a lot of Indian time, what they run into. They ask their questions and no one remembers. When he came back here, I bet he drove, he come across the border with some other folks. He . . ."

They were passing a new building going up. The steel girders were partly assembled. The building wasn't too tall yet. A couple of men lounged far up enough to kill them if they fell, casually as people lean against walls.

"Shit," said Du Pré.

"What?" said Michelle.

"Nothing," said Du Pré.

"Look," said Michelle, "just sign the complaint, please. Humor me. At least if we find him, we can hold him on that."

"Okay," said Du Pré.

"Have Bart bring you downtown," she said.

"I go and sign the complaint, I guess," said Du Pré.

"Now what?" asked Bart.

"I changed my mind," said Du Pré.

"Bullshit," said Bart. "Something changed it for you."

Du Pré sat silent.

"Okay," said Bart, "we go down and play scritchy-scritch on the little piece of paper. While my bullshit detector melts down. *Why did you go and change your mind?*"

They parked by the big building that held Michelle's office and went in. They found her talking quickly into her phone.

"Well," she said, to the phone, "I don't know where he might cross or if he will. . . . I know that. . . . I know that, too. Just hold him. We want to talk to him."

337

She hung up.

"You asshole," she said pleasantly, smiling at Du Pré.

"I will sign your form," he said.

"Shit." Michelle sighed. She took Du Pré by the arm and down a couple long halls and into a courtroom. A judge was waiting. Du Pré signed a complaint.

"Will he be available to testify, Detective Leuci?" the judge said offhandedly.

"If I have to bring him in a sack," said Michelle sweetly.

They walked back out.

"What have you got on your tiny little mind?" she said, hurrying Du Pré back down the hall to her office.

"Couple hundred stitches," said Du Pré.

"I don't fucking believe it," said Detective Leuci.

"You aren't going to catch him," said Du Pré. "You going to try to get the Canadians give him back, when I can't even say for sure it was him who cut me?"

"Motherfucker," said Michelle.

"I can't say," said Du Pré.

"Shit," said Detective Leuci.

Bart was waiting out in the hallway.

They walked up to him.

"Gabriel," said Michelle tiredly, "what are you going to do now?"

"Go see my daughter maybe," said Du Pré. "Get my fiddle first."

"I picked up your fiddle at the hospital," said Bart. "They brought it in the ambulance."

"Then I will go and see my daughter," said Du Pré.

"Don't do this," said Michelle.

"What?" said Du Pré.

"Just don't," said Detective Leuci. She bit her lip and went into her office.

✤ CHAPTER 46 ✤

Y̶ou were right about Gianni and Catfoot," said Bart, looking at
the card in his hand. It was the card the woman reporter had
given Du Pré in the little Inuit village on Hudson Bay after he and
Bart and the Quebec Indians had come down the Rivière de la Baleine.

"I think you find out that Lucky isn't Chippewa and that he came
and went from the village," said Du Pré. "They will cover for him,
but they are not very good at it. I don't think that they talk to the
Mounties, though."

Two percent of Canadians are Indian, one-quarter of prison inmates are, too. So the Indians don't like the Mounties much.

"How's Maria doing?" said Bart. He looked a little shamefaced.
He had been so besotted by Michelle Leuci that he had been thinking of little else.

And I don't blame him one bit, Du Pré thought. He has had very
little love in his life and is trying to do right by it. He remembered
Bart's bloated, sick face, and Bart three-quarters dead from booze.
But Bart was struggling and he had faith in the possibility of love in
the world. Which took a great deal of courage, come to think on it.

"She is fine," said Du Pré. "Little Métis girl from Montana,
where the schools are not much good, trying to go to a tough eastern university. But she will just work till she gets it. She is tougher
than either you or me, I think."

"That would not take very much," said Bart, "as we are nothing
but a couple of middle-aged marshmallows."

Du Pré nodded. Fair enough.

"But you are really going to go and hunt Lucky," said Bart. "You know Michelle will bust you if you kill him. She'll bust you if you threaten him."

"It will be out of her jurisdiction," said Du Pré, "but I have to find him first."

"You won't tell me where you are going to look?"

"I don't know," said Du Pré.

Bart let it drop. Du Pré was lying, sort of. He didn't know where he was going yet, but he'd decide soon enough—as soon as Bart was off to find that woman reporter and go back to the village and hound Eloise and Françoise and Hervé and Guillaume. Bart would not be good at it, but that woman, Sulin Bickhoff, would be very good at it. Strange name. So, for that matter, was Gabriel. Du Pré wondered if Bart's family owned her newspaper. Probably. They seemed to own just about everything.

If Bart and this Sulin Bickhoff found out what Du Pré thought they would, then Michelle would have something better to work with than she had now.

Du Pré's forehead itched. He would not be blending into any crowds for a while. Probably have a narrow white scar across his browned forehead.

I can't even kill the fucker, Du Pré thought angrily. I got to goose him till he screws up, and he is plenty smart for sure.

Du Pré called Maria. She was in her room at the boardinghouse near the school, working hard.

"You be ready in the fall," said Du Pré. "You worry too much."

"I know," said Maria. "I know I worry too much and that I will be ready in the fall. But . . . this is some different place, Papa."

"I got to ask you a favor," said Du Pré.

"Okay," said Maria. She would hear him out at least.

"I need for you to go someplace safe where no one knows you are except Madelaine until I call her to call you. This guy, killing these Indians down here in D.C.? I have found him and he ran. I don't know he even knows about you, but you do me this favor, huh? Just go hide till Madelaine calls you?"

Maria didn't say anything for a while.

340

"Okay," she said. "I will tell you what, I will take some books that I have to read and my computer, I will go someplace—I am not even going to tell you where—and then I will wait. But you got to call Madelaine to call me so I know that you are all right."

"Sure," said Du Pré, not knowing where he was going or if there were telephones there. Or if Lucky would get him, too.

"Where are you going, Papa?" said Maria. "You got to tell me so I can worry about some place."

Shit, Du Pré thought, now she will come after me. Maria, she don't have any fear bones.

"Maria," said Du Pré, "I know how this song ends. Now you going to go and come with me, I guess."

"Papa," said Maria, "you are so smart, I am more proud of you every day."

Why, Du Pré wondered for the ten thousandth time, don't I keep my big fucking mouth shut and not think for my daughter, who will not have it? She would not have it when she was two and she will not have it now.

"I will drive up and get you," said Du Pré.

"I will be ready," said Maria. "Do I need a gun?"

"Christ, no!" said Du Pré. "They are illegal everywhere here, you know."

"What," said Maria, "has that got to do with anything?"

"Where you get a gun, anyway?" asked Du Pré.

"I brought two with me. There are these drug people and burglars and rapists here, you know. I don't like that shit."

Du Pré was speechless. I send my little girl off to get ready for college, she is ready to kill. Where did she learn this? Me. Montana. Your Honor, that asshole needed killing. Case dismissed.

"What kind of fucking guns do you have, anyway?" asked Du Pré.

"I got a nine-millimeter Sig-Sauer and a Colt Python," said Maria.

"You ever shoot them?"

"Sure," said Maria. "I can do a four-inch group at fifty feet with the nine-millimeter. The Python is a little sloppier, but it fits in my backpack, on the side pocket there where it is easy to hand."

341

"Okay," said Du Pré, "I will come and get you."

"Yes, Papa," said Maria.

Du Pré hung up. He rubbed his eyes. When he opened them, Bart's hand was in front of them with the keys to the Rover dangling from his fingers.

"I didn't hear anything," said Bart, "but I just want you to know that I am extremely glad you have an adult along with you. I would worry otherwise, but now I will not. I can't afford to have heard anything, because I would have to tell Michelle, who would go completely batshit. Now, would you please get out of my sight, and do you have enough money?"

"Yes and I don't know," said Du Pré.

Bart went to the kitchen and came back with a wad of hundreds.

"Have you thought of family counseling?" he said, eyes wide.

Du Pré took the money, the keys, his fiddle, then he walked out the door. He got in the Rover and headed north.

He didn't get to Massachusetts till dawn, and it took him a while to find where in Northampton it was that Maria lived.

He pulled over to the curb and got out.

Maria came striding out the front door of the huge old house. She had a backpack and a carryall. She kissed Du Pré on the cheek. He put her luggage in the back.

"You know where them Mohawks live?" said Du Pré.

Maria pointed north and Du Pré started the Rover.

✦ CHAPTER 47 ✦

They went round the southern end of Lake Champlain and then turned north on a freeway. Du Pré was drinking lousy thin coffee from a Styrofoam cup and steering, and what he most wanted to do was pull off and rip the bandage away and scratch his itching forehead.

I got the good healing flesh, Du Pré thought. I can take these damn stitches out pretty soon.

"You maybe ought to change that bandage, Papa," said Maria. "We get you one, fluorescent green like that dragline of Bart's."

Goddamn kid.

"So you will tell me maybe where we are going?"

"Up next to Canada," said Du Pré. "I am thinking this Lucky isn't Chippewa; I think about how he does things. So then I think maybe he is Mohawk."

"Mohawk?" said Maria. "Why them?"

"Lot of them are ironworkers," said Du Pré. "They run around long way off the ground on steel beams, no safety lines, move like cats."

All the other Quebec Indians had moved like woods people, careful not to make noise. But Lucky moved for balance. Lucky grabbed the ground with his feet. Lucky pulled it up to him.

Or maybe I am full of shit, too.

"How you gonna look for him, that flag on your head?" said Maria.

Good question.

"You got a picture of him?" she said.

"In the glove box," said Du Pré. The photos Bart had taken of the crew were there, taken right after they had pulled the canoes out at the bay.

Maria riffled through them.

"It's this guy standing next to you and then here's another of him speaking into a microphone. He's kind of cute," said Maria.

"Christ," said Du Pré.

"You aren't laughing enough, Papa," said Maria.

Du Pré didn't feel like laughing. His head itched.

"So I will be a real pain in the ass till you laugh."

Du Pré laughed at that.

"I don't really know," said Du Pré, "I think he would have left

D.C. right away. I am thinking the Mohawks because they are right next to Canada there and it is so easy to go across the border."

"Okay, Papa," said Maria.

"If we got to go across the border, you leave them damn guns somewhere," said Du Pré. "Them Canadians don't like people have pistols."

"I know, Papa," said Maria. "They don't shoot each other much. We got more murders each year in Omaha than they do in all their whole country. I wonder why Americans shoot each other so much."

"Television," said Du Pré.

"Television?"

"Every time I watch television, it is so damn dumb, I want to go out and shoot somebody," said Du Pré.

"Okay," said Maria, "you are better now."

They drove for a couple of hours, then pulled off to have lunch. Du Pré studied the map while waiting for his cheeseburger.

"Little dinky states back here," he said. "We got ranches bigger than Vermont."

"It's so pretty there, Papa," said Maria. "People have been there a long time, pretty little churches and towns. Makes me think Montana is so new."

Also very old, Du Pré thought. People hunting buffalo there a long time before them pyramids were built. I wonder when Benetsee was born? Long time gone.

They drove on. They had left the interstate and wound along a good two-lane blacktop road, coming to little towns every fifteen miles or so. There were orchards in heavy leaf; the land was rich from rain.

Du Pré found a motel about forty miles from the Mohawk reservation. He rented two rooms for two days. The woman behind the desk gave him the keys and a packet of tourist information. She recommended a little inn just up the road, very good food, though somewhat pricey.

344

Du Pré had left all of his spare clothing at Bart's. He gave some money to Maria and sent her off to buy some spare things, took a shower, and went to sleep. When he woke up it was getting on dark. There was a big paper sack on the suitcase stand.

The clothes had been washed and carefully folded. Du Pré got dressed, pulled on his boots, threaded his belt through the loops on the tan jeans. He put his wallet and keys in his pocket. He knocked on the door connecting the two rooms.

"You up, Papa?" said Maria. "Everything fit?"

"Yes," said Du Pré. He opened the door.

Maria was at the little desk in her room, studying. With a 9mm pistol holding down her notes.

"Where did you get that gun?" asked Du Pré, curious.

"Bought it," said Maria, "if it make you feel better."

"You are not old enough to buy a gun."

"Jacqueline is." She smiled sunnily.

"Okay," said Du Pré. Well, he didn't have to worry about Maria if she was on guard. The girl would consider carefully before shooting, but she would shoot. Probably hit what she shot at, too. Maria didn't like to do anything poorly.

"How many that hold?" asked Du Pré.

"Fourteen," said Maria.

"Four-inch group?" said Du Pré.

"Yeah," said Maria. "Nine, ten seconds. If I rush, I don't hit so good."

If I rush, I don't hit so good. Well, well, well.

"Now we are here, I don't quite know how to do this," said Du Pré.

"He will not be expecting you," said Maria. "Just find him and that will scare him."

"I think I try to call Bart," said Du Pré, "Michelle too, find out anything."

He went outside and looked at the sun. Maybe eight o'clock.

He got Michelle on the first try, at her desk in D.C.

"Where the fuck are you?" she said. "Bart's up in Quebec. He called earlier, but I was out. Now I can't raise him. Some sort of atmospheric problem. I'll try in a while."

"Upstate New York, I guess they call it," said Du Pré. "I wanted to see if you had any suggestions."

Michelle was silent. "No," she said finally. "I don't. We don't have any evidence against Lucky good enough to get a warrant."

"How 'bout assaulting me?"

"Sure," said Michelle, "but if we pop him for that, maybe he just goes to ground. Any attorney will bargain it down to where all he'll have to do is send in a check or forfeit bail. This is D.C., murder capital of the country. The courts are choked."

"Michelle," said Du Pré, "you call Madelaine, see if she can get old Benetsee to call and talk with you maybe."

"Why?" said Detective Leuci.

"Make you feel better," said Du Pré.

He hung up and went back out to look at the sunset.

The food at the old inn was very good and very expensive. Du Pré had some bourbon.

He slept well that night.

✤ CHAPTER 48 ✤

A bright morning with a lot of dew on it. A Friday.
Du Pré rolled a smoke and stood in the cool. He wondered how far north the Saint Lawrence was.

Maria came out of her room, dressed in ragged jeans and a blouse that seemed to be mostly knots. She had a scarf over her forehead and under her hair in the back and big dark glasses and her shoulder bag, the kind photographers carry.

"Yo," said Du Pré. "Morning. You want to go get some breakfast maybe?"

They went back to the inn, but it wasn't open. They found a little working-class restaurant in the town and had big breakfasts of eggs and ham and hash browns. The coffee was good. There was a plate of homemade biscuits.

They stood on the sidewalk out front and watched the little town gearing up. Tourism was its lifeblood. There were galleries and T-shirt shops and "antique" stores. But not too bad.

"You think maybe Lucky is over on the reservation?" said Maria.

"Not yet," said Du Pré. "I think he comes in late tonight, with maybe a carload of high-iron workers from the city. Maybe New York, I don't know. I think he thinks that there are warrants out for him, he will make it back here without using anything he has to buy a ticket for or go to some special place to leave at."

"Are there any warrants?"

"Chickenshit one for assaulting me in D.C.," said Du Pré.

"We got to get you a new bandage," said Maria. "That one looks kind of grubby, you know."

She went off to a drugstore and came back with some tape and gauze and a big, cheap bandanna, white, with blue roses all the hell over it.

"Wish your hair was long enough to braid," she said.

"Oh," said Du Pré, "I look plenty Indian, plenty Frenchy."

They sat in the Rover. Maria tugged Du Pré's bandage off and looked at his wound. She cleaned his forehead with a couple foil-wrapped wet paper towels that smelled like lilacs.

"I think you can take the stitches out, couple days," she said. "It isn't even oozing anywhere."

"I am not oozing, I am happy," said Du Pré.

"I am going to put some aloe vera cream on that," said Maria. "It will make it heal faster."

The ointment felt cool on Du Pré's forehead.

Here I am hunting somebody with my daughter the gunslinger, Du Pré thought, and I am *glad* to have her here. My women, they all

347

have had some common sense. I don't know I do or not.

"You drive me to the reservation and I will ask around," said Maria. "Say I love this man's music and have they seen him. They will think I am a groupie."

Du Pré didn't have a better suggestion.

The car telephone chirred.

Du Pré picked it up.

"Finally," said Bart. "I've been trying for hours."

"Sorry," said Du Pré.

"Okay," said Bart. "You were right. Sulin kept after Eloise until she got so pissed, she screamed that Lucky had come to help them. And then Sulin kept hammering on the murders, especially those little girls, till Eloise went off to talk to Hervé and Guillaume and found out, yeah, he was gone a lot and at those times."

"You find out what tribe he is?" asked Du Pré.

"They say they know nothing at all about where he came from. Just that he was around for a while and talking about the dams and canoes and how to fight it. Sounded good. Well, fighting it is good. But for all they know, he dropped from the fucking moon."

"He won't come back there," said Du Pré.

"Um," said Bart. "Michelle is plenty pissed off."

"Okay," said Du Pré. "She can't do nothing, you know. Pisses me off when I can't do nothing. So maybe you go back and help her out."

"I stay out of her way when she's working," said Bart.

"Good," said Du Pré. "go back and take her to dinner, buy her maybe some flowers."

"So," said Bart, "where are you exactly?"

"Upstate New York, they call it," said Du Pré.

"Alone?"

"I got Maria."

"Well," said Bart, "I won't worry about you then."

"She is one tough lady," said Du Pré. "Got guns enough for a platoon."

"I will never understand you people," said Bart. "Okay. We are

348

on our way back shortly. I am going to tell Michelle everything."

"Of course," said Du Pré.

"You need me there?"

"I don't think so," said Du Pré.

Just me. Just Lucky.

Just the one dream.

I need to talk to Benetsee.

I have already talked to Benetsee.

"Okay," said Bart. "Ain't this a pisser?"

"It is that," said Du Pré.

He put the phone back in its cradle.

"Let's go to that reservation," said Maria. "You drop me off somewhere, give me maybe two hours."

"I want to keep an eye on you there," said Du Pré.

"I will be all right," said Maria. "I am researching this paper and looking for these musicians, you know."

"What if he's here already? He will not like questions about him."

"I am not going to ask him, Papa."

Du Pré didn't have a better idea. He wished, for one thing, that the Rover didn't have D.C. license plates.

"We will go and rent a car," said Du Pré.

"Why?" said Maria.

"D.C. license plates on this thing."

Maria sighed and reached into her shoulder bag. She took out two Massachusetts plates and handed them to Du Pré.

Christ, Du Pré thought, I will just go back to the motel so I don't slow her down so much. Me, I am old, need a nap.

"Good you think of that," he said.

"Yeah," said Maria. "That garage will be pissed off, but we will take them back, you know."

Illegal weapons and stolen license plates, Du Pré thought, and my lovely daughter there. Four-inch group. I don't think she will have any trouble in college. Jesus.

They drove down the road and found a rest area. Du Pré

switched the license plates. The screws went into plastic sets. No rust. It took him five minutes.

"Okay," said Du Pré. "Where you want me to drop you off?"

"They got a high school or a public library?" said Maria.

They drove to the reservation. All such places are sad and in disarray.

Du Pré asked the man at a gas station where the library was and he dropped Maria there.

He drove on, found a place to park off the road, and walked among the wildflowers. He sat on a log and smoked.

The time dragged on.

But then it was time to go back.

When he pulled up by the library, Maria was waiting.

She got in the Rover.

"You were right," she said. "He is expected back late tonight maybe. She didn't know anything about the festival, you know. Funny."

"Why funny?" said Du Pré.

"The librarian," said Maria, "is Lucky's sister."

✤ CHAPTER 49 ✤

Remember your fathers," said Benetsee. The phone was so clear, it sounded as if the old man was lisping wet advice in his ear. So Madelaine had given him wine.

She takes everybody for what they are if they are not mean, Du Pré thought, and so I am very lucky.

"I don't know what I am doing," said Du Pré.

"Nobody knows what they are doing," said Benetsee, "not even the gods. Just remember your fathers."

Du Pré hung up.

"So?" said Maria.

Du Pré shook his head. "I don't know," he said.

"If you feel you are right, Papa, then it will be okay," said Maria.

Du Pré tried to think, but there wasn't much to think about. His forehead itched and so did his thoughts.

"What if he doesn't come?" said Maria.

"Benetsee says he will come," said Du Pré.

"When?"

"The last hour before dawn."

Owl time.

"Some pretty country around here, Papa," said Maria. "Let's drive some and then get a good dinner, maybe you get a little sleep."

"You got to just stay in that room till I come back," said Du Pré.

"Okay," said Maria. She sounded cheerful.

"Balls," said Du Pré. "Now where are those fucking guns?"

"Papa," said Maria, "they are mine. I will stay in the room and only shoot anyone who breaks in, okay?"

"Maria . . ."

But she was looking straight ahead and Du Pré caught himself. Maria was her own and always had been. She would not do what she would not own to, and she would not take orders—from anyone. And no hard feelings, it just happened to be that way.

Du Pré started the Rover. They drove off to the west, found a narrow two-lane blacktop road, and wandered down it past orchards and occasional white frame farmhouses.

"Pretty fat country, this," said Du Pré.

"You aren't happy, can't see prickly pear cactus and sagebrush," said Maria. "Sure are a lot of people here you know."

They found another inn nestled by a clear lake and had supper, good fish and some white wine. The lake was ringed by vacation houses. There were no motorboats on it, just canoes.

After they had finished, they went out on the dock.

"Play me some music, Papa," said Maria. Her lower lip was

351

quivering. She was very tough and awfully young—back and forth.

Du Pré went to the Rover and got his fiddle. He took it and the bow out of the case and carried them back down and they sat on the end of the dock and Du Pré played, not loudly. Jigs and reels and portage ballads, songs of work, songs of longing.

"You girls at home, pull the rope and help us with this big canoe."

Bragging songs, how many packs of furs a voyageur can carry uphill on a bad portage.

Du Pré sang some of them. He had a clear tenor voice.

They waited for the night.

Du Pré sent one last soft, low note across the water. They got up and walked to the Rover and drove back to the inn. Du Pré took a shower.

He left his wallet. He put the slingshot in his hip pocket and the carved stone balls in his left front pocket and thought of drinking some bourbon but knew that he couldn't. He put on the moccasins Benetsee had given him.

He kissed Maria and ruffled her hair, then went out and got in the Rover and drove off.

He parked by the highway leading to the reservation, shut off the engine and the lights.

The hours dripped by like falling water.

Traffic dwindled away.

Du Pré sank into a hunter's half sleep.

And all the hunted had to do was act the innocent, ask why was Du Pré hounding him, and there would be nothing Gabriel could do by law.

The mosquitoes whined through the open windows. They landed on Du Pré and fed. He didn't move.

His eyes flicked back and forth.

A car appeared. It was full of people. The car pulled off right across the road and six men got out to piss.

Lucky was one of them.

Du Pré opened his door, slid out, and walked through the shadows.

They were all standing with their backs to him, watering the barrow pit.

Du Pré crossed the road. He walked to their car.

A couple of the men finished. They zipped up and stretched. Lucky was still pissing.

Du Pré waited.

A man turned round and gave a start when he saw Du Pré.

"Lucky!" Du Pré shouted. "I am here! We dance, huh?"

Lucky whirled, hands at his crotch.

Everybody froze.

"Ho, Du Pré," said Lucky. "You are a fool. This is this guy I told you about." He was looking left and right.

A couple of men came round the car, toward Du Pré. He saw a knife flash.

And then a gun started firing behind Du Pré, in the trees. Fast fire. The slugs were going just overhead but not much.

People scattered. Some dove into the barrow pit they had just pissed in.

Lucky ran. He was there, and then he was moving into the woods, very fast. He sank in the shadow of the trees.

Du Pré waited and then he ran up the road before cutting in.

The gun was still firing behind him.

Wonder how many clips she got for that thing? Du Pré thought. I bet ten; she always was a thorough little girl.

Du Pré slowed down. He stopped and listened. He could hear Lucky moving slowly and softly somewhere in front of him.

He would probably try to make it to the town.

But he could do that on a long hook, sliding around Du Pré.

Du Pré moved forward, spreading the undergrowth with his foot before putting it down.

He waited. Lucky was moving slowly, too.

An owl hooted softly.

Du Pré wondered what the hell Benetsee had meant by remembering his fathers.

Catfoot, of course. When Catfoot walked, he barely ruffled the dust.

Du Pré listened as hard as he could. He thought of Lucky's sounds as music, tried to think where they would go next.

The gunfire died away and all was silent back behind Du Pré.

She's reloading, thought Du Pré. I love that kid. We can visit each other in jail.

He heard the Rover drive off, then stop.

He heard Maria ululating, the blood warble of Indian women, to send their love to their men in battle.

Du Pré felt the earth beneath the soft soles of the moccasins, flexed his toes, and gripped. He breathed deeply. The light was rising; the dew glittered. He felt spiderwebs across his face as he moved, sling loaded and in hand.

I'd rather have a sawed-off shotgun, thought Du Pré. But it would not fit in this song, I think.

The Rover drove back the other way, a door opened, the guns went again, and then the Rover drove away fast.

Du Pré heard sirens faint and far off.

The light rose, flooding. Du Pré smelled ferns and duff and the sour standing water. Pine. A bitter whiff of tobacco, sour, old, sunk in cloth and skin. He heard a rhythm soft and intrusive, like dry, callused palms rubbed lightly over one another, skin rasping on skin, and then what he thought might be a drum.

Benetsee.

Du Pré looked ahead and saw an eye behind leaves spangled with drops of iridescence.

Lucky fired as Du Pré dropped, and the slug went past just over him. Du Pré rolled behind a rotten log, wriggled over to a small gully, went on elbows like a salamander rising in the sun like fire. A snake lifted up its head and then sinuously disappeared into a hole by a tree root.

I want him before them fucking cops get here and grab him,

only to let him walk, Du Pré thought. My fathers, do me honor, guide me now, make my hand strong and my eye keen, and let me use this sling rooted in the earth. I want his blood.

Du Pré stood up quickly, saw the path Lucky had taken, the leaves unwinking with the dew he'd shaken off in passage. Toward a clearing up ahead.

I got to fight him in the open, then I do that.

Du Pré heard Benetsee's bullroarer in his left ear, coming from the west.

Du Pré ran forward, bobbing, crouching, shifting.

He paused and put two of the stones in his mouth.

He raised his head above the clustered prickly ash and saw a junkyard, old cars piled high, several draglines rusting, booms lowered to the earth, blackberry bushes thick over forgotten shells of metal.

Du Pré stood up. He looked toward the rising sun on his right. He glanced to his left.

Bears and bobcats, old dances, warriors slithering in the night to steal horses flashed through his mind.

Du Pré dove hard for the hump of a crumpled car just ahead of him.

He heard the shot and the slug hit the rusty metal and punched a hole on through. Du Pré shoved himself through the blackberry vines; the spines clawed at his hands and face.

Du Pré stood up quickly, staring hard at where the slugs had come from. Lucky was thirty feet up in an oak, straddling a branch and aiming. Du Pré dropped again.

"You are cooked," Du Pré shouted.

The sirens were winding down.

✦ CHAPTER 50 ✦

Y ou don't have a gun," said Lucky. He tossed his off into a mess of blackberries.

Du Pré saw the driving gloves on Lucky's hands. Lucky balled them up and tossed them after the gun. Can't get prints off rough leather so good.

Lucky shifted so he sat legs on one side of the big branch.

"You kill a bunch of people," said Du Pré. "Now why you do that?"

"I like it," said Lucky. "You wouldn't understand."

Fucking right I don't understand, Du Pré thought. He listened for the sound of people coming through the woods, but there was nothing. A car horn blared. Too far to hear people shouting, probably.

"There's nothing you can do, Du Pré," said Lucky. "You could dig the gun out of the bushes, maybe catch me before I got to the road. Shoot me. Maybe, but I don't think so. They got you clear for murder then, Du Pré."

Du Pré heard the hand drum, wings, smelled cedar, blood, earth.

Lucky sat easy on the branch. He took out a cigarette and lit it, drew the smoke into his lungs.

"Fuck you, Du Pré," said Lucky. "Pretty smart of you, figure it out, some folks would say. But you aren't smart enough to beat me. You figure it out, you still got nothing. They can arrest me. They got not one damn thing, Du Pré. I say, no, I did not, they let me go. Can't do anything at all Du Pré. Great country we live in, don't you think?"

356

Du Pré moved round to a clear place. He let the thongs of the slingshot drop slowly.

He prayed. Lucky turned his head; a branch snapped some ways off. Someone was coming.

Du Pré whirled the shot, crouched, rose up, let the thong go. The stone flashed straight and caught Lucky in the temple as he turned his head. His arms jerked up, he quivered, fell over backward, thumped into the damp earth, crushing the underbrush.

Du Pré made his way over to him. His neck was broken, his head bent over too far on his shoulder.

Du Pré looked at the little trickle of blood at the corner of Lucky's mouth. The stone ball lay on the ground, in the center of a maple's leaf, crimson on its etched blackness. Du Pré picked it up, looked at it, put it in his mouth.

"Taste your blood, Lucky," said Du Pré. "I hate you for what you did, you bastard. I hate you for what you did to them and now for what you've done to me."

People were coming. Du Pré didn't care to talk to them. He moved back into the forest, rubbed mud on his face, hid in bushes, watched them pass, starting every time they made a noise themselves. He waited till they found Lucky and began to shout and then calm down and talk into their radios.

Du Pré moved through the forest to the highway, looked, crossed it, took his careful time making his way back to the inn. It was late afternoon. The Rover was parked away from the door; the Washington, D.C., plates were back on it. Du Pré let himself into his room.

"Over now, huh, Papa?" said Maria. She was lying on the bed, reading a book.

Du Pré nodded.

"You hear me do the ululation?"

"Yes," said Du Pré. "Where you learn to do that?"

"You don't learn to do that, Papa," said Maria. "It is in the blood, you know. It just came to me."

357

"Okay," said Du Pré. "Now you tell your papa where you get all them damn guns you shoot off."

"Evidence room at the sheriff's back home," said Maria. "Don't worry, I erased all the records. They were part of a dope bust four years ago, pretty well forgotten. Took them out of the computer, the files."

Maria had done some work for the Sheriff's Department for credit in high school. She'd done some work on the Sheriff's Department, too.

What do I got to say? Du Pré thought. I kill that sack of puke and don't give a shit for the opinions of no one at all in the matter.

"Where them guns now?" said Du Pré suddenly.

"I wipe them off, put them under the seats of that car Lucky and the others drive up in," said Maria sweetly. "You don't think I am a thorough girl, Papa?"

"Shit," said Du Pré.

"Them moccasin do you good there?" said Maria.

Du Pré nodded. "Bunch of things do me good." He told her what had happened.

"I heard Benetsee," said Maria, "heard him here while I wait for you. He told me my warrior be back soon, then he say my papa come a little after. You know you walking different from how you do at home, wearing the boots?"

Du Pré looked down at his filthy clothes, the moccasins all smeared and spattered. He felt tired.

"You maybe wash my clothes while I rest?" said Du Pré.

"Sure," said Maria. "We need to stay another night, anyway, not run off, attract attention. I like this being a crook, you know."

"It is not that," said Du Pré.

"I know," said Maria. "Some crazy country, huh? Too many people in it. Some guy like Lucky, he kills for the fun of it. I wonder how many like him there are."

"Michelle Leuci says about two hundred any given time. Very hard to catch, you know. Most crooks are dumb, but they are not."

Du Pré found some whiskey after Maria had left with his soiled clothes. Wash out the last of it.

If I hadn't killed him, then I would have had to keep on till I could, Du Pré thought, very hard to find the right moment.

The telephone rang. Du Pré nodded and picked it up.

"What the fuck have you been up to?" snarled Detective Michelle Leuci.

"Just woke up," said Du Pré.

Michelle was silent for a moment.

"He's dead," she said.

"Okay," said Du Pré. "Who is dead?"

"Lucky," said Michelle. "But you wouldn't know anything at all about that, I am sure."

"Well, I can't say that I am sorry," said Du Pré. "What happened?"

"I don't know, other than he was DOA," said Michelle. "Maybe the coroner will find something, the ME."

"How is Bart?" said Du Pré.

"Thanks for changing the subject," said Michelle, "since I know what happened enough to know I never will know what happened. So I guess it is fine, I hope, I hope. He's kinda chewed up and feeling ill-used."

"Oh?" said Du Pré.

"Yeah. I couldn't stop you so I dumped all over him. He said you were his best friend and he knew you very well and that if anything bad happened, he would pay for a fine defense for you. He also said that Lucky was dead meat. Did you know you scare Bart?"

"Why should I scare Bart?" said Du Pré.

"Yes," said Detective Michelle Leuci.